The Folly of Eustace and Other Satires and Stories

....

ROBERT HICHENS

Edited by Gregory Shepard

Introduction by S.T. Joshi

Stark House Press • Eureka California

THE FOLLY OF EUSTACE & OTHER SATIRES AND STORIES

Published by Stark House Press
1315 H Street
Eureka, CA 95501, USA
griffinskye3@sbcglobal.net
www.starkhousepress.com

Book design by Mark Shepard, shepgraphics.com
Proofreading by Bill Kelly
Cover art by C. B. Williams

First Stark House Press Edition: March 2024

The Folly of Eustace: Eustace Lane decided at any early age to don the mask of the clown. People began to take notice, calling him a whimsical, irresponsible creature. He reveled in surprise parties and practical jokes, in being silly in unexpected way. Then he fell in love with Winifred Ames, and she with him. But was she in love with the mask… or the man underneath?

The Last Time: While on the train to Calais, Strickland is seated in front of woman who momentarily breaks down in extreme anguish. Embarrassed, he says nothing. But they meet again. And this time Mrs. Armitage explains the tragedy of her life, and her deepest regret.

The Letter: Everyone was surprised when Lena Wareham accepted Eustace Henley's proposal of marriage. Lena is somewhat surprised herself. Then the letter arrives. Eustace has put his true thoughts about Lena in a letter to the woman he really loves, then mistakenly mails it to Lena. Should she let him know she received it, or accept a seemingly loveless marriage?

Enter the compelling world of Robert Hichens. These stories and six more tales of human folly and foibles await you.

Contents

Introduction 7

The Folly of Eustace 13

The Two Fears 33

The Lift 38

The Last Time 51

The Façade 92

The Letter 135

A Boudoir Boy 181

The Piano 192

The Worth While Man 206

Bibliography 222

Introduction
By S. T. Joshi

Robert Hichens (1864–1950) may be known today chiefly for his tales of horror and the supernatural, most notably "How Love Came to Professor Guildea"; but in his own lifetime he was hailed as a distinguished mainstream novelist with a tendency toward social and cultural satire. His first published book, *The Green Carnation* (1894), was a hilarious send-up of the aesthetic pretensions of Oscar Wilde and his circle. The stories in this volume were included in collections published in the first three decades of Hichens's literary career, from *The Folly of Eustace and Other Stories* (1896) to *The Streets and Other Stories* (1928), and exhibit the broad range of his work outside the realm of weird fiction.

What these stories reveal is the delicacy of Hichens's portrayal of character. In this process he generally requires the expansive space of a novelette or novella; some of the best stories in this volume are of this sort. "The Folly of Eustace" is prototypical. This keen portrait of a man, Eustace Lane, who from the age of sixteen onward decides to play the fool and, as an adult, gains the reputation as "a dancy, a fop, a whimsical, irresponsible creature," finds his life changed when he marries Winifred Ames. Should he keep up his buffoonery or settle down to a more orthodox married life? And does his wife suspect that his clownishness is merely an act, or has now become a character trait so ingrained in him that he can't behave as a normal man? The tragedies that befall the couple speak poignantly of the need for honesty in relationships; and Eustace brings his fate upon himself by his unwillingness to be honest with himself.

Another central theme in these stories, as in Hichens's work as a whole, is the role of women. For this lifelong bachelor, women were a source of inexpressible fascination. There is some evidence that Hichens engaged in a sort of essentialism—the assumption that certain habits were endemic to women as women, rather than the product of social and cultural factors specific to their historical era. Certainly, the period in which Hichens was writing—from the late Victorian era to the post–World War I period of slowly broadening political, economic, and sexual freedom for women—was one in which the roles of many women (especially those of the middle and upper class) were highly circumscribed, with a bland assumption of their obvious inferiority to men in various ways. But for Hichens, these circumstances only added to the attraction of the "eternal feminine." The narrator's passing comment in "The Letter"—"Women are the very devil"—is not meant derogatorily, but to indicate the inscrutability of the female, at least to such a hyper-masculine temperament as Hichens's.

Consider "The Lift." This tale is one that approaches psychological terror in its depiction of a young man who finds himself in a stalled elevator ("lift" in English parlance) with a middle-aged woman who, aside from her linguistic difficulties, is married to an apparently insane man who habitually abuses and even threatens to kill her. She begs the young man for help, but the absurdity of the whole situation causes him to laugh uncontrollably. The story does not end with any grand cataclysm, but we are left with the impression of the latent horror of relationships that can descend to this level of domestic warfare.

"The Last Time" may well be the most remarkable story in this volume. Henry Strickland, who briefly met Vivienne Armitage on a train, later encounters again at a house party—and he is keen on investigating the secrets that lie buried in her heart, even though she is outwardly an austere, restrained, and even emotionless woman. She has become a widow between Henry's first and second meetings with her; and as she slowly expounds upon her relationship with her late husband, she reveals the depths of her fiery temperament—but in language that is always of impeccable elegance and grace. This confession could count as one of the most searing passages in the literature of its era, as with ruthless honesty she speaks of what we would today call a bipolar temperament—in particular, a "horrible propensity for being cruel only to those I loved." "It is that, just that," she goes on, "that has ruined my life." Henry's bitter conclusion at the end of her narrative ("Our human lives—how terrible they are!") is a fitting capstone to a tale that in its way is also an almost excruciating venture into psychological torment.

Then there is "The Letter," where many of the prejudices of Hichens's era—especially as they pertain to women—are revealed. It is an open question whether Hichens subscribes to these prejudices; one would like to think otherwise. Here we have a thirty-five-year-old woman, Lena Wareham, who is described as plain and homely, and by the standards of the time already considered a "spinster." To the surprise of everyone, she falls in love with a slightly younger man, Eustace Henley, who asks her to marry him. But then she receives by mistake a letter Eustace has written to a married woman, Enid, with whom he is passionately in love, and it becomes clear that Enid has asked Eustace to go ahead and marry Lena so as to take away the temptation of continuing her affair with him. The critical passage in this letter is Eustace's casual way of telling Enid about his future bride:

> "She's a few years older than I am. She's a thorough good sort, quiet and straight and saner than we are. Nothing passionate and erratic about her. I shouldn't think she's ever had a sleepless night because of a man in her life. She isn't good looking, but she's got a face you can trust, kind eyes with an honest look in

them that tells you what she is at first sight. You'd probably call her a homely sort of woman, and so she is. People all like her, but I don't suppose a man ever went mad over her even when she was a girl."

What woman could possibly proceed with a marriage with a man who writes this way about her? But that is exactly what Lena does—and the relatively happy ending of this story speaks of hidden depths in the human psyche and the way in which people inevitably make compromises for the sake of a cherished relationship.

"The Façade" can be discussed here, although it is really a satire on English class distinctions. These distinctions—as we know from shows such as *Downton Abbey*—were as inflexible as the Indian caste system, and Hichens draws upon many of the English biases (ones that continue to be prevalent right down to the present day) that govern the manner in which the upper class separates itself from their perceived social inferiors. Even today, the enunciation of words—here embodied in the dropping of the *h* in words beginning with that letter, an infallible indication of lower-class upbringing—is made much of, as are such things as one's manner of dress and other key factors. The celebrated stage actress Ariadne Marshall appears to belong to both the social and intellectual aristocracy, as she wishes to appear only in intellectual plays aimed at a select coterie. Why, then, does she choose to star in a play, *Sally Eliza,* whose lead character is a slatternly Cockney woman? As the story progresses, it becomes increasingly obvious that Hichens is engaging in pungent satire against the upper-crust narrator and his ilk, who one and all are appalled at the fact that tickets to the opening night of the play have been sent to all and sundry instead of a chosen few. The fact that the play is a popular success is, to the highbrow coterie that had surrounded Ariadne, a sure sign of the play's worthlessness ("It reeked of the people who like boiled cabbage"). In the end, no one, high or low, is exempt from Hichens's barbed pen.

A similar sort of satire is the focus of the early story "A Boudoir Boy," where an elderly "spinster" pokes merciless fun at the intellectual pretensions of a young man who vaunts his decadent credentials. In "The Worth While Man" we have a scenario where a woman in a country house yearns for intellectual equality with an insufferable know-it-all who calls himself Lord Lionel Danesborough—but he proves to be something very different. Finally, "The Two Fears" is a grim story of World War I, where a mother is afraid of her son's imminent enlistment—and also afraid that he will *not* enlist. This brief tale poignantly hints at the destruction of an entire generation of young Englishmen during this catastrophic conflict.

Robert Hichens's work may seem dated to many of us today, as the social and cultural standards prevailing in his time have given way to a broadly egalitarian ethos that scorns distinction of any kind as inherently elitist or anti-democratic. But Hichens was writing of what he knew—and his intimate familiarity with the members of his class, whether they be intellectuals or aristocrats, allowed him to etch with unerring acuteness the foibles and eccentricities that made that period of English history so unique. But his work has a far broader significance than being merely a portrait of the Edwardian and interwar eras. Human character never changes very much from century to century, and Hichens had the sensitivity to probe the depths of our fears, hopes, and dreams in a way that remains eternally relevant. And how can anyone sensitive to fine literature not fail to be captivated by his graceful, musical prose as it lovingly depicts people and scenes whose utter reality strikes us forcibly with each passing sentence?

—November 2023

....

S. T. Joshi is a freelance writer and editor. He has prepared comprehensive editions of H. P. Lovecraft's collected fiction, essays, poetry, and letters, including an annotated edition of *The Case of Charles Dexter Ward* (2010). He is the author of *The Weird Tale* (1990), *The Modern Weird Tale* (2001), *I Am Providence: The Life and Times of H. P. Lovecraft* (2010), and *Unutterable Horror: A History of Supernatural Fiction* (2012), and has edited *the anthology American Supernatural Tales* (2007).

The Folly of Eustace
and Other Satires
and Stories

....

ROBERT HICHENS

The Folly of Eustace

I

Some men deliberately don a character in early youth as others don a mask before going to an opera ball. They select it not without some care, being guided in their choice by the opinion they have formed of the world's mind and manner of proceeding. In the privacy of the dressing room, the candles being lighted and the mirror adjusted at the best angle for a view of self, they assume their character, and peacock to their reflection, meditating: Does it become me? Will it be generally liked? Will it advance me towards my heart's desire? Then they catch up their cloak, twist the mirror back to its usual position, puff out the candles, and steal forth into their career, shutting the door gently behind them. And, perhaps till they are laid out in the grave, the last four walls enclosing them, only the dressing room could tell their secret. And it has no voice to speak. For, if they are wise, they do not keep a valet.

At the age of sixteen Eustace Lane chose his mask, lit the candles, tried it on, and resolved to wear it at the great masquerade. He was an Eton boy at the time. One fourth of June he was out in the playing fields, paying polite attentions to another fellow's sister, when he overheard a fragment of a conversation that was taking place between his mother and one of the masters. His mother was a kind Englishwoman, who was very short-sighted, and always did her duty. The master was a fool, but as he was tall, handsome, and extremely good-natured, Eustace Lane and most people considered him to be highly intelligent. Eustace caught the sound of his name pronounced. The fond mother, in the course of discreet conversation, had proceeded from the state of the weather to the state of her boy's soul, taking, with the ease of the mediocre, the one step between the sublime and the ridiculous. She had told the master the state of the weather—which, for once, was sublime; she wanted him, in return, to tell her the state of her boy's soul—which was ridiculous.

Eustace forgot the other fellow's sister, her limpid eyes, her open-worked stockings, her panoply of chiffons and of charms. He had heard his own name. Bang went the door on the rest of the world, shutting out even feminine humanity. Self-consciousness held him listening. His mother said:

"Dear Eustace! What do you think of him, Mr. Bembridge? Is he *really* clever? His father and I consider him unusually intelligent for his age— so advanced in mind. He judges for himself, you know. He always did, even as a baby. I remember when he was quite a tiny mite I could always trust to his perceptions. In my choice of nurses I was invariably guided by him. If he screamed at them I felt that there was something wrong, and dismissed them—of course with a character. If he smiled at them, I knew I could have confidence in their virtue. How strange these things are! What is it in us that screams at evil and smiles at good?"

"Ah! what, indeed?" replied the master, accepting her conclusion as an established and very beautiful fact. "There is more in the human heart than you and I can fathom, Mrs. Lane."

"Yes, indeed! But tell me about Eustace. You have observed him?"

"Carefully. He is a strange boy."

"Strange?"

"Whimsical, I mean. How clever he may be I am unable to say. He is so young, and, of course, undeveloped. But he is an original. Even if he never displays great talents the world will talk about him."

"Why?" asked Mrs. Lane in some alarm.

To be talked about was, she considered, to be the prey of scandalmongers. She did not wish to give her darling to the lions.

"I mean that Eustace has a strain of quaint fun in him—a sort of passion for the burlesque of life. You do not often find this in boys. It is new to my experience. He sees the peculiar side of everything with a curious acuteness. Life presents itself to him in caricature. I— Well hit! Well hit indeed!"

Someone had scored a four.

The other fellow's sister insisted on moving to a place whence they could see the cricket better, and Eustace had to yield to her. But from that moment he took no more interest in her artless remarks and her artful open-worked stockings. In the combat between self and her she went to the wall. He stood up before the mirror looking steadfastly at his own image.

And, finding it not quite so interestingly curious as the fool of a master had declared it to be, he lit some more candles, selected a mask, and put it on.

He chose the mask of a buffoon.

From that day Eustace strove consistently to live up to the reputation given to him by a fool, who had been talking at random to please an avid mother. Mr. Bembridge knew that the boy was no good at work, wanted to say something nice about him, and had once noticed him playing some absurd but very ordinary boyish prank. On this supposed hint of character the master spoke. Mrs. Lane listened. Eustace acted. A sudden ambition stirred within him. To be known, talked about, considered, perhaps even wondered at—was not that a glory? Such a glory came to the greatly talented—to the mightily industrious. Men earned it by labour, by intensity, insensibility to fatigue, the "roughing it" of the mind. He did not want to rough it. Nor was he greatly talented. But he was just sharp enough to see, as he believed, a short and perhaps easy way to a thing that his conceit desired and that his egoism felt it could love. Being only a boy, he had never, till this time, deliberately looked on life as anything. Now he set himself, in his, at first, youthful way, to look on it as burlesque—to see it in caricature. How to do that?

He studied the cartoons in *Vanity Fair*, the wondrous noses, the astounding trousers, that delight the cynical world. Were men indeed like these? Did they assume such postures, stare with such eyes, revel in such complexions? These were the celebrities of the time. They all looked with one accord preposterous. Eustace jumped to the conclusion that they were what they looked, and, going a step farther, that they were celebrated because they were preposterous. Gifted with a certain amount of imagination, this idea of the interest, almost the beauty of the preposterous, took a firm hold of his mind. One day he, too, would be in *Vanity Fair*, displaying terrific boots, amazing thin legs, a fatuous or a frenetic countenance to the great world of the unknown. He would stand out from the multitude if only by virtue of an unusual eyeglass, a particular glove, the fashion of his tie or of his temper. He would balance on the ball of peculiarity, and toe his way up the spiral of fame, while the music hall audience applauded and the managers consulted as to the increase of his salary. Mr. Bembridge had shown him a weapon with which he might fight his way quickly to the front. He picked it up and resolved to use it. Soon he began to slash out right and left. His blade chanced to encounter the outraged body of an elderly and sardonic master. Eustace was advised that he had better leave Eton. His father came down by train and took him away.

As they journeyed up to town, Mr. Lane lectured and exhorted, and Eustace looked out of the window. Already he felt himself near to being a celebrity. He had astonished Eton. That was a good beginning. Papa might prose, knowing, of course, nothing of the poetry of caricature, of the wild joys and the laurels that crown the whimsical. So while Mr. Lane hunted adjectives, and ran sad-sounding and damnatory substantives to earth, Eustace hugged himself, and secretly chuckled over his pilgrim's progress towards the pages of *Vanity Fair*.

"Eustace! Eustace! Are you listening to me?"

"Yes, father."

"Then what have you to say? What explanation have you to offer for your conduct? You have behaved like a buffoon, sir—d'you hear me?—like a buffoon!"

"Yes, father."

"What the deuce do you mean by 'yes,' sir?"

Eustace considered, while Mr. Lane puffed in the approved paternal fashion. What did he mean? A sudden thought struck him. He became confidential. With an earnest gaze, he said:

"I couldn't help doing what I did. I want to be like the other fellows, but somehow I can't. Something inside of me won't let me just go on as they do. I don't know why it is, but I feel as if I must do original things—things other people never do; it—it seems in me."

Mr. Lane regarded him suspiciously, but Eustace had clear eyes, and knew, at least, how to look innocent.

"We shall have to knock it out of you," blustered the father.

"I wish you could, father," the boy said. "I know I hate it."

Mr. Lane began to be really puzzled. There was something pathetic in the words, and especially in the way they were spoken. He stared at Eustace meditatively.

"So you hate it, do you?" he said rather limply at last. "Well, that's a step in the right direction, at any rate. Perhaps things might have been worse."

Eustace did not assent.

"They were bad enough," he said, with a simulation of shame. "I know I've been a fool."

"Well, well," Mr. Lane said, whirling, as paternal weathercocks will, to another point of the compass, "never mind, my boy. Cheer up! You see your fault—that's the main thing. What's done can't be undone."

"No, thank heaven!" thought the boy, feeling almost great.

How delicious is the irrevocable past—sometimes!

"Be more careful in future. Don't let your boyish desire for follies carry you away."

"I shall," was his son's mental rejoinder.

"And I dare say you'll do good work in the world yet."

The train ran into Paddington Station on this sublime climax of fatherhood, and the further words of wisdom were jerked out of Mr. Lane during their passage to Carlton House Terrace in a four-wheeled cab.

"What an extraordinary person Mr. Eustace Lane is!" said Winifred Ames to her particular friend and happy foil, Jane Fraser. "All London is beginning to talk about him. I suppose he must be clever?"

"Oh, of course, darling, very clever; otherwise, how could he possibly gain so much notice? Just think—why, there are millions of people in London, and I'm sure only about a thousand of them, at most, attract any real attention. I think Mr. Eustace Lane is a genius."

"Do you really, Jenny?"

"I do indeed."

Winifred mused for a moment. Then she said:

"It must be very interesting to marry a genius, I suppose?"

"Oh, enthralling, simply. And, then, so few people can do it."

"Yes."

"And it must be grand to do what hardly anybody can do."

"In the way of marrying, Jenny?"

"In any way," responded Miss Fraser, who was an enthusiast, and habitually sentimental. "What would I give to do even one unique thing, or to marry even one unique person!"

"You couldn't marry two at the same time—in England."

"England limits itself so terribly; but there is a broader time coming. Those who see it, and act upon what they see, are pioneers; Mr. Lane is a pioneer."

"But don't you think him rather extravagant?"

"Oh yes. That is so splendid. I love the extravagance of genius, the barbaric lavishness of moral and intellectual supremacy."

"I wonder whether the supremacy of Eustace Lane is moral, or intellectual, or—neither?" said Winifred. "There are so many different supremacies, aren't there? I suppose a man might be supreme merely as a—as a—well, an absurdity, you know."

Jenny smiled the watery smile of the sentimentalist; a glass of still lemonade washed with limelight might resemble it.

"Eustace Lane likes you, Winnie," she remarked.

"I know; that is why I am wondering about him. One does wonder, you see, about the man one may possibly be going to marry."

There had never been such a man for Jane Fraser, so she said nothing, but succeeded in looking confidential.

Presently Winifred allowed her happy foil to lace her up. She was going to a ball given by the Lanes in Carlton House Terrace.

"Perhaps he will propose to you to-night," whispered Jane in a gush of excitement as the two girls walked down the stairs to the carriage. "If he does, what will you say?"

"I don't know."

"Oh, darling, but surely—"

"Eustace is so odd. I can't make him out."

"That is because he is a genius."

"He is certainly remarkable—in a way. Good-night, dear."

The carriage drove off, and the happy foil joined her maid, who was waiting to conduct her home. On the way they gossiped, and the maid expressed a belief that Mr. Lane was a fine young gentleman, but full of his goings-on.

Jane knew what she meant. Eustace had once kissed her publicly in Jane's presence, which deed the latter considered a stroke of genius, and the act of a true and courageous pioneer.

Eustace was now just twenty-two, and he had already partially succeeded in his ambition. His mask had deceived his world, and Mr. Bembridge's prophecy about him was beginning to be fulfilled. He had done nothing especially intellectual or athletic, was not particularly active either with limbs or brain; but people had begun to notice and to talk about him, to discuss him with a certain interest, even with a certain wonder. The newspapers occasionally mentioned him as a dandy, a fop, a whimsical, irresponsible creature, yet one whose vagaries were not entirely without interest. He had performed some extravagant antic in a cotillon, or worn some extraordinary coat. He had invented a new way of walking one season, and during another season, although in perfect health, he had never left the house, declaring that movement of any kind was ungentlemanly and ridiculous, and that an imitation of harem life was the uttermost bliss obtainable in London. His windows in Carlton House Terrace had been latticed, and when his friends came there to see him they found him lying, supported by cushions, on a prayer carpet, eating Eastern sweetmeats from a silver box.

But he soon began to tire of this deliberate imprisonment, and to reduce buffoonery to a modern science. His father was a rich man, and he was an only child. Therefore he was able to gratify the supposed whims, which were no whims at all. He could get up surprise parties, which really bored him, carry out elaborate practical jokes, give extraordinary entertainments at will. For his parents acquiesced in his absurdities, were even rather proud of them, thinking that he followed his Will-o'-the-wisp of a fancy because he was not less, but more, than other young men. In fact, they supposed he must be a genius because he was erratic. Many people are of the same opinion, and declare that a goose standing on its head must be a swan. By degrees Eustace Lane's practical jokes became a common topic of conversation in London, and smart circles were in a perpetual state of mild excitement as to what he would do next. It was said that he had put the latchkey of a Duchess down the back of a Commander-in-Chief; that he had once, in a country house, prepared an apple pie bed for an Heir-apparent, and that he had declared he would journey to Rome next Easter in order to present a collection of penny toys to the Pope. Society loves folly if it is sufficiently blatant. The folly of Eustace was just blatant enough to be more than tolerated—enjoyed. He had by practice acquired a knack of being silly in unexpected ways, and so a great many people honestly considered him one of the cleverest young men in town.

But, you know, it is the proper thing, if you wear a mask, to have a sad face behind it. Eustace sometimes felt sad, and sometimes fatigued. He had worked a little to make his reputation, but it was often hard labour to live up to it. His profession of a buffoon sometimes exhausted him, but he could no longer dare to be like others. The self-conscious live to gratify the changing expectations of their world, and Eustace had educated himself into a self-consciousness that was almost a disease.

And, then, there was his place in the pages of *Vanity Fair* to be won. He put that in front of him as his aim in life, and became daily more and more whimsical.

Nevertheless, he did one prosaic thing. He fell in love with Winifred Ames, and could not help showing it. As the malady increased upon him his reputation began to suffer eclipse, for he relapsed into sentiment, and even allowed his eyes to grow large and lover-like. He ceased to worry people, and so began to bore them—a much more dangerous thing. For a moment he even ran the fearful risk of becoming wholly natural, dropping his mask, and showing himself as he really was, a rather dull, quite normal young man, with the usual notions about the usual things, the usual bias towards the usual vices, the usual disinclination to do the usual duties of life.

He ran a risk, but Winifred saved him, and restored him to his fantasies this evening of the ball in Carlton House Terrace.

It was an ordinary ball, and therefore Eustace appeared to receive his guests in fancy dress, wearing a powdered wig and a George IV Court costume. This absurdity was a mechanical attempt to retrieve his buffoon's reputation, for he was really very much in love, and very serious in his desire to be married in quite the ordinary way. With a rather lacklustre eye he noticed the amusement of his friends at his last vagary; but when Winifred Ames entered the ballroom a nervous vivacity shook him, as it has shaken ploughmen under similar conditions, and for just a moment he felt ill at ease in the lonely lunacy of his flowered waistcoat and olive-green knee breeches. He danced with her, then took her to a scarlet nook, apparently devised to hold only one person, but into which they gently squeezed, not without difficulty.

She gazed at him with her big brown eyes, that were at the same time honest and fanciful. Then she said:

"You have taken an unfair advantage of us all to-night, Mr. Lane."

"Have I? How?"

"By retreating into the picturesque clothes of another age. All the men here must hate you."

"No; they only laugh at me."

She was silent a moment. Then she said:

"What is it in you that makes you enjoy that which the rest of us are afraid of?"

"And that is—"

"Being laughed at. Laughter, you know, is the great world's cat-o'-nine-tails. We fear it as little boys fear the birch on a winter's morning at school."

Eustace smiled uneasily.

"Do you laugh at me?" he asked.

"I have. You surely don't mind."

"No," he said, with an effort. Then: "Are you laughing to-night?"

"No. You have done an absurd thing, of course, but it happens to be becoming. You look—well, pretty—yes, that's the word—in your wig. Many men are ugly in their own hair. And, after all, what would life be without its absurdities? Probably you are right to enjoy being laughed at."

Eustace, who had seriously meditated putting off his mask forever that night, began to change his mind. The sentence, "Many men are ugly in their own hair," dwelt with him, and he felt fortified in his powdered wig. What if he took it off, and henceforth Winifred found him ugly? Does not the safety of many of us lie merely in dressing up? Do we not buy our fate at the costumier's?

"Just tell me one thing," Winifred went on. "Are you natural?"

"Natural?" he hesitated.

"Yes; I think you must be. You've got a whimsical nature."

"I suppose so." He thought of his journey with his father years ago, and added: "I wish I hadn't."

"Why? There is a charm in the fantastic, although comparatively few people see it. Life must be a sort of Arabian Nights Entertainment to you."

"Sometimes. To-night it is different. It seems a sort of Longfellow life."

"What's that?"

"Real and earnest."

And then he proposed to her, with a laugh, to shoot an arrow at the dead poet and his own secret psalm.

And Winifred accepted him, partly because she thought him really strange, partly because he seemed so pretty in his wig, which she chose to believe his own hair.

They were married, and on the wedding day the bridegroom astonished his guests by making a burlesque speech at the reception.

In anyone else such an exhibition would have been considered the worst taste, but nobody was disgusted, and many were delighted. They had begun to fear that Eustace was getting humdrum. This harlequinade after the pantomime at the church—for what is a modern smart wedding but a second-rate pantomime?—put them into a good humour, and made them feel that, after all, they had got something for their presents. And so the happy pair passed through a dreary rain of rice to the mysteries of that Bluebeard's Chamber, the honeymoon.

II

Winifred anticipated this honeymoon with calmness, but Eustace was too much in love to be calm. He was, on the contrary, in a high state of excitement, and of emotion, and the effort of making his ridiculous speech had nearly sent him into hysterics. But he had now fully resolved to continue in his whimsical course, and to play forever the part of a highly erratic genius, driven hither and thither by the weird impulses of the moment. That he never had any impulses but such as were common to most ordinary young men was a sad fact which he meant to most carefully conceal from Winifred. He had made up his mind that she believed his mask to be his face. She had, therefore, married the mask. To divorce her violently from it might be fatal to their happiness. If he showed the countenance God had given him, she might cry: "I don't know you. You are a stranger. You are like all the other men I didn't choose to marry." His blood ran cold at the thought. No, he must keep it up. She loved his fantasies because she believed them natural to him. She must never suspect that they were not natural. So, as they travelled, he planned the campaign of married life, as doubtless others, strange in their new bondage, have planned. He gazed at Winifred, and thought, "What is her notion of the ideal husband, I wonder?" She gazed at him, and mused on his affection and his whimsicality, and what the two would lead to in connection with her fate. And the old, scarlet-faced guard smiled fatuously at them both through the window on which glared a prominent "Engaged" as he had smiled on many another pair of fools—so he silently dubbed them. Then they entered Bluebeard's Chamber and closed the door behind them.

Brighton was their destination. They meant to lose themselves in a marine crowd.

They stayed there for a fortnight, and then returned to town, Eustace more in love than ever.

But Winifred?

One afternoon she sat in the drawing room of the pretty little house they had taken in Deanery Street, Park Lane. She was thinking, very definitely. The silent processes of even an ordinary woman's mind—what great male writer would not give two years of his life to sit with them and watch them, as the poet watches the flight of a swallow, or the astronomer the processions of the sky? A curious gale was raging through the town, touzling its thatch of chimney pots, doing violence to the demureness of its respectable streets. Night was falling, and in Piccadilly those strange, gay hats that greet the darkness were coming out like eager, vulgar comets in a dim and muttering firmament. It was just the moment when the outside mood of the huge city begins to undergo a change, to glide from its comparative simplicity of afternoon into its leering complexity of evening. Each twenty-four hours London has its moment of emancipation, its moment in which the wicked begin to breathe and the good to wonder, when "How?" and "Why?" are on the lips of the opposing factions, and only the philosophers who know—or think they know—their human nature hold themselves still, and feel that man is at the least ceaselessly interesting.

Winifred sat by the fire and held a council. She called her thoughts together and gave audience to her suspicions, and her brown eyes were wide and rather mournful as her counsellors uttered each a word of hope or of warning.

Eustace was out. He had gone to a concert, and had not returned.

She was holding a council to decide something in reference to him.

The honeymoon weeks had brought her just as far as the question, "Do I know my husband at all, or is he, so far, a total stranger?"

Some people seem to draw near to you as you look at them steadily, others to recede until they reach the verge of invisibility. Which was Eustace doing? Did his outline become clearer or more blurred? Was he daily more definite or more phantasmal? And the members of her council drew near and whispered their opinions in Winifred's attentive ears. They were not all in accord at the first. Pros fought with cons, elbowed them, were hustled in return. Sometimes there was almost a row, and she had to stretch forth her hands and hush the tumult. For she desired a calm conclave, although she was a woman.

And the final decision—if, indeed, it could be arrived at that evening—was important. Love seemed to hang upon it, and all the sweets of life; and the little wings of Love fluttered anxiously, as the little wings of a bird flutter when you hold it in the cage of your hands, prisoning it from its wayward career through the blue shadows of the summer.

For love is not always and forever instinctive—not even the finest love. While many women love because they must, whether the thing to be loved or not loved be carrion or crystal, a child of the gods or an imp of the devil, others love decisively because they see—perhaps can even analyze—a beauty that is there in the thing before them. One woman loves a man simply because he kisses her. Another loves him because he has won the Victoria Cross.

Winifred was not of the women who love because they are kissed.

She had accepted Eustace rather impulsively, but she had not married him quite uncritically. There was something new, different from other men, about him which attracted her, as well as his good looks—that prettiness which had peeped out from the white wig in the scarlet nook at the ball. His oddities at that time she had grown thoroughly to believe in, and, believing in them, she felt she liked them. She supposed them to spring, rather like amazing spotted orchids, from the earth of a quaint nature. Now, after a honeymoon spent among the orchids, she held this council while the wind blew London into a mood of evening irritation.

What was Eustace?

How the wind sang over Park Lane! Yet the stars were coming out.

What was he? A genius or a clown? A creature to spread a buttered slide or a man to climb to heaven? A fine, free child of Nature, who did, freshly, what he would, regardless of the strained discretion of others, or a futile, scheming hypocrite, screaming after forced puerilities, without even a finger on the skirts of originality?

It was a problem for lonely woman's debate. Winifred strove to weigh it well. In Bluebeard's Chamber Eustace had cut many capers. This activity she had expected—had even wished for. And at first she had been amused and entertained by the antics, as one assisting at a good burlesque, through which, moreover, a piquant love theme runs. But by degrees she began to feel a certain stiffness in the capers, a self-consciousness in the antics, or fancied she began to feel it, and instead of being always amused she became often thoughtful.

Whimsicality she loved. Buffoonery she possibly, even probably, could learn to hate.

Of Eustace's love for her she had no doubt. She was certain of his affection. But was it worth having? That depended, surely, on the nature of the man in whom it sprang, from whom it flowed. She wanted to be sure of that nature; but she acknowledged to herself, as she sat by the fire, that she was perplexed. Perhaps even that perplexity was merciful. Yet she wished to sweep it away. She knit her brows moodily, and longed for a secret divining rod that would twist to reveal truth in another. For truth, she thought, is better than hidden water springs, and a sincerity—even of stupidity—more lovely than the fountain that gives flowers to the desert, wild red roses to the weary gold of sands.

The wind roared again, howling to poor, shuddering Mayfair, and there came a step outside. Eustace sprang in upon Winifred's council, looking like a gay schoolboy, his cheeks flushed, his lips open to speak.

"Dreaming?" he said.

She smiled.

"Perhaps."

"That concert paralyzed me. Too much Beethoven. I wanted Wagner. Beethoven insists on exalting you, but Wagner lets you revel and feel naughty. Winnie, d'you hear the wind?"

"Could I help it?" she asked.

"Does it suggest something to you?"

He looked at her, and made his expression mischievous, or meant to make it. She looked up at him, too.

"Yes, many things," she said—"many, many things."

"To me it suggests kites."

"Kites?"

"Yes. I'm going to fly one now in the Park. The stars are out. Put on your hat and come with me."

He seemed all impulse, sparkling to the novelty of the idea.

"Well, but—" She hesitated.

"I've got one—a beauty, a monster! I noticed the wind was getting up yesterday. Come!"

He pulled at her hand; she obeyed him, not quickly. She put on her hat, a plain straw, a thick jacket, gloves. Kite flying in London seemed an odd notion. Was it lively and entertaining, or merely silly? Which ought it to be?

Eustace shouted to her from the tiny hall.

"Hurry!" he cried.

The wind yelled beyond the door, and Winifred ran down, beginning to feel a childish thrill of excitement. Eustace held the kite. It was, indeed, a white monster, gaily decorated with fluttering scarlet and blue ribbons.

"We shall be mobbed," she said.

"There's no one about," he answered. "The gale frightens people."

He opened the door, and they were out in the crying tempest. The great clouds flew along the sky like an army in retreat. Some, to Winifred, seemed soldiers, others baggage wagons, horses, gun carriages, rushing pell-mell for safety. One drooping, tattered cloud she deemed the colours of a regiment streaming under the stars that peeped out here and there—watching sentinel eyes, obdurate, till some magic password softened them.

As they crossed the road she spoke of her cloud army to Eustace.

"This kite's like a live thing," was his reply. "It tugs as a fish tugs a line."

He did not care for the tumult of a far-off world.

They entered the Park. It seemed, indeed, strangely deserted. A swaggering soldier passed them by, going towards the Marble Arch. His spurs clinked; his long cloak gleamed like a huge pink carnation in the dingy dimness of the startled night. How he stared with his unintelligent, though bold, eyes as he saw the kite bounding to be free.

Eustace seemed delighted.

"That man thinks us mad!" he said.

"Are we mad?" Winifred asked, surprised at her own strange enjoyment of the adventure.

"Who knows?" said Eustace, looking at her narrowly. "You like this escapade?"

"Yes," she answered.

"My mask!" he thought, secretly longing to be quietly by the fire sipping tea and reading *Punch*. "She loves that."

They were through the trees now, across the broad path, out on the open lawns.

"Now for it!" he shouted, as the wind roared in their faces.

He paid out the coils of the thin cord. The white monster skimmed, struggled near the ground, returned, darted again upward and outward, felt for the wind's hands, caught them and sprang, with a mad courage, star-wards, its gay ribbons flying like coloured birds to mark its course. But soon they were lost to sight, and only a diminished, ghost-like shadow leaping against the black showed where the kite beat on to liberty.

Eustace ran with the wind, and Winifred followed him. The motion sent an exultation dancing through her veins, and stirred her blood into a ferment. The noises in the trees, the galloping music of the airs on their headlong courses, rang in her ears like clashing bells. She called as she ran, but never knew what words. She leaped, as if over glorious obstacles. Her feet danced on the short grass. She had a sudden notion: "I am living now!" and Eustace had never seemed so near to her. He had an art to find why children are happy, she thought, because they do little strange things, coupling mechanical movements, obvious actions that may seem absurd, with soft flights of the imagination, that wrap their prancings and their leaps in golden robes, and give to the dull world a glory. The hoop is their demon enemy, whom they drive before them to destruction. The kite is a great white bird, whom they hold back for a time from heaven. Suddenly Winifred longed to feel the bird's efforts to be free.

"Let me have it!" she cried to Eustace, holding out her hands eagerly. "Do let me!"

He was glad to pass the cord to her, being utterly tired of a prank which he thought idiotic, and he could not understand the light that sprang into her eyes as she grasped it, and felt the life of the lifeless thing that soared towards the clouds.

For the moment it was more to her—this tugging, scarce visible, white thing—than all the world of souls. It gave to her the excitement of battle, the joy of strife. She felt herself a Napoleon with empires in her hand; a Diana holding eternities, instead of hounds, in leash. She had quite the children's idea of kites, the sense of being in touch with the infinite that enters into baby pleasures, and makes the remembrance of them live in us when we are old, and have forgotten wild passions, strange fruitions, that have followed them and faded away forever.

How the creature tore at her! She fancied she felt the pulsings of its fly-away heart, beating with energy and great hopes of freedom. And suddenly, with a call, she opened her hands. Her captive was lost in the night.

In a moment she felt sad, such a foolish sorrow, as a gaoler may feel sad who has grown to love his prisoner, and sees him smile when the gaping door gives him again to crime.

"It's gone," she said to Eustace; "I think it's glad to go."

"Glad—a kite!" he said.

And it struck her that he would have thought it equally sensible if she had spoken, like Hans Andersen, of the tragedies of a toy-shop or the Homeric passions of wooden dolls.

Then, why had he been prompted by the wind to play the boy if he had none of the boy's ardent imagination?

They reached Deanery Street, and passed in from the night and the elements. Eustace shut the door with a sigh of relief. Winifred's echoing sigh was of regret.

It seemed a listless world—the world inside a lighted London house, dominated by a pale butler with black side-whiskers and endless discretion. But Eustace did not feel it so. Winifred knew that beyond hope of doubt as she stole a glance at his face. He had put off the child— the buffoon—and looked for the moment a grave, dull young man, naturally at ease with all the conventions. She could not help saying to herself, as she went to her room to live with hairpins and her lady's-maid: "I believe he hated it all!"

From that night of kite flying Winifred felt differently towards her husband. She was of the comparatively rare women who hate pretence even in another woman, but especially in a man. The really eccentric she was not afraid of—could even love, being a searcher after the new and strange, like so many modern pilgrims. But pinchbeck eccentricity— Brummagem originalities—gave to her views of the poverty of poor human nature leading her to a depression not untinged with contempt.

And the fantasies of Eustace became more violent and more continuous as he began to note the lassitude which gradually crept into her intercourse with him. London rang with them. At one time he pretended to a strange passion for death; prayed to a skull which grinned in a shrine raised for it in his dressing room; lay down each day in a coffin, and asked Winifred to close it and scatter earth upon the lid, that he might realize the end towards which we journey. He talked of silence, long and loudly—an irony which Winifred duly noted—sneered at the fleeting phantoms in the show of existence, called the sobbing of women, the laughter of men, sounds as arid as the whizz of a cracker let off by a child on the fifth of November.

"We should kill our feelings," he said. "They make us absurd. Life should be a breathing calm, as death is a breathless calm."

The calm descending upon Winifred was of the benumbing order.

Later he recoiled from this coquetting with the destroyer.

"After all," he said, "which of us does not feel himself eternal, exempt from the penalty of the race? You don't believe that you will ever die,

Winifred?"

"I know it," she said.

"Yes, but you don't believe it."

"You think knowledge less real than belief? Perhaps it is. But I, at least, hope that some day I shall die. To live on here forever would be like staying eternally at a party. After all, when one has danced, and supped, and flirted, and wondered at the gowns, and praised the flowers, and touched the hand of one's hostess, and swung round in a final gallop, and said how much one has enjoyed it all—one wants to go home."

"Does one?" Eustace said. "Home you call it!"

He shuddered.

"I call it what I want it to be, what I think it may be, what the poor and the weary and the fallen make it in their lonely thoughts. Let us, at least, hope that we travel towards the east, where the sun is."

"You have strange fancies," he said.

"I! Not so strange as yours."

She looked at him in the eyes as she spoke. He wondered what that look meant. It seemed to him a menace.

"I must keep it up—I must keep it up," he murmured to himself as he left the room. "Winifred loves fancies—loves me for what she thinks mine."

He went to his library, and sat down heavily, to devise fresh outrages on the ordinary.

His pranks became innumerable, and Society called him the most original figure of London. The papers quoted him—his doings, not his sayings. People pointed him out in the Park. His celebrity waxed. Even the Marble Arch seemed turning to gaze after him as he went by, showing the observation which the imaginative think into inanimate things.

At least, so a wag declared.

And Winifred bore it, but with an increasing impatience.

At this time, too, a strange need of protection crept over her, the yearning for man's beautiful, dog-like sympathy that watches woman in her grand dark hour before she blooms into motherhood. When she knew the truth, she resolved to tell Eustace, and she came into his room softly, with shining eyes. He was sitting reading the *Financial News* in a nimbus of cigarette smoke, secretly glorying in his momentary immunity from the prison rules of the fantastic. Winifred's entry was as that of a warder. He sprang up laughing.

"Winnie," he said, "I think I am going to South Africa."

"You!" she said in surprise.

"Yes; to give acrobatic performances in the street, and so pave the way to a position as a millionaire. Who ever heard of a man rising from a respectable competence to a fortune? According to the papers, you must start with nothing; that is the first rule of the game. We have ten thousand a year, so we can never hope to be rich. Fortune only favours the pauper. I am mad about money to-day. I can think of nothing else."

And he began showing her conjuring tricks with sovereigns which he drew from his pockets.

She did not tell him that day. And when she told him, it was without apparent emotion. She seemed merely stating coldly a physical fact, not breathing out a beautiful secret of her soul and his, a consecrated wonder to shake them both, and bind them together as two flowers are bound in the centre of a bouquet, the envy of the other flowers.

"Eustace," she said, and her eyes were clear and her hands were still, "I think I ought to tell you—we shall have a child."

Her voice was unwavering as a doctor's which pronounces, "You have the influenza." She stood there before him.

"Winifred!" he cried, looking up. His impulse was to say, "Wife! My Winifred!" to take her in his arms as any clerk might take his little middle-class spouse, to kiss her lips, and, in doing it, fancy he drew near to the prison in which every soul eternally dwells on earth. Finely human he felt, as the dullest, the most unknown, the plainest, the most despised, may feel, thank God! "Winifred!" he cried. And then he stopped, with the shooting thought, "Even now I must be what she thinks me, what she perhaps loves me for."

She stood there silently waiting.

"Toys!" he exclaimed. "Toys have always been my besetting sin. Now I will make a grand collection, not for the Pope, as people pretend, but for our family. You will have two children to laugh at, Winnie. Your husband is one, you know." He sprang up. "I'll go into the Strand," he said. "There's a man near the Temple who has always got some delightful novelty displaying its paces on the pavement. What fun!"

And off he went, leaving Winifred alone with the mystery of her woman's world, the mystic mystery of birth that may dawn out of hate as out of love, out of drunken dissipation as out of purity's sweet climax.

Next day a paragraph in the papers told how Mr. Eustace Lane had bought up all the penny toys of the Strand. Mention was again made of his supposed mission to the Vatican, and a picture drawn of the bewilderment of the Holy Father, roused from contemplation of the eternal to contemplation of jumping pasteboard, and the frigid gestures of people from the world of papier-mâché.

Eustace showed the paragraph to Winifred.

"Why will they chronicle all I do?" he said, with a sigh.

"Would you rather they did not?"

"Oh, if it amuses them," he answered. "To amuse the world is to be its benefactor."

"No, to comfort the world," was Winifred's silent thought.

To her the world often seemed a weary invalid, playing cards on the coverlet of the bed from which it longed in vain to move, peeping with heavy eyes at the shrouded windows of its chamber, and listening for faint sounds from without—soft songs, soft murmurings, the breath of winds, the sigh of showers; then turning with a smothered groan to its cards again, its lengthy game of "Patience." Clubs, spades, hearts, diamonds—there they all lay on the coverlet ready to the hands of the invalid. But she wanted to take them away, and give to the sufferer a prayer and a hope.

At this period she was often full of a vague, chaotic tenderness, far-reaching, yet indefinite. She could rather have kissed the race than a person.

And so the days went by, Winifred in a dream of wonder, Eustace in the toy-shops.

Until the birthday dawned and faded.

All through that day Eustace was in agony. He did not care so much for the child, but he loved the mother. Her danger tore at his heart. Her pain smote him, till he seemed to feel it actually and physically. That she was giving him something was naught to him; that she might be taken away in the giving was everything. And when he learnt that all was well, he cried and prayed, and thought to himself afterwards, "If Winifred could know what I am like, what I have done to-day, how would it strike her?"

She did not know; for when at length Eustace was admitted to her room, he trained himself to murmur, "A girl, that's lucky because of all the dolls. The Pope sha'n't have even one now."

Winifred lay back white on her pillow, and a little frown travelled across her face. If Eustace had just kissed her, and she had felt a tear of his on her face, and he had said nothing, she could have loved him then as a father, perhaps, more than as a husband. His allusion to the supposed Papal absurdity disgusted her at such a time, only faintly, because of her weakness, but distinctly, and in a way to be remembered.

She recovered; but just as the child was beginning to smile, and to express an approbation of life by murmurous gurglings, an infantile disease gripped it, held it, would not release it. And Winifred knelt beside it, dead, and thought, with a new and vital horror, of the invalid world playing cards upon the drawn coverlet of its bed. Baby was outside that chamber now, beyond the curtained windows, outside in sun or shower that she could not see, could only dream of, while the game of "Patience" went on and on.

III

The death of the child meant more to Winifred than she would at first acknowledge even to herself. Almost unconsciously she had looked forward to its birth as to a release from bondage. There are moments when a duet is gaol, a trio comparative liberty. The child, the tiny intruder into youthful married life, may come in the guise of an imp or of a good fairy: one to cloud the perfect and complete joy of two, or one to give sunlight to their nascent weariness and dissatisfaction. Or, again, it may be looked for with longing by one of two lovers, with apprehension by the other. Only when it lay dead did Winifred understand that Eustace was to her a stranger, and that she was lonely alone with him. The "Au revoir" of two bodies may be sweet, but the "Au revoir" of two minds is generally but a hypocritical or sarcastic rendering of the tragic word "Adieu." Winifred's mind cried "Au revoir" to the mind of Eustace, to his nature, to his love, but deep in her soul trembled the minor music, the shuddering discord, of "Adieu." Adieu to the body of child; adieu more complete, more eternal, to the soul of husband. Which goodbye was the stranger? She stood as at crossroads, and watched, with hand-shaded eyes, the tiny, wayward babe dwindling on its journey to heaven; the man she had married dwindling on his journey—whither? And the one she had a full hope of meeting again, but the other—

After the funeral the Lanes took up once more the old dual life which had been momentarily interrupted. Had it not been for the interruption, Winifred fancied that she might not have awakened to the full knowledge of her own feelings towards Eustace until a much later period. But the baby's birth, existence, passing away, were a blow upon the gate of life from the vague without. She had opened the gate, caught a glimpse of the shadowy land of the possible. And to do that is often to realize in a flash the impossibility of one's individual fate. So many of us manage to live ignorantly all our days and to call ourselves happy. Winifred could never live quite ignorantly again.

To Eustace the interruption meant much less. So long as he had Winifred he could not feel that any of his dreams hung altogether in tatters. Sometimes, it is true, he contemplated the penny toys, and had a moment of quaint, not unpleasant regret, half forming the thought, Why do we ever trouble ourselves to prepare happiness for others, when happiness is a word of a thousand meanings? As often as not, to do so is to set a dinner of many courses and many wines before an unknown guest, who proves to be vegetarian and teetotaler, after all.

"What shall I do with the toys?" he asked Winifred one day.

"The toys? Oh, give them to a children's hospital," she said, and her voice had a harsh note in it.

"No," he answered, after a moment's reflection; "I'll keep them and play with them myself; you know I love toys."

And on the following Sunday, when many callers came to Deanery Street, they found him in the drawing room, playing with a Noah's ark. Red, green, violet, and azure elephants, antelopes, zebras, and pigs processed along the carpet, guided by an orange-coloured Noah in a purple top hat, and a perfect parterre of sons and wives. The fixed anxiety of their painted faces suggested that they were in apprehension of the flood, but their rigid attitudes implied trust in the Unseen.

Winifred's face that day seemed changed to those who knew her best. To one man, a soldier who had admired her greatly before her marriage, and who had seen no reason to change his opinion of her since, she was more cordial than usual, and he went away curiously meditating on the mystery of women.

"What has happened to Mrs. Lane?" he thought to himself as he walked down Park Lane. "That last look of hers at me, when I was by the door, going, was—yes, I'll swear it—Regent Street. And yet Winnie Lane is the purest—I'm hanged if I can make out women! Anyhow, I'll go there again. People say she and that fantastic ass she's married are devoted. H'm!" He went to Pall Mall, and sat staring at nothing in his Club till seven, deep in the mystery of the female sex.

And he went again to Deanery Street to see whether the vision of Regent Street was deceptive, and came away wondering and hoping. From this time the vagaries of Eustace Lane became more incessant, more flamboyant, than ever, and Mrs. Lane was perpetually in society. If it would not have been true to say, conventionally, that no party was complete without her, yet it certainly seemed, from this time, that she was incomplete without a party. She was the starving wolf after the sledge in which sat the gay world. If the sledge escaped her, she was left to face darkness, snow, wintry winds, loneliness. In London do we not often hear the dismal howling of the wolves, suggesting steppes of the heart frigid as Siberia?

Eustace grew uneasy, for Winifred seemed eluding him in this maze of entertainments. He could not impress the personality of his mask upon her vitally when she moved perpetually in the pantomime processions of society, surrounded by grotesques, mimes, dancers, and deformities.

"We are scarcely ever alone, Winnie," he said to her one day.

"You must learn to love me in a crowd," she answered. "Human nature can love even God in isolation, but the man who can love God in the world is the true Christian."

"I can love you anywhere," he said. "But you—" And then he stopped and quickly readjusted his mask which was slipping off.

From that day he monotonously accentuated his absurdities. All London rang with them. He was the Court Fool of Mayfair, the buffoon of the inner circles of the Metropolis, and, by degrees, his painted fame, jangling the bells in its cap, spun about England in a dervish dance, till Peckham whispered of him, and even the remotest suburbs crowned him with parsley and hung upon his doings. All the blooming flowers of notoriety were his, to hug in his arms as he stood upon his platform bowing to the general applause. His shrine in *Vanity Fair* was surely being prepared. But he scarcely thought of this, being that ordinary, ridiculous, middle-class thing, an immoderately loving husband, insane enough to worship romantically the woman to whom he was unromantically tied by the law of his country. With each new fantasy he hoped to win back that which he had lost. Each joke was the throw of a desperate gamester, each tricky invention a stake placed on the number that would never turn up. That wild time of his career was humorous to the world, how tragic to himself we can only wonder. He spread wings like a bird, flew hither and thither as if a vagrant for pure joy and the pleasure of movement, darted and poised, circled and sailed, but all the time his heart cried aloud for a nest and Winifred. Yet he wooed her only silently by his follies, and set her each day farther and farther from him.

And she—how she hated his notoriety, and was sick with weariness when voices told her of his escapades, modulating themselves to wondering praise. Long ago she had known that Eustace sinned against his own nature, but she had never loved him quite enough to discover what that nature really was. And now she had no desire to find out. He was only her husband and the least of all men to her.

The Lanes sat at breakfast one morning and took up their letters. Winifred sipped her tea, and opened one or two carelessly. They were invitations. Then she tore the envelope of a third, and, as she read it, forgot to sip her tea. Presently she laid it down slowly. Eustace was looking at her.

"Winifred," he said, "I have got a letter from the editor of *Vanity Fair*."

"Oh!"

"He wishes me to permit a caricature of myself to appear in his pages."

Winifred's fingers closed sharply on the letter she had just been reading. A decision of hers in regard to the writer of it was hanging in the balance, though Eustace did not know it.

"Well?" said Eustace, inquiring of her silence.

"What are you going to reply?" she asked.

"I am wondering."

She chipped an eggshell and took a bit of dry toast.

"All those who appear in *Vanity Fair* are celebrated, aren't they?" she said.

"I suppose so," Eustace said.

"For many different things."

"Of course."

"Can you refuse the editor's request?"

"I don't know why I should."

"Exactly. Tell me when you have written to him, and what you have written, Eustace."

"Yes, Winnie, I will."

Later on in the day he came up to her boudoir, and said to her:

"I have told him I am quite willing to have my caricature in his paper."

"Your portrait," she said. "All right. Leave me now, Eustace; I have some writing to do."

As soon as he had gone she sat down and wrote a short letter, which she posted herself.

A month later Eustace came bounding up the stairs to find her.

"Winnie, Winnie!" he called. "Where are you? I've something to show you."

He held a newspaper in his hand. Winifred was not in the room. Eustace rang the bell.

"Where is Mrs. Lane?" he asked of the footman who answered it.

"Gone out, sir," the man answered.

"And not back yet? It's very late," said Eustace, looking at his watch. The time was a quarter to eight. They were dining at half-past.

"I wonder where she is," he thought.

Then he sat down and gazed at a cartoon which represented a thin man with a preternaturally pale face, legs like sticks, and drooping hands full of toys—himself. Beneath it was written, "His aim is to amuse."

He turned a page, and read, for the third or fourth time, the following:

Mr. Eustace Lane.

"Mr. Eustace Bernhard Lane, only son of Mr. Merton Lane, of Carlton House Terrace, was born in London twenty-eight years ago. He is married to one of the belles of the day, and is probably the most envied husband in town.

"Although he is such a noted figure in society, Mr. Eustace Lane has never done any conspicuously good or bad deed. He has neither invented a bicycle nor written a novel, neither lost a seat in Parliament, nor found a mine in South Africa. Careless of elevating the world, he has been content to entertain it, to make it laugh, or to make it wonder. His aim is to amuse, and his whole-souled endeavour to succeed in this ambition has gained him the entire respect of the frivolous. What more could man desire?"

As he finished there came a ring at the hall door bell.

"Winifred!" he exclaimed, and jumped up with the paper in his hand.

In a moment the footman entered with a note.

"A boy messenger has just brought this, sir," he said.

Eustace took it, and, as the man went out and shut the door, opened it, and read:

"Victoria Station.

"This is to say good-bye. By the time it reaches you I shall have left London. Not alone. I have seen the cartoon. It is very like you.

Winifred."

Eustace sank down in a chair.

On the table at his elbow lay *Vanity Fair*. Mechanically he looked at it, and read once more the words beneath his picture, "His aim is to amuse."

The Two Fears

I

Mrs. Allington was afraid. She had always been what is called a nervous sort of woman. Constitutionally delicate, thin, small and pale, with large, anxious, brown eyes, her whole appearance suggested sensitiveness and an almost shrinking timidity. A widow now, she had been married young to a man who did everything "in his own way."

He had loved her, but in his own way. He had been kind to her, but in his own way. He had eaten and drunk, taken his pleasures and undergone his misfortunes, worshipped himself and paid homage to his Creator in his own way. And some had thought that his way was a trying one. Most of his friends and acquaintances had called him at one time or another a trying man. Several had gone so far as to say of him that he had a way with him that would have tried a saint.

Mrs. Allington may, or may not, have been a saint; anyhow, she never said, and never showed, that her husband tried her. She fell in with all his wishes while he was alive, and appeared to mourn him with deep sincerity when he was dead. She had looked very anxious while he was with her, largely presiding over her life; she continued to look very anxious after he was—as Miss Allington, her knitting, charitable sister-in-law put it—"gathered in."

It seemed as if she couldn't look anything else.

A fixed expression may with time become almost as deceptive as a mask. If a woman always looks anxious, nobody bothers about her anxieties; perhaps, indeed, nobody believes in them. By displaying she may actually conceal.

So it was with Mrs. Allington.

When the European war broke out she was living in a small house in Kensington with her only child, Ivo, who was just twenty-five, and who was doing well as a journalist.

Mrs. Allington had just enough for her necessities; but for her comforts, for those innumerable small things which draw some of the austere harshness out of life, which paint in a little warm colour on the grey, she was dependent upon Ivo.

But for Ivo she must have lived in a cheap boarding house instead of in that cherished possession—247, Lenorva Road, West Kensington. But for Ivo really nice dresses—not many, and never expensive, but in a modest way satisfactory—would have been "beyond her." But for Ivo she could not have indulged in occasional visits to the theatre and occasional pleasant afternoons at the Ballad Concerts, followed by tea in Bond Street. Ivo was clever and had the artistic temperament—which implies startling irritabilities and occasional exhibitions of nerves upon the tightrope—but he was very good to his mother in his own way, which was not inherited from his father.

And now Mrs. Allington was full of fear connected with Ivo. Two fears, in fact, possessed her soul. She was afraid that Ivo would enlist in the army Kitchener had begun to form for active service against the Huns. That was fear number one. And she was afraid that he would not enlist. That was fear number two.

She felt that she simply couldn't bear it if Ivo enlisted, and she knew that she just couldn't endure it if he didn't. As she said absolutely nothing about either of her two fears, and merely went on looking extremely anxious, nobody had the least suspicion that she was not "just as usual." Even Ivo, who was supposed to be so intuitive, and to whom human nature was said to be an open book, even Ivo had no notion that his mother was in any way worried. To tell the truth, he thought he was doing all the worrying that was being done at 247, Lenorva Road.

When the war broke out he had had tremendous visions of "finding himself" as the ideal war correspondent. But Kitchener—everything was put upon Kitchener by everybody—had other views. Or so it was rumoured. There were not to be any war correspondents. And so for a time Ivo went on in the old way of a successful young freelance. He wrote about war in West Kensington, and khaki began to appear in the streets. It became more and more mysteriously prevalent. One saw it in the Tube; one jostled against it in the Underground; one sat beside it upon the tops of 'buses; one met it unexpectedly in great abundance on coming round corners; it tramped about the parks, and did remarkable maneuvers in sunlit public gardens, and sang along the Mall, and whistled its way along the Embankment beside the old brown river.

And Ivo began to worry.

He was a clever boy and a good sort of boy, but he was of the intellectual rather than of the muscular type. He was decidedly an individualist, and, though he was a journalist, he was much concerned about art. He knew all the ways of the Cubists, the Futurists, the Vorticists; he was very keen on the Russian ballet; he was deeply interested in what Mr. George Moore was going to do next, and swore almost passionately by Granville Barker.

In music his taste ran rather to Scriabin than to the composer of "Tipperary."

And so he worried quite a good deal.

And in Mrs. Allington fear number two began to grow and to attain conspicuous proportions.

How perfectly terrible it would be if Ivo didn't enlist!

The sons of neighbours and even of friends began to change colour; from the blue serge, or the dull green of Harris tweed, or the black of that cloth which is made up into "morning coats," they faded—or was it bloomed?—into khaki.

And the young men who hadn't changed colour became louder in their assertion that it would be a short war, "all over long before these fellows in a hurry get their rifles.”

Mrs. Allington lay awake night after night, and fear number two crouched beside her pillow.

What would she do if Ivo didn't enlist?

II

She and her son did not talk very much about the war. Ivo honestly thought that she “didn't take much stock of it,” and she thought—well, who knows what little women think about the great things, and the men who are in them? But she noticed the khaki. She noticed it so much that she saw the world clad in it. For her there were no more trousers, there were only puttees.

One day, when fear number two impended over her like a Colossus, Ivo said to her in a very casual way:

“I suppose you could get along on a good deal less than you do, mother—at a pinch, eh?”

Fear number two shrivelled and was gone, and fear number one lifted itself suddenly to the height of Mrs. Allington's heart; but she went on looking anxious, and said in her usual voice—a very light and rather faded soprano:

“Yes, dear, I suppose I could, at a pinch.”

“That's what I thought. It's generally possible to knock off a few things. Most of us wade through superfluities.”

“Dear?”

“My way of saying we complicate our needs.”

“Oh, I see.”

But he felt perfectly certain she didn't. Ivo was apt to think that his mother didn't see things. He loved her more than he knew and more than she knew, but he didn't consider her at all clever. You see, he was clever himself, and that fact shut certain doors against him.

During the next few days Mrs. Allington was never alone. Always day and night fear number one was with her.

How terrible, how almost unbearable it would be if Ivo were to enlist! She looked very anxious and exactly as usual.

Ivo, meanwhile, was going through a mental struggle which actually made him lose weight. He wanted to enlist and he hated the idea of enlisting; he longed to be a patriot and to prove his patriotism, and he loathed the thought of giving up his career, and still more the thought of being a private in the midst of a crowd of privates, of having to live always, day and night, in public, hopelessly and everlastingly mixed up with all sorts and conditions of men with whom probably he would not have an “idea in common.”

At moments he longed to be sixteen, at other moments he pined to be forty-one, and look it. He thought of Mr. Roger Fry and the Post-Impressionists, of Mr. George Moore and “The Apostle,” of the Russian ballet and "Thamar," of the strange and realistic novel he meant to write, the novel which would take him out of journalism.

He also thought of his mother.

Had he the "right" to sacrifice his mother on the altar of his patriotism? He was a freelance in journalism. No one would continue a salary to him if he joined the colours. It would mean pinching by his mother; it might even mean the giving up of 247, Lenorva Road. Could he, ought he to require this of his mother? It would be beastly sleeping in a tent in the damp—perhaps on Salisbury Plain—with a hugger-mugger of fellows who had never even heard of half the things which meant so much to him. Surely an only son oughtn't to do that when swarms of brothers were showing their sleek heads and fancy socks all over the country without a thought of joining the Army.

But the khaki—the khaki! Everywhere it met him like a summons; and at last he said to his mother abruptly:

"They seem to want a lot of men for this war, mother—eh?"

"Yes, dear," said Mrs. Allington, in the faded soprano.

"Kitchener seems very keen on increasing the numbers."

"Does he?"

"Well, you see the appeals on all the walls. That can only mean one thing."

He spoke rather irritably.

"I don't look at the walls very much, dear," said Mrs. Allington vaguely.

Ivo was silent for a moment. He got up, went to the window of the little sitting room, and looked out upon Lenorva Road, that stretching paradise of stucco. His lips were pursed and his brown eyes stared. They saw a black cat, which moved between the expressionless houses like a creature whose nature belonged to the jungle.

"And my nature?" he thought. "Does it belong to Lenorva Road or to England?"

He turned round.

"Would you advise me to join, mother?" he asked.

Then, on either side of her stood the two fears, stiff and forbidding, like sentinels with fixed bayonets. She waited a moment, not looking at them; then she said:

"Well, dear, as you say, they seem to want a lot of men for this war. And if Lord Kitchener is really very keen on increasing the numbers, perhaps—"

But at this point the faded soprano faded quite away.

"I'll join, mother. It may mean leaving Lenorva Road."

"Whatever it means—" said Mrs. Allington.

And there she stopped, perhaps because of surprise. For a strange thing had happened—the two sentinels with the fixed bayonets had vanished.

She never saw them again.

Ivo joined—never mind what regiment. Presently he fell at the

Dardanelles.

His mother received the telegram announcing his death in a cheap boarding house where she is living now in Rova Crescent, Shepherd's Bush.

I saw her walking alone down the road not very long ago. She was dressed in a very ordinary black gown, not such a good gown as she used to wear in the days when she lived at No. 247. But what struck me was her expression.

She no longer looked anxious. If it hadn't been Mrs. Allington I should have thought she looked proud, proud in a beautiful way.

As I took off my hat to her I thought: "So the widow still gives her mite."

The Lift

I

In a red hotel, which used to stand on the sea-front at Naples, I encountered Madame. She was travelling with a remarkable looking man, who drew my attention before I took any notice of her. Indeed, he practically effaced her by his strong personality, as a mighty rock effaces a small plant meekly sprouting in its shadow.

This man was enormous, much over six feet high, with great shoulders, a tremendously deep chest, a vast, jutting out stomach, big, sturdy legs, broad capacious feet. His startling bulk of body was finished off with a head and face which simply demanded your attention; the head covered with dense black hair brushed back from a mighty forehead and worn long over the nape of a thick bull-like neck; the face bronzed, with large, handsome features quivering with expression, and hot, staring black eyes. The mouth and chin were adorned with elaborate moustaches and an ample square-cut Assyrian beard.

The voice and manner of this personage were just what they should be to accord with the rest of him. The former was a sonorous and commanding bass, the sort of bass that would sound just the thing in a finale of Verdi's *Aïda*. The latter—but that's more difficult to describe.

Sometimes it suggested to me an earthquake, at other times a storm at sea. It embraced voluminously, or rejected and dashed down with violence. It was gesticulatory. Hands, arms, head seemed always in movement. Often, too, the great body seemed to quake. The large hot eyes rolled. The Assyrian beard was thrust out this way and that, as if to the four points of the compass. As I watched, imaginations of what Alexandre Dumas *père* must surely have been came to me. Did some obscure black blood, flowing in canal-like veins, cause all this restless, yet not happy, exuberance, hiding deep down somewhere in that gesticulating mass?

I sat not far from him in the restaurant, and noticed that he was a great eater and that he drank like a Russian. Also, he was an epicure and was never satisfied with the cooking. There were perpetual summonses to the *maître d'hôtel*, perpetual arguments, scoldings, and commands. And these upheavals ended invariably in a majestic distribution of largesse. Tipping I cannot call it.

After dinner, when I came into the semi-Oriental hall which occupied the middle of the hotel, I would find the Potentate—as I had secretly named him—protruding from a large armchair, a mighty cigar in his mouth, a magnum of champagne in an ice-pail beside him. Madame had vanished to some distant corner, and was occupied with some foreign newspaper, as often as not held upside-down. But one didn't miss her because one hadn't noticed her. The Potentate had a strange power of making those near him seem so unimportant that they became practically invisible. They were there, but one didn't genuinely see them. I didn't genuinely see Madame till some time after I had minutely observed every detail of her phenomenal companion.

He soon spoke to me. He soon spoke to everyone. Solitude was as abhorrent to him as tranquillity. Despite his evident herculean strength he was, I'm convinced, a martyr to neurasthenia. He had the mania of motion. He couldn't be quiet. He couldn't sit really still. Some malady of the mind or the nerves was forever whipping him. And he was forever responding to the lash. During the day he was heaven knows where; up Vesuvius, one volcano going to another, at Ana Capri, at Sorrento, coasting among the caves beyond Posilippo, visiting the prisons of Niscida, diving into the lowest quarters of Naples, here, there, everywhere. But at eight-thirty he was usually to be found in the restaurant, and generally after dinner he managed to stay in the hall for some time, companioned by the champagne and the ice-pail, and by anyone he could capture to serve as a victim of his avalanche of talk. Later, in a vast overcoat, with an immense black hat spreading wings about him, cigar in mouth, he would pass out by the revolving door and disappear into the night.

When he caught me coming out of the restaurant he poured iced champagne down my throat and smothered me with intimate information. He was a Brazilian, a doctor, a publicist, journalist, politician, millionaire. He owned great tracts of land, large segments of cities in South America, plantations, mines, ranches. He had built himself palaces. He showed me photographs of one of them, apparently all of white marble, with columns, terraces, fountains, bathhouses, lakes, tennis courts, a racing track, exotic gardens. And he was there in the gardens, striking a tremendous attitude, his uncovered head exposed to a tropical sun. The friend of presidents, it seemed that he had made revolutions, and been instrumental in overthrowing governments and placing his nominees in positions of autocratic power. He had travelled all over the world, and was travelling still. He was, in fact, always travelling. He spoke of going from Naples to Japan, Thibet, New Zealand, Central Asia, the islands of the Southern Pacific. The round world shrank to the size of a pea as I listened to his uproar of conversation.

One night, when he caught me, Madame was as usual in the offing, but this time well in sight and well within hearing distance of us. She was sitting on a pseudo-divan, holding the *Berliner Tageblatt* upside-down in front of her. The Potentate pointed at her with a big brown forefinger.

"That package is the curse of my life," he said, in his loud bass voice.

He spoke usually in French, with a tremendously strong accent, but often introduced Italian, Spanish, and English words into the conversation.

I begged his pardon.

"That woman—my wife—she's a package!"

He turned on me. The beard swept about me.

"Look at her. Isn't she a package?" he bayed.

I said I really couldn't agree with him. I went farther. I begged him to remember that the lady could hear everything that was said.

"Hear! She's a fool! She's an ignoramus! She understands no language but Portuguese. Think of being married to a package who understands not one word of any language but Portuguese!"

I did so.

"And isn't she ugly?" he exclaimed, with a violent gesture towards her. "Tell me—isn't she frightful? And I didn't marry her till I was forty and she was forty-three. So she wasn't even young. Look at her!"

Madame, at whom I then was obliged to look, was certainly not a beauty. She was very thin, with an indefinite flat face, powdered here and there in patches, a retreating chin, and coarse, dusty-looking dark hair, so badly arranged that it suggested that hens had been scratching about in it.

"Well?"

What could I say? I said nothing.

"Go on! I tell you she understands nothing but Portuguese!"

"But really—"

"You can shout. She won't understand you."

But politeness prevented me from shouting that I thought Madame a very unfortunate-looking female. Her timid, anxious eyes were upon me, peeping over the upside-down newspaper. And they surely understood a language other than Portuguese.

"Just think!" the Potentate went on. "I have to drag that package there with me all over the world. She's been round the world with me three times already. And she sees nothing, comprehends nothing, enjoys nothing. What does she do? Sits in hotels all over the globe reading papers written in languages she can't understand upside-down! What a life-companion for a man blazing with ideas! But I'll pack her back to Brazil"—he spoke at her across the room—"one day when she least expects it down to the port with her boxes, and" —he actually got up, and extending his right leg brought it back, then shot it forward in a violent kick—"and off to Brazil with you, you package—you!"

He followed up the kick with a movement of his hands doubled up into fists.

"Boum—pouf—and off with you!"

I seemed to see the fists catching her in the small of the back and elsewhere, I seemed to see her shot over the gangplank head foremost into the ship that was bound for Brazil. Then I looked across the hall and met those small furtive eyes peeping over the *Berliner Tageblatt* upside-down, and I believe I reddened.

"Really," I said, turning to the Potentate. "Really, I think we ought to be more—more careful."

It wasn't a very adequate sentence, I know. He swept it away with a blast of withering scorn that seemed to run like fire through pampas grass.

"Haven't I told you again and again that she understands nothing but Portuguese?"

II

It was, I think, two days after this rather unfortunate introduction—if it can be properly called an introduction—to the Potentate's helpmate, that between ten and eleven o'clock in the evening I was in the outer hall of the hotel, in front of the cage that served as the home of the electric lift. The Potentate, after a stormy hour with me by the ice-pail, had just barged out alone into the night, having failed to persuade me to accompany him in a search for the horrors of Naples. Ever since dinner Madame had been sitting by a pseudo hubble-bubble on the usual pseudo-divan, reading the *Echo de Paris* upside-down, while her spouse had been entertaining me with copious iced champagne and a torrent of abuse of her. It seemed that matters matrimonial were moving rapidly towards a crisis in the Brazilian ménage. Monsieur was about to depart for Java—he had suddenly thrown over Tibet—and he had affirmed to me that evening that if he saw Madame sitting about in Java, reading Javanese papers upside-down, he would assuredly strangle her "with his own hands." He had indulged in a violent, and marvellously expressive pantomime of strangling a reluctant consort, during which Madame's small eyes had peeped at us both over the bottom of the *Echo de Paris*. And then, foaming more or less over my refusal to bear him company, he had flung away into the night. Now, feeling really rather unnerved by it all, I was on my way to bed.

I must tell you that in our hotel we sometimes "operated" the lift ourselves, by shutting the gate and pressing a button. I was now bringing the lift down from an upper storey. It arrived empty, and, not seeing any attendant at the moment, I stepped in, shut the cage-gate, and was about to press the button, which would take me up to the third floor, when I saw peeping at me through the bars of the gate the small furtive eyes of the Potentate's wife.

Knowing she understood no language but Portuguese I felt it was useless to address her in English, French, or Italian, the only languages I can speak in, and I therefore asked her by gesture if she wanted to go up. She nodded vaguely, whereupon I opened the gate, let her in, and then by facial expression and hand pantomime, inquired which floor she wished to go to. She pointed to my button, the third-floor button. I pressed it, and the lift immediately began to ascend. We had glided upwards past two floors when the electric light went out, the lift stopped between floors two and three, and the Potentate's wife and I were imprisoned in total darkness. Evidently a short circuit had occurred. Now, while the lift had been in movement, Madame had been sitting on a narrow seat with which it was provided, and I had remained standing ready to open the gate when we arrived at the third floor. Neither of us, of course, had uttered a word to the other. I could not speak Portuguese, and, besides, we had never been formally introduced to each other. Certainly I had been asked in her presence whether she wasn't frightful, and had been told I could shout my acquiescence. I had also been told, when she was there, that she was a package, a fool, an ignoramus, that she had been forty-three when she married, that she read newspapers in languages she didn't understand upside-down all over the world, that she saw nothing, comprehended nothing, enjoyed nothing, that if she went to Java she was going to be strangled, but that in all probability she would be kicked almost immediately on board a vessel bound for South America and exported to Brazil. All this might perhaps be said to have forged a sort of link between us. Still, I must repeat that in my opinion it scarcely constituted a strictly formal introduction. And now we were closeted together in the pitch dark, and might be there, isolated from the outer world, for a considerable time.

I felt, I confess, rather awkward as I remained standing perfectly still.

There was at first not a sound from the Potentate's wife. She mightn't have been there, so mute was she. Not the least whistle of breathing, not the smallest rustle of a gown, indicated her presence in the darkness close to me. And I remember absurdly thinking, "Suppose she's dead!" (Such ridiculous thoughts come to you in the dark.) She might be dead. Some people did die suddenly. She might be one of them. If it were so, if she were dead, should I be compromised? I found myself asking that question of myself. A comparatively young man is discovered shut up alone in a pitch-dark lift, between two floors, with a dead lady from Brazil, whom he has been seen to let into the lift a few minutes before in apparently perfect health!

It hadn't at all a nice sound about it! I had to admit that to myself. It didn't suggest a nice character at all. And how would the Potentate take it? I knew, of course, that he was anxious to strangle the lady, but I knew also that his intention was, if the strangling were to be done, to do it with his own hands. He had expressly said so, and more than once. If he thought he had reason to suppose that I had stepped in and taken the matter into my own competence, he mightn't like it. He mightn't like it at all. He might consider that I had played false with him, had as it were stolen his idea and used it before he had had leisure to. He might turn nasty, and if he did I should probably have an exceedingly unpleasant time. I was beginning to feel extremely apprehensive when out of the darkness came a thin soprano murmur of words which I didn't understand. Madame was not dead, and was saying something to me, doubtless in Portuguese.

"I'm so sorry I don't understand Portuguese," I replied politely.

The murmur came again.

"*Je le regrette beaucoup mais je ne comprends pas la langue Portugaise,*" I said.

For the third time the voice spoke.

"*Mi rincresce tanto tanto, ma veramente non capisco la bella lingua di Portogallo,*" I exclaimed in desperation.

To my intense surprise the voice said:

"'Elp me! I spik little Inglis, French, Italian, little German, too. 'Elp me! *Aidez moi! Sauvez moi!*"

There was a second of deep silence. Then came a sort of thin cry out of the darkness.

"*Aiutate mi, Signorino!*"

"I don't understand German," I said hastily, fearing that Madame would break into that language, and then go on possibly to Spanish, Russian, Greek, Roumanian, Dutch, and other European languages. "But don't be afraid. It's only a short circuit. I'm convinced of that. Probably in a few minutes it will be all right. Meanwhile there's no danger."

"'Elp me!" the voice replied. "*Sauvez moi!*"

"I assure you, Madame, I gladly would if I could do anything. But we are between two floors, and there's no possible means of getting out. You see the lift—"

"'E is mad!"

"No, no! What I mean is that the lift—"

"I not understand!"

"*L'ascenseur! L'ascenseur! L'ascensore!*"

"'Elp me! 'E is mad! *Il est fou. 'E pazzo!*"

"But it isn't the lift's fault, really, Madame. What has happened is this. There has been a short circuit, and—"

"I say 'e is mad."

"But it's the electricity which has—"

"You tink not. 'E give you champagne. *Vous en buvez. Vous pensez qu'il*—you tink 'im good man. But 'e is mad."

"Oh, I beg your pardon. You are speaking about your husband. I thought you were upset about the lift."

"'Elp me! *Bitte helfen Sie mir! Helfen Sie mir!*"

"Madame, I'm very sorry, but I don't understand Ger—"

"'E is mad. *Er ist verrückt!* 'Elp me, Sair!"

Now that I understood the exact meaning of this oft-repeated exclamation I began to feel extremely uncomfortable. I was very sorry for the poor lady. Her situation awoke all my chivalrous feelings. The prospect, before her if, as was at least possible, she did ever reach Java with the Potentate, was certainly very far from reassuring. No one likes to be strangled, and she was probably as averse as anybody else from such an end. Nevertheless, I really didn't quite see what I could do.

"Per-raps you—*peutêtre vous comprenez* Spaneesh, Sair?" the voice broke in on my anxious self-communing.

"I don't Madame, not one word! I must ask you to stick to English, French, or Italian."

"'Elp me! 'E is mad!"

This reiteration of a very unpleasant, even sinister, statement, began to get on my nerves. Things always seem worse in the dark. At least I think so. Even a cold in the head seems a tragedy in the dark, suggests pneumonia, galloping consumption, all sorts of horrors. And the darkness in the lift was what is called in the Bible "thick darkness." It seemed almost tangible. The heat, too, between the narrow enclosing walls of the shaft was overwhelming. I felt beads of perspiration starring my forehead. And hideous visions of the Potentate mad rose before my imagination. Such a large man—mad! It scarcely bore thinking of. A moderate-sized man gone crazy is all very well, but dementia on such a scale as the Potentate's would be altogether too much, a thoroughly inartistic piece of exaggeration.

"'Elp...."

"Madame!" I exclaimed, "I only wish I could, but you must realise how very difficult my position is in this matter. I know your husband so very little. And besides"—suddenly the ice-pail rose before me in the darkness—"besides, I have received nothing but hospitality at his hands. I have drunk his champagne. How can I interfere? How can I take any steps which might end in his incarceration in a lunatic asylum?"

"When you spik I understand no ting."

I realised that in my excitement I had been talking with voluble rapidity. Now I bent forward in the direction in which I believed Madame to be located—I was beginning to get confused, to lose my bearings, as one easily may in the dark—and said very slowly and impressively:

"Your husband has given me champagne, *iced* champagne. That makes my position very delicate. Champagne! You understand? *Champagne!*"

That word pronounced first English, then French fashion, evidently got home to what Madame no doubt thought of as her brain. For she replied, with unexpected lucidity:

"*Il donne toujours champagne.* 'E give champagne to all. In France 'e give champagne, in Italie, in Japon, *dans les Indes*. When I say, ''Elp!' everyone 'e say, 'champagne!'"

This was a veritable heart-cry, and it did not leave me unmoved.

There was something genuinely pathetic and terrible in the thought of this poor and ineffective lady being whirled about the habitable globe by the extraordinary being she had somehow—how I could not conceive—had somehow married, being whirled about the globe, and, when she appealed in all the languages of the nations for help in her doubtless very grave dilemma, being met always by the same very brief remark, "Champagne!" Something terrible in it, but something irresistibly comic, too! And in the dark I saw men of all nations, in all quarters of the world, being caught by the Potentate as they emerged from the restaurants of hotels-de-luxe, and held captive by the ice-pail, while Madame sat in the offing, peeping at them over the upside-down newspaper, and realising that yet another possible rescuer was being rendered impotent by the cruel generosity of the Brazilian phenomenon. And the comedy, the farcical comedy of it, struck away the tragedy out of my mind, and in the dark I began to laugh. That was dreadful, but I couldn't help it, any more than a man with a keen sense of humour can help laughing in church when anything ridiculous happens there. I laughed. I shook with laughter. My whole body quivered and was convulsed with laughter. And tears of laughter ran out of my eyes and down my laughing face. But through it all I was intent on not making a noise. Some, I hope gentlemanly, instinct prompted the avoidance of the roar. And all the time I laughed I was making a most strenuous and persistent effort to have my fit out in a respectable silence. And I believe this praiseworthy endeavour would have been crowned with success if, just at the crisis of my convulsion, the thin voice out of the darkness had not exclaimed:

"'Elp me, Sair! *Aidez moi! Aiutate mi Signorino!*"

And then, though she surely knew by this time I didn't understand German:

"Helfen Sie mir! Er ist verrückt! Bitte helfen Sie mir mein Herr!"

I think it was the German that finished me off. Anyhow, when she said the last words, I saw all the nations, represented by their male population, round the Potentate's ice-pail, and I let out one of the biggest bursts of laughter that probably ever broke from the frame of a man.

Long ago in a French farce, called *Les Surprises du Divorce*, I saw Coquelin *aîné* in a laughing scene. He began to laugh and he couldn't stop. His laughter escaped entirely from control, like Frankenstein's monster. It dominated him, it devastated him, it ransacked him from top to toe, it reduced him finally to a sort of human jelly, but still he went on laughing. The mind had long since ceased from laughing, but the body couldn't stop laughing. It was doubled up with laughing while the mind looked on shocked at the ghastly spectacle.

So I laughed that night in the lift with Madame. I thought of her marriage to the Potentate at the mature age of forty-three, and laughed. I thought of her travelling three times round the globe with him, doing nothing except read foreign newspapers upside-down, and laughed. I thought of the Potentate's gradually going mad under the stress of her impotent companionship, and laughed. I thought of the Potentate's rendering all the Knights-Errant, who might have succored the poor lady, innocuous by means of iced champagne, and laughed. I thought of her being kicked on board a ship bound for Brazil, and laughed. I thought of her being strangled by the Potentate in Java, and shrieked with laughter. Yes, I grieve to say it, that final vision of tragedy made me throw back my head in the by then almost suffocating darkness and laugh till my knees gave way, and I was obliged to lean against the wall of the lift for support.

How long I laughed I shall never know. In pitch darkness one loses count of time. But at length human nature seemed to go on strike from sheer exhaustion. My mind had long since stopped laughing, or even smiling. Now the last drops of laughter oozed—so I felt it—out of the squeezed sponge of my body. The tears of laughter began to dry on my cheeks, and in another moment I should have returned to my normal self-possession, when just at the psychological moment I heard the thin voice say in the darkness, "Why you laugh, Sair?"

And that set me off again.

When at last I did finally and permanently stop, stop "for good and all," I felt physically exhausted and mentally very much ashamed of myself. I realised that I must have made a quite tremendous row, and wondered whether my terrible outburst of merriment had been carried by the lift shaft, as by a sound conductor, into the farthest corners of the hotel. If so, what would people think? What would they think in the Bureau? What would be the general impression in the semi-Oriental hall? Certainly not a good one! When a man shouts with laughter in a dark lift stuck between two floors the most natural supposition would surely be that he is singularly devoid of proper feeling. And when it is known—as I realised that it must by this time be known in the hotel— that his companion in misfortune is an elderly Brazilian lady, of permanently lugubrious temperament, and entirely devoid of all sense of humour, and, moreover, that this lady is a total stranger to him, how must his conduct appear to all decent and right-thinking people?

My own laughter had rendered me deaf to any outside happenings, though not to the still, small Brazilian voice enclosed with me in the lift; but now I found myself listening intently in the darkness for noises from the hotel. Madame, after the question which had renewed my convulsions, had subsided into the death-like silence which had alarmed me at the beginning of our adventure. I conceived of her as finally stricken dumb by my shameless hilarity. But I was now concerned, not with her, but with the hotel. Our imprisonment could not be permanent. We should presently be enabled to emerge once more into the outer world. How should I be received there after what had just taken place? I listened as I don't think I have ever listened either before or since.

III

It seemed to me then that my ears had to get gradually accustomed to something else than terrific peals of laughter before they could be of any real use to me; that I had to wait patiently before they began to perform their normal function of registering ordinary sounds. But, presently, I supposed that they were at their usual work, and they seemed to be conveying to me a very peculiar and very unpleasant impression. I seemed to become aware of great confusion at a distance, of a confusion manifesting itself in multitudinous noises, which were all blended together into something that was neither sound nor silence. It was as if I did not actually hear, but felt through the agency of my ears, this mingling of many noises. And I was obscurely conscious that the hotel must be in an uproar.

Now, what could be the cause of an uproar in the hotel? I asked myself the question, and I immediately thought of the Potentate.

I had now lost all count of time, and really had not the remotest idea how long we had been shut up in the lift. Had we been there for a quarter of an hour, for an hour, for two hours? The Potentate had flung out into the night some time after ten o'clock, and I had thought to retire to bed almost immediately after his departure. If Madame and I had been in the lift for half an hour or so it must be about eleven o'clock. But it might well be later. Possibly, it was near midnight. I began to wonder at what hour the Potentate usually returned from his nocturnal excursions. Beneath us, it seemed to me now, the muffled uproar in the hotel was growing in volume. What could be the cause of such mysterious confusion in a hitherto well-ordered establishment? Had the Potentate—

But I put the ugly thought from me and tried to concentrate on the mishap to the lift. Such an accident, involving the comfort, and it might almost be said the safety, of two guests would, of course, rouse a certain anxiety in the Bureau. The Director would be summoned. There would be a conference about what was to be done. There would—but I now realised that I had no definite idea what happened in a first-class hotel when a lift, containing an elderly lady from Brazil and a comparatively young Englishman, stuck fast in the dark between two floors. The matter was outside my experience of life. I could only guess and imagine. But guess and imagine as I might the ugly conviction remained with me: "The Potentate has returned and has found out about the lift."

What he was doing, in consequence of having found out, of course I couldn't know. But having observed his demonstrations in the restaurant when an omelette was lacking in truffles, or when a bottle of Burgundy wasn't warmed to a nicety, I could deduce from them what he might well be capable of if he imagined that his honour was in question. And he wouldn't be reasonable. At all times he was like a thoroughly unreasonable volcano. It would, I knew, be quite useless for me to tell him that I hadn't deliberately arranged for a short circuit in order that I might secure an undisturbed *tête-à-tête* with Madame. He wouldn't believe me. I remembered my reiterated refusal to go out with him that night. By Jove, that would look bad, too, if he suspected anything I. He would certainly bring that up against me.

I found myself sweating profusely with heat and apprehension.

"Why you laugh, Sair?" said the thin voice in the darkness.

I began to understand in some degree why the Potentate had at any rate thought of strangling my companion. Why will women go back upon the past? Why will they rake up memories which are far best forgotten. It seemed to me now incredible that I had ever laughed, and I was intensely irritated by this cross-examination upon a matter which was, as I recognised, very little to my credit, and which it was quite impossible for me to explain to anyone, least of all to Madame. For how could I possibly tell her the simple truth, which was that I had nearly died of laughing because I had been visualising her assassination at the hands of the Potentate in Java?

"I can't explain, Madame," I said. "Please don't ask me. Please forget all about it. And now I beg you to tell me something. At what time does your husband usually come back to the hotel?"

"Sair?"

"At what hour does your husband generally come in to go to bed?"

"Sair?"

I clenched my hands.

"*A quelle heure votre mari—votre mari! Comprenez vous?—à quelle heure se couche-t-il généralement?*"

"Sair?"

I raised my fists, as the Potentate had raised his in the pantomime of the exportation to Brazil.

"*Vostro marito—capisce Lei? Vostro marito—a che ora va a letto?*"

"Sair?"

"At what o'clock—*à quelle heure—a che ora—*"

"I understand no ting!"

"But you told me that you spoke Inglis—I mean English—French, Italian, and even German. But you assured me—*mais vous m'avez assuré que—ma Lei mi ha detto che Lei parlava quattro lingue, quattro lingue—*"

"When you spik I understand no ting."

The perspiration was dropping from me. I was bathed in it, partly on account of the intense heat generated in the lift shaft, but partly also, I am certain, on account of my mental exasperation, my fear of the immediate future, and my inability to induce my extraordinary companion to comprehend any mortal thing I said. That was it then! She was one of those intolerable women who can't comprehend one word of any language spoken to then. And I remembered that the Potentate had told me that Portuguese was the only language she understood, not that Portuguese was the only language she spoke. For all I knew she might be able to speak badly in all the living languages extant. But it was quite certain that she was totally incapable of grasping the meaning of the simplest sentence in any one of them, however carefully spoken to her. My English accent was excellent. My French I flattered myself was more than passable. My Italian had in the long-ago years won a word of praise from no less a judge than the famous Madame Ristori. And yet all my efforts were greeted with the intolerable comment, "When you spik I understand no ting."

Suddenly, however, desperation rose in me. I resolved that somehow I would make this extraordinary being understand me. And I recollected having been told that the best way to force a very stupid, or very ignorant or very obstinate person into comprehension of your meaning is to speak of something which vitally affects his, or her, comfort, safety, or happiness: of money owed for instance, or of food long overdue, or of personal insecurity—such as danger to life or limb. I therefore crouched forward in the darkness towards where I supposed Madame to be and said in a penetrating voice:

"If you value your life on no account go to Java!"

"Sair?" came, to my great surprise, from immediately behind me.
I spun round.
"N'allez pas à Java, je vous en prie, Madame! N'allez jamais à Java!"
"'Elp me, Sair!"
"I'm trying to help you. *Lei non deve andare à Java ! Ha capito Lei?"*
"When you spik I understand no ting."
"Don't go to Java!" I roared.
"'Elp me, Sair!"
"I'm telling you—"
My voice failed me.
"Aiutate mi, Signorino! Helfen Sie mir!"
"I don't understand Ger—"
"Er ist verrückt! 'E 'ave give you champagne but 'e is mad. 'E pazzo. 'E pazzissimo! Monsieur, c'est un grand fou! Ich fürchte mich vor ihm. Aber was soil ich tun? Niemand hilft mir, weil sie alle zusammen von seinem champagner getrunken haben. Ich bitte sie—"
"Madame, how many times must I tell you that I don't under—"
"Wenn mir niemand helfen will weiss ich wirklich nicht was ich tun soil. Er ist mein Mann aber er hat mich nicht lieb. Wenn sie nur—"
But at this point in our conversation a diversion occurred. Suddenly the darkness vanished. The electric light gleamed out once more, and I found that I was standing up in the lift with my back to Madame and my face to the folding doors. I was about to turn round when the lift moved upwards and stopped with a jerk. Concluding that at last we had reached floor number 3, I pulled the doors inwards and was confronted by a wall. We had stuck again. But something—it seemed fatally—drew my glance upwards, and I saw above the wall, through the bottom of a grille, a pair of enormous feet and the beginnings of two mighty legs. They were immovable, like things put outside a bedroom door at night to be cleaned. I examined them with agonised attention, craning my neck to get a better view. Despite the bars which partially concealed them I knew them for what they were—the Potentate's feet and ankles, and I looked round at Madame.
"For mercy's sake," I whispered. "Don't—"
The lift moved with a jerk and stuck again. I was now confronted by a mountainous protuberance decorated with a cable-chain of gold and a whole family of seals of various shapes and sizes. Again I turned my head.
"For heaven's sake!" I whispered urgently, "mind you don't—"
"Sair?"
"Dites lui que—spiegate the quando voi siete venu—"
The lift glided smoothly upward, stopped gently, blandly almost, and I was face to face with the Potentate. His enormous black eyes were staring into mine. His Assyrian beard was thrust out towards me. He still wore the vast overcoat and enormous hat in which he had passed out into the night.
"It isn't my fault!" I began through the bars. "I assure you solemnly

that—"

He flung open the lift-gate. I thought, of course, that he was going to assault me, but his eyes travelled fiercely beyond me to Madame, who was still seated in the corner, and who now peeped out into the regained world exactly as she peeped over her newspapers.

The Potentate looked at her and then at me, in deadly silence. "I positively assure you," I began again, "I solemnly swear on my honour that—"

He swept aside my excuses with a gesture. I stepped meekly out on to the landing. Exactly what happened then I don't know. I was feeling quite unnerved. But I suppose Madame must have summoned courage to get out of the lift of her own accord, for the next thing I remember was seeing her thin back and scratchy head of hair disappearing in the distance of the corridor. She seemed to creep round the corner and was gone. I was alone with the Potentate.

He took out an immense gold watch and looked at it.

"The electric light and power failed all over Naples at twenty minutes to eleven," he said, in the *Aïda* bass.

"It's twelve o'clock now. You've been shut in there alone with her for an hour and twenty minutes."

"It wasn't my fault! I positively assure you, I swear on my sacred honour that it wasn't my—"

"For an hour and twenty minutes—and you haven't strangled her!"

He stared into my eyes like one who regards a phenomenon, something which he sees, but in which he finds it almost impossible to believe.

Then, without another word, he turned, and walking as it seemed to me with majestic contempt, disappeared round the corner of the corridor.

I kept my room all next day. On the following morning, when I ventured out, I learned from the polite young man at the Bureau that the Potentate and Madame had just set sail for Java.

The Last Time

I

The romance of autumn lay over the land.

Already the September gales, which attack the trees and shake from their branches the weakling leaves, were over, and the stealthy peace of the new season was stealing along the ways. Mists lay at dawn and at eventide in the folds of the hills and along the sedgy banks of the streams. Heavy dews bathed the grasses. Colours were creeping among the woods. The days were rapidly getting shorter. And the minds of men were changing with changing Nature, were turning inwards a little like curling leaves, were becoming more aware of themselves than they had been in the season of open-air joys.

With the first fires crackling on the hearths there came the autumn thoughts, which are strangely different from the thoughts of summer.

Harry Strickland noted that difference as he sat before his fire with a pipe, in his house in Chelsea, looking out on the river. He had been up north, fishing in Cumberland with a friend, and climbing Scawfell Pike, Pillar, and other craggy hills of the Lake District.

Their last nights had been spent in the inn at Wastdale Head, and at the Scawfell Hotel at Seascale. The weather had been wild. But up north at that season one expected wild weather. They had bicycled from Wastdale to Seascale to take the train to the south. All along the great sands, which stretch from St. Bees Head to Ravenglass and beyond, the sea had shown line behind line of tossing white foam, and had roared with a voice which had sounded full of mysterious invective. The gulls of the Muncaster Gullery had swept down the wind uttering their cry, which was like a cry of the wind and the driven sands. And at sunset, in a pageant of cruel gold, the Isle of Man had showed for a few moments only far off beyond the roaring waters, like some terrible legendary land, then had been swallowed up by great clouds and the night.

The north had been harsh, almost wintry in those last days; yet it was not until their train had run into the homelands of Southern England that Strickland had suddenly realized the flight of a season. He had gone up north in full summer. He returned to find deep autumn enfolding the land. And now, while he sat by the fire, he felt the autumn harbouring among the chimney pots of London and in the small gardens of Chelsea, felt it hanging over the Thames and creeping about the bridges. Things were dropping, dropping, dropping down. Tawny colours and decay made the great town rich and strange. The wild and vital cries of the north had given place to that stillness which belongs only to autumn days and nights, a stillness not breathless, as sometimes in winter frost-time, but heavy and almost foreboding.

Wastdale Head and the mountains and the wild weather of the so-called northern summer! London—autumn in the city and the south!

The fire crackled on the hearth. Outside the black river was at almost full tide. Autumn recollections flowed upon Strickland. And nearly all of them were a little sad. For he was one of those more or less imaginative people who feel a sadness in autumn, and are apt to connect the season with the swift fading of life, with the falling away from a man of his strong activities, his high hopes, his keen pleasures of the body, his animal spirits, his thoughtless gaieties, even his loves. Among these autumn recollections of his one stood out, was more vital just now than the others, was oddly persistent. His mind left it, but again and again returned to it.

He had gone over to Paris on some business connected with an electrical company of which he was a director. Towards the end of September he had set out on his return to London. The *rapide* from Paris to Calais, often crowded, had chanced not to be full that morning, and Strickland had found himself in a first-class carriage with only one other traveller, a woman. She had sat next the window on the far side of the carriage with her back to the engine. He had sat also next the window, exactly opposite to her.

When she got in he had cast a swift but casual glance at her, and had noticed that she was well, but simply dressed, that she was tall, handsome but rather austere looking, and that she had the peculiar distinction of being obviously young and yet having snow white hair. He had guessed that she was an American who had lived usually abroad, probably one of those cultivated American women who make Paris their home.

Then he had gone on reading.

At that period he had been half-way through Rolland's "Jean Christophe," a book which had interested him profoundly. He was a man who could forget everything in a fine book. That day he had forgotten for a long while the woman sitting opposite to him.

She was not reading. He had been vaguely aware of that, and had noticed that two or three magazines lay on the seat beside her. She must have sat very still. For no movement had recalled him to recollection of her when he became absorbed in his book. The deep thoughts of Rolland about life and human nature, profound, cynical, often very sad, had carried him away into vastness. He had been entangled, as it were, in the immense and intricate complications of existence. Paris, which he had but just left, was all around him in the book, Paris which he had thought he knew, but now felt that he did no really know at all.

Presently he had come to the end of the volume, "*Les Amies.*" He read the last words, "*Elle ne bougeait point, les yeux à demi fermés. Enfin, it se releva, et, sans la regarder, it sortit rapidement.*"

He closed the volume.

Above him, in the rack, shut up in his dressing case, was the next volume, "*Le Buisson Ardent.*" He meant to get hold of it, to go on with his reading. But for a moment he had sat quite still, staring before him, thinking about the episode on which he had just been concentrated. And in that moment he had gradually become aware of the tremendous forward movement of the train, of its noise, of the flying landscape at his side, and then of his silent and still companion. And he had looked up with now seeing eyes.

The tall woman with the young face and the white hair—he remembered it all sharply now by the fire on this autumn day—was sitting upright and absolutely still, with her hands calmly folded on her lap. He had glanced at her face, and noticed its refinement, the slightly aquiline nose with sensitive, narrow nostrils, the curved, closely meeting lips, the marked, very dark eyebrows, the rather large dark eyes, the broad, low forehead. The whole aspect of the face was reserved, dignified and, he had thought, almost singularly tranquil. The woman was not looking at him but downward.

For some time they had sat thus quite still, but his thoughts had become busy about her for the first time since they had left Paris.

A cultivated, probably high-minded, woman he had thought her, married, far above the groping hands of want, intellectual, tranquil, very reserved, perhaps even a little cold and distant in her relations with other human beings, yet ardent somehow, in some secret moments, and very, very self-possessed.

And just then a strange and horribly tragic thing had happened.

The face in front of Strickland had suddenly contorted itself in a grimace, had worked violently for two or three ugly seconds; it had become suffused with blood; it had swelled; and then the woman had burst into a passion of tears. She had wept as Strickland had never seen a woman weep before, with a face convulsed, a body shaking.

That had been strange enough. But a stranger thing still had been this: that Strickland had said, done nothing; had not bent forward in pity, sympathy; had not spoken a word of enquiry, a word of human gentleness, or chivalrous courtesy. He had wanted to, had had the immediate natural impulse to, had even intended to. But something— and it must have been something in the woman's mind or soul—had absolutely prevented him from either acting or speaking.

Simply—he had not dared to.

When he had realized this—his impotence to dare, he had got up quickly, taken his dressing case down from the rack, opened it, pulled out of it *"Le Buisson Ardent,"* and gone on reading Rolland, while his companion had gone on weeping.

And—and that had been all!

He had never spoken to the woman; he had never known what was the matter. The train had rolled on to Calais. Before it had reached its destination, aware at last of absolute silence in the carriage, apart from the noise of the train, he had glanced up over his book. And he had seen once more a tall, handsome, rather austere looking woman, sitting perfectly still, with an air of dignity and of strong self-possession.

The train had stopped. A porter had quickly opened the door, had taken the woman's belongings. She had stepped down, had mingled with the crowd. And Strickland had never seen her again.

Why was he thinking of her on this autumn day with such persistence? He wondered. The episode dated back three years now. His life had been fairly crowded up since then, one way and another. And yet the woman was there before him, convulsed, shaken, crying horribly.

Somehow ever since that day of travel he had connected her in his mind with the autumn, with the season of heavy sadness and decay; he had seen dead leaves falling round her life, rains blurring her fate as they blur a window pane, the twilight that holds the dark night in its hands settling about her.

Poor woman!

Strickland had seen perhaps as many sorrows as the average man, but he had never felt tragedy so strongly as he had felt it in that railway carriage with that stranger. What could it have been that had so suddenly, so utterly overcome such a woman as that? and how had she been able, through her breakdown, to inhibit him from any demonstration of sympathy? In her collapse she must have been strong. He still felt curiosity about her. Now he got up, walked over to the window and looked out on the river. Then he opened the window. The autumn came in breathing its many regrets. Barges went by in the twilight. A hoarse voice cried out from the water. A bell rang thinly and was drowned by the rolling of wheels. A little wind came, a little low wind as if out of the earth, and shook some damp yellow leaves from the lowest branches of a sycamore tree. And a shiver went through Strickland. He shut down the window.

As he went back to the fire he thought of Jeanne, the girl wife he had parted from in anger a couple of years ago.

What was Jeanne doing now? It didn't matter to him. They could never get on together again after the unholy row they had had.

And yet they had loved one another, had been terribly near to one another at times.

Yes, there was something terrible in drawing quite close to the soul of another in the dark. It showed one the horrible gap that lies between each human being and any other.

Autumn thoughts—damn them!

Three days later, when he returned from a tiresome meeting in the city, Strickland found a letter lying on his hall table.

DENBURY HOUSE,
DENBURY, KENT.
September 28.

DEAR MR. STRICKLAND,
If you are free do you feel inclined to come down to us from next Thursday or Friday till the following Monday? There is a good

train down to Applethwaite from Charing Cross at four-thirty. You change at Ashford. We would send the car to meet you. Only three or four people in the house. We have a hard tennis court now, and it is in perfect order. So bring your racquet. Mrs. Ingleton, who plays splendidly, will be with us, an American friend who lives in Paris, Mrs. Armitage—she married an Englishman and is a widow—and probably a couple of men. Dick says you can't get out of it. What do you say?

Yours very sincerely,
MINNIE LAPARAIS.

Strickland had no country engagement for the following Saturday and Sunday, and he decided to accept the Laparais' invitation. He had been to Denbury before and was fond of the place. They made him feel at home there and Mrs. Laparais never put on any frills. Dick, her husband, was an excellent fellow, and knew good wine from bad better than most men. A hard tennis court was an attraction, too, for Strickland was an ardent tennis player. And grass courts were impossible now. He wrote that he would be down on the Friday. And when Thursday came he felt such a longing to be away from misty London that he got out of two Friday morning engagements and wired that he would be at Applethwaite station at six-thirty that day.

And he duly arrived there at the appointed hour.

As he got out of the train a keen wind, which more than hinted at the nearness of the sea, welcomed him blowing across the wide green marshes, and he turned to look over them.

"Good evening, sir," said the gateman, an acquaintance of his, who lived in a cottage on the edge of the flats by the crossing. "Glad to see you in these parts again."

They had a few words together.

"Are you still contented down here?" asked Strickland. "No longings for London?"

"No, sir. I'd never go back to London now. It's cold here in the winter, but it's quiet. And I can breathe here. My wife likes it, too."

Strickland glanced at the little cottage by the roadside.

"It's a home," he said.

"That it is, sir."

Strickland took a good look at the man, and thought that the country had got at his face. There was nothing of the town in his weather-beaten, fresh-coloured features, his gently smiling eyes, the stubbly grey hair which fringed his lined cheeks and chin.

"Good night."

A blue motor was waiting. In a moment Strickland was being whirled along the narrow lanes, past the tree-edged canal, towards the upland on which stood Denbury House, looking south over a wide Kentish landscape. Soon the bold grey tower of the church, dating from somewhere about 1200, rose into view above the big old trees which surrounded it. The tiny village came in sight. A dog barked at the gate of a cottage garden full of stocks, hollyhocks, nasturtiums. The country postman passed on his bicycle. Then the blue car turned to the right between two low white gate posts, swung round sharply to the left of a sundial, and drew up before the Lutyens front of a red brick house with a porch and stone pillars.

The church clock struck seven.

In the square drawing room with its Italian furniture, its black panelled walls, its window curtains the colour of a cardinal's hat, Strickland found his hostess by the side of a blazing wood fire, with belated tea ready for him if he wanted it. With her were Mrs. Ingleton, a tall, handsome woman, not unlike Britannia, and two men; Arthur Liggan, known in London as "the intellectual stockbroker," a thin, wiry, brown man, with thick white hair, short white beard, and unusually bright and intelligent eyes, and Barclay Carrow, of the F.O., about thirty, large, sallow, with black hair parted in the middle, long fingered hard hands, melancholy eyes, and a quiet manner, which partially concealed a sometimes severe cleverness.

Minnie Laparais, about forty years old, dressed badly but always looked distinguished, had practically no manners yet was obviously a thorough lady, was almost too unselfconscious, very human, very keen, and extraordinarily kind to those she liked. Those whom she didn't like she seldom seemed to be aware of. She didn't attack them; she just forgot about them. They didn't appreciate it.

After tea Mrs. Laparais said:

"You'll see Vivienne Armitage at dinner. You are next to her. Dick has been out on the marshes after wild duck, and may be a minute late. You know how careless he is. We shan't wait for him. I'll show you your room."

And, very casually, she showed it to Strickland and went away with her "what does it matter?" walk.

Strickland's clothes had all been put out and he dressed quickly. Dinner was at half-past eight. Soon after a quarter-past eight he went downstairs and opened the drawing room door.

A tall woman was standing alone by the fireplace with her back to him. She had on a black dress. Her hair was snow white. Hearing the door she looked round. It was the woman who had cried so terribly in the railway carriage on the way from Paris to Calais. Strickland recognized her at once. But he didn't know whether, or not, she recognized him. He was inclined to think she did not, for she showed absolutely no sign of recollection of him. No sudden movement betrayed surprise. Her face was absolutely non-committal. She just looked at him politely, tranquilly, a little coldly perhaps, not speaking but ready to speak, not smiling, but ready to smile if necessary.

Strickland shut the door, came up to the fire, and introduced himself.

"You are Mrs. Armitage?" he said.

"Yes."

"Mrs. Laparais told me I should meet you. I believe you live in Paris."

He could not resist saying that, though, on reflection, he thought it would perhaps have been more delicate if he had avoided the remark.

"Yes," she said. "I am a Parisian-American. I hope you don't dislike the type? I believe some English people find it trying."

"I hope I am not so insular."

The rest of the party came in—Mrs. Laparais and Dick last of all.

Then they went into dinner.

Dick Laparais' chief claim to distinction was as a player of games. He had evidently been born to do astonishing things with balls; cricket balls, tennis balls, golf balls, racquet balls, footballs. He could always get the better of a ball. So he was famous and beloved throughout all England. He was a dear fellow, too, not a bit conceited about his prowess, indeed decidedly modest and at times apologetic—when he beat other fellows to love on his own hard court, or bowled men out first ball middle stump on his own cricket ground.

"Chance!" he would say. "All chance! My dear chap, the luck was with me."

How could he help being loved, in England the paradise of balls and players with balls?

In person he was short, deep in the chest, muscular yet extraordinarily quick on his feet, bald, rosy and beaming, with large ears, a round nose and a small, determined mouth. Someone had said of him, "He simply seethes with vitality!" And it was true. Of course he had had "good luck" on the marshes, and had brought home several brace of wild duck.

"Dick always seems to have luck with the birds," observed Minnie Laparais casually.

"He happens to be an exceptionally good shot," murmured Barclay Carrow to Mrs. Ingleton. "I don't believe in luck."

They began an argument on that subject. It presently spread, and everyone was asked to give an opinion on the matter. When Mrs. Armitage's turn came she said:

"I believe in evil chance."

"Well then—in good luck too—eh?" said Dick Laparais in his loud, rather throaty voice.

"I don't know about that," said Mrs. Armitage.

As she spoke, rather softly, her dark eyes happened to meet the eyes of Strickland, who was sitting beside her and he surprised—or believed that he surprised—in them a furtive expression, which was gone almost instantly.

"Perhaps she did recognize me!" he said to himself.

And he was conscious of a slight thrill. He discerned in Mrs. Armitage a surreptitious character, mingled of strength and perhaps of the weakness which goes often with passion, that generous monster which gives away too much. Her defences seemed perfect, yet—he had reason to know it—she was subject to storms which could sweep them away in a moment. Behind her austere mask there lay burning fire. Perhaps of all her companions in the long white dining room only he guessed that she was one of those immensely deceptive women who spend half their time sitting alone with their secrets, in the peopled solitude inexorably created for them as a dwelling place by character.

He wondered just how much she hated him, if she recognized him. For he felt that she must hate him. Hadn't he seen her soul practically naked? That was surely unforgivable. There could be no possibility of friendship between such a woman, full of reserves and sensitiveness, and Peeping Tom.

When his eyes met hers now he felt they were looking guilty.

But she seemed to notice nothing.

She talked agreeably and with serene self-possession. She was evidently cultivated, slightly critical, quite pleasantly sure of herself yet without arrogance. He found out that she had been brought up in Paris and knew very little of America.

"My husband loved France," she said. "His mother was French. And so, oddly enough, was mine. Our blood was all mixed up."

"Many people think that is an advantage," said Strickland.

"Well, I don't," she replied. "I think it a disadvantage to possess two strong strains of blood differing tremendously the one from the other. It may make for intelligence possibly, but it also makes for fever."

"Fever! But—dare I say it?—you look very tranquil," said Strickland.

There was just a touch of the lightest irony in his voice.

"Fevers die out when the hair turns white," she said.

"I don't think so. The fires of a human temperament, I fancy, burn even on the edge of the grave," said Strickland.

"And besides you are young."

He lowered his voice in saying that. At that moment he felt that somehow, during dinner, a sort of understanding had been established between him and his neighbour.

And that night, when he was up in his bedroom, he said to himself, "I believe we shall speak of the journey we made together from Paris to Calais."

They had played bridge all the evening. He and his partner, Mrs. Ingleton, had lost to Mrs. Armitage and Dick Laparais. When they got up from the table Dick had said:

"Ah, well, Mrs. Armitage and I had all the luck of the cards."

And then he had actually been banal enough to add the everlasting, "Lucky at cards, unlucky in love!"

Mrs. Armitage had said nothing. But Strickland had noticed that immediately after he had spoken the tiresome words Laparais had fallen silent and had looked oddly embarrassed—rather like a well-meaning boy who had said the wrong thing.

"Was it the tragedy of an unfaithful husband and one of those inexorable loves of which only women are capable?" Strickland thought as he got into bed.

II

On Friday morning Strickland, Mrs. Ingleton, Barclay Carrow and Laparais played tennis on the hard court. Mrs. Laparais was in the house and about the village (she was nearly always busy and never made a fuss about it). Arthur Liggan and Mrs. Armitage went for a walk. After lunch Strickland suggested to Mrs. Armitage a stroll about the garden, but she said she had some letters to write, and Mrs. Laparais offered to come with him. Later there was going to be more tennis.

"How do you like Vivienne Armitage?" asked Mrs. Laparais, as they walked over the stone path under the Pergola towards the swimming pool.

Strickland, who now believed that Mrs. Armitage had made up her mind to avoid being alone with him during the visit, answered:

"I scarcely know her yet."

After a moment he added:

"I should think she is rather a difficult woman to know."

"You never met her in Paris, I suppose?" said Mrs. Laparais casually.

"I have never seen her about Paris," returned Strickland.

As he spoke he saw his hostess's large grey eyes resting upon him, and he was moved to add:

"Did you think I had?"

"I don't know why, but during dinner last night it came into my head that perhaps you had seen Vivienne Armitage before."

"Did she say so?" said Strickland.

"Oh, no. But I didn't speak about it to her."

They walked on for a moment, passed through a tall, iron gateway and came to the swimming pool. There, on the stone coping which edged it, they stood still.

The motionless water was now discoloured. Dead leaves floated on its surface. Water insects straggled across it. The trees which drooped over the end where the diving board projected from the bank above the deepest part were yellow and brown, and reminded Strickland of a withered old woman's face. It was difficult to think that this pool a few weeks ago had called men to swimming, had been clear and green and inviting. Now it looked sad, even almost repellent.

"I have seen Mrs. Armitage before," said Strickland now, gazing at the water. "But I'm not positive that she knows it."

"Yes?" said Mrs. Laparais.

"But I had never spoken to her till last night. About two years ago I travelled with her in the express from Paris to Calais. Her appearance struck me; perhaps because of her white hair. For her face looks young."

"She is youngish—about thirty, I think. I wonder if she remembers you."

"I'm not sure."

"I think she does."

"Good heavens! Why?"

"I don't know. Would you like to see my white Leghorns?"

They went through a gateway into a field and came to a large chicken run.

"They are certainly beauties," said Strickland.

They talked for a few minutes about the chickens, then went on into the big kitchen garden.

"Has Mrs. Armitage been a widow long?" asked Strickland presently.

"Rather more than two years. Her husband died suddenly—I think it was in the month of August. Was she in black when you saw her in the train?"

"Yes, but not in deep mourning."

"I don't think she ever wore mourning for him. I believe they got on very badly together. Probably it was a relief to her when he died. I don't know exactly where the fault lay. But people who have known her much longer than I have say that she used to be very fiery and to have a tremendous temper. I only met her after her husband's death, and I have never seen a sign of it. She seems to me to have supreme self-control. I cannot imagine her being out of temper. Can you?"

"I don't know. You see I scarcely know her. What are those?"

"That's spinach."

"Does—does Mrs. Armitage know about me?"

"About you and Jeanne?"

"Yes."

Mrs. Laparais nodded.

"She has met Jeanne in Paris."

"In Paris? I didn't know Jeanne was there."

"It seems she is."

"Hullo! What about some more tennis?"

Dick Laparais stood before them racquet in hand, red, beaming, looking almost as eager as a spaniel who sees his master walking towards a gun case.

"Mrs. Ingleton's on the lawn already."

"Right you are!" said Strickland.

And he went off to get his racquet.

Strickland did not play his best game that afternoon. He found it difficult to concentrate. Many of his volleys went wide, and not a few of his forehand drives were held up by the net. Dick Laparais, who with Liggan opposed him and Mrs. Ingleton, remarked at the close of play that he and Liggan had had all the luck of the game. But Strickland, with a glance at Mrs. Armitage, who had been watching the struggle from a garden chair in the company of her hostess, said:

"Not a bit of it. I'm quite off colour this afternoon. I ought to go on my knees to Mrs. Ingleton."

"You did play badly," said she, with a good-natured smile. "But you should have seen me at Eastbourne this year. I couldn't hit a ball right.

And two days before I could almost have stood up to the Lenglen. You were thinking of something else."

And she strode off cheerfully towards the house.

"What were you thinking of?" asked Mrs. Laparais.

But Strickland gave an evasive answer and went in to have a bath and change.

When he came down again Arthur Liggan tackled him on an important financial question, and then Laparais suggested they should get in an hour on the marshes with guns before dark. The motor would "run them down" in a jiffy, and the birds were simply asking to be shot. Strickland opened his mouth to refuse, but shut it again when he saw his friend's face. One couldn't refuse such an expression.

Dick's "hour" meant shooting till the night was too black around them for them to distinguish a bird from a tree. They were even late for dinner.

That evening Strickland sat between his hostess and Mrs. Ingleton. After dinner Laparais begged him to play bridge, which Mrs. Armitage refused to play with the plea of having a slight headache, and when the women went up to bed Strickland had found no opportunity of a quiet word with her.

He did not sit up very late that night with the men, but when he went to his bedroom he found a wood fire burning, and he resolved to smoke a last pipe "up the chimney." Minnie Laparais wouldn't mind. She never seemed to mind anything men did. That was why they all liked her. He got into his dressing gown and slippers, lit his pipe and sat down in an armchair.

And he sat there smoking till two, although he was decidedly tired. Perhaps he was too tired to leave his armchair and get into bed.

He slept till very late the next morning, disgracefully late. It was half-past ten when he went down the broad staircase to breakfast. Just as he came into the long corridor from which most of the sitting rooms opened he heard the purr of a motor car, Dick Laparais's genial voice crying out, "Good-bye! Too bad! Too bad! Sorry you're going!" the toot of a horn, then the diminishing noise of a car in swift movement. Finally there was silence.

So one of the party had left—on a Saturday!

He knew at once who it was, and when Laparais met him at the door of the breakfast room with, "Isn't it too bad? Mrs. Armitage has had a letter obliging her to go back to town. London on a Sunday! Poor woman. I pity her. She asked me to say good-bye to you for her. Come along! You must be as hungry as a hunter after all that exercise yesterday. We'll see who has the luck at tennis to-day"—he simply shrugged his shoulders.

Dear old Laparais! He was a splendid fellow, but really—

"I'll play up to-day, old chap, never fear!" he said, after a moment. (One must live up to a fellow's character when he's your host and the kindest fellow on earth.)

And that day Strickland played, ferociously, his best and won the approval even of Mrs. Ingleton, who was ever chary of praise, but whose stalwart appearance and Britannia-like mien seemed to demand the last ounce of effort from everyone who played with her, or against her.

After tea that day Laparais came up to the armchair in which Strickland was lounging by the fire.

"Well, old chap, what do you say to another hour with the birds? Bob's in the hall barking himself into a fit by the guns." (Bob was Laparais's brown spaniel.)

"All right—" began Strickland mechanically, almost hypnotized by the eager, dog-like expression on the beaming face which impended above him.

Then a sudden revulsion seemed to take hold of him, almost as if by the throat.

"Why the devil should I say 'yes' to everything? I won't. Damn it, I will not!"

He had already half got out of his chair. Now he dropped back.

"My dear fellow, I've played so hard to-day that I'm quite on a rough edge. I really think I'll lie low if you won't think me a molly-coddle."

Dick Laparais's face fell for a moment. It was very difficult for him to realize that any man had ever had enough exercise. But in an instant he beamed again.

"Of course! Of course! Keep quiet! Perhaps—I'll do the same? Eh, Minnie?"

A loud, though distant, barking was heard.

"Poor old Bob! 'Pon my soul I don't like to disappoint the dog. Eh?"

He hesitated. His wife smiled. Nobody said anything.

"Well, I'll—I'll just go for half an hour, only to keep poor old Bob in health, you know. A dog needs exercise. I hate to see a dog going to pieces for lack of exercise. Eh?"

He was gone. Minnie Laparais laughed heartily, and somehow there was love in her laughter.

"Poor old Dick! Isn't it sad to be the victim of a dog?" she said.

And then she rang for the tea to be taken away.

"Have a game of billiards?" said Mrs. Ingleton to Arthur Liggan. "Just a couple of hundred up?"

"Certainly. I shall be delighted. But you'll beat me. You are worse than Laparais. You beat me at every game, even at spilikens."

"Now that isn't true. I've never really studied spilikens."

"Don't!" said Liggan. "You'd become English champion in a day."

They went off together amicably.

Barclay Carrow sat for a little while, to save appearances, as Strickland decided. He never did the wrong thing, not even in an examination. They talked of books. Mrs. Laparais was an ardent reader. Then they spoke of people.

Presently Carrow said:

"What a singular charm your departed friend has."

"Vivienne Armitage! I think so too. Yet she makes little effort to please."

"I dislike all social effort that is apparent."

"So do I. But perhaps because I am incapable of it. I know I am often horribly rude by being too passive. Dick calls me 'the unself-conscious jellyfish,' that is of course when I get among the wrong lot. I lose my voice with a bore. A country garden party has exactly the same effect upon me as a bad attack of laryngitis."

"That is carrying things rather far, isn't it, Strickland?"

"Yes. But even that is better than having an acute attack of social hysteria, which so many of us are subject to."

"Vivienne Armitage never has that. How quiet and still she is, and yet I never find her dull."

"I think I know why that is," said Carrow, getting out of his chair.

"Why?"

"Because on her hearth a fire is always burning."

Without making any excuse he went slowly out of the room.

"Do you agree?" said Mrs. Laparais, when the door shut behind him.

"Yes," said Strickland.

"It may be so. I don't know Vivienne Armitage really well. I don't know anyone who does."

"I am sorry she went so suddenly," said Strickland.

"So am I."

He fidgeted for a moment, hesitating whether to say a certain thing or not. Finally he said:

"I have a ridiculous idea that she went because of me."

"Because of you! Why should she?"

"Perhaps she didn't like meeting me."

Mrs. Laparais asked no questions. She only leaned forward and said in her self-possessed and rather deep voice:

"I feel like telling you something. Before she went she asked me for your London address."

"For my—how very odd! But perhaps—does she know Jeanne well?"

"I have no idea. When I told her a man called Henry Strickland was coming she said: 'Is he separated from his wife?' I said you were. Then she said: 'Is she called Jeanne?' I said she was."

"And then—then—"

"Then she merely said: 'I have met her in Paris.'"

"And that was all?"

"That was all. She never alluded to you again."

"Perhaps she—I daresay she thinks I have behaved like a brute."

"I daresay she does," said Mrs. Laparais calmly. "She may be a feminist."

"Oh, I don't think so! I don't know, of course."

"No more do I. Anyhow she has your address."

And she changed the conversation, without taking the trouble to try to find a bridge from one subject to another.

III

Strickland left Denbury House early on Monday morning. He travelled up to town with Arthur Liggan and Barclay Carrow, and they agreed that they had had a pleasant time. Carrow, however, added: "in spite of the abrupt defection of by far the most interesting member of our party." They discussed Mrs. Armitage amiably. Arthur Liggan, although he had never met her before, had heard a good deal about her. The ramifications of his acquaintanceship with all manner of people were so extensive that he had heard a good deal about almost everyone above a certain level in Europe. Carrow showed interest in this hearsay and edged Liggan into talk. The most striking fact which emerged from Liggan's report was this: that there was an extraordinarily marked difference between Mrs. Armitage married and Mrs. Armitage widowed.

"They all tell me so," he asserted, stroking his silky white little beard.

"They?" questioned Carrow, cocking up his left eyebrow in a manner difficult of achievement by any but a Foreign Office man.

"People who know her in Paris. Armitage was very rich and knew all the American Colony there, and most of the best French people, barring the Jews."

"And what is the difference between Mrs. Armitage the wife, and Mrs. Armitage *veuve*?"

"Some such difference as one notices between a volcano and an Alpine snow peak," said Liggan.

"A volcano in activity or an extinct volcano?"

"Oh, the former, very much the former."

"Does Mrs. Armitage suggest an Alpine peak to you, Strickland?" said Carrow.

"Not altogether. But she is more like that than like an active volcano. She suggests to me great self-possession, great self-control."

"And she was, I understand, noted for her lack of self-control," said Liggan. "She and her husband used to have tremendous rows. I believe the Armitage rows were almost notorious in their set. But since his death she has seemed another woman."

"Probably she married the wrong man and has only known happiness since she got rid of him. Armitage may have been an irritant. And it must be exquisite to lay an irritant to rest in the grave, or to place the ashes of an irritant reverently in a pretty little urn. Mrs. Armitage may have known that joy. Call no woman happy till she is a widow. Hullo! Ashford and the papers!"

At Charing Cross they separated and Strickland was free.

He often enjoyed a country house visit, but he was generally glad when it was over. Even the most delightful country house had a faint flavour of the cage for Strickland—after two or three days.

Free! He got a taxi and drove to his house. It was a very charming and well-arranged though quite small house, and he had never lived in it with Jeanne. So it possessed no tragic memories for him. Nevertheless he thought it looked almost drearily empty as he carried his kit bag into the hall and put it down. He spoke a few words to Ellen, his parlour maid, and to his housekeeper, Mrs. Fry, ran through the letters that were lying on the hall table, then went off to the City.

It was a mercy to have plenty of work.

About five that day he was walking home by the river side.

In the country he had thrown off the depressing effect which autumn had had upon him. Laparais had kept him very busy. And at Denbury he had seldom been alone. But now again he felt his loneliness acutely, and the soft, and yet heavy, depression of the season flowed over him.

And so Jeanne was in Paris! And the woman of the railway carriage knew her. Strickland wondered how intimate the acquaintance between the two women was, and what Jeanne had said about him. For no doubt she had spoken about him to Mrs. Armitage. The latter, he felt sure, had left Denbury because he was there. Nevertheless she had asked for his address. She must then surely intend to write to him, or perhaps to see him again. Her going away so abruptly, and her asking for his address, seemed to him, in consideration of the two facts, to show a contradictory mind and disposition. But then all interesting, all really attractive women were contradictory. Jeanne had been contradictory. He remembered, when they were engaged, that he had often been taken aback by her apparently opposing moods. And after their marriage he had not always understood her. And he doubted whether she had ever understood him, although she had certainly loved him, even with violence. Violence! There had always been a certain violence in their relation to one another, in their intimate intercourse. Perhaps that fact had lain at the root of their disagreement which had ended in rupture.

He paused by the river not far from Battersea Bridge and looked over the water. It was very dark and very calm, almost horribly calm—like his life now that Jeanne was out of it. During his married life he had often felt terribly impatient, had often longed for quiet and peace. Now that he had them he was acutely dissatisfied.

"I must be a difficult beast," he thought. "I suppose I want to eat my cake, and have it, and give it away."

A great barge went by drifting in the middle of the river with the tide which was going out. He looked at it and saw two figures of men upon it, and a sort of reckless and absurd longing to be one of them came to him. For the moment he felt sick of his life, and that theirs must be far more interesting and attractive than his. To get on that barge, and float away down the great river, away from the huge city with all its troubles and hindrances, away to silent places, to a distant life, to sea marges! Wouldn't that change a man?

The barge grew dim on the river. It had passed under Battersea Bridge. The pace of it on the water seemed to quicken. It was escaping from London furtively.

Yes, he envied those men who moved to and fro on it, busy with mysterious tasks.

He turned, crossed the road and went into his house.

"If I wasn't tied by business I'd get away and travel for a year!" he said to himself.

In the hall he looked for a letter. Since he had returned to London he had begun to expect a letter. But there was none. Perhaps, after all, the woman of the railway carriage would never write to him. She had asked for his address. But that might have been merely a whim.

He began to think it was merely a whim when a month had gone by and he had not had a word from her. The hard winter, with its fogs, and its ineffable dreariness and oppression, got London well into its grip, and Mrs. Armitage made no sign. And at last Strickland ceased to expect any word from her. She had fled from him at Denbury and he would probably never see her again. He would certainly never hear from her. The lines carved by dissatisfaction deepened in his face. Often, thinking of life, he said to himself, "*à quoi bon?*" What was the good of it all? Existence was a stagnant thing.

On the day when he had parted from Jeanne his life had been divided into two parts as if by a sharp sword. The past had been intense, violent, full of fierce ups and downs, tortured sometimes, sometimes ecstatic, always quivering with vitality, with love, with tempers, with tears. The other part, well, it was very Anglo-Saxon. And Strickland knew that he found it very dull. When he entered his club too often he saw boredom towering up like a heavy monster. The routine of society was becoming very insipid to him. Even his work not seldom seemed stale and flavourless. And when he put the key in the door of his house he did it without expectation. Indeed, often he thought, as the door yielded to his touch: "What on earth am I going to do in here?" Life had lost its savour for Strickland, and life without savour is not merely dull. Very soon it becomes hideous.

It was becoming almost hideous to Strickland, when one evening towards the end of January, on coming home from the City, he found a large square envelope lying on his hall table. He took it up. He didn't know the handwriting, which was firm and clear. On the front of the envelope in small letters was printed "Claridge's Hotel."

An invitation no doubt. He opened it and read:

CLARIDGE'S HOTEL.
Thursday.

DEAR MR. STRICKLAND,

I met you last autumn staying at Denbury. Do you remember? I am in London for a few days and should like if possible to see you. Can you suggest an hour if you have any free time?

Believe me, yours sincerely,

VIVIENNE ARMITAGE.

So—she had written!

Suddenly the flatness of life seemed to disappear. Strickland carried the note into his library, where there was a big fire.

"What can she want to see me for?"

He reread the note and felt intense reserve almost bristling in it. She did not suggest a place for their meeting. The natural thing would be for him to offer to go to her hotel. But since she had not asked him to do that he resolved to follow his impulse, and to ask her to come to him. Possibly she really wished to visit him, as she had not hinted at his going to Claridge's.

He sat down at his writing-table and wrote a note inviting her to tea the next day. He sent it off by a messenger boy whom he told to bring back an answer. The boy returned in about an hour with a note.

CLARIDGE'S HOTEL.
Thursday.

DEAR MR. STRICKLAND,
As you kindly ask me I will come to tea with you to-morrow. Many thanks.
Yours sincerely,

VIVIENNE ARMITAGE.

On the following day Strickland had a talk with his housekeeper, Mrs. Fry, before he went to the City. He came back earlier than usual, with a quantity of flowers which he had bought in Covent Garden. Mrs. Fry was ready with vases and specimen glasses, and helped Strickland to arrange the flowers and to distribute them about the room. A big fire was burning. The tea-table was ready. The sofa cushions were "plumped" out, the blinds and curtains drawn, a few books put about to make the room look lived in. Some wax candles were lighted.

"It looks all right, Mrs. Fry, doesn't it?" said Strickland.

"Very nice indeed, sir," said Mrs. Fry.

"When the lady—Mrs. Armitage is her name—comes please tell Ellen to bring her up at once. And I am not at home if anyone else calls."

"Yes, sir."

Mrs. Fry departed, and Strickland went to stand by the fire.

He felt strongly expectant, even a little excited. The smell of the flowers was strong in the room and reminded him suddenly of Jeanne.

If, instead of Mrs. Armitage, it were Jeanne who was coming back! How different the house would seem in a day, in an hour even. Although he lived alone Strickland had never recaptured the bachelor feeling. Once married that was surely destroyed in a man forever. A bachelor might, probably often did, feel complete. A married man—Strickland judged the matter from his own experience—separated from his wife felt somehow lopsided. And a woman separated from her husband?

But Strickland was sure that he would never know how women felt about such things.

A bell sounded thinly below. He took his hands out of his pockets and looked towards the door.

IV

"Mrs. Armitage, sir," said Ellen's thin voice.

Mrs. Armitage came into the room looking grave, self-possessed, austere, but still young under her crown of white hair.

"Bring up tea, Ellen."

"Yes, sir."

Strickland held out his hand.

"I am glad to meet you again. You went away from Denbury so suddenly."

"That there was no time to say good-bye."

"Do sit here by the fire and take off your coat."

She slipped out of her long dark fur and sat down.

"Did Mrs. Laparais tell you I asked for your address before I went?" she said, without looking at him.

"Yes, she did."

"You must have been surprised."

"I was rather. But it made me hope we might perhaps meet again someday."

The door opened and Ellen came in with tea. When she had gone out Strickland said:

"We shall not be disturbed again."

Mrs. Armitage glanced round the room. Her dark eyes, Strickland thought, looked anxious and strained, and a slight self-consciousness hovered about her; but her lips looked determined. He felt self-control in her almost as if he had his hand on a bar of steel. But he remembered the railway carriage, and he knew that this woman was full of violent feeling. After giving her tea and helping himself, he sat down by the tea-table and said:

"May I ask you something?"

"Why I have come here, why I wished to see you?"

"No, it isn't that. What I want to ask you is this. Do you know that you and I had met before we met at Denbury?"

"Yes."

"I fancied you knew. But I wasn't quite sure."

"I recognized you directly you came into the drawing room at Denbury. That was really why I left on the Saturday morning. I—I tried to stand being with you, but I couldn't. It was too painful."

There was a silence. He broke it by saying:

"But you are here!"

"Yes. I'm not so weak now. Besides I have learnt a good deal since then. During a great part of my life I think I learnt practically nothing. I was perhaps almost incapable of learning. But now I am learning all the time. My eyes are open on life. That is because I have suffered terrifically."

"I know."

"Yes, you know. You are the only one who does know, you a stranger. And that is why I am going to speak to you as I should never be able to speak to anyone else. You have seen the truth of me. I hated you for it once. But I believe now it was all arranged. It was necessary that it should be so. There was something I had to do, and, with my nature, I don't think I could ever have brought myself to do it if you had not seen the truth of me first. I am generally too reserved. It's almost an illness with me. If you had spoken to me in the train I don't know what would have happened. But you were reserved that day—and now I shall speak to you. I have come here to speak to you."

She leaned forward in her chair. She had taken off her gloves, and her long narrow hands were clasped lightly together—with a delicate lightness. She looked into the fire.

"How much do you know about me?" she asked.

"That you were married and lived in Paris, that your husband died suddenly about two months, I suppose, before we met in the train,"

"Yes."

"That—that —" Strickland hesitated.

"Oh, don't hesitate, don't choose your words. I have come here to—tell you. So you can tell me."

"I was told that you and your husband hadn't got on at all well, that probably it was a great relief to you when he died."

"Oh!"

It was almost a cry, and vibrated with irony. After a pause she said:

"Were you told that I was a difficult woman, that I had a bad temper?"

"Something of that kind. But people, even quite dear people, often talk maliciously. I don't think they mean to do harm. They just run on and say anything that comes into their heads."

"Yes—yes, I know I have done it. We have most of us done it. But they spoke the truth. I was a terribly difficult woman. I had a very bad temper. And I have been punished for it. I have been scourged for it."

Her long hands twisted for a moment, gripped each other almost fiercely.

"I don't want anyone else ever to be punished as I have been."

She was silent, still gazing into the fire. Then she said, looking up at him with steady, wide opened eyes:

"Mr. Strickland, I know your wife."

"Yes," he said.

"Minnie Laparais told you?"

"Just that, nothing more. She did not say how well you knew her."

"I did not tell her. But I will tell you. I know your wife very well. That is why I am here."

"Yes?" said Strickland, feeling very uncomfortable, but trying to look quite unembarrassed and calm.

"Of course at first I had no idea her husband and the man I met in the Paris-Calais *rapide* were one and the same. I only found that out when you walked into the drawing room at Denbury."

"Yes?"

"After that I was for the time occupied, as I suppose most of us usually are occupied. I was given over to my own egoism. I knew you recognized me as the woman who had shown you herself though we had never spoken to one another. A storm swept over me that day in the train. I don't know why. Till that moment, even when I was alone, I had not broken down—in body. Then I broke down. It had to come I suppose. And it came in front of you. My soul had wept many times, tears of blood. Only then did my body weep. And you saw it. You—you behaved with true delicacy—like a gentleman if I may say so. You recognized instinctively that you couldn't help me, and you didn't try to. I shall always be grateful for that."

"I—I felt like a brute."

"I know—for being there. That wasn't your fault. But at Denbury, as I say, being full of egoism, I couldn't forgive you. And I went away as soon as I could. I didn't really think I should ever see you again of my own accord. But I took your address. Even then I had some faint pushing instinct, I suppose. We are often a little better than we want to be. We struggle against it. I struggled. But now—here I am. Do please give me a cigarette if you have one."

"Please forgive me!"

He held out a box. She took a cigarette quickly, lit it and went on.

"Mr. Strickland, you heard that I was probably relieved when my husband suddenly died. This is the truth: it broke my heart."

Strickland looked away from her. In a moment he heard her say again:

"It broke my heart. You have heard that we didn't get on well together. That's true. We often quarrelled. It was my fault. I loved him so much that I didn't care really at all for anyone else. My love for him was so great that perhaps it exhausted my power of loving. I don't know. Anyhow everyone else was really indifferent to me. And yet we didn't get on. Because I had a horribly difficult temperament, and was born with an exceptionally violent temper. I was by nature highly nervous, exacting and irritable. But no man can ever have been loved by a woman more than my husband was by me. I am absolutely certain of that."

She paused, and as the pause was prolonged, Strickland said:

"We cannot help our natures."

"Yes, we can!" she said, almost sharply. "We ought to. If we don't we may quite easily bring hell here on earth. Were you thinking of your own nature?"

"Perhaps I was."

"I want to make you feel differently, Mr. Strickland, I must make you feel differently about that. Do you ever read the Bible? Lots of men don't, I suppose. But do you?"

"Not very often," Strickland acknowledged. "But of course I have read it. A good deal of it is familiar to me."

"Yes, I know. We read it, and think, 'That's true enough. There's something in that.' Or, 'That might apply to many people.' Or if we come on a text that is an admonition we say to ourselves, 'Many of my neighbours might do worse than take *that* to heart.' And there it ends. It was so with me. There's a text that I should think practically everyone knows—"

She broke off. Her face suddenly twisted, almost as it had twisted in the railway carriage.

"Do please—do tell me which text that is!" said Strickland quickly.

"Wait a moment," she said, in a muffled voice.

He waited. He knew she was making an almost terribly strong effort to retain, or to regain, complete self-possession.

"It—it—it is that old text, 'Let not the sun go down upon your wrath—let it not go down.'"

"Of course I know it."

"Everyone knows it."

She gazed at him, and now a deep solemnity had come into her eyes.

"Everyone knows it and probably few bother about it. I was one of those. I—*I* let the sun go down on *my* wrath."

Her eyes were flooded with tears, but she looked at Strickland through her tears, steadily.

"And then I was stricken to the dust. Yes. Has it ever occurred to you how all through our lives we are perpetually being taken unawares."

"Sometimes I have thought of that."

"We are seldom or never prepared for the big things which happen to us. They come upon us as suddenly as bullets fired by enemies in ambush. And too often we aren't ready. We aren't ready to die."

It seemed to Strickland that another woman was emerging in his companion, was coming out of the reserved, almost austere woman who so few minutes ago had entered his drawing room. And she was strangely unreserved. There was something of the seer in her manner, something of the teacher in her voice. She spoke evidently out of the depths of a heart knowledge which rendered her passionately sure of herself. Beside this woman Strickland began to feel very ignorant.

"'Let not the sun go down upon your wrath,'" she went on. "Those words are never really out of my mind now. But they can do me no good. I disobeyed them and my punishment will last as long as I live. And afterwards? Mr. Strickland, is there an afterwards for us, do you think?"

"I hope there is."

"There must be!" she said, fiercely almost. "Otherwise we cannot ask for pardon, we cannot explain, we cannot— There must be! there is! I will believe it! If science could even disprove it by proving that all a man is and has dies with the body, ceases to function when the last breath is drawn, I would not cease to believe. I long so much for the hereafter that there must be the possibility of it. Such longings have their goal, or else God is the most absolutely merciless power in all creation. For He is in Creation."

She laid down carefully the end of her cigarette, cast a swift glance at Strickland, and said in a quieter voice:

"Now I am going to tell you!"

And again he was conscious of almost rigid effort, of the almost hard exercise of will.

"I'm half American, half French; Southern American, Southern French. From Nice my French ancestors are. I was brought up chiefly in France. I was born—at least I suppose so, as it manifested itself when I was a mere child—I was born with a terrific temper and a highly impulsive nervous temperament. On some days I felt buoyant, joyous, full of hope, kindness, good nature; on others I was miserable, full of blackness, angry suspicious thoughts and imaginings, impulses to unkindness, intense irritability. On such days I was caged in darkness and nothing seemed right to me. I felt injured without reason, or even abandoned. I couldn't believe in the love of anyone for me, and yet morbidly I desired love. But I felt unworthy of it, uncertain of myself, shrinkingly useless and incapable, and yet arbitrary and full of vehement yearnings.

"These violent and sometimes opposing feelings bred in me an impulse to be morally cruel—and always to those I loved. When I was in these moods I tried to hurt those I loved, and in hurting them I wounded myself, I thrust daggers into my own heart. For I thought I had made myself hated by them and that they could never tolerate me again. And yet somehow I was forgiven! I have often asked myself why. I think it must have been because, in spite of all, I knew how to love. I had a passionately warm heart, and was really loyal under all my almost infernal tempers and moods.

"Sometimes, Mr. Strickland, I am inclined to believe that there are possessions of the devil even in these modern days, and that I was often possessed of the devil.

"Of course I was punished sometimes for my tempers, but on the whole my parents spoiled me. We were generally in Paris, where I was educated. I was an only child and, because of my temper, I suppose, had things very much my own way. Often I have noticed that if in a family, or in a community, there is one person with what is called a strong temper, and a difficult nature, that person usually rules the others. The average human being has a horror of scenes, and would rather be ruled than often endure them. I think I ruled in my family. And yet I was loved, because I loved. I was often horrible to my father and mother, but I adored them both. They are dead now, but *they* died with me beside them, able to ask forgiveness of them for all the pain I must have caused them. They knew—before they died."

All the self-consciousness of which Strickland had been aware when Mrs. Armitage came into his room had vanished from her now; all reserve seemed to have died out of her. They sat by the fire in the delicate light shed by the wax candles like two intimates, and Strickland no longer had any acute sense of strangeness in listening to this revelation of moral defects by a stranger. He knew that she had a very definite purpose driving her on, and that presently he would know what that purpose was. Meanwhile he was content to listen absorbed, undesirous of making the least interruption. But now she paused and looked up at him, almost expectantly, almost as if she were waiting for some comment, or some question from him.

"You—you—" he began, and hesitated. She was still silent and still kept her eyes fixed on his, with a curious half-expectant and—he thought—half-inward look.

"I understand those moods of yours," he said, at last. "I have known something of the same kind myself. One day everything seems right; another day everything seems black and infernal."

"Yes. But do you understand my horrible propensity for being cruel only to those I loved?" she asked, in an earnest low voice. "For picking them out as my victims? It is that, just that, which has ruined my life. Can you understand it?"

He thought of certain episodes in his life with Jeanne.

"Yes," he said, reddening slowly. "I believe there are many people who are only really unkind to those whom they love."

"Isn't that from the devil?" she said.

"I don't know. I don't think I believe in a personal devil."

"Why is it then?"

"In some way—somehow it doesn't seem worthwhile to be cruel to those who are nothing to us. It is those who are very close to us, whom we have wrapped up in our lives, who give out music when we touch the keys. And so I suppose we are moved to touch them."

"But why should we, why do we deliberately strike horrible discords? Why can't we be contented with the beautiful harmonies of life?"

Again Strickland thought of his life with Jeanne.

"I don't know," he said. "It often seems as if we were driven."

"That is our fault. We should not let ourselves be driven. Look at me, Mr. Strickland."

"Yes?"

"Perhaps you will think me very arrogant for saying what I am going to say. I could never be driven again. I was one of the most uncontrollable women, at moments, that there can ever have been in civilization. For I am highly civilized."

"I can see that."

"And now I have absolutely complete control over my behaviour to other people; not always over my own emotions, the emotions that are entirely mine, that I don't share with others, but over my actions in connection with others. People are safe with me now. I had a lesson which in one moment changed me—broke me. Do you understand— broke me?"

"What lesson?"

"It was this. I loved a man. I am thirty-two now, though of course I look much older. Then I was twenty-three. Although I believe my temper must have been notorious among my friends, and was certainly known about by all my relations, although I was considered an alarming type of girl, several men had seemed to be attracted by me before this time. I had not cared for them—and with me it has generally been all or nothing. It isn't love or hate, but love or tremendous indifference, a dryness of the desert in my heart. Now I met the man to whom afterwards I was married, and I loved him. Mr. Strickland, at first he didn't care for me. I was the first to love. It often is the woman, often she draws the man to her by that, by loving him desperately, and wanting him desperately, and saying nothing about it, and acting, and pretending. But it oozes through all the acting and the pretending, and it drops on the man—drops—drops—and mysteriously, occultly almost, he feels wanted, desired, and it warns him, and it makes him know that he has been lonely in all his freedom, lonely perhaps in his intrigues and his vices, lonely with his bachelor friends—and he begins to want the woman who wants him so terribly. Often it's like that."

"Is it?" said Strickland, wondering at this woman's amazing frankness, a frankness which seemed for the moment to free her from the bondage of sex.

"Yes. I think women want—much more than men. As a sex we are not, and never shall be, independent. Men often set out to conquer us when we are conquered already. I loved for nearly a year before I was loved. Often I thought I never should be loved. I believed the legend of my horrible temperament had gone before me to him, that it repelled him. And I was frightened, terrified. For the first time I looked my temperament in the face as it was, and saw it as a great danger, as a dragon in my path of life. For the first time I wanted to kill the dragon because I thought perhaps he knew of and hated it. My love grew for a year, and side by side with it grew my first real moral effort. I don't know—I can't remember how far I succeeded in what I was trying to do, but one day he told me he loved me. He asked me if I could ever love him! That is how men know us! I was quite frank. I told him I had loved him for a whole year, and of my fears that he knew about my violent nature. I humiliated myself perhaps. But I loved too much to mind. I made the very worst of myself. Something inside me warned me to do that. Something said to me, 'Don't let him misunderstand you. Show your sores! If he can stand the sight of them and still wish to be with you he loves you indeed.' And I was brave. But cowardice isn't my fault, I think. I am not often a coward."

"I am sure you are not," said Strickland. "And he—how did he take it? Had he known?"

"He had heard rumours, but he told me he had only half believed them. I assured him that they were true. I tried to let him into the ugliest secrets of my temperament. You may say no woman would ever do that with a man she loved. But I did do it. I was so afraid of his finding out ugly things later and hating me because I had concealed them that I was frank as few women are ever frank. I told him that I couldn't govern myself but that I would try to, that I would make the greatest possible effort to overcome my temper and banish my desperate moods. He said it would be all right, that he would help me. I must tell you that he was a man with enormous self-control, but a very, very sensitive man. I believe I told you at Denbury that his mother was French?"

"Yes, you did."

"His father was English but a great lover of France. My husband was in some ways more French than English. He had the Frenchman's sensitiveness to women, quick intelligence, swiftness of vision, and understanding of subtleties, but all the Englishman's sentiment, straight-forwardness and loyalty. He had a splendid nature. I wasn't like many women. I loved something worth loving. He was incomparable, Mr. Strickland, indeed, indeed he was! People felt that he was. They loved him instinctively. But not as I did. I worshipped him. I pray sometimes that no poor woman may ever worship as I did. For even in happiness there is something terrible—there is almost a menace in loving like that. I think—and I am almost sure I am right—that it is only a few people who know how to love. I believe the greater number of people live and die without ever knowing the depths and the mysteries, the ecstasies and the horrors of love. Few would acknowledge it. Practically all men and women, if asked, would say that they had loved. But I don't think the answer would be true. Great love is, I am convinced, a very rare thing unknown by most of us."

She looked at Strickland questioningly, then added, with a sort of diffidence:

"Jeanne knows it, I think: she is one of the few."

Strickland flushed deeply, but kept his eyes on her. Before her amazing unreserve he scarcely dared to be reserved. When, he wondered, was this extraordinary interview going to end?

"Mr. Strickland, we were married, Andrew and I. We gave ourselves up to happiness as I think few people ever can have given themselves. My love had waited a year, had had to wait a year in absolute uncertainty. So I had to pay it back. At any rate if I am a dead woman now I haven't died without living. But—but we never, never have enough happiness, true happiness, because we always feel, all those of us who have ever had it, that it ought to be eternal, somehow must have been originally meant to be eternal. What has happened we can't know. But I am sure when happiness was designed, invented—whatever you like to call it— it was designed to last. That design has been frustrated. It doesn't last. It never lasts. But we are aware of a scheme gone somehow awry in that. Don't you feel it?"

"Yes," said Strickland.

"The strange thing is that we make ourselves the instruments to frustrate the original design. We work, instinctively, it often seems, to destroy what we live by. We undermine our own happiness in a thousand ways, sometimes secret, sometimes violently open—according to our temperaments. Coral insects work unwearyingly to build. We work almost as unwearyingly to bring down. We plant and we tend the seeds of our own destruction. It wasn't enough for me to be happy—apparently. Looking back it seems so. My love grew, and in growing it became destructive. At first I held my natural temperament—the bad dangerous part of it, I mean—in check without difficulty. Happiness seemed to lay my nerves to rest, to smooth out my prickly irritabilities. Changing moods didn't beset me at first. I had no days of unreasoning depression. I had no impulses towards unkindness, or even cruelty. I was tender to Andrew then. I submitted myself to him with that wonderful happiness in submission which only a loving woman ever feels. But that perfection of being didn't last on my side.

"Presently it was as if I swung back to my original temperament and way of being. I thought then it was inevitable, that I couldn't help it, that I had to be as God had made me. (That's the excusing phrase, the miserable cliché of the sinner!) I know now I simply didn't continue an effort I had made, and that I could have continued it if I had chosen. Mr. Strickland, most of us don't try enough. We are morally lazy. We compound with our worst part. We take hands with our natural vices, the vices that are natural to us. That is what I did to my damnation on this earth. Oh, how I should love to save others from doing that! I have paid. I shall go on paying all my life long. But I don't want others to pay. I believe many who suffer long for others to suffer too. I don't. I don't want anyone else to suffer—no! That's why I am here to-day."

"Yes—yes. I—I begin to understand."

"Do you?"

"I think at least, perhaps I do."

She sat very still for a moment. Apparently she was thinking deeply, profoundly. At last she said:

"In daily life with anyone—I don't care who it is—there are many difficult moments when human forbearance only—nothing else—can save the situation. And if one has a highly-strung, naturally sensitive and irritable temperament, and is liable to lose control, those moments are terribly dangerous. Although I loved my husband exclusively, although my love grew in marriage rapidly, fiercely, often things in my husband irritated me, not the deeper me, but the me on the surface. Sometimes one seems two, I think, an underneath, abiding, eternal entity, very deep and persistent and still, and something else, something capricious—I scarcely know how to say—fashioned in such a way as to be swayed, got at, by all the passing littlenesses. There is the water at the top that is caught by the breezes and the winds and the tempests, and the water far down in the depths that knows not of them.

"The deeper me, I think, loved my husband in perfect unity always, through everything. But as our life together went on, lengthened out, that other one, horribly sensitive, irritable, nervous, uncontrolled, began to criticize, to find fault, to chafe at certain things, to be restive, even to be angry, bitter, condemnatory. We had no child. I was horribly sensitive about that. Oh, if you knew what some childless women endure in eternal silence! And I was jealous—that is the curse of sensitive women—jealous without reason, and knowing really I had no reason. When he died I felt he had died absolutely true to me. I couldn't prove it. No woman can ever prove such a thing. But I just know it, Mr. Strickland—as I daresay you know a somewhat similar thing."

"Yes," said Strickland, in a low voice.

Without asking permission, mechanically almost as a man does an accustomed thing, he pulled his pipe out of his pocket, began to fill it with tobacco carefully. She sat watching him.

"We so often sat like this," she said.

"What?"

He looked up from his pipe startled almost by her intonation.

"So often I watched him doing what you are doing. I can see his hands now—just the movement of them and the shapes they took. When those we love are dead we often see their dear hands moving in the firelight, or in the candlelight. And then we remember their eternal stillness and—"

She broke off.

Strickland had paused. This woman moved him strangely by the depth of sincerity in her emotion, and by her extraordinary simplicity. Now, with an effort, he went on with what he had been doing. Presently he lit his pipe. Then she spoke again.

"Those we love can irritate us as no other human beings can irritate us. Can't they?"

"Yes."

"We want them to be perfect, I suppose, and so their imperfections strike us like little hammers. I was horribly critical in spite of, or perhaps because of, my great love. But I can't be sincere about this part of my story. I was so unworthy of him. He was so far above me, so far too good for me. But there are human beings who criticize God. Put me among them, Mr. Strickland—me as I once was. Then you'll know. All I can tell you about that is that I criticized my husband, often and even bitterly. He bore with my hatefulness in that respect wonderfully, but not meekly. He wasn't a meek man, or I should never have loved him. He did not return criticism for criticism, and so I suppose it seemed as if I were the superior one of us two. How often that happens when two people live together. It is the inferior, the mentally and morally inferior, who crazily assumes the position of the superior. Perhaps it is a miserable futile effort to get up higher. I don't know. Anyhow, although I knew in my heart that my husband was far above me both in character and in intellect, I was the one to criticize. He seldom, scarcely ever, criticized me. When I was intolerable he would get up in silence and go out of the room, out of the house, stay away for a time, come back and meet me as if nothing had happened.

"Often I tried to provoke him into passion. I played, as it were, for scenes. Something in me at certain times seemed to demand a violent scene. He would not give me what I demanded. He thought it degrading for two people linked as we were to mingle love with its hideous opposite, anger, recrimination. There was a certain almost spiritual dignity about him—absolutely unostentatious—which sometimes provoked me almost to fever, I think because I had none of it, and because his having it made me feel how inferior I was to him. And yet I loved him for it all the time—underneath. Really I loved even his faults, his tricks, his little mannerisms. I know that now. I knew it directly I heard—"

She got up suddenly. For an instant Strickland thought that she was going to leave him, that she had suddenly repented of her frankness, and would not stay. But she only went to stand by the fire. For a moment she stayed with her back to him. Then she turned round. Her face was very pale, and her eyes were burning with emotion, and an energy of feeling such as he had never seen before, he thought, in a woman's eyes, except perhaps at moments in Jeanne's.

"Directly death comes knowledge comes," she said. "Probably few, or none, of us ever know exactly what we feel about another until death takes that other away. But then, immediately I think, we know. We know what that other meant to us. We know what that other was. We look right into the eyes of truth. Death veils and unveils, throws a veil over the body and tears it away from the soul. That at least was my feeling. Mystery and nakedness are there together in one and the same moment, and we cry out the truth only when there is no voice to answer us. But—oh, if only we didn't wait for death! If we would only speak when there was still time for the answer! I said to you that all through our lives we are perpetually being taken unawares. That happened to me in a most terrible way, the most terrible way possible. Our married life went on—mine with Andrew—in the way I have tried to indicate. I was a horribly difficult wife. People knew it. It was generally supposed, I am sure, that we got on together badly, that we were very unsuited to one another. I hadn't even the art to hide my ugly temperament from my friends and acquaintances. Many of them knew, must have known, of our disagreements. But I was never disloyal. I never was so vile as to speak against Andrew in secret. Still people knew. That accounts for what you have heard—the hideous supposition that Andrew's death was probably a relief to me. For though I never spoke against Andrew many people have seen me when I was angry with him, when I was irritated by him. I didn't know sometimes how to hide my tempers, and my moods of the devil.

"Looking back now I often wonder how Andrew was able to bear with me as he did. Not that he was a plaster saint with me. He was sometimes very angry. He never let me rule him as some miserable husbands allow themselves to be ruled by their wives to their own undoing. He was always a thorough man with me. But he bore with me wonderfully.

I think perhaps because he knew how exclusively I loved him. You see, Mr. Strickland, I had told him what I was before I married him. I don't think he ever forgot that. He had promised to try to help me to be different. And often he tried to help me. After my hatefulness I was sometimes—not always as I ought to have been—terribly ashamed, contrite. I could ask for pardon. I'm not one of those who are unable ever to do that. And with a man of his nobility to ask for pardon sincerely was to be forgiven immediately and absolutely. Each time, after I had said and shown how soul-sorry I was, I thought I should never sin in that way again. But I did, always I did sin again.

"My jealousy made him very miserable. It seared him. But he would have his decent freedom, the freedom every man, married or not, ought to have. He told me that he should go on behaving as if I trusted him, even if I could not trust him. He would never give me an account of his doings if I cross-examined him out of jealousy. Otherwise he was always willing to tell me anything. One thing in him which sometimes irritated me to the verge almost of madness was his marvellous self-control. I don't believe anything irritates an uncontrolled person so much as complete self-control in another. It is such a stinging rebuke. That rebuke he gave me many times, but not deliberately. He never tried to irritate me though I tried over and over again to irritate him. Once he frightened me.

"We were in a château on the Seine. There was a little wood in the grounds near the house. It was in autumn, on an autumn afternoon. That day I was in one of my worst moods. Autumn is a season that always depresses me, that inclines me, I suppose, to morbidity."

"I know—I know!" said Strickland, quickly breaking in upon her speech. "It seems to take away hope. One hears all the doors shutting against one. I, living here alone by the river, I know that."

"Ah!"

She gazed at him.

"Yes—you who live here alone!" she said. "And"—she paused; he waited—"and need not live here alone!" she added.

Strickland looked down, and pulled at his pipe.

"God sends loneliness to some of us," she went on. "I think it is one of the greatest punishments of God, perhaps the greatest of all. But why anticipate God?"

She was silent. Strickland said nothing.

"In Paris I know someone who is lonely," she said, sombrely, almost fatally. "But I don't think it is God's punishing hand laid on her, as it is on me."

She bent her head a little. Then she lifted it and went on.

"That autumn day he and I were alone in the château. We had had some guests with us but they had just left. They had been with us for shooting. One of them was a beautiful woman who was extraordinarily amiable, kind and gentle—the reverse of myself. She was almost universally beloved for her sweet disposition. While she had been with us I had secretly compared her with myself. Then I had gone a step further. I had imagined her as the wife of my husband (women often give themselves to such imaginings). How different Andrew's life would have been with her! I had dwelt on that thought. At night I had lain awake with it. She would have surrounded Andrew with the warmth of endless kindness, delicate and unwearied tenderness. She was not a dull but a clever woman, clever in goodness—a rather rare combination. She would never have trampled on his sensitiveness as I did, as the Devil drove me to do. She would have made him far happier than he was, or could ever be, with me. Often—I knew it as I pondered over this other woman—often he must be very unhappy with me. And then came the thought 'I am comparing myself with this woman. Probably Andrew has been comparing her with me.' Such a thought was like a sudden dagger thrust. I writhed under it.... I felt certain that Andrew had secretly compared me with this woman to my detriment. For as I was exceptionally violent and in many ways unamiable so she was exceptionally serene and beautifully poised. We stood out from the mass of women in our different ways. And what a way was mine!

"I had brooded over all this during the visit of our guests, until I had come to the horrible, morbid conviction that in very truth Andrew had been comparing me with our friend, and that he had been wishing that he had chosen differently when he married. I felt positive that the visit of this woman—she had never stayed with us before—had opened his eyes to facts, perhaps never clearly seen before by him, and that now, through her, he had realized the disaster of his life. All this may seem absurd to you, Mr. Strickland, but it just happened as I tell you. I could not help almost hating this dear woman. And I bade her good-bye conventionally, but feeling that I was bidding good-bye to an enemy.

"That day blackness encompassed me. It was one of my terrible days. I felt hopeless, a slave of my hateful character, angry with the Creator who had made me as I was, totally impotent to change, or even to put up a fight against myself! Andrew no doubt noticed the condition I was in. He was but too accustomed to my black dog moods. But he said nothing and seemed as cheerful as usual. After lunch, however, he said he was going out shooting and would probably be back late. He would shoot till dark, he said. I scarcely know why, but this announcement of his suddenly brought my misery to a climax. I suppose I felt that, now we were left alone, he was longing to get away from me. I could not contain myself and I broke out into a torrent of reproaches with which I mingled the name of our departed guest. I can't tell you what I said. I believe I launched contemptible and absurd accusations against him. In spite of his marvellous self-control he was this time driven into real anger. He told me to be silent, and not to dare to malign the name of a woman who was above reproach. I persisted. He went quite pale. Finally he left me. He was away a long time. I did not know whether he had gone out shooting. At last I went to ask. I found the keeper who usually accompanied him. The man told me that his master had left the house alone and without his gun, and had gone in the direction of the wood. I did not follow him. I did not dare to.

"Towards evening Andrew returned and came into the room where I was. He was still very pale, but his eyes were red and bloodshot. He looked terrible, I thought, as if—as if he had been crying. Then I broke down completely. I humiliated myself and begged him to pardon me. I asked him where he had been. He told me he had been sitting in the wood for hours, trying to make up his mind "what to do." This reply terrified me. I looked again at his eyes. I remember that I muttered: 'Why are your eyes so red?' He put his hand up to them quickly and turned his head away from me. Then I knew that he had been crying. Mr. Strickland, the knowledge that I had reduced such a man, a real man if ever there was one, to such a condition of despair, broke up all the hatefulness within me. And I—I showed him my utter contrition. But I had hurt him so much that he could only say: 'It must stop, Vivienne. From this moment it must stop. I find I can't bear it anymore. I am losing control. And if I lose it then the end will come quickly—I know that.' Mr. Strickland, from that day I was a different woman. For I had been terrified. I forced myself to govern my moods, to hold my temper in check. Things were better, much better between us. He knew the effort I was making and he helped me in every way he could.

"There were certain things in him which always irritated me, little habits, little ways. I needn't, I can't tell you. He tried to change them. He tried to change them! Oh, if only I could have them in my life now, every one of them! I should bless God for them! To me his faults, if they were faults, were really dearer than the greatest virtues of other men. I know that now. He did everything he could think of to make things easy for me. He was touchingly good to me. There is something so wonderful in the conscious effort of a man to be all that a woman wishes him to be. When I think—when I think —"

Sudden tears rushed to her eyes. She drew out a handkerchief quickly and wiped them away. Her face flushed, grew red to her temples. At that moment Strickland felt almost as if he were again in the Paris-Calais express.

"Oh, it hurts you too much!" he said. "Don't let us—"

But she interrupted him quickly, impetuously.

"No. I came here to make you understand. I have nearly finished. It doesn't matter about me. Don't trouble about me and what I feel. I am on the other side of sorrow."

She rolled up her handkerchief and put it on the mantelpiece.

"This is how the end came, Mr. Strickland. It was again autumn. The shooting season had begun and we were in the château. We generally had a few shooting parties every autumn. Andrew and I consulted together as to the people we would ask. Remembering the horrors of the preceding autumn he did not suggest asking that sweet woman about whom we had had that terrible scene. Her husband was a great shot. Our shooting was exceptionally good. It would have been natural to ask him and his wife. But Andrew made up the lists without alluding to them. I said nothing at the time. But on the evening of the day on which we had decided whom we were going to ask I remember thinking that it was cowardly of me to allow Andrew to be so far more magnanimous than I was. And I resolved to prove my goodwill and my absolute contempt for the accusations I had made the preceding year, to prove my absolute trust in Andrew, and in myself, by begging that Madame de V.—I cannot tell you her name—and her husband might be invited to come to us.

"Next day I told Andrew of my wish. He looked surprised, doubtful for a moment. 'I know what you are thinking,' I said. 'You are wrong. Andrew, I have conquered myself. I want them to come, partly that you may know it.' He looked pleased, almost—almost as if he were a little proud of me. I wrote the invitation. It was accepted. They came to us."

She came away from the fire slowly and sat down again in her chair. The flush had died out of her face, which looked now almost hard.

"This is what happened," she said. "I had miscalculated my own powers for goodness, for reasonableness. I thought I had changed. Really I had not changed. I thought I could absolutely trust myself. I was wrong. I thought I was now incapable of being jealous of Andrew. It was not so. The effort I had made for so long, a successful effort, instead of strengthening me, as I thought, must really have tried me to the point of exhaustion! Our friends arrived on a beautiful autumn day. I welcomed them, as I believed, with genuine pleasure. Perhaps really it was only with a conscious, strong effort to be pleased, which for a moment deceived myself. Madame de V.—who, of course, could have had no idea what my former feelings towards her had been (for I feel sure I had concealed them effectively while she had been in our house) seemed happy to be with us again.

"She was a radiant woman, getting, I think, light and warmth from the beauty of her own disposition. Our other guests were cordial and in fine spirits, the men looking forward to their sport, the women to the pleasures we were able to provide in plenty for those who visited us. Everything seemed to promise well, and my husband was gayer, more carefree than I had seen him for some time. Nevertheless, even on the first night after their arrival, I was conscious that for me all was not going to be well. The sight of Madame de V. recalled to me in a strange and dreadful way my past jealousy. I knew it to be evil and absurd. I had believed it to be utterly dead and done with. Yet already I began to feel it again. Again her serenity and charming good nature, which produced happiness all about her as light produces beauty in a landscape, marked for me the contrast between her temperament and disposition and my own, underlined for me, and as I fancied for others, my own defects. She made me feel my own moral inferiority to her. The light of her showed to me, and I thought to others, the shadows in which I was enveloped. I wished she had not come. I wished I had never suggested the invitation.

"When I compared myself with her—and I did this again as on the occasion of her former visit—I felt that such a woman must be a danger to me. Whenever I saw my husband with her, enjoying himself in the beams of her clever kindness, I trembled. Oh, Mr. Strickland, it is impossible for me to make you, or any other man, understand what I went through. It is all so horribly absurd and yet, in a woman such as I was then, so horribly natural. I—I—only a vulgarism can express what I felt. It seemed to me that Madame de V. showed me up."

She looked towards Strickland with a sort of shamed and almost wistful enquiry.

"I know exactly what you mean," he said, in answer to her look.

"It was a cruel feeling. It ate its way into me. It made me almost hate her for being what she was, one of the most good and delightful women in the world. Why, I asked myself, should she have been born, as I am sure she was born, naturally good, delightful, happy, a cause of happiness in others, without effort, while I, with all my efforts and struggles and even prayers—for I had often prayed to be different from what I was— could never extricate myself from my ugly temperament, never free myself from the curse of my uncontrollable irritability and evil humour? Madame de V., I felt sure, never suffered from jealousy. Why should she? Why should she fear any woman? The love of others was her natural birthright. And, thinking that, I felt, as I had often felt before, that it was impossible that anyone could really love me.

"Long ago my husband's love for me must really have died, when he found out what I was. I imagined him acting what perhaps once had been reality. I remembered all the scenes I had made with him, all my attacks on him, all my sarcasms, all the bitter words I had spoken to him in bad temper when my only desire had been to wound him. How he must hate me in his heart! Perpetual forgiving must weary out a man's love. Thinking back I tried to fix the moment when my husband's affection for me must inevitably have died. And immediately I thought of the day when he had gone out alone into the wood and had come back to me with red eyes. I remembered his words, that he had been sitting in the wood for hours trying to make up his mind 'what to do.' I knew now exactly what they meant. He had been debating with himself how best to get rid of the burden that weighed him down—me. On that afternoon in the wood he had realized that his love for me was dead. My despair, my pleading, my promises of amendment had been effective on his sense of chivalry, and he had shouldered the burden again. That was what had happened. I knew it now. And Madame de V. had been the cause of this disaster to me. It was she who had wrecked my life.

"Something seemed to crash in me, as I said this to myself, bringing everything to ruin.

"This crash, as I can only call it, happened on the second night of our house party, and not when I was alone. It occurred when I was sitting in the midst of our guests after dinner, listening to a pianist whom we had engaged to come out from Paris to play to us. I shall never forget that moment.

"My husband happened to be sitting on a sofa by Madame de V., who was herself a fine pianist and devoted to music. I was at some distance from them, but could see them both without turning my head. The pianist played first a sonata by Mozart, clear, gay, delicate, happy—full of spontaneity and sunshine, it seemed. Delight in it, and understanding of it, shone on Madame de V.'s beautiful face, and I saw her, from time to time, look at my husband, as if she were summoning him to share in her pleasure.

"'She is like that music,' I thought, as I sat in the midst of the ruin which nobody saw, which no one was aware of but myself.

"When the sonata was finished there was a short pause, during which I talked to my neighbour, Madame de V.'s husband. What I said I don't know. I believe I spoke mechanically, forced myself to speak because it was required of me. My husband meanwhile was talking animatedly with Madame de V. I saw him smiling, then laughing. It seemed to me that he looked almost boyish. Had I ever seen him look like that with me? Mr. Strickland, in my misery I told myself that I had never been able to bring such an expression into his eyes, such an emancipated expression. My whole body turned cold as I watched, but I went on talking. Some part of me, I suppose, was able to listen to what was being said to me. Presently the pianist began to improvise a short prelude and everyone was silent. Then he played something of Liszt's. I can't tell you its name, but it was a stormy, passionate thing, with occasional bits of romance in it, fleeting moments of sweetness, but a great deal of violent ugliness. It showed off marvellously the great executive powers of the pianist, but it was tormented, lowering, full of thunder clouds, fierceness, unrest, the very antithesis of the piece which had preceded it.

"I thought to myself, 'And that is I!' Again I looked at Madame de V. and my husband. She was listening intently with a grave, almost puzzled expression on her face. Her brows were drawn a little together. Her lips were pressed together. I felt that the music interested her, but that she disliked it. While I was feeling this I saw my husband steal a glance at me; a strange, furtive glance—I thought it. It was almost as if a stranger looked at me, but a stranger who knew, or had gathered by means of secret observation, much about me—to my detriment. Then he looked at Madame de V. I shut my eyes. In darkness I heard the remainder of that tempestuous music—music with no foothold anywhere for the soul that wants to rest. And in that darkness all power of moral control, of effort such as I had made during the last year, seemed to leave me. I was conscious of a terrific departure.

"I don't know how I got through the rest of the evening. The end came at last. I was able to say 'good night' to our guests. I pressed Madame de V.'s hand. (I can feel that pressure still.) I remember hearing her pleasant, clear voice say, concluding some discussion of the music, 'Mozart for me!' My husband added a comment that made me quiver. It was: 'One sees you reflected in Mozart as in a mirror. But in Liszt one sees only a stormy petrel.'

"That is meant for me!' I thought.

"Then we separated, going upstairs to our different rooms.

"My husband and I had a set of rooms in a tower. It was almost like a small flat, with a lobby, two bedrooms and a sitting room, quite separate from the rest of the house. That night I went quickly up to my bedroom, sent away my maid, and then locked both the doors of my room. When my husband came up to change into a smoking coat he tried my door. Finding it locked he called out to me. I didn't move or answer. He called out again. Then, as no one replied, he went to his room. I didn't see him again that night. I didn't want to see him. I was afraid to see him. A savage was awake in me. I sat up nearly all night. I can't tell you all that passed in my mind. But I'll tell you this—I felt I hated my husband."

Her eyes seemed to ask Strickland a searching question. At last she added:

"One can only feel as I felt then towards the man, or woman, one really loves best in the world. Mr. Strickland—do please forgive me—haven't you hated Jeanne like that?"

"I—I scarcely know," he said.

He paused; then as if making a strong effort over himself, he added:

"Perhaps I have, now and then."

"I remembered that look he had given me, and I hated him—or said to myself that I did. I summed up all my long love for him, all I had given him, all I had suffered because of him; not, I mean, because of any fault in him, but inevitably because of my type of nature, and my type of love, brought into close connection with him. And this was the end of it all—a look like that, the look of a stranger who knew bad things of me. For how long had his mind been working about me in a way secretly hostile to me? For how long had he gazed at me across a dividing gulf? The thought came to me that, on that day a year ago, when I had humbled myself to him after he came back to me from the wood, he had been bitterly sorry at the contrition which had prevented his final release from me. He had, I felt sure, hoped to win his freedom that day. But he had not won it.

"Don't think that even then I believed that Andrew could ever be false to me with Madame de V. I was not so mad as to think that. What I believed was this: that he wished he had married such a woman as Madame de V.; that she had made him long for such companionship as she could have given him; that she had unconsciously taught him to hate such a woman as I was. That was all, but that was enough.

"In the morning I only came down just before the men went out shooting. I saw Andrew only when I saw him among our guests. I thought he looked at me anxiously, as if he were almost in dread of something. But I smiled at him and managed, I believe, to hide what I was feeling. Some of the women were going to walk with the guns, Madame de V. among them. Andrew asked me if I were coming. But I refused. I said I had things to see to in the château.

"'Of course you'll be with us at luncheon?' he said.

"I said I would. But when the brake was starting for the rendezvous agreed on for lunch I didn't go. I made an excuse to the two or three women who were driving, said I wasn't feeling very well, and stayed behind by myself.

"That day I had a horrible feeling which I suppose is very rare in a woman brought up as I had been among refined people, always taught to hide their passions, to behave in a certain way whatever happens, to have at any rate complete control of manner except in moments of what is called privacy, that is in moments when they are with their own family, or most intimate friends. I felt as if I were losing hold of the conventions, as if I should be obliged to do something desperate. All these people whom I was entertaining—what were they to me? Why should I eternally act before them? I hated them. I dreaded their return to the château, because I didn't know whether I should be able any longer to be ordinary, civil, agreeable to them. I imagined myself breaking down under the strain I was enduring and doing something terrible before them all. Nietzsche has said that in every woman there dwells a tyrant and a slave. I believe that in almost every woman there dwells a primitive being who isn't really far removed from a savage. Perhaps the savage usually sleeps, or drowses. I felt my savage was awake.

"The afternoon wore on. I looked at the clock and knew I hadn't long to wait. My guests and Andrew would soon be home. Presently I heard the grinding of wheels on the gravel, the sound of horses' hooves, then, a moment later, the note of a motor horn, of laughter and gay voices, a barking of dogs.

"Mr. Strickland, at that moment I couldn't stand the routine of civilized life. The crash I told you of had evidently carried away something on which I had been able to rely till now—what's generally called 'myself.' I knew I could no longer rely on myself, and I went upstairs and hid myself in my room. I got into a dressing gown, quickly made all dark, and lay down on my bed.

"Presently I heard a knock at the door. It was my husband. I was obliged to let him come in. Finding me in the dark he asked what was the matter. I told him I had a violent sick headache and felt feverish. He wished to send for the doctor. I refused. I begged him to make my excuses to our guests, to send up my maid and then not to disturb me again. I said my nerves were all to pieces from the pain in my head. We spoke to each other in the dark. But I felt energy, cheerfulness, the open air had come into my room with him, and I bitterly compared my misery, my almost madness, with my husband's sanity and poise. I was a moral wreck. He stood there near to me—a man, a sportsman, full of the glorious sense of well-being, physical and mental, that the exercise of the bodily powers gives to a man.

"He stood there filling the dark room with an atmosphere of health and strength. Mr. Strickland, in less than a week from that moment he was dead.

"Our guests had been invited to stay for four days. During the rest of their time I did not face them. I never went downstairs. But I saw one of them. Madame de V., in the most charming way, I believe, insisted gently on coming up. This was on the evening before she left the château. She sent up a message begging to be allowed to see me. And my husband also brought a word from her. I remember he said to me:

"'Do see her, Vivienne. She is so calm, such a sweet woman, she can only do you good. I often wish you knew more of her.'

"(That's how men are with us, Mr. Strickland! But how often I long to be misunderstood by Andrew now! We love men partly because they haven't got our horrible subtleties.)

"I consented to see Madame de V., and she came up to my room. It wasn't quite dark. There were two shaded candles lighted. She sat down by my bed, and stayed perhaps for half an hour. But it seemed a very long time to me.

"I couldn't ever tell a man what I lived through during that little visit, Mr. Strickland. I suppose, to an onlooker, it would have seemed a happy little interview between two women who were good friends. Madame de V. perhaps felt it to be so—perhaps not. For I don't know how well I acted. She must, I think, in spite of my efforts have realized that there was something very wrong with me. But she may have attributed it to my bad health. I don't know. I don't suppose I ever shall know. She was marvellously kind and sympathetic. I believe she liked me. I believe she wished to be a good friend to me. That I couldn't help, at that time, hating her was not her fault.

"While she was with me, talking in her pleasant, sweet voice, I kept thinking of the look my husband had sent to me during the piano playing. Innocently she had surely prompted that look. I believed she had done me a deadly harm and merely by being what she was. My whole body shrank from her. Her nearness to me put my nervous system into a sort of tumult. Her goodness called forth all my evil, but I didn't show it to her. No, I lay there very still, and listened to her quiet voice, and forced myself to speak quietly, gently in return. It's strange how sometimes goodness rouses evil. It's terrible. Some people ought never to meet each other, never to know of each other's existence. Fate brought Madame de V. and me together. It ought to have kept us forever apart. It was she who made me destroy the foundations of all the happiness I could ever have in this world. She tempted me to evil as no devil could ever have tempted me. Isn't it an irony that a saint, who means nothing but good, can bring about such a tragedy as mine?

"At last she left me. I have never seen her again.

"That day the house party broke up. All our guests left the château. They went away in the morning. My husband had some business to attend to in Paris. He came to my room to bid me good-bye. Somehow— he only stayed a few minutes—I managed to seem calm and casual while he was with me. As he was going out of my room he said: 'I shall motor up with the De V.'s and come back by train.' With an effort—for I felt as if I had received a blow over the heart—I asked him when I should expect him. 'To-morrow morning in time for lunch,' he answered. 'What—not to-night?' I said. My throat felt all dried up as I spoke. 'No; I'm afraid I can't get through all I have to do in time to get back to-night,' he answered. I remember I opened my lips to beg him not to spend the night in Paris, but I shut them without speaking. He bent to kiss me, but I turned my head brusquely away. At that moment I felt I would rather be touched by a snake than by him.

"I can't tell you much about the following night. I didn't sleep. In the dark hours I reviewed my life and its utter failure, and in my madness I attributed its failure to my husband. I no longer blamed myself. I blamed him. My tortured nerves drove me into fierce condemnation of him. Everything was distorted by my imagination that night. I saw nothing as it really was. Evil boiled up in me—evil."

She stopped abruptly. Strickland could see in her face that in imagination she was literally living through again that bit of her past life. She stared before her while he waited, not moving. His pipe had gone out, but he still kept it between his lips. At last she looked at him as one who again sees the reality of the moment.

"I told you that when my husband was going to kiss me I turned my head away brusquely. I told you that at that moment I would rather have been touched by a snake than by him—"

She paused.

"Yes," Strickland said.

"That was the last time he ever bent down to kiss me."

"Do you mean—didn't you ever see him again?"

"Oh, yes. We had a last interview, but there was nothing but hatred in it—what seemed hatred, I mean—on my side. No man could have wished to kiss, no man could ever have even thought of kissing, the woman I was in that last interview. Oh, Mr. Strickland, the last time— the last time—and not to know it, not even to suspect it! Our poor human lives—how terrible they are! If only we could know a little more, if only we could know! We should be so different. But take a warning by me. With one you love always say to yourself: 'It may be the last time!' And put your true heart, your love, the best part of you into it. And you will be thankful. Even you may bless me some day. When you say good-bye, if it be only, as you suppose, for a day—an hour—remember that it may be for the space of a lifetime—even forever. Do we know?"

For a moment her face was tormented.

"Let your last time be sweet and tender. Otherwise you go into hell here on earth. I have done that.

"In the morning I got up. I was restless, like a driven fury. I waited for him to come back. I did not know what I was going to do. But I knew I was going to do something drastic, perhaps horrible. I knew I needed to do something horrible as one needs to eat when starving. The whole of me seemed possessed by an absolute need to chastise, to scourge, to use the lash, to draw blood—blood from the soul (for the soul can bleed). Because I was tortured I longed to torture—not any friend, or casual acquaintance, not a servant, not some stranger, but the one I loved. That, and only that, seemed my horrible necessity. I was—I must have been—possessed that day.

"I came downstairs. I went out. I walked in the garden. I went into the wood where he had once stayed so long—thinking 'what to do.' Where was it he had waited, thinking, devising plans for his freedom from me? The golden leaves were falling. I stood among them and asked myself, 'Was it here?' I went on, deeper into the wood, to the inmost recesses. Again I stood still, and said, 'Was it here?' Nothing answered. Nothing told me. But I thought, 'I'll bring him here. I'll torture him here, for wishing to get away from me, to rid himself of me, who have loved him exclusively.' (I can hear the leaves falling now, and the shrill cry of birds in the coverts.) Presently I looked at my watch. It was nearly noon. I returned to the château.

"I found a telegram there. It told me that he was delayed in Paris for a few hours, but would be down by an afternoon train. I thought, 'I don't care. When he comes I'll take him into the wood. Even if it's night, I'll take him into the wood.' The idea of the wood obsessed me.

"Twilight was beginning to fall when at last he came back. It was cold that evening, cold with the strange earthy chill characteristic of autumn, compounded, I always think, of the differing coldnesses of many things dead or fading rapidly into death. I was dressed for walking when he came into my sitting room. He seemed surprised at seeing me up, still more so at seeing me dressed for going out. He came towards me, perhaps intending to kiss me. But something in my look must have stopped him. For, when he was near me, he stood still. He asked me if I was better. I said I was quite well, and wanted him to come out with me. He said of course he would come if I wished it, but added a doubt as to the wisdom of my going out at such a late hour after my illness.

"I told him I wished to talk to him and preferred to do it in the open air. He asked me why. I said, imperiously, even violently, I believe, that I wished it and that was enough. He said nothing more and we went out together. I led the way towards the wood. Mists were beginning to rise from the Seine, which flowed not far from the château. We walked in silence side by side. When we drew near to the trees he said that we had better remain in the garden, on one of the terraces, where it would be dry underfoot. I said that I wished to go into the wood. 'It is madness in your condition,' he said. But I persisted and we followed a winding grass path among the trees till we came to a clearing. Woodcutters had been at work there. Several trunks of poplar trees, stripped of their branches and leaves, lay on the damp ground. Here I stopped and stood still.

"'Do you remember coming into this wood last year?' I asked. 'After Madame de V.'s visit to us?'

"He answered, 'Yes.'

"'Was it here you sat for hours considering what to do?' I asked.

"'It may have been here,' he answered. 'I can't remember exactly. But what does it matter?'

"'I only wanted to tell you here in this wood,' I said, 'that this time I shall not humble myself. I shall not beg forgiveness. You can do what you like. I understand the whole situation now clearly. Last year you wanted to get rid of me. You were hoping to get rid of me. But I didn't let you. I didn't give you the chance. Because then I still loved you. But now it's different.'

"Mr. Strickland, I can't tell you any more of the words I said. But I poured forth all the bitterness in my heart. Instead of humbling myself and showing my love, I called pride to me in my jealousy. I pretended that it was I who was weary of him, that it was I who longed to get rid of him. Always I saw before me the face of Madame de V. like a smiling vision in the mists—"

She stopped speaking and stared before her for a moment. Then she got up and again stood by the fire with her hands gripped tightly together.

"Mr. Strickland, do you know how in such moments of madness, of love, intense love, turned, twisted all awry, the tongue finds instinctively all the most horrible words, all the words that are like spears to lacerate and draw blood? Do you know?"

"Yes," said Strickland.

"They say—some people say—that the other side of love is hatred. If it is so then, in such moments, we turn love inside out, we show the side that is hideous. I did. You know what the intimacy of marriage is, how it arms one with knowledge that others haven't got, knowledge of the little human failings, of the secret weaknesses, that everyone has, however dear, however noble. Tricks, mannerisms of body and soul, physical things—who knows them quite as the husband does, or the wife? And the repetitions—the things that come again and again! The husband knows them of the wife, the wife of the husband, as nobody else ever can, I think. Every wife has weapons which perhaps no other living woman has against the husband. I used all mine. I can't tell you more than that. And all the time I loved every hair on his dear head. That's how a woman can be! God's curse must be on us from the beginning, I sometimes think.

"He didn't speak—not a word. He just stood there looking absolutely stricken—with a sort of terrific surprise in his eyes. But the terrible, the frightful thing is, that I know at that moment he believed that I hated him. (Men can believe such a thing!) At last when I had emptied myself of hatred and bitterness—hatred of the moment, false hatred, madness simulating its opposite—I stopped speaking. He stood for a moment. Then he turned. I heard his feet trampling on the brushwood. The trees and the mists took him.

"When I went back to the château night had fallen and his servant came to tell me his master had left in the motor for Paris.

"'Who went with him?' I asked.

"He told me no one. Andrew had gone alone, driving himself. Mr. Strickland, that same night he was killed on the road to Paris, near a village. Two villagers saw it. They said he was driving fiercely, at something like seventy miles an hour. A dog ran out. He tried to avoid it. The car struck a bank. It was the end.

"It was the end for him.

"I received his dead body, Mr. Strickland—that was all."

Strickland, without knowing why, had instinctively got on to his feet. She held out her hand, put it on his arm.

"They laid him down before me, and I couldn't tell him the truth. Can you understand what that meant to me?"

"Perhaps—partly," he almost whispered.

"That's all I can tell you. Mr. Strickland, whatever people may say— and modern people say a great deal—against what they call emotionalism, sentimentality, and so forth, some of us live by feeling, I think. We have to. There isn't a pulse beating in the brain as there is in the heart. Don't be false to your heart. That is death. Jeanne loves you. She is ill—"

"Ill!" said Strickland.

"Yes—because she is starving, I think. That's why I came. That's why I have told you. I don't know of course how much you love her, or if you love her. But I thought I would just give you the chance to profit by my tragedy if you care at all. That day, in the Calais express, before you, I went down into the bottom of understanding of what I had done, and what it meant. I wonder now whether you had anything to do with that. I don't know. All I know is that till that moment, since Andrew's death, I hadn't shed a tear."

She went to the sofa and picked up her fur coat. Strickland helped her to put it on.

When she said good-bye she gave him a slip of paper.

"Jeanne's address in Paris," she said.

Those were her last words to Strickland.

On the following morning Strickland started for Paris.

The Façade

I

When I met Ariadne Marshall for the first time she was, I suppose, almost at the height of that peculiar career which had made her notorious. Everyone in London who knew of anything—there are of course millions who don't—knew of her. She represented intellect upon the stage. She was renowned for plastic grace. Her taste in costume was considered extraordinary. She followed no fashions. She was above that sort of thing. Besides her beauty—if indeed it were beauty—was too peculiar to be pulled about by the dressmakers, the *modistes*, the hair specialists. It demanded a very special treatment. Some said it was Byzantine; others thought it early Egyptian. Anyhow it would have been ruined by "bobbed" hair, and devastated by a short skirt, a fish tail, a jumper or a "tailor-made." As to hats—well, Ariadne designed her own hats with the help, it was sometimes said, of Cambridge professors.

Ariadne knew a large selection of professors. All the intellectual men who had never heard of Delysia, who didn't know that London contained a theatre named " The Gaiety," were to be seen at her "first nights," and frequented her small panelled house in Marmion Street, Westminster; a house of austere aspect and frugal charm, with a minimum of furniture, but containing some priceless "bits," a collection of jade and another of amber which caught the sunlight—when there was any—and one, only one, picture which was said to be a Leonardo da Vinci. Who said so I can't remember at the moment. But I believe it was a Portuguese expert who lived in Corfu, and who was considered by a small clique of the elect to know more about Leonardo than any other human being, either in Corfu or out of it.

In this small and delicately mysterious house, with its black and purple dining room (upstairs), its misty blue and green drawing room (downstairs), its long orange-coloured bedroom without any bed—Ariadne slept on a divan raised about half a foot from the floor—and its tiny garden—"the hanging garden of Westminster," Ariadne's circle called it—on the leads, Ariadne dwelt alone like a chaste priestess, ministered to by some two or three respectable women dressed in plum colour and with reassuring Scottish accents.

Ariadne was a widow, and had been a widow for a tremendous long time, though she was only in the beginning of the thirties. She had been married very young, she said, long before she knew what she really was. To whom? Nobody seemed quite to know. But it was understood that the husband had been that most dreadful of all created things—a Philistine. If any question were asked about him, such as: "What did he do?" the answer would be, "She never says, but—he was a Philistine." Or "Did he understand her? Was he unkind to her?" "She never accuses him of anything, but—he was a Philistine." Long ago, it was whispered, before Ariadne had ever thought of going upon the stage, the grave had most fortunately closed over him, and now he slept with his fathers in Philistia. Even his name was unknown to Ariadne's circle. It had not been Marshall. That much was certain! Johnnie Dean, a devoted adherent of Ariadne's, always spoke of the deceased as, "That man whose name wasn't Marshall." For the rest Ariadne had a right to her secret. She had married a Philistine and had emerged into what she was, untouched, untainted, with no mire of Philistinism clinging to the skirts of her garments. Her marriage must have been a great melodrama, one of those melodramas which one doesn't care to think about, but the curtain had long since been rung down upon it. And Ariadne was what she was.

Ariadne—I am speaking of the time when I first got to know her—was "in management"; that is she had power over a building fitted up as a theatre and called "The Parthenon Theatre," which was frequented by the elect of London, Oxford, Cambridge, and other centres of taste and intellect. Over the portico of this temple of art was the name "Ariadne Marshall," which at night was illuminated with dull red light. On the programme was the announcement: "Sole Lessee and Manager, Ariadne Marshall." And whatever play was being given one read the statement: "The play produced by Ariadne Marshall," and lower down: "The costumes designed by Ariadne Marshall."

There was no doubt therefore as to who had power over the Parthenon Theatre. As Johnnie Deans said: "Ariadne is the theatre, and the theatre is Ariadne." And this declaration evidently covered the whole matter.

The Parthenon Theatre was in a by-street—that coarse-tongued fellow, Sam Hartlebury, in consequence always spoke of Ariadne as "the widow in the by-street"—but quite near to the centre of things, and at the time I am dealing with was enjoying a nice little intellectual success with a play by Ezra Green called *Realistic and Idealistic Love*, in which Ariadne was never off the boards. She was alone there when the curtain went up, and alone there when the curtain came down, both times in the centre of the clever little stage which was copied from one in Moscow. The play was still running to quite fair houses, but Ariadne would be wanting a new piece soon, and Professor Simeon Jenkins hadn't yet finished the translation he was making from the Dutch for Ariadne. Therefore she had to look about for something suitable. Now I had just written something. The question was whether it was suitable. Only Ariadne could decide that. We didn't know each other. But an introduction was "brought about" by Johnnie Dean. And that was how and why I came to know Ariadne.

Johnnie Dean took me to Marmion Street on a Sunday afternoon about three o'clock at Ariadne's special request, and I brought the play I had written with me.

"She'll judge it at a first reading," said Johnnie, with a wise smile. "Ariadne's extraordinarily swift. No hesitations—no shilly-shally. Her intellect goes straight to the point."

"That's more than one can say of most actresses," I remarked, trying to cover uneasiness with cynicism.

"Oh, Ariadne's much more than a mere actress. She's a highly intellectual woman with a marvellous sense of art. Here we are!"

The front door was black, with a silver knocker, the head of a Dryad. There was no letter box.

"The postman has to ring and give the letters in," observed Johnnie, gravely.

"Dear me!" I remarked, impotently.

A Scottish woman in plum colour opened the door.

"The drawing room's downstairs," said Johnnie.

"Dear me " I again said, laying down my hat on a black marriage chest which stood in the minute square hall.

"And the dining room's on the first floor."

"Dear—"

But at this moment Ariadne was disclosed by the Scottish woman, who had opened the drawing room door, and my remark was truncated.

Ariadne was standing erect by a tall chimney-piece of carved wood, with panels and thin fluted columns. A wood fire was burning behind her. She looked very tall against that background of flame. She wore a black velvet dress with very long tight sleeves, and in her red-brown hair, which completely covered her ears, and which appeared to me amazingly thick and mysterious, there was fastened a large and learned-looking red jewel in an extraordinary setting of gold. I felt at once that it had been dug up out of a tomb by an Egyptologist who was a friend of Ariadne's. Her irregular features—she has, or had, a rather pointed nose with arched nostrils, a wide full-lipped mouth, a small round chin, and narrow green eyes slanting downwards under thin slanting eyebrows—were set in a serious carven expression like that of a muse who was thinking deeply and tranquilly. In her right hand, on which was one extraordinary ring, which I felt sure also came from a tomb, was a book bound in some dull brocade with gold clasps, a Greek testament with a "crib" as I found out later. Near to her, sitting in a misty blue armchair, was a little old man, dry as a Saharan lizard, with expressionless blue eyes, a mouth like a purse with no money in it, and bright pink hands.

As Johnnie introduced me to Ariadne she gazed at me steadily, not piercingly but with strong earnestness, and shook my hand with a sort of calm authority, after laying her book aside on a small antique table, which looked as if it had come out of the vestry of some ancient church. Then she introduced me to the little old man—Mr. Murryan was his impressive name. (I thought it sounded like the name of a pestilence.) I bowed, wondering why he was there and whether he was going to stay, and Mr. Murryan nodded, suddenly caught hold of his nose, seemed to ring it, and turned in his very long feet, which had previously been arranged in what used to be called "the first position."

"Have you brought the play?" asked Ariadne, in a deep and sonorous voice, still looking earnestly at me with the carven expression.

I said "Yes."

"Well, then—thank you, John."

And to my surprise Johnnie evaporated while Mr. Murryan remained.

"A Murryan upon him" I remember saying to myself.

When Johnnie was gone Ariadne took a long deep blue taper from a silver casket which stood alone—no doubt it was priceless—on a bracket under the supposed Leonardo, a long-faced woman either smiling or not smiling—one couldn't tell which—and lit three candles of deep blue wax.

"Please sit in this chair," she said, pointing to a high chair just in front of them, "I shall give you all my attention."

I glanced at Mr. Murryan, who was pulling one of his exceptionally large ears with his brilliant pink fingers. Who was he? I couldn't divine. Anyhow he was there. Then I sat down and took hold of my play. As I did so Ariadne sank upon a very low-cushioned settee near the fire, clasped her hands round her knees, and gazed into my face with an unwinking fixity which was almost, not quite, oriental.

"The Parthenon Theatre!" I thought. "And she is as still as the Parthenon—on a height, too. For she must be tremendously intellectual."

As I began to read it seemed to me that this play of mine was great rubbish.

That impression of my work deepened in me while I read the three acts. As I finished each one I paused for a moment and looked first at Ariadne, then at Mr. Murryan. The latter seemed to be wrapped in a deep and trance-like sleep, for his eyes were shut and no breathing was audible. The former was evidently wrapped in high thought and profound contemplation. For she never moved—as far as I could see—and never took her eyes from my face. There was something tremendously impressive in her intense concentration on the matter in hand. She seemed literally to loom over me and my play. And again I was reminded of a temple set on a height.

At last I had read the final word, and I crumpled the manuscript up in a pair of decidedly nervous hands. A deep silence ensued.

"That's all!" I said.

I corrected myself quickly:

"That is all."

Mr. Murryan got up, rang his nose, and slipped out of the room, like a lizard slipping over sand, I thought. I was alone with Ariadne.

When the door was shut on her enigmatic friend I thought she would speak. But she didn't. She sat still wrapped in thought. Evidently she was mentally summing up my play preparatory to delivering a verdict. I imagined her powerful mind busily and relentlessly at work, its brilliant operations masked by the mysterious physical frontage presented to my view.

"Well," I said, at length, feeling that someone must speak. "Well, Miss

Marshall, what do you think of the play?"

She moved and now faintly smiled.

"I've taken it all in," she said, calmly.

"I realize that fully."

"We won't talk about it."

"What?" I exclaimed, surprised, even taken aback. "You think it so—"

"To-morrow morning you will know what I think. To-morrow morning, perhaps by the second post, you will receive a letter from me going thoroughly into your work. I shall write to-night when the house is quiet. The brain, I find, works best at night when ordinary folk"—she allowed herself a faint and compassionate smile—"are sleeping."

She paused for a moment. Then she got up slowly, plastically, stretched out her fine arms, touched her voluminous hair gently, and said:

"Now shall I show you my few treasures? That is a Leonardo."

And we went to look at the picture.

I thought it had something of Ariadne's mysterious grace and poise.

II

On the following morning, by the second post, I received a large, square and evidently well-filled envelope, butcher blue in colour, and directed to me in the small, clear writing which is characteristic of Oxford and Cambridge. The address indeed looked as if it had been written by a Don. I opened the envelope eagerly and took out a long letter which began:

"Dear Man"

I was already—I confess it—much impressed by Ariadne's remarkable personality, but when I had finished reading her letter I suppose I felt about her much as Johnnie Dean did. For the butcher blue pages set forth a minute, powerful, logical and deeply subtle criticism of my play.

"As it is it won't do," Ariadne wrote. "The psychology is in places too cloudy, sometimes even contradictory—the contradictions unintentional on your part of course. Let me point out precisely what I mean."

And she pointed it out with really remarkable perspicacity. I saw my play with new eyes—hers, judged it with a new brain—again hers. Of course it wouldn't do as it was. The only marvel to me was that I hadn't seen that before. Ariadne had opened my peepers with a vengeance!

At last I laid the letter down and looked, stared, at the last words, as the blue paper reposed on my writing-table.

"But don't be discouraged, dear man. I am sure you can get it right. What it needs is more *thought*, more fundamental brain work. Give it that—how few folk ever give that to anything—and it may yet be possible to produce it in the Parthenon Theatre. I dare say any other manager in London would be satisfied with it as it is now. But that is not my case. —Ariadne Marshall.”

Fundamental brain work! There wrote no doubt the true Ariadne. In thinking over the many actresses I knew—and I knew, oh, so many—I could not come upon her peer. People of the stage hitherto had always seemed to me extraordinarily haphazard in their mental processes. They were many of them gifted, no doubt, but they seemed to rely on their gifts rather as a bird relies on its wings—without thought. They chanced their flights. Ariadne was more like a powerful aeroplane than a bird. But she was the skilled mechanic too, and the pilot and the observer. A most remarkable woman, a woman with brains!

After smoking a pipe I telegraphed, answer paid, to Ariadne:

“May I come to you and discuss the play?”

Within a short time I received this reply:

“I never discuss plays. My business is to judge the finished work. Greetings. —Ariadne Marshall.”

I was deeply impressed by this telegram. In a way it disappointed me. Yet it was admirably to the point. It is for the author to do, for the actress-manageress to judge of what he has done. Discussion is a sort of collaboration. I felt rather humiliated by being thus set right. But Ariadne had gone to the core of the matter.

Fundamental brain work! That was the thing. The worst of it was that I felt rather like a reluctant day-labourer, who, in a warm feather bed, hears the first strident notes of intolerable chanticleer.

That evening I bought a stall for the performance at the Parthenon Theatre.

Now, as everyone knows—except those who know nothing—the Parthenon Theatre has a majestic façade which gives nobility almost to the by-street in which it unsuitably stands. The façade is a Greek Temple. But when you get inside the theatre is surprisingly small, indeed almost pokey, with narrow corridors, a rather mean staircase, and a very poor foyer. Unless the play being done requires incidental music there is no orchestra. The lighting of the stage is perfect. But the lighting of the theatre, though adequate, is not brilliant. The decoration is good but very simple, almost austere. The stalls and dress-circle seats are upholstered in black with dull gold sparingly used. There is no pit. The walls are panelled in dark wood. The curtains which hide the stage are of a dim purple hue. I need not say that no plush is to be found in the theatre. Ariadne would as soon connect herself with plush as with *The Soul’s Awakening* in painting, *The Rosary* in literature, or “The End of a Perfect Day” in music.

There was a fair, though not crowded, audience that night, and I was very much struck by its appearance. It was not an ordinary audience. There was something earnest, almost reverential—suggesting clasped hands and upraised eyes—about it. As I glanced at the rather dowdily clad men—many of them young with students’ eyes and locks—at the women with Greek fillets in their hair and deep-hued, though not strictly modish robes, I muttered to myself, “fundamental brain work!”

This was not a common or garden theatre for light-hearted fools. This was a place of aspiration, of intellect, a place where you could put your teeth into something which might be gritty but which would certainly prove to be substantial.

What would my play be—here? Not up to the mark, I said to myself, not up to the mark at all!

Realistic and Idealistic Love was enormously intellectual, and Ariadne's performance in the chief part was enormously intellectual, too. At least I thought so. One did not feel a woman's heart beating in it so much as a man's brain working in it. And yet the attitudes, the poses, were almost voluptuous at times, but with a sort of classical and statuesque voluptuousness. I remember in one scene she opened a door and I felt that it gave upon something tremendous—the desert, perhaps, or the interior of an academy for the study of occult sciences. In another scene she shut it, and I felt that she was shutting out immensities. She was calm in the part, quite passionless; but this absence of passion was striking. She looked wonderful, as wonderful as the façade of her theatre.

During the *entr'actes* few people went out to the bars—if there were bars. They sat still and talked earnestly in subdued voices. I heard such expressions as, "food for the mind," "full of grey matter," "the inner workings of a restless but controlled intellect," "a grand exhibition of the serpentine convolutions of that marvellous piece of mechanism the modern brain."

Yes, there was fundamental brain work here.

At the close of the performance an attendant came up to me and said: "Are you Mr. So and So?" I said I was. "Then will you kindly come to see Miss Marshall."

I followed the woman through a doorway, and was shown into a long narrow room, sparely furnished and lined with books, where I found Ariadne lying on a divan almost level with the floor in her stage dress. In a corner of the room was a young man, with a white, round face, a high, round and protuberant forehead, and large sunken brown eyes, who was holding in both hands a small statuette of Circe. Ariadne introduced him as Mr. Leo Fanning. He bowed but said nothing.

"Sit down, dear man!" Ariadne added, slightly moving her feet.

I sat down on the end of the divan with my knees nearly touching my chin.

"So you saw me," I said.

She shook her head compassionately.

"I never see anyone when I am acting. How could you suppose so? The artist who sees the audience can never hope to accomplish anything. No. The man at the box office recognized you and told me you were here. You read my letter carefully?"

"I did indeed."

"You took it to heart and brain?"

"Certainly I did."

"You realize now what I need to work upon? Brains there must be in any play I produce, a high intellectual standard. I am not here for the silly people."

At this moment there was a knock at the door, and on Ariadne's replying, "Come!" a very thin, middle-aged man, with a marvellous round black beard, critical dark eyes, and an almost femininely prim gait and manner came in. He walked sideways to Ariadne, bent almost double over her, and said in a high careful voice:

"My sweet lady! You were never more forthright than to-night. Your whole performance was axiomatic. The exquisite dryness of it was a tonic after the slush in which playgoers—I only come here of course—wade year in year out. A touch of emotion would have ruined it. But you held back. No saccharine from you! The finest caravan tea without even the smallest lump of sugar—that was what you gave us. Pure thought divorced from emotion! Kindling to the mind!"

"My dear!" said Ariadne. "My dear!"

Then turning and leaning on her elbow she said to me:

"Professor Huskin Repps, of the British Museum," and uttered my name to the professor.

In the brief conversation which followed, and which was I must say almost entirely over my head and beyond my competence, Ariadne said very little, and Mr. Fanning, whom the Professor already seemed to know well, nothing except once "I can't agree with that." Ariadne was apparently not a great talker. But one felt her thinking hard when others were in talk, thinking ahead of them, above them, under them, all round them. The Professor talked, and I spoke a few times tentatively. Then a maid with Titian hair brought in a tall glass of something which looked like thickened milk.

"My Bransonia!" explained Ariadne.

"The best brain builder science has so far discovered," said the Professor. "Well, we must leave you."

As he was about to go Ariadne said of me:

"He has submitted a play to me."

The round beard was suddenly projected towards me, and the dark eyes interrogated me with a sharpness that seemed almost hostile.

"Indeed!"

He turned primly round to Ariadne and cocked two questioning eyebrows of bushy black.

"Not quite!" she answered. "Not quite! But with more thought, more brain work, more of that wrestling of the mind with the problem which *we* know—perhaps!"

"Ha, ah?"

He gazed down at her.

"The mind and the problem! Forthright! Forthright! And the grit of it between one's teeth, like the finest sand!"

He pushed out the beard towards me again.

"Perhaps?" he said.

And once more his critical—and it seemed to me rejecting—eyes busied themselves to my thinking about my very entrails.

"That's something to spur on the most laggard mind!" he said, in an almost piercing soprano—and was gone.

I prepared to follow him discreetly and Ariadne did not try to detain me. She was already sipping her Bransonia and seemed sinking into reverie.

As I pressed her soft white hand she said:

"*He* knows!"

"He?"

"Huskin Repps."

"Yes? What?"

"The value of a tingling dryness in art. Beware of saccharine, dear man. Fools love it; but I don't want fools in the Parthenon Theatre. There are plenty of styes in London."

"Styes!" I said, somewhat startled.

"Where the offal is profuse. Let the fools go there. They must not come near me."

She drew her robe closer about her feet with a carefully splendid gesture, and turned her head away with a deep sigh.

I went out reverently, quite forgetting to nod to Mr. Leo Fanning.

III

From that evening onwards I was included in Ariadne's circle.

It was an understood thing that Ariadne considered me a "promising" man and that I was toiling hard o' nights on a play which she earnestly hoped might eventually come up to her standard of what a play ought to be, but which didn't do at all as yet.

Although I was over thirty, and had published several books which had attained success, and had also had two plays produced in London, both of which had made a good deal of money, I felt now like a youthful beginner, who might perhaps have some talent but who had yet to prove himself. So great was the spell of Ariadne upon me, so high did I feel her standard to be.

She never mentioned my books. Perhaps she had never heard of them, for she told me once quite frankly that she only found time to read the few great classics which were in accord with her temperament, "perhaps a peculiar one." But she knew of my plays. This I know, because she once said in the presence of a few of her intimates, who were gathered together in the hanging garden of Westminster: "He has tried already, the dear man!" And then she had given me a wonderful smile of mingled pity and encouragement.

Her circle was not very large. How could it be when far the greater number of people are fools? But it included distinguished men and women, professors, poetesses, painters, sculptors, scientific men, a musician or two, a decorator or two, an architect, one novelist—Jasper

Trent, of America—and several "thinkers" who were also very well-born and very much in society. Some top-hole politicians might also be seen in Marmion Street from time to time, but never an actor or an actress. Ariadne was very sorry for her comrades of the stage.

"All thought processes seem quite alien to them," she sometimes said. "I have infinite difficulty in finding suitable people to act with me. I am always searching for minds but I seldom find them. So I try to find wax upon which I can set my impress at rehearsal."

She was said to be "very wonderful" at rehearsal.

Mr. Murryan and Mr. Leo Fanning I had never encountered again. They were evidently not of the habitués of Marmion Street. Professor Huskin Repps, however, was continually there, and I began to think that he was delicately in love with Ariadne, for he hung about her in a prim and yet at times almost ecstatic way, and showed himself intensely critical of most of those who were admitted to her intimacy.

"It is a very precious mind!" I have heard him say: "It must not be contaminated by folly or ignorance. One must watch over it and guard it."

In Ariadne's circle there was one figure which intrigued me.

This was a man of perhaps about thirty, or thirty-two, called Augustus Transome, whom I might possibly have thought almost second rate if I had not met him in Ariadne's house. He looked to me like a Jew, but I was not certain that he was a Jew. His nose was not predatory, though it was slightly upturned and unduly prolonged, a characteristic of certain Jews of the less aristocratic type. But his back, his walk, and a peculiar way in which his small dark eyes flew from side to side in their sockets, as if looking this way and that for good opportunities, strongly suggested Israel to me. He was always very well, even smartly dressed, was quiet, and wore a carefully trimmed moustache. His voice was rather thick and slow, and really I could not help thinking sometimes that he had the ghost of a cockney accent. He said very little.

In this he was not unlike Ariadne, who was not a great talker, and who, I knew, disdained what she called "cackle." But his silence did not seem deeply intellectual like hers. There was something sly, something almost furtive and underhand about it. I never heard Mr. Transome speak about money but I felt that he was rich. Nobody in Ariadne's circle explained him to me, but everybody seemed to take him for granted. So of course I took him for granted too. He took very little notice of me though he was always very polite, but now and then I observed his small eyes fixed upon me, and I thought there was something appraising in their gaze, as if Mr. Transome—"Augustus," Ariadne called him—were considering what exact value I represented, or might eventually represent, in hard cash.

Ariadne never spoke to me directly of the play I was trying to bring up to her standard, but she often made me feel that she was thinking deeply about it and about me, was mentally perhaps trying to help me with it. I felt sure that she knew exactly what ought to be done to it, but after that telegram I dared not attempt to discuss it with her. The play was my job; the judgment of it was hers. To each one a different task. I had once heard her say: "Those who try to help and lift others up with their own superior gifts and powers only put a top varnish on natural incompetence." And it had struck me as a very just, and even a very subtle remark. So I knew I must work out my own salvation.

But my desire to reach intellectual heights worthy of Ariadne made me work very slowly, and my play was not ready when "Realistic and Idealistic Love" began to stagger on its last legs. Professor Simeon Jenkins's translation from the Dutch was not finished either. Another play must be found at once.

On a memorable Sunday afternoon the question of the next production at the Parthenon was discussed by a select segment of Ariadne's circle. There were present Professor Repps, Professor Simeon Jenkins, Mrs. Lascelles, the poetess and essayist, Lady Burnett, the well-known portrait painter—who had painted Ariadne three times—Eustace Delminius, the composer, Jasper Trent, and Augustus Transome. Myself, of course, though I scarcely knew why. I think it must have been because I was working for Ariadne and she wished to help me by as it were identifying me with her art and her future.

It was really a conclave. We sat round a narrow oak table, oblong in form, in the dining room upstairs, and Ariadne told us frankly that she had a very serious, a vital question to put to us.

She was looking remarkably handsome that day in a robe of cloudy red brocade, with her magnificent hair parted in the middle and drawn into a Grecian knot at the back of her head.

The question she had to put to us was this.

Someone called "Jock Jonesmith," who had never been heard of anywhere, either in London or out of it, but who had been—according to his own written account of himself—bred and brought up in the inner depths of Whitechapel, had written a four-act play, and had actually had the cheek to send it to Ariadne, with a letter which stated that his Whitechapel pals thought it prime, that a "Whitechapel School," akin to the "Manchester School," of playwrights would shortly claim the attention of the world, that Mr. Jonesmith was considered, in Whitechapel, to be the most fit and proper person to be the leader of this as yet unheard-of "school," and that Ariadne—of all people—had been selected by Mr. Jonesmith and his pals as the most suitable manageress and actress in London to make him, his work and his school known to the public. Ariadne had read his play, and had now gathered us, a few of the really mattering intelligences, together to consult us as to whether she should put it on at the Parthenon immediately after the imminent withdrawal of *Realistic and Idealistic Love*. The play was called *Sally Eliza,* and dealt mainly with Jewish pugilists and their female adherents. The heroine was unable to pronounce an "h," even when under the influence of drink, and was a pure-bred cockney. Was it possible, or was it not possible, for Ariadne to undertake such a part in such a play?

I shall never forget the expressions upon the faces around the oblong oak table while Ariadne was telling us all this and when she had told it. Beads of perspiration stood out on the small, but bulbous forehead of Professor Huskin Repps; Professor Simeon Jenkins, who was totally bald, flushed violently all over his usually milk-white head; Mrs. Lascelles, a woman dark as the night with wildly rolling black eyes, looked tormented, like a pythoness suffering from a severe attack of indigestion; Lady Burnett, who resembled a remarkably well-made cottage loaf drawn fresh from the oven, seemed to "give" as if her dough had suddenly suffered a mysterious change; Eustace Delminius, who was exactly like an Anglo-Indian major brought up from the cradle on curry, drew his enormous moustaches into his mouth and sent them forth again with epileptic regularity. As to Jasper Trent, a big, clean-shaven, Italian-looking man, with a figure like a vat, and a countenance as expressive as Naples on a hot day, he got up and rolled up and down the room, holding his hands to his sides as if about to loom into a fit of hysteria.

Only Augustus Transome seemed unmoved. He sat perfectly still. But his small Israelitish eyes darted to and fro in their sockets as if good opportunities were presenting themselves to him from all the points of the compass. I couldn't of course see myself. But I know I was thoroughly shocked, and the world seemed to founder about me at the thought of Ariadne appearing on the stage of the Parthenon in a piece called *Sally Eliza*.

When Ariadne ceased from speaking there was an awful silence, which was broken by two high soprano notes, almost like an emotional hiccough, from Professor Huskin Repps. Ariadne turned to him with an amply gracious, almost an embracing, gesture.

"I know!" she said. "Blessed man—I know! But wait a moment before you condemn your Ariadne. I never act upon impulse. I am always guided by pure reason backed up by clear intelligence. I have studied this play alone minutely. And I have written out an analysis of it, which I have here."

She produced from a large blotter bound in old silver, which lay in front of her, some sheets of manuscript closely written in her minute, Don-like calligraphy.

"Hear me before you condemn me as a madwoman!" she said, with a noble sonority which made the small room vibrate. "And when I have read, answer me this"—her narrow eyes swept over our faces—"Is the fact of a cockney accent an insuperable objection to my playing the part of Sally Eliza?"

With that she began to read.

Her analysis of my play had been masterly, but this was more masterly still, because more elaborate, more searching, more minute. The whole of young Jonesmith's play was in it with all Ariadne had thought about it. Whitechapel literally seemed to rise up and to live in it, with all its amazing vitality, its crudity, its black charm, its hook-nosed and thick-lipped and shining-eyed and crinkly-haired fascination. I have never been more enthralled in my life than I was by that manuscript and by Ariadne's calm and clear and completely unbiased reading of it.

When she ceased Jasper Trent broke into a roar of:

"A masterpiece! A masterpiece!" which was like an eruption of Vesuvius. Mrs. Lascelles was in tears through which she murmured, "Prose as perfect as 'Will o' the Mill,' or one of the Meynell essays!" As for the rest they simply "went for" Ariadne in a spontaneous outburst of delicately executed and beautifully bloodless adoration. But then came the great debate. *Could* Ariadne play a part with a cockney accent, and *could* she leave out her "h's"? Was it possible? Was it to be done? Even if it were possible and were to be done could she ever learn to do it, she who was the fine flower of intellectuality and scholarship upon the London stage, she whose "note" was so loftily aristocratic, so rarely expressive of the only true aristocracy, that of the educated brain?

The debate was hot and tremendous. We all took part in it, except Mr. Augustus Transome, and it lasted till the day fell into evening, and the pale lights were lit in Marmion Street. Even then it was not over, for we had only reached the point when Professor Repps, in his most shrieking soprano, was exclaiming:

"Before deciding we must hear you drop an 'h'! That is essential! Ariadne must drop an 'h'! Till that has been done no decision is possible!"

On this a plum-coloured Scotswoman appeared at the door and asked if she might bring in supper.

Supper! Was there indeed to be supper? There was, and it was a champagne supper from the Ritz!

I shall never forget that supper. It was really a delicate uproar of intellectuality such as Westminster can have seldom heard. Everyone was brilliant at once—except Augustus Transome, who scarcely spoke a word and who drank nothing but barley water. Jasper Trent bellowed epigrams, marred only by parentheses. The two professors talked one against the other while I persistently tried in vain to interrupt them. Lady Burnett sketched Ariadne in charcoal with one hand while she carried mayonnaise to her fiercely chattering mouth with the other. Mrs. Lascelles—yes, believe it, for it is true—laughed, actually laughed till she cried at the frantic witticisms of Delminius, and over the ice pudding made a pun in Italian which ought to be handed down to the coming generation. And Ariadne, enthroned in a great Venetian chair, and trifling with a peach, a nectarine, a nut as the case might be, dreamed over the wondrous scene which she had evoked, and wove her thoughts about us, tranquilly, steadfastly, unrestingly.

But at last there came a pause in the delicious tumult. Professor Repps had struck upon the uncovered supper table with a small knife of Georgian silver.

"We are here for a decision," he said. "And it is time we came to it."

He wiped his face with a handkerchief of Surah silk.

"I have invented a sentence for Ariadne to say to us. It is this: 'Hi, Henry, here! Has hideous Horace had his hateful ham'? My sweet lady"—he swung primly, yet worshipfully, towards Ariadne—"Can you memorize that?"

"Please repeat it again, blessed man!" said Ariadne, leaning forward with a look of intense concentration on her face, while we all sat breathless.

"Hi—Henry—here! Has—hideous—Horace—had—his—hateful—ham?" repeated Professor Repps, gazing at her with the feverish anxiety of an author asking great things of his interpreter.

Ariadne sat back and shut her eyes for a moment. Then she opened them and a startling change came into her face. It seemed to me that the lofty intellectuality faded gradually and completely out of it, that its place was taken by a—dare I say it?—by a curiously common, almost a vulgar, look that was nevertheless enticing because it was— apparently—so entirely natural. It was almost as if I had seen the noble façade of the Parthenon Theatre fade away into the twinkling, cheerful and unpretentious, street frontage of a Whitechapel public house. Then she twisted her generous lips sideways, leaned forward, cocked her Grecian head to the right, and said in the most authentic cockney I ever heard:

"'Ello! 'I, 'Enery 'ere! 'As 'ideous 'Orace 'ad 'is 'iteful 'am? 'Ello! 'I 'Enery, 'ere! 'Ello! 'Ello!"

We gazed at Ariadne and at one another so amazed that we were all stricken speechless, till at last the well-known sonorous voice, with its strongly intellectual and cultivated intonation, broke the spell.

"Tell me, dear things," it said. "Is it possible? Can I drop an 'h' upon the stage of the Parthenon Theatre?"

"I have never in my life heard 'h's' dropped to such absolute perfection," said Mrs. Lascelles.

And as if moved by an irresistible impulse she rose from her seat, went to Ariadne and kissed her just above the left eyebrow.

"It's pure genius! It's absolutely forthright!" exclaimed Professor Repps.

There was not one dissentient voice in our company.

"Then the play is to be done!" said Ariadne, with a sudden, keen look in her face, which seemed to be unnoticed by the others, but which startled me. "You pass it? You have my word for its value as a human document and as a piece of instinctive art in its genre. Pass the dropped 'h' and the cockney accent and I put the play into rehearsal to-morrow."

Never before had I seen Ariadne display such swift energy. It is true that the supper from the Ritz—a champagne supper—had rendered us all intellectually and vocally energetic that evening. But Ariadne seemed to have sprung into an almost startling life which owed nothing to champagne, mayonnaise and ice pudding. There was something I thought of for a moment as released in her manner. A shutter seemed to drop and a strongly lit window to take its place, with a view into a sharply defined room beyond—a room in which no Leonardo hung upon the wall, but something quite different.

But her energy had the effect of rendering her auditors suddenly anxious, timorous, undecided.

A long and agitated debate ensued, which gradually centred round one terrifically important question.

If *Sally Eliza* were put on at the Parthenon would it bring "the wrong people" to the theatre?

That was the great fear of Professor Repps, Mrs. Lascelles and Professor Simeon Jenkins, partaken of, though in lesser degree, by Eustace Delminius and Lady Burnett. Jasper Trent declared that even a dropped 'h' would never induce that contemptible and corrupt spawn of ignorance mated with brutality, the average playgoer, to put its nose— if indeed it might be said to have a nose, having rather a snout—into the precincts of the Parthenon Theatre. And I scarcely knew what to say, or even to think, so confused and excited was I by this time. As to Augustus Transome, he said nothing at all, but lay back in his chair watching Ariadne with his little keen eyes half-shut, and one side tooth showing under his carefully-trained moustache.

The "wrong people" in the Parthenon Theatre! Could that risk be taken by Ariadne? Suppose that Whitechapel were to arise out of its darkness lit by the flares of gin palaces and to assail those doors through which had entered hitherto only the elect of London, the University towns, Manchester, and the few other centres of earnestness and intellect? Suppose that "bruisers," and their terrible females wrapped in shawls and crowned with feathered hats, should be drawn to a "show" in which their psychology was dissected and their crude passions were— in a masterly way, of course; we had Ariadne's word for that—laid bare! Suppose the flappers of the West End, and the degenerate "nuts"— Professor Repp's word, of which Mrs. Lascelles had to ask an explanation—who ministered to their anemic pleasures, were to follow in their wake in search of a new sensation? Suppose—worst supposition of all—"Smart Society" were to hear of the hubbub and roll up in its motors to "see the fun"? Ariadne would be ruined, utterly ruined! Her unique position would be lost forever. She was the actress of the fit, though few. She disdained the herd. But how could she keep the herd out if it came bellowing to seek her?

The question might have been hotly debated all night if it had not been for a clinching sentence uttered by of all people—Mr. Augustus Transome.

He suddenly ran a pointed tongue over his rather protruding lips, and said in his husky voice:

"They won't come! Miss Marshall"—he always called Ariadne, Miss Marshall—"Miss Marshall will know how to keep them away."

And abruptly the debate collapsed, as if a Lloyd George had found time to pay a visit to "the House" and say a couple of stinging words to the Commons.

We looked upon Ariadne, who said nothing but merely returned our look with her unfathomable, though not large, eyes, and suddenly we knew that Augustus Transome was right. There was something about Ariadne, her aura perhaps—yes, that was it, her aura—that would inevitably prevent the Philistines from drawing near.

Ariadne would know how to keep them away!

IV

The rehearsals of *Sally Eliza* had begun and meanwhile I was working feverishly to finish my play. Somehow the success of a young man from Whitechapel with such an unheard-of name as Jock Jonesmith had stung me in my tenderest part, my vanity I suppose I must call it. I have said "the success." This may seem perhaps to some a premature word, but not to me. This fellow, this Jock, had achieved the greatest possible success already; he had succeeded with Ariadne; whereas I, a man of parts, a man with a decent Christian name, and a surname which did not combine in ridiculous juxtaposition two gross familiarities, had not succeeded. I was toiling to get a thing right while Jock—the name was in my ears abhorrently day and night—had got it right at the first go off. Ariadne had "passed" him, and she had not "passed" me. With Jock it was "yes," with me it was "perhaps." I detested Jock; but he made me work as I had never worked before, with green tea and wet towels.

I must confess also that at this tune I was the victim of jealousy. For I now saw but little of Ariadne, while young Jonesmith no doubt was with her every day. *Realistic and Idealistic Love* was still running, but feebly to its end with a daily waning vitality, and *Sally Eliza* was being moulded into shape by Ariadne—and Jock Jonesmith. I imagined them together in the darkened and shrouded theatre, she directing, he agreeing, metaphorically on his knees to the mistress of his destiny. I saw them standing together in "the wings," sitting together far back in the auditorium, with only charwomen and black cats as chaperons. And my heart was hot within me.

Was I then in love with Ariadne? Did my daring leap so high as that?

I remembered her lofty abhorrence of saccharine, her distaste even for sugar. I remembered Professor Repp's contemptuous allusion to "slush" and, following on it, Ariadne's praise of "tingling dryness," and I realized that I was nearing dangerous ground. Ariadne was a great intellect, but I did not know that she was a great heart. And in any case I was wholly unworthy of her. I bound a wet towel around my fevered brow, drank a brew of green tea, seized my "relief pen" and strove almost ferociously to be intellectual. I would take my play to the heights. I would show Jock Jonesmith what grey matter really was.

Now and then I was privileged to see Ariadne in Marmion Street during this time, but only for a few minutes, and I never met Jock Jonesmith there. Ariadne seemed remote when I saw her. She was gracious as ever. She looked quite wonderful; but she said very little, and was evidently drowned in deep thought, was immersed in reflection.

"I am wrestling," she said one day, as if in explanation of her demeanour, "as Jacob did with the angel. At night I am Realistic and Idealistic Love; by day I am Sally Eliza. It stretches the brain almost to snapping point."

"I am wrestling, too," I ventured to say.

"You?" she said, vaguely.

"With the play."

"The play?"

She laid an emphasis on the definite article.

"My play."

"Oh—yes."

She sighed, with her eyes upon me. It seemed to me that there was a thin light of sarcasm in their gaze. I dared not say more.

One day when I saw her for not more than five minutes a strange thing happened. She dropped an "h" in the twilight.

We had been speaking of the expression of the emotions and, in an effort to live up to her standard, I had quoted Charles Darwin's remark about fear causing contraction of the platysma myoides muscle.

"I know!" she answered negligently. "I know!" She was silent for a moment and then she said: "A similar effect is often brought about by 'orror."

"By—" I stammered, and paused.

"I said by 'orror," she answered tranquilly.

I scarcely know how I took my leave and got out of the house that day; I scarcely know how I reached my flat in Jermyn Street. But when I was there shut in I knew that Jock Jonesmith must be responsible for what had just happened; I recognized his influence in that twice-dropped "h." I didn't blame Ariadne for it. Indeed, I admired her more than ever, seeing in her lapse a great piece of art. She was already living Sally Eliza. Jock Jonesmith's heroine was becoming part of her very life. She was assimilating this Whitechapel woman, was drawing this creature so utterly remote from her real self into her very blood, was thinking her thoughts, was even dropping her "h's." It was magnificent—but it was terribly trying for those who worshipped her and who now must feel shut out, while Jock Jonesmith was at the very door of the Holy of Holies.

One day she spoke of "Jock." Her exact expression was, "Jock won't allow an arranged first-night audience. He says a theatre is a public place and must be at all times open to the public."

I reported this to the "circle." I could do no less. I drove in a fast taxi to the British Museum and demanded to see Professor Huskin Repps. After a long delay they said that they did not know where he was, but that he must be somewhere in the museum. I searched. I caught him at last in the midst of the Elgin marbles. I drew him into the refreshment room, the only place in the museum which is practically never visited, and there, among the famous relics of what the human family was wont to eat in the long dead past, I told him what Ariadne had said. He was thunderstruck. I have scarcely ever seen a man so affected. I was obliged to take desperate measures, to call for a cup of museum tea. This made him very angry—in his distraction of mind he inadvertently drank it to the dregs—but it brought him round. He thanked me eventually almost cordially for what I had done, and we parted with the understanding that he would at once take "all necessary steps" to frustrate the extraordinary machinations of young Jonesmith. The Professor had never seen him. None of the "circle" had seen him, for Ariadne, as her custom was, never permitted even her dearest friends to come to rehearsal.

No one who went regularly to Marmion Street had ever seen her rehearse so far as we knew, although everyone who went there said she was "wonderful" at rehearsal. This privacy at the Parthenon was therefore no new departure. But it was now evident that young Jonesmith must be made to understand his place. The fact that Ariadne had evidently not made him understand it was terribly ominous. I could see that Professor Repps feared the worst, and I taxied back to Jermyn Street in a condition which was certainly not conducive to fundamental brain work.

However I set to at the play there and then, with such sacred fury that, after sitting up the whole of the succeeding night, I finished it as the voice of the last milkman woke the echoes about St. James' Street.

Jock Jonesmith had caused me to be the victim of a tremendous spasm of intellectuality such as had never shaken me before. This unknown genius from Whitechapel had released my genius unwittingly. My intense jealousy of him had enabled me to make the effort of a lifetime. As I looked at my manuscript I knew that never again should I be able to pour such a torrent of grey matter upon paper. I felt as if the whole of my burning brain lay there in those lines of ink. Even Ariadne, I felt, would be proud of me now. For a moment I triumphed. For a moment I defied Jock Jonesmith, felt him to be far below me. Let him do what he would I was positive that I was his superior. It was impossible that any man born and bred in the depths of Whitechapel could rise to such heights of pure intellectuality as I had done in the at last finished play which lay on the table before me, so modestly, so unassumingly. In the heat of that almost delirious moment I was moved to strong action. That marvellous invention, a telephone, stood on a side table near me. I sprang upon it, gripped the receiver, and rang up "No. 2, Marmion Street." After a prolonged pause, partially filled up by several wrong numbers kindly arranged for by the operator, a voice with a Scottish accent enquired what it was. I gave my name and demanded Miss Marshall. The voice said that she was engaged. I was in such a state of excitement that for a moment I was the victim of delusion, and was guilty of the exclamation:

"Good God! Not to Jock Jonesmith!"

"Yes, sir!" replied the voice.

I believe I reeled at the receiver. Nevertheless I had the strength to say:

"Impossible! I will not believe it. The—the 'circle' will never stand it."

"Sir," said the voice, severely I thought, "it is as I say. Miss Marshall is engaged with Mr. Jonesmith at the moment. They are breakfasting together in the dining room."

Engaged *with* Mr. Jonesmith! The relief was so immense that I nearly broke down, but I managed to control myself and whispered:

"I'll telegraph. Good-bye!"

And I rang off and fell into a chair by my writing table. Ten minutes later from the St. James' Street post office I sent the following telegram to Ariadne:

> "Completed the play this morning at seven forty-nine after working on it all night. When may I come and read it to you?"

Then I returned home, plunged into a cold bath, did electric face massage, parted my hair with a trembling comb, dressed in a dark suit, drank five cups of strong coffee, tried in vain to swallow a kidney, and sat down to wait for the answer to my telegram with the manuscript of my play in my hand.

It was nearly noon when there was a knock on my door and a telegram was handed to me. It ran as follows:

> "Not till after the first night of 'Sally Eliza.' The true artist never mars a major with a minor impression. Greetings. — ARIADNE MARSHALL."

"Damn *Sally Eliza!*" I exclaimed.

And I am ashamed to say that I flung the telegram on the Turkey carpet and set my left foot on it.

That evening I again went to the Parthenon Theatre. I felt that I must see Ariadne if only upon the stage. There was scarcely anyone in the house, for *Realistic and Idealistic Love* was now practically moribund, but I saw in the left-hand grand tier box next the stage Augustus Transome with a most strange looking companion beside him.

This companion was a short, but enormously broad and tremendously strong-set man, with a neck like that of a Herefordshire bull, two thick ears, a huge broken nose, tiny eyes, and three teeth of pure gold, which glittered in his enormous mouth with swollen lips when the lights were turned up. On his hands he wore two diamond rings. His big bullet head looked as if it had been shaved about a week ago. Augustus Transome of course was in evening dress, but his friend wore a light suit of an enormous checked pattern. And when he stood up in the first *entr'acte* I perceived that the coat was divided at the back into voluminous square tails, above which appeared two yellow buttons far larger than the average half-crown piece.

What could this personage be doing in the Parthenon Theatre?

For a moment I thought of going upstairs to the box and seeking an interview with Augustus Transome. But the presence of the other man held me back. What could I say to such an one if I were introduced to him? What topics could he and I have in common?

He stood there in the box with his huge hands thrust deep in his pockets, staring about the house with an expression so surly that it bordered on the malignant. Then he swung awkwardly round and went out, followed by Augustus Transome, who looked like a midge in the wake of a bull.

Should I follow them? Had they gone to the bar—if there was a bar? I thought it most probable. I could almost see the big fellow spreading himself with a glass containing "a drop of Lizzie" in his gigantic red fist. I could almost hear his thick voice uttering coarse witticisms to the barmaid. And I refrained. I could not desecrate the impression Ariadne's art had just made on me by seeking such company, and I stuck to my seat till the curtains parted on the second act.

But as the evening wore on it seemed to me that this same art of Ariadne was not quite what it had been. Perhaps she was tired after the long rehearsals, or perhaps the emptiness of the house affected her. Whatever the reason I could not help noticing that the intellectuality of the performance was less marked than formerly. It seemed really to come and go, like the fitfully genteel accent of a naturally vulgar person carrying on conversation with someone above her to whom she is trying to live up. This distressed me, got almost on my nerves. And I asked myself presently whether even an empty house and the fatigue of rehearsal would account for it sufficiently. Looking about me as it were for some more cogent explanation of this painful phenomenon my eyes strayed to Augustus Transome's box. Most of the lights in the auditorium were turned out, but sufficient illumination remained to define the tremendous figure of the stocky Herefordshire bull in the checked suit. Could he be the reason? Could this unwonted personality be subtly overwhelming the sensitive artistic temperament of Ariadne?

The wrong people in the theatre! I remembered the debate over the supper table in Mansion Street, and I trembled.

I think it was at that moment that I realized how important an audience is to an artist, how dependent the highly-strung and delicately-balanced soul of the supreme creative executant—for I contend that a great artist is just that—is upon the crowd assembled to receive its revelation! Not that the creature in the checked suit amounted to a crowd! But even I was conscious that there was something vulgarly powerful, I might go so far as to say coarsely tremendous in his personality, and this might well be felt by Ariadne.

In the third act of the play a catastrophe happened. Ariadne dropped an "h" upon the stage. The line was, "How can you expect a woman who is guided by pure reason to love at first sight?" Ariadne distinctly said "'ow"! From that moment I was mentally prostrate. I sat with shut eyes waiting for the curtain to descend. When at last it fell I got up mechanically. My eyes instinctively went to Augustus Transome's box, and I saw the woman who had once asked me to come and see Miss Marshall speaking to the man in the checked suit. He nodded, throwing his dented chin upward; she turned; he followed her out of the box. Augustus Transome vanished behind them. His back looked more Israelitish than ever.

As I went out a horrible supposition came into my mind, a supposition so horrible that it seemed to turn my bones almost to wax.

Could Jock Jonesmith and the man in the checked suit be one and the same?

When I was out in the street dwarfed by the noble façade of the theatre I stood still and hesitated. If I went home in uncertainty I knew I should be unable to sleep. Yet Ariadne had not sent for me. Perhaps, however, she did not know that I had been in the theatre. She never saw people in the audience. I had her word for that. The box office man this time might have missed me. I resolved to give her the benefit of my doubt, and I went round to the stage door and sent in my card, on which with a trembling hand I had written: "May I see you?" Almost immediately the answer came back: "Miss Marshall's cordial greetings and she is very sorry she is engaged on a matter connected with *Sally Eliza.*"

As I turned away—it was beginning to rain—I muttered between my teeth, "Damn *Sally Eliza!*"

The phenomenon in the checked suit—with tails and yellow buttons—was Jock Jonesmith. I could doubt that no longer.

V

But I was wrong and I found out my mistake at breakfast next morning. When I opened my *Daily Mail* the very first paragraph that caught my eye was this:

GREAT REVIVAL OF BOXING.

A great revival of the noble art of boxing is imminent. Mr. Frederick Catford, who now owns seven London theatres and is building three more, has taken Olympia and intends shortly to hold a great Boxing Festival there. He is arranging a match between Pug Bullen, the champion English heavyweight, and Tim Milligan, the great Australian boxer, who knocked out Bert Lockford in seven rounds in Tasmania in 19—.

By the way, the arts seem drawing together in a manner which promises well for the future. Last night Mr. Pug Bullen was present in a box at the Parthenon Theatre to see Miss Ariadne Marshall's highly intellectual performance in *Realistic and*

Idealistic Love. We understand that Mr. Bullen expressed his appreciation of the actress and the play in his own hearty and unconventional manner.

It is rumoured that Miss Marshall will shortly present a new play at the Parthenon which is not wholly unconnected with the noble art of which Mr. Pug Bullen is such a proficient exponent.

So the creature in the suit was not Jock Jonesmith! My relief for a moment was intense, but it was succeeded by a keen anxiety, which I knew the "circle" would share. Mr. Pug Bullen's presence in the Parthenon Theatre, in a box, too, was certainly of ill omen for the future. Knowing my England I knew that where Mr. Bullen went his admirers and adherents were certain to follow. And for a moment I saw a hideous vision—the Parthenon Theatre crammed with an audience such as assembles on a "star" night at the "ring" at Blackfriars; the wrong people enthroned to the ruin of Ariadne.

None of the circle "read" *The Daily Mail,* but it seems that they all "saw" it, and this paragraph, backed up by the information about Mr. Pug Bullen's appearance, dress and general personality, which I considered it my duty to give, roused the keenest alarm among them. It was obvious to us all that the circle must take the field for the defence of Ariadne and her interests even against herself.

"If we only knew Mr. Jack—"

"Jock!" I interposed.

"Is it? Mr. Jock Jonesmith, we might know better what should be done!" wailed Mrs. Lascelles.

But not one of us knew or had ever seen the gentleman in question. He kept himself strictly secret. So we were forced to act without any sufficient groundwork of personal knowledge, "a severe handicap to the trained intellect," as Professor Repps very aptly remarked to Professor Simeon Jenkins.

During the three weeks which elapsed before the production of *Sally Eliza* at the Parthenon a painful contest of, I should suppose, an unexampled nature raged between the circle and Ariadne, raged politely, obscurely, almost subterraneously, but raged nevertheless. It was led on our side by Professor Huskin Repps, and it was concerned with the seating arrangements for the first night of *Sally Eliza.*

Hitherto Ariadne's "first nights" had been almost holy occasions, functions deliberately kept sacred to the elect. The distribution of the seats for them had been as carefully discussed, as methodically carried out, as that of the seats for a Coronation in Westminster Abbey. Professor Repps, Professor Simeon Jenkins, Mrs. Lascelles and others to the number, I think, of six, had always sat in committee with Ariadne to supervise the arrangements. And, except of course to the Press, not one seat had ever been allotted to anyone who had not been considered absolutely worthy of being present. The result had been that the audience at the Parthenon on a first night was utterly unlike the audience one sees at any other first night in London. Instead of rows of smart, and would-be smart women, of "resting" actresses and their cavaliers, of fashionable lawyers and their wives, of theatre owners, rich Jews and tea-party young men with narrow foreheads and "waisted" coats, one saw serried ranks of professors, men of brain from Manchester, members of the Atheneum Club, essayists, poets and poetesses, grave women from Edinburgh, and even from as far as Dublin, come up specially for the occasion, writers on *The Quarterly* and *The Round Table* and even *The Hibbert Journal,* with a few choice members of the aristocracy, not the new, but the ancient and real aristocracy which still values brains and can find time for serious reading. Now and then a Prime Minister, if judged suitable, came, and it was rumoured that once an Archbishop of Canterbury had had an armchair provided for him in the "wings" on the prompt side. On one forever memorable occasion, too, the whole of the gallery had been allotted by special request to members of the Savile Club, headed by a celebrated caricaturist and writer whose name is a household word wherever artistry is prized.

Was the first night of *Sally Eliza* to be an exception to the golden rule which had hitherto been observed religiously in Dominion Street—the street honoured by the presence of the Parthenon? The "circle" was determined that it should not. Hence the struggle with Ariadne. Or was it indeed rather with the unseen power behind the throne, Jock Jonesmith?

The struggle raged by letter. For Ariadne, in response to repeated and earnest requests by the circle for personal interviews, alleged that "as a true artist" she dared not "disperse" her energy at such a moment by seeing even her dearest friends and loyal adherents. "I must follow my invariable custom," she wrote to Professor Repps, "and keep my entire brain and soul for the work in hand. It taxes the whole of me. I need not tell you what the wrestling of the mind with the problem means to those of us who are true to ourselves." In reply the Professor pointed out that on former occasions Ariadne had always thought it a sacred duty to go personally into the matter of the first-night audience. Why make a change now? This brought Ariadne more into the open, as it was intended to do, and elicited the statement that on the first night of *Sally Eliza* she had decided to take a new departure and to let the seats for the first night be sold in the ordinary way.

"After long and deep consideration," she wrote, "I have come to the conclusion that I have made a mistake in always surrounding myself with my beloved friends and adherents on a first night. To do this is not to show true courage. The theatre is a public place and a new piece ought to be submitted to the judgment of the ordinary public. I have therefore decided that the seats for the first night of 'Sally Eliza' shall be offered for sale in the usual way."

It was the voice, as we all knew, of Jock Jonesmith speaking from the lips of Ariadne, and we could not sit down under it. (If my metaphors are mixed I cannot help it; the recollection of it all brings back the agony of mind I suffered at that period.) Jasper Trent was put up to protest against such a Philistine departure from the custom of the past, a custom which ensured a solemn verdict of the elect instead of the judgment of fools in their folly. He received a typewritten reply from Ariadne's secretary, saying that Miss Marshall was very sorry but she was not at liberty to change her decision.

This phrase, as may be supposed, roused the circle's protective instinct. It was now obvious that the remark which had originally roused my anxiety and driven me hotfoot to the British Museum accurately expressed the present truth of things. Ariadne was held in durance by this Whitechapel interloper. She was no longer a free agent. She must be freed. But how?

Someone thought of Augustus Transome. It was Lady Burnett, I think. Mr. Transome had taken no part in our struggle. He was in a way "suspect." For it was with him that I had seen Mr. Pug Bullen at the theatre, an unexplained mystery which had affected us all most painfully. So we had not sought his adherence to our campaign. But now in our distress we turned to him. He was a very old friend of Ariadne, and someone—Delminius, I think, or it may have been Johnnie Dean—said that he had "great weight" with her. To my surprise I was chosen to interview Mr. Transome and endeavour to enlist his assistance. Professor Repps, of course, wanted to go. He always wanted to take the lead in everything connected with Ariadne. But the circle interfered. Jasper Trent said that the Professor was already on the verge of a nervous breakdown and must keep himself for his letter writing to Ariadne. And Lady Burnett was good enough to say that "when I liked" I had "a way with me" which might "come round" Augustus Transome.

Mr. Transome was communicated with by telephone at his flat in Maida Vale and said that he was laid up with a sharp attack of lumbago but would see me if I would call.

So I went to Maida Vale.

I found him in bed wrapped in hot flannels and steeped in Elliman's Embrocation, and at once told him my errand. He listened, showing one tooth. I don't know why but I considered this a bad sign. When I had put the matter fully before him he was silent. I waited patiently for some sign from him. It came at last. He was good enough to say:

"I am too ill to interfere."

"But," I said, "Ariadne will be ruined if she carries out this plan."

"Why?" he said.

"Why? God knows who will get in on the first night. Anybody might be there."

Suddenly I thought of Mr. Pug Bullen. It may have been rude, considering all the circumstances, but I was carried away by my feelings, and I exclaimed:

"Pug Bullen might be there!"

Augustus Transome's small eyes darted sideways and back again.

"Why not?" he said.

"Why not?" I ejaculated. "A man like that would ruin the appearance of any audience, even the most intellectual. He stands out like a cairn. He might come in checks. He has three gold teeth, two thick ears, two diamond rings, yellow buttons. You must see—"

"Pug Bullen's a national hero," said Augustus Transome.

"Do you mean to tell me you are so mad that you wish to see a national hero at one of Ariadne's 'first nights'?" I said, with scarcely restrained passion. "Why it would be her ruin."

"I am too ill to interfere," repeated Mr. Transome.

"Do you wish to interfere?" I said, looking him squarely in the face in a thoroughly manly way.

Augustus Transome let his small eyes rest upon me for the fraction of a second. Then he made a remark which I shall never forget as long as I live:

"Miss Marshall has been interfered with long enough," he said.

"But Jock Jonesmith—"

He narrowed his eyes.

"Please ring," he said. "I want some camphor liniment."

When I reported the result of my embassy—it was at Mrs. Lascelles' house in Argyll Road, Kensington, celebrated for its collection of Blake's pictures and its bust of Duse—there was consternation in the circle.

"That man has gone over to the other side," said Lady Burnett. "He has betrayed us."

"I never believed in him!" cried Professor Repps. "He was never forthright. His intellectual processes were always cloudy."

"He mispronounces the word 'how,'" murmured Mrs. Lascelles. "I detected it at once;—'now,' too—but Ariadne would never allow that I was right."

"I believe him to be a Jew!" said Professor Simeon Jenkins. "And *Sally Eliza* is a Jewish play. Who knows if he may not wish to have a Jewish 'first night'?"

I believe we all turned pale. I know Professor Repps did. A Jewish "first night"! Yiddish spoken in the stalls of the Parthenon Theatre! Young Israel let loose in the gallery!

"I shall see Ariadne," exclaimed Professor Repps, "and I shall see her to-day."

"I advise against that, Huskin, old friend!" said Professor Jenkins, firmly.

"Why?" yelped Professor Repps. "Didn't I discover Ariadne? Wasn't it I who first took her to the British Museum? Haven't I formed her mind into the wonderful intellectual engine it has become? Didn't I show her the right path to tread in her art? Wouldn't she have tried melodrama, or even musical comedy, but for me? Didn't I keep her out of Shakespeare for fear she might be called an echo of Ellen Terry? Didn't I bring the right people about her and keep out all the wrong ones? Didn't I—"

"You did, Huskin, old friend, you did! We all know it. Your influence, the influence of the British Museum, has made Ariadne what she is.

But that's just it—"

"What's just what?" cried Repps. "Think clearly and express yourself in a forthrightly way or I can't undertake to follow you."

"You feel too strongly about Ariadne to be the best person to make her see the abyss on the edge of which she is standing. She has always distrusted passion. I have heard her say: 'Passion is the condiment which conceals the real flavour of the meat!'"

"A true saying! A true saying!" murmured poor Repps. "Let someone else go."

"I will go," said Professor Jenkins.

He looked round the "circle" and his eyes fell on me.

"We are both working for Ariadne," he was good enough to say. "She may listen to us. Come with me to Marmion Street."

VI

Professor Repps—we had to let the poor man be doing something—was allowed to write to Ariadne on behalf of the circle begging her to receive us if only for five minutes. An answer was returned that as the rehearsals of the play were interrupted for two or three days on account of the illness of Jock Jonesmith, Ariadne would be "at liberty"—again that sinister phrase—and would see us. A time was appointed. (It was all done by Ariadne's secretary.) At that time Professor Jenkins and I repaired to Marmion Street.

We were shown into the drawing room by one of the Scottish women and sat down to wait for Ariadne. We sat in silence for two or three minutes. I think we were both feeling nervous. I know I was. I had felt ill at ease when I entered the house; with each passing second the sensation grew. It seemed to me that there was a different atmosphere in this house from that with which I was familiar, that this austere drawing room, a soft cloud of blues and greens in a setting of almost ecclesiastical brown, was subtly changed. I glanced about me. My eyes fell on remembered objects, on a *Book of Hours* bound in gold, a jade idol, the collection of amber faintly lit by the fading sunlight. What was the change? Or was it only in my imagination? I glanced up at the wall and started.

"Look!" I whispered to my companion.

"Eh—what?" he said loudly.

"Hush!" I pointed. "There!"

He followed my eyes.

The famous supposed Leonardo was gone. In its place hung a very bad copy of Frith's terrible picture, long since buried in the National Collection, *The Derby Day*. At this moment the door opened and Ariadne came in.

She was dressed in a coat and skirt!

We stood up—somehow. (I shall never know how I did it.)

She came up to us briskly and shook hands. "Well, here you are!" she said.

And I thought that her voice was altered. Its slow resonance was surely gone. The peculiar culture of the intonation, something almost carefully delicate and precise, seemed tarnished though perhaps not wholly lost.

"And now what is it?" she added, sitting down in a business-like manner.

I looked at Professor Simeon Jenkins. He cleared his throat and plunged in. I must say that he spoke eloquently. He is, as everyone knows, a highly-educated man, and he was obviously moved by deep feeling. Without any redundance, indeed with extraordinary economy of words, he exposed to Ariadne the deep anxiety of the circle at her new departure, their conviction that she was rushing to—I believe he said "moving towards"—her ruin, their desire to safeguard her from any evil consequences of her own actions. He pointed out to her that she occupied a unique position upon the British stage, as the only thoroughly cultured, the only deeply thoughtful, the only rigidly self-respecting—in the purely artistic sense, of course—actress England possessed. She had never bowed down to the popular idols of the market place. She had never sought the applause of fools or the vacant laughter of "groundlings." (He repeated the word "groundlings" more than once.) The pursuit of money had been always abhorrent to her. All she had ever sought was the applause of the fit though few, the approbation of the highly-cultivated minority, who would as soon set foot in Gehenna as in Drury Lane Theatre or the garish palaces of the Strand and Shaftesbury Avenue. He alluded to *Sally Eliza*; and acknowledged that the circle, carried away by her reading and her masterly analysis of the piece, and perhaps also influenced to some extent—for are we not all human at certain moments—by the champagne supper from the Ritz, had bowed to her obvious desire to produce it, trusting implicitly in her hitherto unerring judgment of artistic values.

Even now, he said, we were all ready and eager, even those of us who had plays waiting for Ariadne to produce in the fullness of time—a touching allusion to his translation from the Dutch and my original play—we were all ready and eager to find merit in *Sally Eliza*. But it must be given a proper introduction to the small public which worshipped regularly at the Parthenon. And this could only be done if the time-honoured procedure at that theatre was adhered to on this occasion, and the seats for the first night "fell into the proper hands." (This was, perhaps, a slight error in style.) He was sure that Ariadne could not mean to throw herself, a pearl, before the—the—he hesitated, but went on—before the swine of London. He was sure that the distribution of seats would, as always before, be supervised by—

But at this point Ariadne interrupted him.

"There will be no careful distribution of seats, my dear Professor," she said. "The seats will be sold in the ordinary way."

"As they are at the Criterion?" said the Professor in a voice that vibrated with feeling.

"As they are at the Criterion, or anywhere else," said Ariadne.

"The dress circle perhaps—"

"And the stalls."

"But not the boxes! Impossible—the boxes!"

"And the boxes too!"

"But Repps's box!"

"Professor Repps's box too."

"And mine? and Mrs. Lascelles's? and—and—"

"All the boxes!" said Ariadne with a sort of fatal decision.

The Professor got on his feet.

"It is not you who has done this!" he said, with fervent conviction. "I know—we all know that we must look elsewhere for the hand that has done this thing."

Here again his style perhaps deviated slightly from the impeccable accurate.

Ariadne was silent and I saw her eyes stray to the dreadful picture on the wall.

"It is Jock Jonesmith! It is he!"

"I must consider my author, Professor."

"Does he consider us? Does he consider that man who has steeped you in culture, who has shed the atmosphere of the British Museum about your gift! Does he consider Huskin Repps?"

"I am very sorry, Professor. It must be as I say. Indeed, you come too late in any case."

"Too late?" I said.

"Yes. The box office was opened to the public for *Sally Eliza* this morning at ten o'clock."

Both of us realized in a flash that there was only one thing to be done now, and we did it. We got out of the house as quickly as possible, hailed a taxi and drove at full speed to the Parthenon Theatre.

We were too late. The box office for *Sally Eliza* was already shut for that day. Till to-morrow we could do nothing.

That evening there was another meeting of the circle held at Professor Repps's house in Bedford Square, that wonderful house in which culture and intellect seem literally to stalk through the lofty rooms, to dream in the vast library, to lie at rest on the deep sofas among the Oriental china, the Burne Jones pictures, the etchings by Brangwyn, and the portraits of beautiful and intellectual women by Sargent, by Lavery, by McEvoy, by Augustus John. (For Repps is no hater of the moderns, and he loves to have beautiful women around him.) Most poignant touch of all in that house—and I think we all felt it that evening—was the statue of Ariadne, as Venus draped, by the Balkan sculptor Meštrovi , which brooded over the second drawing room.

When all were assembled, and we had drunk Egyptian coffee out of cups of Sévres, the truth was put before the circle, and we told what we had done.

"When will the box office open to-morrow?" asked Lady Burnett, who was a practical woman although a great painter.

"At ten o'clock," I replied.

"There's only one thing to be done now," began Lady Burnett.

"We must buy up as many seats as possible!" roared Jasper Trent.

We all agreed. But the question of money arose. Some of us were not very rich. Intellect of the purest kind does not grasp after money. But we all resolved to be ready with the uttermost farthing, and it was understood that each one should bring a cheque-book to the Parthenon Theatre on the morrow. All the boxes, of course, would be bought in by us, and as many of the stalls as our money would "run to."

We separated about midnight with the noble feeling that, even at great cost to ourselves, we should yet be able to protect Ariadne from utter ruin.

But on the following morning the tragedy deepened. When we assembled before the box office precisely on the stroke of ten, and Professor Repps, as our leader, presented himself at the small opening behind which stood Digby, the business manager, with a request for all the boxes and as many stalls as possible for the first night of *Sally Eliza,* the reply was:

"All seats gone for the first night."

The Professor held on to the jutting piece of wood with both hands.

"All seats—" his voice failed him.

"All seats sold for the first night!"

"Impossible!"

"Very sorry, Professor Repps, but by twelve o'clock they were gone."

"It cannot be!"

"It cannot be, Mr. Digby," wailed Mrs. Lascelles behind him.

"Very sorry, Mrs. Lascelles, but—"

"But *my* box—*my* box!" shouted the Professor.

"Box A next the stage?"

"Yes, Box A—next the stage!"

Digby glanced at a sheet.

"Taken by Mr. Pug Bullen," he answered.

"Pug—Pug Bullen—is it—in *my* box?" yelped Repps, still holding on to the wood.

"Yes, sir."

"And B—box B? " cried Mrs. Lascelles from the back.

Again Digby glanced at the sheet.

"Sold to Miss Tottie Willoughby, the music hall star."

"Tottie—what? Tottie what?" cried Mrs. Lascelles.

"Willoughby, the male impersonator, madam," said Digby. "I'm sorry, but all the boxes are gone."

"Who has box C?" demanded Trent, shouldering his way to the front.

"Sol Israel Isaacstein, Mr. Trent, the owner of the oyster shops in the Strand and the Boxing Palace in the Commercial Road, Whitechapel."

It was enough. This last announcement was enough. We wished to hear nothing more, lest worse should befall us.

We retired in open order, beaten from the field.

But there was still a last chance and we resolved to take it. We would not be utterly ousted from the theatre which we had come to consider almost as our own.

The gallery seats would be on sale at the doors. We would be there betimes. The front row of the gallery should be ours. So it was agreed. There was no wavering, no chicken-heartedness. Even Mrs. Lascelles, the most frail and ethereal of women, thistledown with the brain of a muse, did not shrink from the ordeal of beating her way up into that so-called place of the gods, where the gods never dream of going. Even Huskin Repps, the most fastidious of men, who was laid up if he heard a false quantity, and who had never mingled with a crowd, or rubbed shoulders with the proletariat in his life, did not hesitate for a moment now his duty was plain before him. There was no need to say "Be British" to anyone in our circle. The old spirit of those men who conquered India, and laid hands on all the fairest portions of the globe, was awake in us again, reincarnated, as it were, in our ultra-civilized bosoms. They had fought for plunder. We were fighting for art. But it was the same old spirit that prompted us.

We went away from the Parthenon undefeated to buy camp stools, thermos bottles, meat lozenges and sticks of chocolate. Professor Repps bought also a tweed cap with flaps that could be folded over the ears and Lady Burnett a man's mackintosh coat.

The morning might be inclement.

VII

It was inclement.

The dawn broke grey and lowering, with a yellow tinge in the atmosphere and a damp threatening of rain. I was on my feet early and tapped my glass. It was going rapidly down. At first this fact appalled me. I thought of Mrs. Lascelles, of Professor Repps, exposed to the fury of the elements on the greasy pavement of Mug Street. (The gallery entrance to the Parthenon was in a side slum off the main street.) Lady Burnett could take care of herself. She had once roughed it in Abyssinia. The others were mainly men, and I didn't care in the least what happened to me. But Mrs. Lascelles! The Professor!

I looked out of the window. A soft rain was beginning to fall.

At this moment my telephone sounded and I hastened to it. Jasper Trent's roar sounded through it and told me that he had been in communication with Repps as to the right hour for our assembling in Mug Street. He, Trent, had suggested four o'clock in the afternoon, but the Professor, who it seems had had wind of an extraordinary crowd for the gallery, was urgent for a much earlier hour. One o'clock, the Professor said, was the latest. It was essential that we should be there in "a solid body." Would I, therefore, be in Mug Street by one. This would mean six hours and a half of waiting, but it couldn't be helped.

"Mrs. Lascelles can never do it," I said into the telephone.

"She says she will!" roared Trent. "She has got a camp stool and is sending out to buy a pair of goloshes."

"Noble woman!" I thought. "One never knows what these thistledown creatures are capable of."

"I'll be there at one," I said.

And I sat down, like the camel, to eat for a desert journey. But before I had finished the telephone bell rang again. This time it was Professor Repps speaking from Bedford Square in a piercing soprano.

"I have conclusive evidence that one o'clock won't do for our assembling!" he cried. "An immense crowd is expected. To be sure of the front row we must be in Mug Street by ten-thirty."

"But Mrs. Lascelles!" I cried.

"I'll brave it out," he replied. "I'm taking a box of Proteid biscuits."

"No, no! Not *you!* Mrs. Lascelles!" I exclaimed.

"She is buying goloshes and will be there by ten-thirty."

And he rang off, with extraordinary abruptness, I thought.

It was now raining quite heavily, and my heart was beginning to sink, when I bethought me that this miserable condition of the weather might turn out to the circle's advantage. For it might deter people not moved by our high ideal from coming to Mug Street until the last possible moment. Perhaps no one besides ourselves would be there before the day was well advanced. We should have a horrible time no doubt, but at any rate we might not have to endure the prolonged and dreadful press of perhaps Hebrew humanity. We might have the pavement almost to ourselves, and might be able to get in by the narrow doorway that led to the steep gallery stairs without being almost trampled to pieces by the wrong people. For the wrong people would be in full force to see *Sally Eliza.* There was no doubt about that. With Pug Bullen, Tottie Willoughby and Sol Israel Isaacstein in the boxes I knew, of course, what we had to expect in the gallery.

About ten o'clock I put on a stout suit of Harris tweed, a pair of brogues, a mackintosh coat, and a soft hat—I couldn't bring myself to the wearing of a cap on such an occasion—filled my capacious pockets with sandwiches, biscuits and a flask of the best old brandy, and set out on foot for Mug Street. (I didn't take an umbrella, but carried a thick stick of the blackthorn type.)

When I reached Mug Street I saw a sight that genuinely moved me. Mrs. Lascelles and Professor Repps were already there, pressed closely against the shut door of the gallery entrance, as if ready to burst in directly it should be opened. Mrs. Lascelles held her camp stool folded over her left arm and a small string bag containing edibles over the right. On her feet were the goloshes, and she was clad in a black waterproof and had a black scarf tied over her hat. The Professor wore a thick overcoat with the collar turned up, worsted gloves, and the cap with flaps turned down over his ears. Raindrops nested in his round black beard, and a thermos bottle and a box of Proteid biscuits bulged out of his side pockets. On his refined and almost prim face, with the fastidious lips and the critical dark eyes, there was an expression of ferocious determination. He looked like a fanatic as he stood with one foot on the stone step of the door, but I had never before admired him so much.

There was not another soul about in Mug Street. Only a tabby cat was visible in the distance crouching in a squalid doorway over a wet dead mouse.

Our greetings were almost emotional. We pressed each other's hands in silence, but our faces, I think, were eloquent.

As time passed on, other members of the circle turned up, until we were a compact little crowd of some twenty to twenty-five intellectuals. Lady Burnett, Jasper Trent, Eustace Delminius, Professor Simeon Jenkins, Johnnie Deans—they were all there, with a few devoted ladies who worshipped Ariadne and several young men who cared for the things that matter.

As time wore on, and no one else appeared, we began to suppose that the report of a crowd which had reached Professor Repps had been grossly exaggerated. We had had two little meals; Mrs. Lascelles had long since sunk exhausted upon her camp stool; tea-time was drawing near; and not a creature outside the circle had put in an appearance. True it was raining heavily and persistently. (We were all practically wet to the skin.) But nevertheless this marked absence of the public was strange and almost ominous. Not even a policeman had thought it necessary to roll up in order to regulate us. We might just as well have been comfortably at home for all the good we were doing in Mug Street, yet not one of us complained. Even Professor Repps, whose beard was now matted with wet, and whose cap had totally lost its original grey colour and looked like a shrunken black pudding, said never a word. I could not help admiring the stuff in the man, and realizing how great may be the forces of the soul hidden underneath a prim, and even at times almost old-spinsterish, exterior.

At five o'clock we had our tea out of the thermos bottles, and Mrs. Lascelles ate two meat lozenges and took a sip of brandy from my flask. Six o'clock struck—seven o'clock; the circle was still by itself. Mrs. Lascelles had closed her eyes, and was leaning with her head against Professor Repps's wet knees. The rest of us pressed together for human warmth and bodily support. Conversation had long since died out among us. We merely lived on by willpower for the opening of the gallery door, kept up by the now almost certain knowledge that we should have the front row to ourselves, and should be able to direct the jury assembled to give a right verdict on the work of Jock Jonesmith.

At a quarter past seven two young Jews of unmistakably East End appearance, with large hooked noses, crinkly black hair and protruding lips, swung round the corner of Mug Street, walked impudently up to the circle and immediately began to jostle it.

At seven twenty-five Mug Street was a solid mass of the wrong people, struggling, fighting, making determined "rushes" for the gallery door, heads down, shoulders forward, fists clenched, jowls protruding. At half-past seven it was—the word must be set down—it was Hell.

It is difficult to judge accurately of values in the midst of imminent personal danger, but I should think that practically all the impecunious pugilists of London were numbered among that crowd. Need I say that the circle suffered? I hardly know what happened. It was like being in the falls of Niagara, only worse, for there was nothing fluid about it, though whirling force there was, together with deafening uproar and the most violent movement the human mind can conceive of. All the statutes of the boxing ring were ruthlessly broken. Hitting below the belt was the rule rather than the exception, as poor Mrs. Lascelles, Professor Repps and indeed all the circle knew. Even the savate, hitherto as I understand a mode of attack considered peculiar to the French nation, was brought freely into play. There were now some policemen on the scene, but they were totally powerless. Young Israel dealt with them faithfully, while the main portion of the boxing and bruising confraternity led, as I learned afterwards, by a well-known Hebrew heavyweight called Pedlar Piekmann, devoted their undivided attention to us.

The issue could not be long in doubt. From the moment when Mrs. Lascelles's hat was torn off her head, and Professor Repps's overcoat was reduced to half a pocket, a couple of buttons and a square inch of velvet collar, the game was up—as I heard someone say in strictly metaphorical language. In the very height of the conflict, when Professor Simeon Jenkins, Delminius, Lady Burnett, and others of the circle had long since totally disappeared, when all our thermos bottles, brandy flasks, biscuit boxes, etc., had been ground to atoms under the charging feet of Whitechapel, and when I, for one, was beginning to see Catherine wheels and unknown groups of stars dancing before my nearly bunged-up eyes, the gallery door was suddenly opened, or gave way before the determined onslaughts of Pedlar Piekmann and his adherents. I was conscious of a frantic movement; the back of my head caught a doorjamb; I was forced furiously upward by a press of seething Jewish humanity; I remember trying to be honest—the moral sense is strangely persistent in some of us—and feebly throwing one and sixpence in the direction of a small opening, which I judged to be the gallery paybox; I reached a height (the back of the gallery), and was then flung down a steep descent, bounding and rebounding from the spines of backs of seats; finally I landed on my hands and knees in a narrow space at the edge of a precipice. Miraculously, as it seemed to me, I was in the front row of the gallery of the Parthenon Theatre. When I realized this I hauled myself up, hanging on to the narrow curved ledge in front of me with both hands, and sank down into the lap of someone who said:

"Where the 'ell are *you* a-comin' to? You got—nice manners, I *don't* fink!"

I was reposing on the bosom of a well-known "bantam" from Shoreditch.

Somehow, I shall never know how, I managed to squeeze into an interstice beside him, from which I had an excellent view of the house. When I had collected myself and fastened the two ends of my collar together with a pin, which I fortunately found in the lining of my Harris tweed, I looked round for the circle. Not one of them was visible at first. But as my eyes, ranging over the rows upon rows of Whitechapel faces, male and female—for feathered females were there in mobs—grew accustomed to the semi-obscurity, I perceived one countenance which I recognized, familiar I cannot call it. At the extreme back of the gallery Professor Repps was leaning sideways against the wall, wedged in among a dense throng of standing pugilists, wiping the streams of perspiration from a face which resembled a futurist painting with one hand, and trying to fasten a waistcoat from which every button had been forcibly removed with the other. He, as I learned subsequently, was the only one of the circle, excepting myself, who assisted at the first night of *Sally Eliza.* The rest knew of what occurred in the theatre only from the Professor's and my report of it, mine necessarily much fuller than his, since I had a good view of all that occurred, while he only caught, as it were, broken glimpses over the shoulders and under the arms of the bulky bruisers who surrounded him.

When I had recovered some equanimity after my horrible experience, and was able to breathe deeply once more, I endeavoured to detach myself mentally from my uproarious companions in the gallery, and to take a calm and discriminating view of things below me. The upper boxes and dress circle I could not see, as they were directly under me, but I saw several rows of stalls and all the boxes. As I watched, the stalls filled up rapidly. In them I perceived a few decent-looking and quietly-dressed men, who no doubt were dramatic critics. Two or three of them were accompanied by well-dressed women—their wives I suppose. I also saw a few women who came in unaccompanied and who had little books and pencils in their hands. These, I have reason to believe, were lady journalists, and I have nothing to say against them.

But what of the rest of the audience?

The circle had feared, and had fought against, the presence of the wrong people in Ariadne's theatre, but when fearing most and fighting hardest we had surely never conceived that people could be so wrong as those who poured into the Parthenon that evening, many of them being greeted with stentorian applause and catcalls from the gallery. I don't know who most of them were, though some of those around me sought to instruct me by such cries as: "'Ere's our little bit of all right!" "There comes old Ma Parsons! Three cheers for old Ma!" "'Ow's yerself, Boy Bert, an 'ow's yer Missis?" "Blimey, Bill, if it ain't the Lucky Trickster!

Caps off for the Trickster!" "There's Sunshine Jine with a new boy! Gawd sive old Sunshine!" and the like. I gathered, however, by bits of talk from my neighbours, and by my own close and tragic observation, that they were well-known publicans, pawnbrokers, pugilists, bookies, music hall stars at that moment out of an engagement or taking a holiday, boxing promoters and the like, with their women-kind, legitimate and, I fear, illegitimate. The appearance of most of these personages was devastating. The men—such of them as were in evening dress; many were not—wore coloured waistcoats, frilled shirts ornamented with enormous studs gleaming with stones which I suspected to be false, turned down, or possibly celluloid, collars, made up white, or yellow, or even mauve ties bought apparently to "match" the waistcoats. Not a few "shot" their cuffs as they swaggered into the stalls, or stroked their enormous and oiled moustaches with thick fingers on which glittered diamond rings.

Their countenances were mostly bold studies from the Hebraic world. (Or shall I call it rather the Hebraic underworld?) But some were of the British bulldog species, with pug noses, enormous jaws, large cheek bones, small eyes, and big, hard-looking, round heads, with low foreheads ornamented with streaked forward strands of sticky hair.

The women who accompanied these worthies I must be excused from describing lest I seem to be adverse to the sex. I will merely say that they were remarkable, far too remarkable, to be in place in the Parthenon Theatre, where the "note" had always been a subdued, a "piano" note, and where intellect, even in the feminine sex, had bees looked for and invariably found. Not one of the ladies whom I gazed down upon from the gallery had probably ever even heard of the British Museum; not one, I am quite positive, had ever been there.

Until close upon eight o'clock the boxes remained untenanted, and the attention of the gallery was eagerly fixed upon them, while nuts were being busily cracked, bananas stripped of their mottled skins, oranges sucked and mysterious bottles drained dry. Peppermints spread their pungent odour abroad upon the air. And a small instrument called, I believe, a "fuzzywuz" or "Whitechapel Tickler," was playfully used to keep the more sedately inclined portion of the audience, myself included, from "going to bye-bye."

Just before eight there was a sudden roar of applause, mingled with shrill cries from the women, and many people stood up. Mr. Pug Bullen, accompanied by two females, had entered Box A next the stage. I stood up with the rest, not I need hardly say to do honour to Mr. Bullen, who from the front of the box was ducking to the audience, but to send a passionate glance of sympathy towards Huskin Repps, whom I caught a glimpse of with his sensitive face thrust forward, his round beard resting on the broad shoulder of a typical heavyweight, and his dark eyes almost protruding from his head in an effort to see what was happening. As I looked shouts of "good old Pug!" "Three cheers for old Pug!" "Give it 'em, Pug!" and similar exclamations from all parts of the house enlightened him as to the reason of the uproar, and I saw a quiver of exquisite pain pass over his delicate features. The man's cup was full! I knew it and turned away, just in time to see Tottie Willoughby, the male impersonator, accompanied by Conk Lutkins—who, as I afterwards found out, was a famous female impersonator, of strictly Jewish antecedents—come swellingly into Mrs. Lascelles's box.

Miss Willoughby was a formidable-looking woman with an immense fringe in which was entangled the sort of tiara the fairy queen wears in a Drury Lane pantomime. She had the attitude and manner of a determined—even an aggressive—man, but was attired in an amazingly low-cut dress of vermilion satin, profusely embroidered with heavy gold bullion and trimmed with tassels of gold. She wore long gloves of vermilion kid.

Need I say more about her?

Her companion, the female impersonator, who was saluted by the audience as "Curly Conk!" "Kent Road Conky!" and "'Elio, Queen Elizabeth, 'ow's yerself and the kiddies?" was a tall, impudent-looking man with a bulging eye and a protuberant bust, who wore elaborate evening dress with a coat cut in to an evidently steel-clad waist, and who swayed to the applause which greeted him with an easy familiarity which struck me as the crude acme of supreme vulgarity.

Poor Mrs. Lascelles!

As Sol Israel Isaacstein, whom I shall not describe, rolled into his box accompanied by his wife and his lustrous offspring, a hidden orchestra struck up a popular tune.

Ariadne, for the first time in her management, had debased herself to the lowest theatrical taste in music!

Then the curtain divided and *Sally Eliza* developed before my astonished eyes.

There is no need for me to attempt to analyse *Sally Eliza,* and I have no intention of doing so. The annals of the British theatre are open to the curious, and the matter is sufficiently recent to be within the recollection of a very large portion of the public. It is not for me, a playwright myself, and even one who has endeavoured to write a play suitable to the talent of Ariadne, to praise or to condemn a work which might possibly be supposed by the ignorant to have stood in the way of my own. I will merely state a fact which, in my view, and in the view of the circle, sums up the whole matter.

Sally Eliza was a popular success.

Pug Bullen liked it; Tottie Willoughby liked it; it was approved by Sol Israel Isaacstein and his entire brood; Conk Lutkins thought it "fine." (This I know for I heard his powerful voice, like a strong dramatic soprano enlarged by a megaphone, reverberate through the theatre with the word at the close of the performance.) The gallery "took it to its bosom." Knowing who was in the gallery it is surely unnecessary to say much more. The play had every low and common feature which makes for popular success. It was like the banana among fruits, the kind of thing which is appropriately sold from a barrow, and devoured publicly on the pavement by the teeming vulgar in search of sustenance with a flavour that suits the slum. It reeked of the people like boiled cabbage. It was the peppermint among bon-bons. Vinegar seemed to drip from it on to steel knives. One slipped up on it as upon orange peel in the gutter.

In short it was what the public wants.

This was terrible enough, but far more terrible was the popular success of Ariadne.

When she first came on to be received with an uproar of coarse applause, in which whistling and catcalls were prominent, I did not recognize her, and for one instant supposed that some popular favourite had been engaged as a member of her company. It was only by remarks of my neighbours and then, almost immediately, by certain intonations, certain movements, by a certain carriage of the head, that I knew the woman before me must be Ariadne. It was Pug Bullen who led the applause, gave the signal for it I might say, when Ariadne shuffled in, blowing her nose in a manner indescribable, which at once took the fancy of the house. And soon the shout went up: "'Ere's Sally Eliza!" A shout which seemed to me, and I doubt not to Huskin Repps, to sound the death knell of a great career. Yes, it was indeed Ariadne, that frowsy, towsle-headed, dirty-faced, grimy-handed, husky-voiced girl of the slums, the gin palaces, the boxing ring and the fifth-rate picture palace; a girl who carried her arms akimbo, wore a feathered hat when she went out, cheap earrings, and a rabbit skin boa; a girl without an "h," and, worse, without an intellect or a desire for one; a girl without, indeed, either aspirates or aspirations, whose one aim in life was to have a husband who was strong enough to knock her about, and clever enough to "down" his rival in the boxing ring. It was tragic to see such a woman as Ariadne in such a role, but the greater tragedy was this—that she played it as if she were born for it, with a zest, a gusto, an apparent high-spirited enjoyment of it, which almost paralysed my senses. At first I tried to think that I was merely witnessing a clever tour de force, an exhibition of real acting as opposed to the mere exploitation of a powerful personality, but as the evening wore on I was forced to another and very painful conclusion.

Ariadne—I felt it in my very depths—was revelling in the part of Sally Eliza, revelling like a creature released, from whose back a burden had roiled away and fallen into an abyss. There was no intellectuality here—and she was glad of it. There was no grey matter here—and she was at ease. Everything here was crude, indelicate, mindless. The passions of the illiterate were laid bare like a row of prominent teeth. The commonness of the mob, of those swarming millions from whom we of the circle instinctively shrank away, metaphorically holding our noses, was enthroned and Ariadne was happy in the enthronement. It was incredible and yet I could not deny it. The impossible was accomplished before my eyes.

Ariadne was enjoying Sally Eliza as much as, or more than, the audience was enjoying it; she was enjoying it like one of them.

The curtains met on that most hateful of all things in art—a popular triumph. There were vociferous cries for the author. Instinctively I stood up and leaned forward over the ledge of the gallery, straining my eyes.

"Jock! Jock! Jock!" barked the audience in unison. And I found myself barking with them: " Jock! Jock! Jock!"

But no Jock Jonesmith appeared. Only Ariadne came forward and said, still in the tones of Sally Eliza:

"Jock Jonesmith ain't in the 'ouse! But I'll tell 'im yer likes 'is ply!"

There was a roar of laughter, a shout of applause and Ariadne retired. Immediately afterwards from the wings a foot and a short length of leg were protruded and shaken hard at the audience, producing another shout.

This was the finishing touch to the awful evening. When at last I crept out of the theatre the clouds had cleared and the stars were shining. As Israel gradually melted away into the shades I saw a broken-down figure leaning against the wall of an adjacent public house. It was Huskin Repps.

I got him home to Bedford Square somehow, and left him there, crouched in front of Ariadne, as Venus draped. Then I went back to Jermyn Street. I took out my play and looked at it for a long time. My brain seemed numbed. Huskin Repps, I knew, had lost the ideal of his middle life. But I was still a comparatively young man, and youth is stubborn. I was a playwright, too, which Repps was not. My play lay there before me, witness to my long agonies of intellectuality in the service of Ariadne. Was she indeed doomed, as I knew Repps thought she was? Was she destined to pass the rest of her life in the Augean Stables of popular success? Or was there one who might rescue her? The morrow would show. I was too exhausted to do more than wonder just then. But I remember laying my hand on my play with a gesture which was like a mute prayer.

VIII

That night I made up my mind what I would do on the morrow, and so decisively that I slept well, as men do when they have shaken hands with their manly resolution.

I woke refreshed and calm. My face, it is true, was discoloured by the events of the previous evening. I had taken a scratch or two from the professionals of the ring; over my right eye there was a protuberance the size of a thrush's egg. But my head was clear, my brain cool, my resolution unabated. I was able even to eat a moderate breakfast.

Some papers lay on my table. I did not open them lest I should see the flaming accounts of the hideous and detestable triumph of the previous night. These might have unnerved me. I needed to have all my weapons in order, sharpened and bright. Nothing which might possibly dull them must be allowed to come near me. I attempted no intercourse with the circle by telephone or otherwise. Its members were probably prostrate both mentally and physically. At any rate for the moment they could do me no good. It were better to ignore them. I felt lonely but brave in my loneliness.

Toward eleven o'clock I walked down to Marmion Street and used the dryad's head on Ariadne's black door. A Scotswoman came. I asked to see Miss Marshall. I was told that she was not up. The excitement of the preceding night had tired her. She was still asleep.

"Eh, mon, but it was a braw night the night for Miss Marshall!" said the Scotswoman.

I made no comment on this astonishing announcement, but left a note which I had written at home and brought in my coat pocket in case of eventualities.

"Please give this to Miss Marshall directly she wakes," I said. "And tell her I shall be here again punctually at four. I know she will see me."

Without waiting for another word from the woman I turned on my heel and walked calmly away.

Exactly at four I was there again, this time with my manuscript play neatly rolled up in my hand. While at home a new idea had come to me, which had led me to bring my play.

When the door was answered I said:

"I have made an appointment with Miss Marshall. She is at home no doubt."

"Yes, sir. Miss Marshall is in—"

"That's well!"

I stepped into the hall.

The woman, I thought, looked rather more Scottish than usual at me, but she seemed overawed by my manner and shut the hall door.

"I'm not pair-r-r-fectly certain that Miss Marshall will see ye!" she said.

"I'm perfectly certain that she will!" was my simple and manly answer. "Where shall I wait?"

"In here, sir," said the woman, looking rather subdued.

And she showed me into a little room off the hall, where Ariadne studied and, I supposed, wrote those masterly analyses of plays which had so much impressed me.

I had seen this sacred room once, but had never sat down in it. I did so now, resolutely holding my play on my knees.

The room was simple, but deeply impressive, the room of a thinker, even it seemed of a scholar. I saw a large plain writing table covered with neatly arranged and important-looking papers, docketed, tied with blue tapes; many pens; big sheets of blue blotting paper; masses of butcher blue stationery; a statue of Minerva in marble presiding tranquilly over all. On the wall were books, the classics which suited Ariadne's temperament, "perhaps a peculiar one." From my mahogany chair with carved claws of a lion I perceived the works of Strindberg, of Ibsen, of Hauptmann, of Sudermann, Schopenhauer's *Essays*, Tolstoy's *What is Art?*, Gorki's *Asile de Nuit*, Barker's *The Voysey Inheritance*—a tremendous array of intellect and deep thought. But—another book caught my eyes. It lay on a sofa face downwards and open. My curiosity was aroused. I got up and went towards it. Bending down I read the title: *The Naughty Monk, Rasputin. His life faithfully and minutely recorded by William—*

Before I could read any more the door opened and Ariadne stood before me.

Her hair was "bobbed"!

For a moment that was all I saw. Then she came forward briskly.

"Hello!" she said.

After an instant I answered: "Halloh!"

"What have you got there?" she added.

"I've brought my play."

"What for?" she said. "My dear chap, let me tell you something. *Sally Eliza* will run for a year, perhaps two years."

"No, no!" I ejaculated. "Impossible!"

"But it will! Haven't you seen the notices?"

"I shall never see them!" I answered strongly.

"The papers are all over me, simply all over! *The Times* says that I've brought the reek of Whitechapel across the footlights. The *Pink 'Un* declares—"

"Ariadne!" I exclaimed in my deepest bass.

"Well, what is it?"

"You quoting the *Pink 'Un*!"

"And why shouldn't I?"

She stretched out her arms.

"My dear boy, I've found my freedom at last! Here—sit down."

I sank down between the mahogany claws. She threw *Rasputin* on the floor and curled up on the sofa.

"Were you there last night?" she asked, leaning forward,

Her face between the bobs of her hair looked quite different from usual; sharp, shrewd, almost gamine, I thought. Her eyes had lost their deeply reflective expression and sparkled with cockney mischief. Even the timbre of her voice was changed. The sonorities had sunk away from it. It was lighter, it was full of satirical notes.

"I was there."

"How on earth did you get in?"

"By the gallery door."

"And the rest of them?"

"They were swept away—except the Professor."

"Which one?"

"Huskin Repps."

"He was there!"

"He stood at the back of the gallery."

"Poor old bean!"

"Ariadne!"

"Poor old fruit! But it was all his fault."

"His fault?"

"Why couldn't he leave me alone?"

"Leave you alone? But he made you!"

"Made me a sham!"

"A sham?"

"Made me a façade like the façade of the Parthenon. I was only a frontage on the street till last night; all columns, and broad steps, and pediments, and architraves, and Gawd knows what! I was false British Museum till last night, and he made me it."

I was so astounded that I was literally unable to speak. My voice seemed to dry up in my throat.

"Look here!" she went on confidentially. "I'm not really an intellect. I'm a natural talent. See the difference? I'm a gift, not a brain. He couldn't see that. He would have it that I was a great brain. I came across him when I was an ignorant girl, and he said I looked like a muse. I was in melodrama then on the other side of the water, but I didn't let him know it. I said I was 'resting.' I was as poor as a rat and I saw my chance with him."

"You don't mean to say—"

"What old Repps?"

She broke into a laugh.

"Not a bit of it! My dear, he's a spinster in trousers. No, it was all art with him. He introduced me to the highbrows. He brought me books. He took me—my Gawd!—to the British Museum. He talked to me—oh, how he talked! And I sucked it all in. I thought it was my chance to stand out from the rest and get cackled about among clever people. And I went for it for all I was worth. And I got there. I never made big money, but I got a big name. I stood for intellect on the stage. The highbrows were all over me. I made love to the Professors and they helped me along. All the authors who can't get a popular success brought me their plays. Then I got backed."

"Backed! Who backed you?"

She shut one eye and put her forefinger near her nose.

"Never mind! But it wasn't the Professors! That put me into the Parthenon Theatre. And there I struggled along with the highbrow stuff the big public detests. What do you think's been lost in the Parthenon Theatre?"

"Lost?"

"Money!"

"I don't know."

"Something like five thousand a year, take one year with another! Well, it couldn't go on. But I was afraid to make a change till I was just pushed to it."

"Who pushed you?"

"What about the backer?"

I was silent.

"Even then I'd been a frontage on the street for so long that I was afraid to show 'em that there was anything to be made of me. That was why I got you all in that Sunday evening. Remember?"

"The supper from the Ritz?"

"Ah! That was *his* idea."

"Whose?"

"What about the backer?"

Again I was silent.

"Well, after supper it went *his* way, and then I was all in. I never looked back after that. And I've got there. I've showed 'em what's inside of me, and they jolly well like it. No more Corinthian pillars for me! Walk up, walk in, and see the bar parlour! No more eating of husks— why, his very name's Huskin!—but have a good warm and a jolly good drink and go home with a belly full!"

"Ariadne!" I started to my feet.

"Well, what's the matter? Are you like the rest of 'em? Can't you stand a bit of the truth?"

"Tell me the truth," I said. "Who is the backer?"

"What about Augustus?" she replied.

"Augustus Transome!" I cried. "It was Augustus Transome who got you to put on *Sally Eliza*?"

"Got me! What do *you* think?" she replied. "Why, he wrote the old thing."

"Augustus Transome is Jock Jonesmith!"

"Ra—ther! But even I didn't know it at first."

"Well, I'm—"

"That's it, my boy! Be natural for once and tell us you're damned!"

Instinctively I made for the door. Those weapons of mine were blunted in my hand. I had meant to unroll my play, to read the new intellectual parts, to dwell on the grey matter. I had thought to recall Ariadne with my play to her better self. But now—!

At the door, however, I turned, moved to do so by a recollection.

" But—but—" I stammered. "Your letters!"

"My letters! Whatever do you mean, boy?"

"Your analysis of my play! Your analysis of *Sally Eliza*!"

"Oh, old Murryan wrote those. He did everything to keep up the highbrow legend of me. He bolstered up the façade. I only copied 'em out. I went by him in most everything. When I acted he stuffed all the bow-bow intellectual rot into me. He was the wonderful Ariadne— excepting the production and the costumes and all that. Young Fanning looked after those."

I had heard enough and I laid my hand on the door knob. As I did so Ariadne called out from her sofa:

"I say, I like you, boy! The circle hasn't quite done for you yet. Now you take my tip. Scrap all the intellectual rot in your play. Leave the situations as they are, work up the comic bits, stuff in plenty of laughs and some more spooning, and then bring it along to me again. But scrap all the intellectual rot! See?"

I believe I bowed. I know I was far beyond speech. I opened the door, held it, and looked back.

Ariadne had picked up *The Naughty Monk, Rasputin*, and was eagerly turning over the pages, evidently to find her lost place.

My tale is nearly at an end. I gathered the circle together. I told them who Jock Jonesmith was and who Ariadne's backer was. They were horror-stricken. But when I explained to them the nature of the change in Ariadne, the mental and moral change, even the physical change, they were appalled.

"Her hair bobbed!" wailed Mrs. Lascelles, who was stretched upon a sofa with her poetical head swathed in wet bandages by doctor's orders. "It is the end!"

And, like Hezekiah, she turned her face to the wall.

"She says she is really a bar parlour," I said. "And that you"—I turned to Huskin Repps—"made her a sham. She mentioned the word façade. She spoke of columns, architraves, pediments—"

"My words, my words!" murmured Repps. "She had never heard of a façade, of an architrave, till she met me!"

"Had she ever heard of anything till she met you?" asked Lady Burnett.

"Perhaps not! Perhaps not!" said poor Repps. "but she had a forthright brain and—"

"That's just what she denies!" I exclaimed, moved to interrupt him almost in despite of myself. "She swears she hasn't got a brain. She said to me: 'I'm a gift, not a brain.'"

There was a moment of dead silence. Then Jasper Trent roared the circle's epithet over the grave of Ariadne:

"She's a popular success. *Requiescat in pace.*"

The Letter

I

Lena Wareham was very happy, and as she was not accustomed to happiness the sensation was tremendous, startling. It almost frightened her at moments. She asked herself whether this new warmth, as of a bright fire on a hearth that had long been cold and cheerless, could possibly last for more than a short time. Might it not soon die down, flicker out leaving only a dust of grey ashes? She had been used to think that the joy many women are given was not intended for her, and she knew that her friends and neighbours had thought the same thing. They were at home with her loneliness, were thoroughly satisfied with it, thought it quite the right and natural thing. She was there in her pleasant old house on the outskirts of the village, living with her servants, her dog and her horses for company, looking after her garden—she was very clever at gardening—receiving her acquaintances and friends with unfailing hospitality, enjoying a quiet and well-ordered life in the midst of the beautiful and characteristically English scenery in which Sutton Dering stands, a well-off spinster lady of thirty-five. She was there and she would always be there as long as she lived, a part of the village life, almost a part of the village landscape.

One saw her working in her garden, with a shady garden hat on her smooth brown hair, on her bicycle going to the post office, walking to church up the long village street, with its Tudor houses and old creeper-covered cottages with jutting-out windows, driving her phaeton to the country houses round about, or to the market town of Brinkton, where she did the chief part of her shopping; one saw her playing tennis with the neighbours, on the links golf club in hand, in the village hall at the occasional concerts and theatrical performances which "livened things up" at Sutton Dering. And one thought she was a dear, pleasant, comfortable creature, absolutely suited to the pleasant life she was living.

Certainly she was not married. But why on earth should she be married? The papers stated that there were thousands of "superfluous" women in England. Unless Parliament brought in polygamy, which seemed quite unlikely, it was impossible for every woman to find a husband. Besides, well-off spinsters, with kind hearts, smiling faces and excellent health, are very useful and acceptable in country places. You can turn to them for all sorts of things which married women, mothers, cannot be expected to bother about. As Mr. Portyon, the Rector of Sutton Dering, said emphatically, they have their "place in the scheme," like beetles which mysteriously appear in back kitchens one doesn't know why. Miss Wareham's place in the scheme of Sutton Dering had long been well defined and nobody wanted to see it empty. Providence had doubtless designed her for it, and everybody, including it was supposed Miss Wareham herself, was thoroughly satisfied with the forethought of Providence.

Lena Wareham was one of those women who somehow are not "expected" to marry. Not that she was ugly. She had a pleasant and healthy-looking face, with quite nice features and agreeable grey eyes. Her hair, too, was nice though she dragged it back too much from her forehead. She had a well-knit figure, and was active on her feet. But she was "homely." She dressed quite well but she never looked fashionable. There was absolutely nothing alluring about her. Even when she wore silk stockings they might almost as well have been made of worsted for all the effect they produced. Her "note" was neatness, but it was somehow a spinstery neatness, as any knowing flapper would have told you after one comprehensive glance at it. Her hats were not all wrong, but they never looked really smart. And her whole demeanour was simple and without the least tinge of enticement.

"She can never have known how to flirt!" Mrs. Parkins, the wife of the master of hounds, had been heard to say.

And the remark was quite true. Lena never had known how to flirt.

Most women, even plain women, have, or have had "little ways with them" which make an effect on the masculine animal, a small armoury of feminine weapons which sting, or prick, or, more subtly, stir the male into alert attention. Miss Wareham had no such little ways, had no armoury of weapons to keep sharp and bright. She always wished to please in a thoroughly human way, for she was warmhearted and fond of her kind, but she was strangely devoid of subtleties where the other sex was in question. She had, perhaps, something of the simple honesty of a nice English boy. And that sort of thing, as Mrs. Cheelsman, the rector's sister-in-law, said, doesn't go far with the modern man nowadays.

"He looks," said the lady, "for a good deal more than that."

And perhaps he didn't find it in Miss Wareham. Anyhow, although she had always been on pleasant and friendly terms with all the men she had known, she had never been run after by men.

In fact—and this was deadly in connection with an unmarried and not old woman—when men sought her out it was usually to tell her about their love difficulties with other women.

So at thirty-five Lena Wareham was still unmarried and not a soul in Sutton Dering ever expected her to marry. It might even be asserted that not a soul in Sutton Dering imagined that she had the least desire to marry.

And this was just where everyone was wrong.

Miss Wareham had been in love for years with a man whom her neighbours all knew, if not personally at any rate by sight. And not one of them had suspected it. So disarming, even so deceiving, may be simple honesty when it is coupled with delicate reserve, and with a natural lack of self-consciousness, and with a strong inward humility.

For though Miss Wareham had fallen in love with Eustace Henley it had never occurred to her as possible that he could ever fall in love with her. For one thing he had been numbered among the men who had come to have tea with her in her pleasant garden and had told her about their difficulties with women.

She remembered that day very well. It had been a trying day for her, though she had not shown it. They had sat in the summer house at the edge of the lawn and, after the second cup of tea, Eustace had remarked in a casual way that it was very difficult for a fellow to understand women. That had been enough for Miss Wareham. She had known at once what was coming. She was going to be consulted about another love affair with which she had nothing to do. At that moment a silent voice within her had set up an outcry which only she had heard.

"Why? Why?" it had cried. "Why do they confess to me? I'm not a priest! I'm not even an old woman. Why have I to bear this?"

And then she had sat very still, with a pleasant, earnest look of sympathetic attention on her kind face, and had heard it all, and had afterwards done her best to be explanatory of the mentality of other women, and had even given advice as to what it would be best for Eustace Henley to do under the difficult circumstances. And Henley had eventually gone away quite soothed and hopeful, and had afterwards said of Miss Wareham that she was the best little woman in the world, and would have made some fellow "a damned good wife" when she was a bit younger.

Well, Henley hadn't married that other woman, and now he was actually going to marry his mother confessor! It seemed incredible, but it was true. In that same garden he had told Lena Wareham that he loved her and had asked her to be his wife. And she had said yes, marvelling at the wonder which had come to her. The old life of loneliness, which she had hated for over twelve years, since her parents had died, would soon be at an end forever. She would have a companion at last.

Eustace was a gentleman farmer, and had a small estate on the top of the hill which rose above Sutton Dering. He had not been born in the neighbourhood, but had lived there for over eight years, ever since he had purchased the property of Easton. He loved country life, loved hunting, shooting, fishing; but he was not one of those rather dull, healthy animal men who let their minds go to sleep while their bodies are active. There was something of the faun in his appearance, something slightly wild and exotic in his personality, something quick and whimsical in his mentality which marked him out from the ordinary country gentleman who lived about Sutton Dering year in year out. He read books as well as the papers. He had travelled. He often ran up to London.

There was nothing stagnant about Eustace Henley. But he preferred the country to town and chose to sink his money in land rather than to dispose of it in the City. He was not good-looking. He was tall, thin, even scraggy, with auburn hair, a brown face covered with freckles and irregular features. His eyes were large and red-brown in colour, full of light and changing expressions. And he had a big mouth with splendid white teeth, under a short auburn moustache. His small ears lengthened at the top into shapes that some people called pointed.

Such was the man whom Miss Wareham had fallen in love with at first sight. He was thirty-one, four years younger than Miss Wareham.

His proposal had surprised her. She had never suspected that Eustace cared for her, although she had noticed that a change had come into his manner when he was with her. Formerly he had been friendly but casual. He had treated her in a rather impersonal way, had usually talked to her as if she were there to be talked to, or occasionally listened to, but not as if she were a very definite woman totally different from all the other women whom he knew, Lena Wareham, a friend whom he could never confuse with other women friends, someone requiring from him a special treatment, a special tone, special subjects of conversation.

This change in him had at first rendered their intercourse less easy than before. Henley had often seemed slightly self-conscious when they were together. His conversation had become difficult. Often it was interrupted by abrupt and uneasy silences. Sometimes Miss Wareham had felt that while Eustace was talking his mind was at work on some problem which he had not mentioned to her. Now and then she had seemed to be aware of some inward debate which was perplexing him. And more than once she had expected a renewal of that old topic long ago broached in the summer house, had feared yet another confession of difficulties with a woman.

But to her great relief it hadn't come. And she had wondered what was the matter. Eustace was certainly very often preoccupied. People had noticed it, people in the village. And one day Mrs. Cheelsman had said so to Miss Wareham.

"It's my belief that Mr. Henley has either lost a lot of money or that he has fallen in love. Nothing else can account for his absence of mind. Depend upon it, it's one or the other that's troubling him, love or money."

It had turned out to be the former. For shortly after that remark of the rector's sister-in-law Eustace had ridden down to Chilham Corner and had proposed to Miss Wareham.

She had been tremendously astonished, but not too astonished to accept him.

That was a week ago. And now the engagement was given out and the whole neighbourhood knew of it.

II

It was a warm June day and Lena Wareham was alone in the afternoon, expecting the post which was due between three and four o'clock. Eustace Henley was away in London. He had had to go up on business, but she was expecting him back almost directly. Meanwhile he had promised to write to her and tell her what he was doing and how he was getting on without her. The letter might perhaps come to-day with the London papers.

Lena had never yet had a letter from Eustace, but she had in a locked drawer several short notes written in his large, erratic handwriting, accepting, or refusing, invitations to tennis or dinner, notes to "Dear Miss Wareham" from "Yrs. sincerely, E. Henley."

How would he begin his letter from London, and how would he end it? She was wondering now as she strolled about the garden looking at the very fine roses. (Her roses were noted in the county and had won many prizes at local flower shows.)

There had been plenty of wondering during the last few days in Sutton Dering. The astonishment of the village and the neighbourhood at the engagement had been intense and ill-concealed. "We never expected it!" had been the universal cry of the gossips. Some people had seemed almost injured by the announcement that Miss Wareham and Mr. Henley were going to be wife and husband. But no doubt they would settle down to it presently. Anyhow, Lena was too intensely happy to be upset by the not very flattering surprise that a man wished to link his life with hers. In her joy she was almost indifferent to opinion. Besides, she was secretly wondering, too. For, like the gossips, she had never expected it. She must have been strangely blind, she supposed. Now she saw, realized, and was gloriously alive. The garden seemed new to her. Every rose had a different look. The velvety grass of the lawn was strange to her feet, strangely delicious. And she felt very young, full of the ardour of youth.

How would he write to her now? She thought of different beginnings, different endings. There were a good many ways of opening and closing a letter. Which would be his?

She heard beyond the privet hedge the sharp ting-ting of a bicycle bell in the lane that led to the house, and stood still. No doubt that was the postman. She waited, looking towards the long Tudor front of the house with the narrow terrace bordering it, and the white garden benches. The arrival of the London post had always been a pleasant little episode in her quiet day, but how strange it was to expect it as she was expecting it now! Love changed everything, lifted everything into light, emphasized everything, made everything vital, important, underlined as it were all the meanings.

Love even made old Jennings, the red-nosed postman, seem a marvellous emissary to her now. He had surely the letter, the only letter in the world, in that brown bag of his.

Susan, the parlourmaid, appeared in the doorway that led to the terrace. Lena had told her to bring the post into the garden, and now she stepped primly out. She had several missives in her hands, long shapes of papers, small squares and oblongs lying above them.

Lena looked very calm.

"Thank you, Susan. Oh!"

She had dropped *The Daily Telegraph.*

"That's it. Thank you. I'll read them out here."

"Yes, ma'am."

The maid went away.

"There's two letters from *him!*" she remarked a moment later in the servants' hall.

"Well, I never!" said the cook.

"But I didn't put them on the top of the others—not me!"

"Where did you put 'em, then?" asked the cook.

"Bottom of all."

"You are an artful one, Sue," said Minnie, the housemaid. "You do know a thing or two."

"I know that sweetest had better come last—like it is with a dinner."

In the garden Lena had hidden herself away at the end of a long alley bordered with low hedges of yew. Here there was a semi-circular bench of stone with a stone sundial in front of it. The bench was warm from the sun. She sat down there, put aside the papers, and quickly began to look at the letters.

One, two, three, four—hadn't he written? She turned over the fifth letter, which was lying on the top of a sixth with the address facing downwards. Yes, there was a letter from him! She didn't look at the sixth letter, which had also been turned with the address downwards. His was the only letter that mattered. She held it for a moment tightly, whilst she gazed at the erratic handwriting. How she loved it!

> "Miss Wareham,
> "Chilham Corner,
> "Sutton Dering,
> "Worcestershire."

How absurd she was! And how glorious it was to be absurd!

Resisting a strong desire to put her lips to the envelope, she opened it and took out Eustace's letter. She unfolded it gently and looked at the opening: "My darling." She blushed. She didn't know what she had expected, but she felt now that she had not expected that. She turned the sheet over and looked at the end.

> "In spite of all,
> "Yr. lover always, forever,
> "FAUN."

In spite of all? What a strange thing to put! And the signature was strange. Neither she nor anyone else in Sutton Dering had ever called Eustace Henley "Faun." Some people certainly had said he had a look of a faun, but she had never said so. She had never hinted to Eustace that she thought he bore any resemblance to the half-developed creature of the woods. And—in spite of all! Evidently the letter must contain some self-reproaches, perhaps even some relation of past episodes in his life which he had thought it honourable to tell her of now that they were lovers, were going to be married.

She turned back the sheet and again read "My darling." "It's all right," she said to herself, "Nothing matters but that. I don't mind his sins."

And then she began to read on.

My darling, —I've done it at last. For more than two months I've been thinking over it, trying to make up my mind to it, shying away from it. Sometimes I felt that it couldn't be done, that I must keep my freedom in spite of all, that it was the only thing worth having now in this damned world where everything seems to go wrong for some of us. But at last I've done it. As you couldn't bring yourself to pay the price that the bold step would have cost us both, and as you begged me to raise the barrier between us higher, I've taken you at your word.

Lena Wareham had become very pale. Her brows were drawn together, and the hand which held the letter in the sunshine was trembling slightly.

"What does this mean?" she was saying to herself. "What does it all mean? It can't—it can't—"

Something told her that she ought to stop reading the letter, insisted that she must stop, put it back in the envelope, return it to the writer, or destroy it. It was addressed to her, but it could not be meant for her. There must be a mistake, the most hideous mistake that had ever been made. Now she meant to obey her instinct, the simple, honourable instinct of a woman who was a lady, and who had never in her life done a dirty action or yielded to a low desire against which the best part of her had rebelled. She meant to do this, but her own body seemed to defy her. She tried to force her hands to fold up the letter, hiding the words which his hand had written for other eyes than hers. But her hands didn't move. She turned her eyes away from the page, but her eyes came back to it, stared at it. Then she tried to shut them and failed. And all the time something ugly within her, which must have risen into life with the new chance of happiness on which she had counted—how passionately in the last few days!—something greedy, violently alive and defiant, said to her, " Go on! You have a right to go on. This was written by the man who has told you he loves you. It is addressed to you. Who has the right to read it but you? You can only understand it if you read on to the end. Then the meaning will be clear, and it is absolutely essential for you to know what the meaning is."

The struggle within Lena Wareham was intense. It felt to her like the legendary struggle between good and evil. She knew, absolutely knew now, that Eustace had made a terrible mistake, that he had written a letter to some other woman about her, and had, by accident, enclosed it in the wrong envelope. If she went on reading, therefore, she would be deliberately reading a private letter belonging to someone else; she would be deliberately doing an absolutely dishonourable thing.

Of course she couldn't do that. It wasn't in her nature to do such a thing. If she did it she would be in the mire. Her own eyes would see herself muddy, filthy. She had once caught a servant reading a letter of hers on the sly, and had never forgotten the sensation of creeping disgust, and even of shame, which had come upon her and had made her almost feel guilty herself in realizing the low guilt of another. When the woman had turned and had seen her it was she who had reddened to the roots of her hair. But that red had flooded her face for another. And she could never—

She got up from the bench, left the letter and the envelope lying on it with the rest of the post, and walked down the alley. There was no wind, and the letter lay still. She went right down the alley between the yew hedges. At the end of it was a small piece of water in which water lilies grew. Beyond was a copse of hazels and larches. When she reached the edge of the water she paused. It was shallow and clear. As she looked down she saw a goldfish flick his tail and glide slowly away into the shadow with an air of mysterious purpose, as if he were away on an errand which must be surreptitiously carried out. And suddenly, for the first time, she realized the sharp separation between worlds in the world, the complete separation, for instance, between the life in the pond at her feet and the life in the garden in which she was standing, each of them a little world made intense and mysterious by the breath sent into organisms placed in it. This realization seemed to have something to do with the violent pain she was suffering, which had apparently given her new faculties. She felt like a stranger to herself.

She turned, and was now facing the sundial which she saw in the distance. It was rather large, and hid that bit of the bench on which Eustace's letter was lying. Nevertheless, she felt as if she saw the white paper with the sunlight streaming over it. It was useless to stand where she was, thinking vaguely of the goldfish now concealed in the pond somewhere under the water lilies. She must do something. And she began to walk down the alley again. When she was midway in it she heard a genteel voice call gently, discreetly:

"Ma'am! Ma'am!"

She started violently, but immediately controlled herself and answered:

"Yes, Susan … what is it?"

The maid's head appeared above the yew hedge on her left.

"Mrs. Portyon and Mrs. Cheelsman are in the drawing room, if you please, ma'am."

"I'll come directly—in a moment. I'll just get my letters."

"Yes, ma'am."

The maid went away, walking with an acquired dignity and holding her back very flat. Then Lena went slowly to the bench. She put Eustace's letter back into the envelope and pushed it inside her dress, gathered up the other letters and the papers, walked to the house, went into her writing room and carefully laid them down on the writing table. This done she looked at herself in the glass. Did she look odd? Was there anything?

She did not know, was not sure. She put up her hands to her head and smoothed her already smooth hair. Mrs. Portyon and Mrs. Cheelsman mustn't see anything—notice anything.

She felt very furtive, horribly furtive.

At last she turned and went into the drawing room.

III

The good ladies stayed for a very long time. Lena was obliged to offer them tea. They accepted it eagerly. It would help them to talk—to talk about the engagement.

Mrs. Portyon, the rector's wife, was enormously stout and enormously voluble. Conversation with her was rather a disease than a distraction. There was something almost vicious, almost unhealthy, in her enjoyment of talk. Her sister, Mrs. Cheelsman, who was less furiously powerful over the parts of speech but not less desirous to be getting rid of words, was always greatly irritated by Mrs. Portyon's superior energies, and showed her irritation by sarcasm. She strove to make up for being knocked on the head by reviving with ferocity. If she could only get in a word edgewise she was resolved that at least it should be a devastating word.

Lena always felt tired after half an hour with the sisters, but to-day they exhausted her. They had of course only the one topic, her engagement to Eustace Henley. It had surprised them both immensely. To tell the truth, though they really thought they were as sharp as most people and sharper than some, they had never suspected that Lena and Mr. Henley cared for each other. They had supposed that Lena was too comfortably settled at Chilham Corner, too fond of being her own mistress, to wish for the uncertainties—for uncertainties there were though some people might not think so—of marriage. And Mr. Henley had always seemed to them to be quite contented as a bachelor and not to be looking about for a wife. Of course it was rather lonely on the top of the hill, especially in winter when the winds blew so often straight from the Cotswolds. But then Mr. Henley had so many animals, and they were company for those who liked them, especially horses and dogs; cows much less so of course, though Mrs. Portyon had known a woman once who had got very fond of a Jersey, or was it an Alderney cow and—brainless, utterly brainless, the cow, but now this really was interesting.

Mrs. Cheelsman had met a man, quite a gentleman, in Devonshire—close to Chudleigh in fact—who used to go out walking accompanied by a Berkshire pig. But that was a very special case and Mr. Henley—Mrs. Portyon was wondering whether Lena would go up the hill after the wedding or whether Mr. Henley would come down it. There was much to be said for Easton, but on the other hand Chilham Corner had great advantages. Doctor Mills declared, and always had declared, that the air at the top was far more tonic than the air at the bottom, containing indeed special properties—ozone, she believed, was the term—which were lacking from the air at the bottom. But it was not everybody who could stand the strong air. She remembered a baby—embryos babies every one of them! Mrs. Cheelsman was acquainted with a full-grown woman, very much of Lena's age, too, who on removing from Tunbridge Wells to Brighton, Hove to be exact, found her liver—Mrs. Portyon hoped that Lena would think it well over before deciding on any step. Women were more fragile than men as a rule, though when a man was a delicate plant, like poor Mr. Brinkton, of Bramham Shotwell, for instance, he was apt to go off quite as suddenly as any woman of them all, which reminded her that when she was a girl she had known a young fellow who, after being operated on for appendicitis, which had only just come into fashion at that time, had lost all his energy and had been totally incapable even of holding a golf club, although before the operation he had been a great athlete, which really seemed to prove, in spite of what the doctors said, that there was really something in the appendix after all—absolutely useless and futile, the appendix!

Mrs. Cheelsman begged Lena to put it from her mind. She was of opinion that Lena would be wise to bring Mr. Henley down the hill, for this reason, that—Mrs. Portyon was anxious to know when the wedding would be as the rector meant to take his summer holiday this year at the end of August and go to Bath to take the waters, as he had had more than a touch of sciatica of late, and of course he would never hear of anyone but himself uniting Lena in the Holy Bond to Mr. Henley. When would it be? The rector—the rector must take his chance for once in a while! But Mrs. Cheelsman specially wished to know the date of the wedding, because Miss Pyefield, of Arrow in Arden, one of the Pyefields, had implored her—the rector, Mrs. Portyon was positive, would give up Bath altogether rather than—

"Thank God they are gone!" said Lena, putting her hands to her temples at half-past five.

She stood for a moment. Then she rang the bell and told Susan she was not at home to anyone else.

"I haven't even had time to read my letters," she said, not looking at the maid.

"No, ma'am. The fact is, ma'am, everyone is so interested—"

"Yes, yes. I think I heard the bell, Susan."

"I'll say not at home, ma'am."

When she was gone Lena went to the writing room. She hadn't decided what she was going to do, and, perhaps to delay matters, to give herself time, she looked at the letters on the table, one by one. On turning over the fifth the blood rushed to her face. Another letter from him! She sat down. She was trembling. Then she tore it open.

"Dearest Lena,
Yr. deeply affectionate Eustace."

It was not a long letter. She read it through. It was cheerful, cordial; it told of his doings. Here and there she found affectionate phrases, allusions to the future, to their common life in Sutton Dering. Towards the end he expressed a hope that they might be married very soon. He didn't believe in waiting once a thing was decided upon. The last four words of the letter were emphasized by the prelude, "with love."

When Lena had finished reading it, she was possessed, as she had never before been possessed, by a desire which was like a physical power against which her strength wouldn't allow her to struggle. But for this second letter she might possibly have resisted the temptation to read the first through. Now she couldn't resist it. She was a loving woman and she had to compare the two letters, had to—at whatever cost to her self-respect. She tried to palter with herself, to tell herself that she had a right to read the first letter because it had been sent to her, and because of the circumstances in which she was placed. She said to herself: "It isn't as if it were an ordinary letter. It isn't as if Eustace were not engaged to me, had not asked me to be his wife. I have promised to marry him. I must know how I stand. A woman has a right to know the truth of the life of a man she is going to give her life to. And he sent the letter to me."

She even said to herself:

"Perhaps it is not a mistake. Perhaps he sent it on purpose—as a way of letting me know without actually telling me."

Of course she knew the utter insincerity of such a pretended supposition, and immediately she had said it she abandoned it for the brutal frankness of a jealous woman, stabbed in the moment of her greatest happiness.

"I must—I will know about the other woman."

Nevertheless Lena's cheeks burned as she drew the letter out of her dress, and sat down in a low chair near the casement window to pore over it, to compare it with the other letter—to her.

It was a much longer letter than hers, and the tone of it was quite different from the tone of hers. There was an intense vitality in it which made her letter, despite its cordiality, its affectionate phrases, seem almost dead. As Lena held the two letters side by side and compared them with feverish concentration she felt that one was a living thing, the other a decorated corpse.

A living thing—yes, into which love had breathed the breath of life!

She gathered from the letter, which was full of such allusions as only an intimate of the writer could thoroughly understand, that the woman to whom it was written was a young married woman whose husband had been separated from her for a long time but had now rejoined her. It was fairly evident that in the husband's absence Eustace Henley had had an intrigue with her, but that on seeing her husband again she had been conscience-stricken at what she had done, and had resolved absolutely to give up the illicit connection. Lena gathered this from various expressions in the letter, some rather vague, some more definite. But though she had to guess at certain things, and could only surmise others, one truth glared at her from the paper which she held with shaking fingers. It was this: that Eustace was marrying her in obedience to the urging of the woman he loved; he was marrying her to make the other woman's position safer; he was marrying her because she would be a barrier between him and a possibly dangerous sin. The other woman was afraid of her own weakness and of Eustace's passion, and from fear she wanted him to be tied as she was, by matrimony. There were expressions in the letter which left no doubt of this.

But it was the last part of the letter which held the most painful, the most burning interest for Lena, because it dealt directly with herself.

> "And now you may care to know what she is like—the woman who will stand, with your husband, between me and you. She's a few years older than I am. She's a thorough good sort, quiet and straight and saner than we are. Nothing passionate and erratic about her. I shouldn't think she's ever had a sleepless night because of a man in her life. She isn't good looking, but she's got a face you can trust, kind eyes with an honest look in them that tells you what she is at first sight. You'd probably call her a homely sort of woman, and so she is. People all like her, but I don't suppose a man ever went mad over her even when she was a girl. She isn't that kind a bit. She's all right at games, likes horses, gardening, a quiet life—the sort you'd call dull, but there's something in it. (You know you always said I was a rustic at heart.) People about Sutton Dering never expected her to marry, and there's the devil of a surprise in the village about our engagement. She's not a feeble nature I should think. I can imagine her helping to keep a fellow very straight if she cared for him. She cares for me—God knows why. I guessed it somehow so that's why I asked her when—when you were determined to lay me out. Of course I shall stick to her when the knot's tied. But—"

And there followed a passage which made Lena tremble all over, and which, just because of that, she read again and again.

The clock was striking seven when at last she put the terrible letter back into the envelope which was inscribed with her name.

Then she sat back in her chair and tried to think. What was she going to do?

No answer came to that question, and presently, almost directly, it was succeeded by another.

What would he do?

She did not of course know exactly how the hideous mistake which had enlightened her had occurred. But she imagined that Eustace had probably sat down, in a violently excited state of mind, to write several letters, including the two which she had received, and, having her strongly, painfully, in his mind, had written her name on the wrong envelope as well as on the right one, and had then—it must have been so of course—posted the letters without knowing what he had done.

But when he found out what he had done?

Suddenly with that thought there came to her a dreadful sense of shame as she realized the possibility, the probability, of being found out. She had done a loathsome thing, but as yet nobody knew that she had done it. If he knew—what then? She remembered the last few words of his letter to that other woman, all he had written of her, "A face you can trust"—"eyes with an honest look in them which tells you what she is at first sight"—"a thorough good sort"—"straight."

Straight! When a man said or wrote that of a woman it meant a great deal. She had always been straight as a die. Looking back on her quiet life she could not recall having ever before to-day done a deliberately mean action, an action of which she was thoroughly ashamed as she was ashamed now; she could not recall even having done anything which she dreaded being found out.

But would he find out?

She tried to think clearly but her mind was confused. She had had such a shock that she was not her normal self. When she strove to follow a train of thought her mind faltered, then became blank. She realized Eustace's mistake; she saw him in imagination posting the two letters; she allowed for an interval of time—for two or three days, a week perhaps. And then what would happen? The woman would not have received the letter he had written to her. Was she expecting it? If not she would not miss it. But would she write to Eustace? And if she did then— Or would he, without her writing, realize what he had done? Didn't people sometimes make mistakes and then, although no one pointed it out, and nothing occurred to draw their attention to—

But here her mind stopped dead, seemed to become flooded with nothingness. And she knew that her head had begun to ache.

Usually she dined at half-past seven, and she always dressed for dinner. Now she heard the music of the Japanese gong. She got up from her chair startled. Quickly she put all the letters she had had by the afternoon's post into a drawer of the writing table and locked it, drawing the key out of the lock afterwards. Then she went into the hall.

Susan was standing by the dining room door.

"I've been busy, Susan," she said. "To-night I'll dine just as I am."

"Yes, ma'am."

"Did anyone call?"

"Yes, ma'am. Mrs. Parkins and Lady Darby."

"Any message?"

"No, ma'am. They just left their cards and were very sorry you were out."

Lena sat down at the table and forced herself to eat. On the previous evening she had dined alone and had thought, "How soon all these lonely meals will be a thing of the past!" She remembered that thought now. When the short meal was over she went out into the garden. The June night was warm and the garden was full of lingering perfumes. She strolled about for a long while, then sat down on a bench and again tried to think.

What was she going to do?

She must give Eustace up, must break the engagement. Of course now there was nothing else to be done. He would understand the reason. But would he understand it? She couldn't tell it to him. She knew that. To do so would be to tell him she had deliberately read that letter. No— but he would guess her reason.

And again her mind was busy about the letter. Was he certain to find out the mistake he had made? Unless the other woman wrote to him, unless they were in correspondence, it was possible that he would never find out. The woman could not answer a letter she had never had. She might not write to Eustace.

Lena remembered the newspapers which had come that day and which she had not yet opened. An announcement of her approaching marriage with Eustace had been sent to *The Morning Post*. It might have been published that morning. She got up, went quickly to the house and tore open *The Morning Post*. She looked. Yes, the announcement was there.

No doubt the woman would see it. Women always saw things of that kind. Or someone else would see it, and tell her. Anyhow she would know. And, knowing, she might never write. She would realize that Eustace had done what she had asked him to do, and she might let the matter rest. For she was afraid—she was afraid.

And she, Lena, was afraid too. She shivered with fear of the future, of Eustace, of herself. But, perhaps strangely, the greatest fear she had was lest Eustace should ever know what she had done. Knowing his guilt—for surely it was guilt to trick a sincere loving woman as he had thought to trick her—she could only think of her own at this moment. That was ridiculous, contemptible, perhaps. She knew almost every woman would think so. Yet it was so. Her sense of her own guilt was so strong that it almost overpowered her sense of his—just then.

But when the deep night had come, and she was alone in her bedroom with the door locked a reaction set in, and out of her depths it seemed that a woman she had never before known arose, a woman fierce and tenacious and bitter, a woman who might be capable of some terrible action. This woman said to Lena:

"Cast away all the delicate niceties, all the foolish, impotent absurdities of conduct and breeding that are expected by village fools and county nobodies from the 'ladylike' woman. They are no good to you or to anyone else who has blood in her veins and a heart that can feel and be outraged. That man is pledged to you. Hold him to his pledge. Don't say a word of what you know. Don't betray by a tremor or a look or even a sigh your knowledge. Be perfectly natural. Be as you have always been with him. You have never acted in your life—act now! You can do it because you are a woman. The woman you are must play the part of the woman you were. Marry him in spite of that letter."

And Lena listened in the night to this woman and felt as if she must obey her.

IV

Four days had gone by and Eustace Henley was in the Brinkton express going home from London. He was travelling second-class in a smoking carriage, and happened to be alone. As he half sat, half lay, on the seat with his long legs stretched across the passageway, and his feet on the opposite cushion, he looked remarkably lean and remarkably muscular, a strong, healthy, active man, of the country rather than of the town. He had a briar pipe in his mouth and a cap on his thick, rather rough auburn hair. On his brown, freckled face there was what is sometimes called a "strained" expression. Despite his obvious health of body he looked like a worried, almost like a desperate man. He had *The Times* by his side, and a book on his knees open, but he was not reading. He pulled hard at his pipe and stared at the opposite wall, then out of the window, then again at the wall. On it hung a long photograph of Furness Abbey. He gazed at the Abbey with all his might. He had never seen it, probably never would see it, but he was sure he would never forget what it was like. It seemed to be connected with his thoughts and his troubles, mysteriously like a building in a nightmare.

Furness Abbey—and doubt! Furness Abbey—and dread Furness Abbey—and a trap! Furness Abbey—and the end of a dream! Furness Abbey—and damnation!

But he had obeyed! He was proving his love by his obedience. She had begged him to help her by doing a certain thing and that thing he was going to do, if nothing had happened.

And that was just what he didn't know yet, whether a terrible thing had happened or had not happened. Well, he would be sure one way or the other in a very short time, to-night probably, at latest to-morrow.

No—he put it at to-morrow. The train didn't get in till six; then there was the drive in the dogcart. It would be better to call in the morning. Lena wouldn't expect him that evening, perhaps wouldn't expect him at all. He might find a word from her lying on his table at Easton. She hadn't written to him in answer to his letter from London. Certainly he had meant to be back two days ago and had been delayed. Still there might have been a letter.

And then another letter of his hadn't been answered. Not that it had required an answer exactly. Indeed, when he wrote it he had wondered whether he would ever get a reply to it, or whether a silence would mark the end of an episode which had turned up his heart as earth is turned up by a plough. He had wondered then, but now he had a knife-like reason for wondering, a reason that seemed to cut into him and that hurt him devilishly. This reason was an uncertainty.

Presently he looked down at the book on his knees. It dealt with the conflict between Religion and Science, and his eyes fell on the words:

> "But the Universe is nothing more than such a cloud—a cloud of suns and worlds. Supremely grand though it may seem to us, to the Infinite and Eternal Intellect it is no more than a fleeting mist."

A fleeting mist—the Universe.

"And I in it," thought Henley, trying to feel his nothingness. "And I sit here almost in a sweat because I don't feel sure whether I addressed an envelope right or wrong!"

The mind does odd things, unaccountable things, at times. Henley's mind had done this: it had led him to write Lena's name and address on an envelope intended by him for another woman. But perhaps that was not very strange. For that day he had been in an excited, emotional condition, and had written five letters at a sitting. With his mind painfully full of Lena in connection with another woman he had by accident written her name and address on two envelopes, and had stamped and posted them with no suspicion that he had made a dreadful mistake. His mind had been, or had seemed to be, quite at ease about that matter. That night he had slept well. But apparently during the hours of sleep a part of his mind, the subconscious part, must have been at work and troubled, for when he woke in the morning his very first conscious thought had been:

"I don't remember writing Enid's name and address yesterday afternoon!"

He had sat up in bed stung by this thought, and then his mind had seemed to make the announcement to him:

"You didn't write her name and address yesterday."

Ever since then he had been mentally disturbed, almost distracted. He might of course have written again or have telegraphed to Enid. He had not done so for fear his strange suspicion might be confirmed, and lest the confirmation might horrify her. If he asked her whether she had received the letter he had written to her, and she had not received it, he knew she would be in an agony of terror lest it had fallen into other hands. That must never be. If he had made this dreadful mistake Enid must never know of it.

Who had the letter if it had not gone to Enid? Could he possibly have addressed it to Lena? That was the question which haunted him perpetually. The most subtle part of his mind, that part which retains all knowledge of what a man has done, learnt, experienced, in his life, would not be frank with him about the matter. Again and again he seemed to be on the very edge of clear knowledge, and again and again something seemed to intervene between him and it. He knew nothing. But he felt that if he had not sent the letter to Enid it had gone to Lena and to no other.

But perhaps the whole thing was rot. He had been terribly upset lately. Life had gone hard with him, and when life goes hard with a man he often loses complete control of his faculties. Perhaps his nerve force had been weakened without his knowing it, and now his nerves were playing him tricks. Probably it would turn out all right and he would be able to laugh at himself in a few hours. For of course he would know for certain, at latest by to-morrow, whether he had been the damnedest fool that had ever walked on the earth or whether he was merely thrown off his balance by the pressure of circumstances. He would know, he would very soon know.

The train drew into Harley Junction and stopped. This was the last stop before Brinkton. Eustace got out, went to the refreshment room and ordered a cup of black coffee and a glass of brandy. He tipped the little glass over and let the brandy run into the coffee, then drank it off. The engine whistled, and he hurried back to his compartment. "How on earth would Lena take such a thing?"

He had a great opinion of Lena though he did not love her. It would hurt him terribly to hurt her. And it would hurt him terribly to be known by her as what he was. Suddenly he saw himself in a new light— as a blackguard.

"But I meant all right!" he said to himself, "I was trying to do the best for Enid."

But somehow that didn't console him, and he ended with a thorough man's thought:

"Women are the very devil."

He stared out of the window. The country was growing terribly familiar to him. He had hunted over those fields, had shot those coverts. There was old Pennywell's stud farm.

"Good God, if I've really done it!"

He had a writhing sensation in the pit of his stomach, and suddenly jerked his feet off the opposite seat and sat straight up. His kit bag was up on the rack. He stood up, stretched out a long arm and hauled it down. Then he knocked out his pipe, looked at his watch. The train was a bit late, ten minutes or so. All the better! Lena wouldn't expect him that evening.

Perhaps she would never expect him again.

He took off his cap, exchanged it for a soft hat, and began to whistle.

"It'll be all right … my nerves have been playing me tricks."

The train began to slow down.

"What on earth will happen with Lena if I have done it?"

The whistle died away on his lips.

"I should hate to hurt a woman like that. And what a last of blackguards she will think me."

There was the south signal box.

He turned to gather up all his things. The book he had taken with him to read lay, open still, on the seat. He picked it up and before he shut it again looked at the page.

"The Universe is nothing more ... than a cloud of suns and worlds—"

Then what does it matter if things do go wrong? If the Universe is only a cloud, a fleeting mist, what are we? Nothing matters.

He repeated that to himself, but it didn't convince him. He felt that what happened to him was terrifically important. And when he thought of Lena knowing, the Universe seemed as nothing beside one woman with eyes that looked at him, a mind that knew just what he was, and a heart that, perhaps, he had irreparably injured.

When he got out at the station he ran across Mrs. Parkins, who had come down from London first class, having been up for the night. She was a hard-bitten, good-hearted woman, with a figure like a ramrod, and a face which looked as if all the storms had gone over it.

"Ah!" she said. "Back again! Do you know why I went up—the chief reason?"

"I haven't an idea."

"One can't get wedding presents in Brinkton."

"That's too good of you."

"I went to a music hall, too, but that was by the way."

In the station yard he found his high dogcart waiting, with his groom, Scawling. He pitched in his bag, took the reins and sprang in, thankful to be doing something definite. The blue roan pulled at the bit. They were off.

"I shall soon know now," Eustace said to himself.

On the way he talked to the groom. Anything to keep his mind busy and off that infernal subject.

Not long after half-past six they turned a corner and came into the long village street, or rather road, bordered by stretches of grass and narrow paths, from which the houses were set back, many of them in small gardens. Eustace saw several acquaintances. There was Mrs. Portyon, majestic in corpulence, talking volubly over her double chin to Mrs. Pratt, the wife of the veterinary surgeon. She saw him and bowed with a smiling dignity which looked somehow official, yet intimate too.

"A married man soon!" that smile seemed to say. "How will you like it?"

Mrs. Cheelsman was close to the post office, with a string bag in her hand. She was seldom seen in the village without a string bag. Her greeting eyes were sharply inquisitive.

"Have you been getting the ring?"

A little further on he saw Miss Vyner, with a racquet in her hand, walking with young Chetwood. No doubt they had been up to tennis at

Sutton Grange, the last house in the village, where the Arlingfords lived. Miss Vyner waved her hand, and young Chetwood playfully shook his fist as the dogcart spun by. Why? Chetwood was always doing some absurd thing for no particular reason. His aim was fun, fun at all costs, fun though the world ceased from revolving.

There was little Doctor Mills driving his Ford.

"Hullo, Henley! Been up to get the trousseau?"

In the distance now Eustace saw a woman walking alone. Could it be Lena? His heart gave a thump, then seemed to stand still. No, it was only Miss Pyford, probably coming from the new cottages on the Lington Road after sitting with some old woman. Her figure was something like Lena's but her face wasn't half so pleasant, though no doubt she was a good sort in her way.

Out of the village at last!

Soon he pulled up the horse at Easton on the top of the hill looking down on the village.

His housekeeper met him at the door.

"Well, Mrs. Green! How are you?"

"Quite well, thank you, sir."

"Any letters?"

"A few, sir, in the study."

"Ah! Any—any notes?"

"There's one, sir, from Miss Wareham."

Eustace stood still.

"From Miss Wareham! When did it come?"

"This morning, sir. I was wondering whether it might be to ask you to dinner to-night."

"Oh, no—not likely! However, I'll just see."

He walked slowly into the study, went straight to the writing table, and took up Lena's note, which was lying apart from the letters. He looked at the address, then turned, went to the door and shut it, after calling out:

"No tea, thank you, Mrs. Green. It's too late."

"Well, I should think so!" thought the housekeeper to herself. "What a funny thing for Mr. Henley to trouble to say!"

When the door was shut Eustace went slowly back to the table, took up the note and held it for a moment in his hand, without opening it.

"What's in it? What the devil is in it?"

Looking back at that moment he could not remember ever before having felt that he was a coward. But he felt a thorough coward now. He was afraid to open that note. His touch on it told him nothing of what was inside the envelope.

"I'm certainly not occult, or psychic, or whatever they call it!" he thought. "Well, here goes!"

He drew a long breath, tore open the envelope and swiftly glanced at the note. Then he threw up one arm with a muffled exclamation which he would have liked to turn into a shout.

"Thank God! Thank God! I didn't! She doesn't know! It's all right! It's jolly well all right!" His relief was so immense that just then, in spite of his great trouble—the breaking with Enid—he was a joyful man. He threw himself down in an armchair and read the note through again.

> CHILHAM CORNER,
> SUTTON DERING.
> *June* 20, 19—.

DEAREST EUSTACE,

I got your dear letter, and would have answered it had I known you would be delayed in London. Do forgive me. I have been replying to letters of congratulation all these days and have had many visitors. How kind people are! If you feel inclined do come down and dine with me to-night, about eight. Don't trouble to dress. You won't have much time I know. With love,

> Yr. very affectionate
> LENA.

"Mrs. Green! Mrs. Green!"

He was at the study door calling.

"Sir?" said the housekeeper in answer.

"I'm dining out—with Miss Wareham. Just tell Scawling to bring round the dogcart in half an hour."

"Very well, sir. I thought as much."

"You're wiser than I am, Mrs. Green! Now for a bath!"

He ran up the stairs singing.

"He is glad to be back!" said Mrs. Green in the servants' quarters. "It's a pity the dinner will be wasted."

"I expect most of her dinner would be if he wasn't to go," returned the cook, who knew what it was to love.

After his bath Eustace came down looking grave. Already the exultation caused by his sensation of escape from a horror had abated and he was thinking of Enid. But he still felt much happier than he had, till that afternoon, since he had asked Lena to marry him. And then he felt so much less of a blackguard now he realized that he had not been found out.

"I am doing the right thing by Enid," he thought. "And now Lena will never know that I'm doing the wrong thing by her."

Then he got again into the dogcart and drove down the hill.

V

Not long after ten Eustace was back again at Easton. He got into an old smoking jacket, lit a cigar and went into his study. He wanted to think about the evening.

Lena had been charming to him, perfectly charming. He had never known her to be so vivacious, so lively before. And she had looked unusually nice, too, better looking than usual, he thought. What had she done to herself? He wasn't quite sure. Her hair—he fancied she had done something to her hair, pulled it out a bit, made more of it. Her complexion was always good, but he had never noticed it so much as to-night, never realized before its smoothness, its delicacy. It hadn't looked countrified to-night although it had looked delightfully healthy. And she had worn a particularly pretty dress, which he didn't remember having seen before, a new dress no doubt. For she had dressed for the evening although she had told him not to. She had excused herself by saying that the day had been so hot and that she felt cooler in a low gown.

Women loved clothes, and after all Lena was a thorough woman. He had noticed that fact to-night, too, more sharply than he had noticed it before. Perhaps being engaged was making a difference in Lena. What more likely? He thought about her eyes. He had never thought much about them hitherto, to tell the truth. They were not brilliant, extraordinary eyes like Enid's, eyes that played on a man's senses, that drove him to folly or to deadly earnestness. But there was a lot of expression in them. At least there had been to-night. Two or three times they had looked at him very strangely, with a sort of intense observation. He had been thankful then that she did not know, thankful that those eyes would never see him as a blackguard.

He wondered exactly what she thought of him, whether she had ever tried to sum him up. Women were given to that sort of thing, to trying to get at the heart of a man, at the heart of a man's secret. And they always thought they had the power to do that.

If they only knew! If Lena only knew!

Very likely she thought she had summed him up and knew his nature to the core. She would never know that.

He stretched out his long legs. The house was perfectly quiet. His servants went to bed early, the three women who looked after him.

The talk had run easily enough at dinner. Lena had talked the most, had been quite brilliant in her quiet way. She was certainly not a dull woman. He had spoken to her of the book he had taken in the train down, and had even quoted to her that passage about the Universe being only a cloud, a fleeting mist. Her eyes had looked particularly strange at that moment. And she had said:

"Some of the mist can feel very much, can't it?"

And then they had had a sort of argument about how much things mattered. That had been nearly at the end of dinner, just before they went into the garden. He had said that it was a great mistake to take life too seriously, too egoistically, as if what occurred to one were of tremendous importance. He had spoken quite like a philosopher, he believed, and had striven to give the impression that whatever happened to himself in the course of his life he would endure it with a high courage, even with a light heart.

And all this talk of his had really been a sort of lecture addressed to himself, an admonition after the events of that day, which had exposed to him his own weakness, his keen sensitiveness, his unexpected faculty of fear.

Lena had listened to him attentively, and when at last he had asked for her opinion on this high matter of the conduct of life she had said:

"Perhaps men feel things less than women do. I don't mean physical pain for I often think they feel that more than we do. I mean mental things. I don't believe any woman who is actually unhappy has ever been able to feel as if it didn't matter."

He had been rather startled for a moment by her tone and had said:

"But surely, Lena, you've never been specially unhappy!"

And then she had said, smiling:

"Oh, I've had a very prosperous, comfortable life. But I have observed other women in my small way. Women are terribly individualistic. Even in games one sees that."

And then she had got up and they had gone into the garden. He had smoked there. They had gone to sit on a semi-circular bench in front of a sundial. Lena had led the way there when he had been inclined to sit down on one of the benches on the terrace. And he had fancied that perhaps she had—well, anyhow he had given her a kiss there.

There was something decidedly strange about Lena. He didn't know exactly what it was, but he had felt it just then, had felt that she was not the ordinary type of good-hearted, countrified, thoroughbred but somewhat inexperienced humanity that he had imagined her to be.

"There's more in her than I had supposed," was his verdict on her now, as he sat thinking things over.

Certainly she had interested him more to-night than she had ever done before, but possibly that was because of his own peculiar state of mind. The revulsion of feeling which he had experienced from fear to relief had made him exceptionally alive to-night, exceptionally sensitive to impressions.

And he had felt so thankful to her all through the evening for not knowing!

The dinner had been excellent. Even the wine had been sound. And how very comfortable and cosy the house looked.

He had suggested a speedy wedding and she had quickly agreed. Why should they wait? He would settle that matter to-morrow.

Married to Lena! How would that be?

He lay back and followed the floating smoke of his cigar as it rose mysteriously in the air, widening out furtively, thinning, fading away.

How much did she love him?

Till to-night she had never debated that question. She loved him. If he had to marry at least he must have a loving wife. Otherwise he couldn't stand being married for a moment. She loved him and that was enough. It would, he supposed, later on be his only solace, his only reward, for having sacrificed himself for Enid.

Enid had one fault; she was undoubtedly a coward in love.

He began to meditate about Lena's courage, or lack of courage. What, for instance, would she sacrifice for him, the man whom she loved?

Enid wouldn't sacrifice her reputation. Perhaps there was always something a woman wouldn't sacrifice; perhaps the legend of woman's marvellous unselfishness in love was solely a legend propagated by women for their own purposes.

He couldn't imagine any man asking Lena to sacrifice her reputation for him. She was not the sort of woman who gets asked to do that sort of thing.

But what sort of woman exactly was she? Funny that when you get engaged to a woman you begin to ask yourself such questions! Formerly he had felt that Lena belonged definitely to a country type very familiar in England. Now, for some reason which he couldn't quite define, he felt that she was not wholly typical, at any rate not so typical as he had always supposed her to be.

Surely Enid would answer that letter of his, the letter which had given him such a devil of a time. She was bound to answer it if she cared for him at all. Mere decency would prompt a reply to a letter in which he had told her that he was obeying her, was sacrificing himself because she asked him, implored him to do so. But she certainly wasn't in any very great hurry to reply. Four days had gone by since his letter was sent. And she lived in Sussex—not far off. He wondered how his letter had struck her; whether it had been a great blow to her to learn that he had taken her at her word, that he was going to be married. Women were so damned odd! They sometimes begged you to do a thing and then, when you did it, they were as upset as the very devil! Men weren't like that.

Now a man, for instance—would he have done what Enid had done? Apparently she had never thought how cruel it was to give another woman a husband who couldn't love her!

But, come to that, no more had he—until he was afraid that perhaps he had misaddressed that letter!

"Jolly odd we human beings are!" was his mental comment at this point.

Enid had certainly thought a great deal about herself in spite of being so much in love with him. Perhaps she wasn't the unselfish type of woman. He had been ready for the plunge, but she hadn't. That was the difference between them. He had had more courage than she had. No doubt about that!

He happened to forget just here that Enid was married and that he was not—yet.

But Enid had not a strong character. Perhaps part of her fascination lay in that. It might be so. Difficult to know!

Lena's character, he fancied, was strong. To-night he had seemed to gather that from her. He didn't quite know why.

What on earth could have put it into his head that he had not sent that had letter to Enid? He couldn't understand it. His mind had never played him such a trick before, had never made him sweat with fear for no reason at all. For there could have been no reason for his panic. He had written three other letters that day, but he felt positive he had not addressed Enid's letter to any one of those friends. He still couldn't remember ever writing Enid's address on any envelope while he was in London, but since—thank God—Lena had not received his letter to Enid it must have gone to the right address. His mind was now quite at ease about that.

And probably to-morrow his certainty would be made doubly sure. Enid was pretty certain to write. If she didn't he would feel that she had treated him damned badly after all he had done for her. But she would write. Not a doubt of it!

His cigar was smoked out. He threw away the end and got up.

What a quiet finish to a day he wouldn't forget in a hurry! He looked round his room. It wasn't uncomfortable but Lena's rooms certainly looked far more attractive. Her house of course was better than his and better run, too, though Mrs. Green didn't do at all badly.

Lena certainly knew how to run her house.

He went slowly upstairs to bed.

Enid was bound to let him have a word in answer to his letter. He counted on that to-morrow, at latest after to-morrow.

When he was between the sheets he realized that he was unusually tired.

"Worry takes it out of a man more than anything else," he thought, "and I worried like hell in the train down."

It was almost joy—the death of the reason for worry.

But there never had been a reason. His mind had created the bogy which had put him into a sweat.

Lena was not an ordinary woman—something odd about her—

He slept.

VI

The marriage of Miss Wareham and Eustace Henley was fixed for the twenty-fifth of July. Mr. Portyon would therefore be able to celebrate it without breaking his cure at Bath, "a manifest advantage for everyone" as Mrs. Portyon was good enough to say.

Wedding presents began to flow in. It became evident that Lena was a popular woman. Not only did she receive an astonishing number of gifts—that was perhaps to be expected because she knew almost everybody in the southern part of the county—but they were handsome and carefully chosen gifts, evidently selected with affection. As Mrs. Arlingford, of Sutton Grange, remarked, "Folks didn't merely sling blotters at Lena Wareham." And the messages which accompanied the various parcels were exceptionally warm, not formal, but genuinely cordial.

Lena was surprised and touched by all the friendliness and affection directed to her address. She was rather a humble woman by nature and she had not expected them. And yet they made life bitter rather than sweet to her. For there seemed a great irony in this outpouring from the hearts of people she was merely fond of, or not even that—just kindly disposed towards, while the one human being on whom she could have concentrated the whole of her love was only pretending to her. Often she wondered how many of these kind people could have continued to care for her if they knew her as she was, knew what she had done and what she was doing, if they could penetrate her motives, trace her actions to their source. What was she? A woman who from indignant curiosity and jealousy had deliberately possessed herself of a secret affecting two lives, and who was about to marry a man who not merely did not love her, but who was going to become her husband in obedience to the whim of the woman he did love. She would become Eustace's wife because a woman whose name she did not know was afraid.

Or—would she become Eustace's wife?

She had allowed the wedding day to be fixed, but she didn't know whether she would go to the altar, absolutely she didn't know.

Her life seemed to have escaped from her control ever since the night when she had done something which, so she often said to herself, it wasn't in her real nature to do. She had defied her real self and the result was that she had lost control of the good and evil which made up the whole called Lena Wareham. Love, it seemed, had betrayed her into the mud, and now she remained there, not knowing whether at the last moment she would make an effort to struggle out, or whether she would sink lower in it. Sometimes she was tempted to tell Eustace what she had done, was on the edge of telling it, but always the woman whom she had never known, or even suspected the existence of, till the night when she had gone up to bed after reading the letter—it had become the only letter that existed to her—intervened and prevented her, as if forcibly, from the revelation of the truth.

She still loved Eustace.

That was astounding to her and made her sometimes feel a contempt for her womanhood. Of course she had read, and heard of, many women who once their affections are fixed on an object cannot detach them whatever happens. She didn't admire such women. It seemed to her that they illustrated a sort of mania which was totally undeserving of either admiration or respect. By nature, and perhaps also because of her way of life, she was a very modest woman, and a love which drove itself into an object and which couldn't be extricated, or extricate itself, seemed to her immodest. She could never wish to hate Eustace, although the woman who was part of her and who yet seemed strange to her, sometimes tried to whisper suggestions of hatred in the night, but she did wish to unlove him. For now she condemned him.

Her feeling of her own guilt—for she called it that—had not lessened, but the feeling of his guilt had increased. She saw herself on the level of that servant whom she had caught reading one of her letters; but she also saw Eustace on a level with men whom in theory she despised, with liars, deceivers of women, the root-and-branch insincere of the world.

Nevertheless she continued to love him, and couldn't conceive of ever loving another man, of ever allowing any other man to be her husband. His body was the only body in the world she could ever give her body to. And as for the soul—well, that strange and apparently wholly physical conviction of hers seemed to comprise in some mysterious way the soul's meanings, too. She didn't understand it; but it was so.

All this time she was of course acting a part. Nobody found that out. But almost everybody noticed a change—some called it a great change—in her. This was generally attributed to the action of love.

"Love always changes a woman!" said Mrs. Cheelsman, in her most definite manner. "It changed me."

"Lena is certainly different," said Mrs. Parkins. "She was asleep, and now she's awake. And I for my part prefer wide-awake people."

"It's had an extraordinary effect on her clothes," observed Miss Vyner to young Chetwood. "They fit her quite differently. They used to hang on her. Now they seem moulded to her."

"Jolly odd that!" he returned. "I wonder if I should get rid of the crease my tailor always leaves between the shoulders if I got thoroughly spoony.... What?"

"Lena Wareham is much more definite than she was," said Mrs. Portyon to the rector. "Young Henley is not marrying a nobody. Far from it. Lena may turn out quite a remarkable married woman."

"Remarkable my dear! Oh, I trust not!" said the Rector. "I like the womanly woman."

"You surely ought to know, if anyone does, that it is quite possible for a woman to be both womanly and remarkable," said Mrs. Portyon, with some acerbity, as she took up a half-knitted stocking of brown wool.

Henry was a good man but he could be very irritating at times. And he would never be a Bishop.

"I wonder whether he will come down the hill or whether she will go up?" she presently murmured to herself.

That was a great question in the village, and it had not been decided yet.

"We shall have to settle where we are going to live, Lena," Eustace said to Miss Wareham one day.

Two or three times already he had alluded to this obviously important matter, but each time she had managed subtly to get away from the subject.

"And where shall we go for the honeymoon?" he added.

"The honeymoon!" she said, almost as if she were startled.

"Well, we must go somewhere."

"Yes, of course. I'll think it over."

"Do; and about our home?"

After a pause she said:

"Where do you wish to live?"

"I'm very fond of Easton, of course. But Chilham Corner is a much better house, and I suppose you're attached to it."

They were in her garden, and now she looked round over the lawn, the bright flowerbeds, the yew hedges, the copse at the end of the pond.

"Yes; I've always been here. But—how would it be if we tried another place?"

"Left Sutton Dering?" he said, astonished. "But all your friends?"

"We shall be starting a new life. Wouldn't it be better to start in a new place—perhaps?"

"And you mean—let Easton and Chilham Corner?"

"We might. Places let very easily round here."

"I'll do what you wish," he said. "I want to make you happy."

"I'll think it over," she answered.

When he had gone she walked up and down in the garden for a long time. It was dreadful how she shied away from that new life of which she had spoken. She dared not contemplate it even now when the wedding day was so near. In her writing table drawer was the letter locked up. She had not destroyed it though several times she had thought of doing so, but she had never read it again. It was in her memory, almost every word of it. There was no need to keep it. Always she would have it with her whether she burnt it or not. As long as she lived it would be her horrible possession. Evidently the other woman, whose name she didn't know, had never written to Eustace since the day when he wrote that letter. Otherwise surely he would know what he had done. And she felt sure that he didn't know. On the evening when he dined with her after his return from London she had detected a change in him, as he had fancied he detected a change in her, but she had not entirely understood it. When they had first met he had sent her, she thought, an almost furtive searching glance, and during the evening he had often seemed to be watching her more closely than usual, with a concentration which had seemed to her new in him. But perhaps she had imagined that, knowing what she knew. Her own furtiveness might have deceived her. And since then he had seemed natural enough. He could certainly act well. Of late, in spite of what she knew, he had seemed quite fond of her. He was a wonderfully good actor.

Presently she went into the house.

Where were they going to live together, he and she? Or were they going to live together at all?

It was the fifteenth of July, only ten days to the wedding day, and, owing to her, they had not even decided on their future home. When the neighbours had been inquisitive she had put them off. She had said she was so busy that she hadn't dealt with that question. They would have two houses. Perhaps they would live first in one, then in the other, going up the hill when the weather was hot, coming down it when the weather was cold to be sheltered. They would, perhaps, try the two houses together before deciding on a permanent home. And they might travel a little before settling down.

"She knows what she means to do, but she won't tell us!" was the general opinion in the village.

"Love has made Lena turn whimsical," said Mrs. Cheelsman.

"Perhaps they're quarrelling about it," observed Miss Pyford, who having now made up her mind that spinsterhood was her permanent lot looked with a jaundiced eye upon matrimony.

Ten days more! What would happen in those ten days?

As the wedding day drew nearer Lena had become more acutely aware of the horror of her situation. Often an intense desire to change it by telling Eustace the truth possessed her. If she hadn't loved him so much—so contemptibly she often said to herself—she might, perhaps, have told him already. But she had a great fear of lowering herself in his opinion.

"At least he respects me," she said to herself. "He doesn't love me but he admires my character. He believes in me. He thinks me sincere, honest, straight. And am I to lose all that?"

And then memory gave her his words in the letter: "a thorough good sort.... a face you can trust.... kind eyes with an honest look in them.... I can imagine her helping to keep a fellow very straight."

Straight! How could she tell him she had been crooked with him?

And yet that was the only straight thing to do. She unlocked the drawer and took out the letter.

"Suppose I tell him? How will he take it? What will he think of me?"

She unfolded the letter and held it on her knees, looking at a phrase here and there. The large erratic writing brought back to her sharply the memory of the shock she had had when she opened it in the garden.

"Faun."

That was what he was to the other woman, while to her he was Eustace. She had never given him a nickname, had never even thought of doing so. Had they ever been intimate? Were they intimate now? Were they not two strangers about to marry each other? Quite certainly she was a stranger to him. But is a man, can a man ever be a stranger to a woman who really loves him? Lena asked herself that question and something within her said "No." It seemed to her then that she did understand Eustace. He was weak in a certain way, swayed by his passions, erratic, quick enough but not brilliant, good at all sports, not far from nature, thoroughly masculine, an ordinary man enough, but very much a man. She read the letter right through again. And to-day she felt impartial enough to understand how it would have appealed to the other woman if she had ever read it. Probably she would have cried over it; perhaps she would have been angry at it. But she would certainly have felt that the man who had written it meant chivalrously towards her. He was doing his best by her against his own desires, in defiance of his root inclination.

Would that woman have liked the closing part of the letter

Lena read it carefully, read it twice.

"No, she wouldn't have liked it. Probably she would have hated it. The praise was too strong. But it was only praise really of moral qualities. Perhaps the woman wouldn't have minded it very much. For what are moral qualities in a woman to a man when compared with physical qualities?

"Nothing passionate or erratic about her. I shouldn't think she's had a sleepless night because of a man in her life."

Suddenly Lena felt a burning wish that Eustace could know her not as she had been once, but as she was now. For she had developed in the last few weeks, developed tremendously. He would be surprised if he knew what lay beneath the surface of "the homely sort of woman," who was so quiet, who was all right at games and fond of gardening.

All right at games! That praise stung her specially to-day. She was glad that other woman had never read about her.

"But he didn't think I had a feeble nature even then," she said to herself.

And then presently came the thought: "Suppose I tell him!"

All she had to do was to enclose the letter in an envelope and write Eustace's name and address on the envelope.

There was stationery on the writing table. She stretched out her arm and took an envelope from the case, put the letter in it, stuck the envelope down. After a pause she got up, reached for a pen and sat before the writing table. She leaned her head on her hand.

"What will happen if I send this?" she thought. Finally she wrote Eustace's name and address on the envelope.

"But I won't send it to-day," she resolved. "Perhaps to-morrow. Yes— to-morrow."

In an upstairs room in the house the wedding presents were gathered together. She left the letter lying on the table and went upstairs to look at them again, and she realized all the horror of a broken engagement, the scandal in the county, the talk in the village, the questions, the lies which would have to be told. For to tell the truth would be absolutely impossible.

One departure from the rule of a lifetime, the rule of absolute sincerity, and what a train of insincerities in its wake!

"Can I ever do it?" she thought.

And her courage seemed to fail. Would it not be easier to persevere along the path of deception?

At this moment Susan came in to look for her and smiled at seeing her among all the gifts.

"They do make a fine show, don't they, ma'am?" she said. "No wonder you like to look at them. I'm sure no one ever—"

"Yes, they are beautiful. Did you want me?"

"Mr. Henley has called again, ma'am."

"Mr. Henley? Where is he?"

"He went into your room, ma'am."

"My room!" said Lena, turning pale.

The maid looked surprised.

"The writing room, ma'am. The door was open and—you're not feeling unwell, ma'am?"

"No, of course not! I'll go to him."

The letter on the writing table—had he seen it?

If so, had he opened it? He had the right to. It was addressed to him.

For a moment she felt paralysed with fear, and did not know how to move.

Susan looked at her in wonder.

"Oh, ma'am, what is it? I'm sure you're not well! Let me—"

"No, no, I'm perfectly well. I'll go down to Mr. Henley at once."

With an effort she forced herself to move, to descend the stairs. But she kept her hand on the balustrade all the way down.

VII

When Lena came into the writing room Eustace was standing by the table with the letter in his hand as if about to open it.

"Don't, Eustace!" she said sharply. "Don't open that letter!"

"But isn't it—"

"Yes. But don't open it now."

She went up to him and took the letter out of his hand.

"But why not? You addressed it to me?"

"I know."

His large red-brown eyes were looking at her with a sort of searching surprise.

"And I'm not to read it!"

"Not to-day."

"But Lena—what's up? What have you been writing to me about?"

She forced a smile.

"That's my secret for the moment."

With a hand that shook in spite of her effort to keep it still she laid the letter down on the table.

"What is it, Eustace? Why have you come back?"

"I don't think you're very glad to see me," he rejoined, in a voice that sounded hurt.

"Of course I am glad. But what is it?"

Instead of answering her he said:

"You look odd to-day."

"Odd?"

"Yes. What's the matter?"

He looked towards the letter.

"Why should you write to me? We see each other every day."

"Yes."

"Then what can there be to write about?"

"You mustn't expect women to be like men."

"I don't."

"There are things women don't care to speak about."

"But to the man who is going to be your husband!"

"Going—but we aren't married yet."

He looked uneasy, impatient.

"I can't understand it," he said. "And I don't like secrets."

"Have you never had one?"

"I!" He lowered his eyes. "Well, if it comes to that I suppose almost everyone—"

"Then leave me mine for—for a little while."

After a slight pause he said:

"Very well. I came back to ask you if you could possibly put up my married sister for the wedding. You see Easton's so small, that with my mother, Lily, my unmarried sister, and Arbuthnot, my best man, the place will be full. Of course, we weren't sure Margaret could come. But I found a letter at the post office, just arrived. And she will be here."

"I can put her up."

"You don't mind I hope?"

"How—how could I mind such a thing?"

"I don't know. I hate to put you to any inconvenience. But—"

"There's plenty of room for her here."

"Then—thank you very much," he said, uncomfortably. "Well, I'll be off now."

He moved, but again looked at the letter.

"Good-bye, Lena."

And he went away without even touching her hand.

When he was gone Lena said to herself desperately.

"I can't give it to him. I can never give it to him."

The mention of his people seemed to have made things worse. She realized now more sharply than ever what a scandal there would be if the match were broken off. The wound to her own heart, the injury to her life, she did not envisage so clearly just then, perhaps because she had been wounded already so deeply that she had become hardened, had given up the woman's natural quest for joy. The thought of parting from Eustace was agony to her, but she knew quite well that she couldn't be happy with him. She would always know that he hadn't wanted to marry her.

And yet during the last few days she had had moments when she had felt that he had a certain genuine fondness for her. He had seemed really to depend upon her, to value her society. In spite of what she knew she did not feel that he was bored with her, that he wanted to get away from her.

"He respects me!" she said to herself. "He likes me as a friend. Perhaps—perhaps someday he might—"

But not if she ever gave him the letter!

Eustace went back to Easton wondering about Lena. What could she have written to him about? Was it possible that she had a confession to make—Lena a confession? The idea seemed absurd. And yet the letter seemed to suggest something like that. A thing a woman can't say to the man she is going to marry in ten days must surely be a confession of some kind. And her look and manner had certainly been very strange. But Lena couldn't possibly have ever done a wrong thing—dear old Lena! If ever a woman was above suspicion she was! Everyone respected and many loved her. She was a thorough good woman. That was something to be proud of in a wife after all.

Suppose Enid had given in to him and had left her husband for him! What a scandal there would have been. Later on, of course, they would have been married, as soon as Enid had been divorced. But people would always have known, have looked askance at Enid. Many would no doubt have refused to know her, and even those who hadn't refused would have regarded her with a certain moral condescension, priding themselves on being "wide-minded" and expecting gratitude from the erring sister.

It would all have been a bit awkward. He hadn't thought of it at the time. He had been too much in love. But now, definitely confronting married life, he realized how very important it was for everything to be quite above board. His wife would be respected and sought after by everyone who knew her. She was immensely popular in her circle. He was glad of that. Lena's popularity made things much pleasanter for him.

Now what on earth could there have been in that letter?

By this time Eustace was at the top of the hill and entering the garden of Easton. As he went into the little hall the parlourmaid met him.

"There's a package for you, sir," she said. "I laid it on the table in your study."

"Oh! Perhaps a wedding present, eh, Annie?"

"That's what I was thinking, sir."

"Well, anyhow, I shan't have many. You should see Miss Wareham's."

"Oh, yes, sir. The whole village is talking about them. But she is that popular with everyone, isn't she? And then gentlemen don't never have so many as ladies, do they?"

"Rather not!"

He strolled into the study.

On his table lay a good-sized square parcel, done up in thick brown paper and sealed with blue sealing wax.

Blue sealing wax! Enid always used that. He snatched up the parcel. Her writing!

So she had sent him a wedding gift though she had never troubled to answer that letter of his. He stood and stared at the familiar handwriting, spidery and irregular, with its oddly formed r's, and its thickly crossed t's. Somebody had once said to him that Enid had a fantastic nature. Her handwriting seemed to bear that out. It was all over the place, but it was very characteristic. The sight of it moved him. Almost like a scent, but not so vividly, it brought back the past and a little of the wildness of life. Enid was a mixture of wildness and conventionality, but in her at the critical moment conventionality had triumphed. And perhaps it was as well that it had. He wasn't sure about that. For wildness had something sweet in it; something sweet that might, however, turn damnably bitter in the end. One never knew! He took out a pocketknife and cut the string of the parcel.

As he did this it occurred to him that there might be a letter inside enclosed with the wedding present. Probably, almost certainly, there would be a word of some kind. He threw the string aside and pulled at the wrappings. Under the brown paper there were some sheets of tissue paper. His strong fingers made short work of them. In a moment there was a litter of twisted shreds on the carpet, and a gold cigarette box with a monogram cut on the lid was exposed to his eager eyes.

He stared for a moment; he recognized the monogram. It was Enid's. Instead of a wedding present she had sent him back the gold box he had given to her after their first—well, when they had first come to an understanding.

"Damn!" he muttered.

He sat down, took hold of the box and mechanically opened it. Inside lay a folded sheet of pale yellow, thick, faintly scented notepaper. He lifted it out, unfolded it and read these words:

> I send you back your box. Of course, I need not say that I wish
> you happiness, but I think you might have sent me a line to tell
> me you were engaged instead of leaving me to find it out from
> the Morning Post. —E.

Eustace read the words twice, steadily.

"What the devil!—but she's mad!" he muttered. "But I—she can't mean it. It's a joke. She's malicious. She's trying to take a rise out of me."

The blood mounted to his face. He tingled all over, remembered his horrible suspicion in London, his fears in the train on the journey down to Sutton Dering, his immense relief when he found Lena's note asking him to dine.

"Oh, she's trying to take a rise out of me!" he repeated to himself desperately.

But he didn't believe it. He knew quite well he was telling a lie to himself. His fears had been well founded. He had really committed that incredibly careless action in London. He had really put his letter to Enid in the wrong envelope. He had always thought it strange that Enid had never replied. It was unlike her to take no notice of such a letter from him. Now he knew why she had never answered him.

"But where is the letter? Where the devil did I send it?" he thought.

He got on his feet and stood twisting Enid's note between his fingers. "Who has got it? Where did it go?"

He realized that someone had probably read it and kept it, someone who must certainly know by whom it had been written. But on that fatal morning he had only written to Lena and one or two of his intimate friends.

"Let's see! Whom did I write to?"

He had an excellent memory. He remembered quite clearly. He had written to Lena, to Arnuthnot, who was going to be his best man, to an old college chum, Henry Taylor, and to a married woman, Mrs. Clynes, who was an intimate friend of his and of his family's. Not one of them surely would have read and then kept such a letter.

Certainly neither of the men would have done such a thing. He had known them both nearly all his life. Even if they had glanced at the letter and realized its purport they would have sent it back to him. He could imagine Arbuthnot enclosing it with a remark to the effect that he, Eustace, was a damned careless fellow and ought to be ashamed of himself. Taylor might have taken such a thing rather differently. He would probably have suggested to Eustace that Eustace wasn't playing the game, and had better think things over before he made a good woman unhappy. Arbuthnot might have laughed at him, Taylor have read him a lecture. But neither of his friends would have kept silence.

There remained Mrs. Clynes. Eustace thought hard about her.

She was a charming woman, of the country, not of the town type, sensible, level-headed, kind, warmhearted. (He had always thought how well she would get on with Lena.) She spoke her mind freely, being essentially sincere, but she was never bigoted or disagreeable. How would she take such a letter as he had written to Enid? Well, she wouldn't read it—except the opening words by accident. He felt quite certain of that. He saw Mrs. Clynes glancing at the beginning, raising her rather arched eyebrows, stopping, laying the letter down and realizing things, then quickly slipping it into an envelope, addressing it, and promptly sending it back to him. That was what Mrs. Clynes would have done. He felt it in his bones. She had not done it; therefore she had not had the letter. He remembered her warm letter of congratulation to him in reply to his telling her of the engagement. No; he had not addressed the letter to Mrs. Clynes.

Well, but then the process of elimination was complete, and he was back again with—

He tore up Enid's note, the damnable note which had suddenly plunged him into misery, shut the cigarette box up in a drawer, picked up his cap, and went into the air. He passed through his gate, walked a little way up the country road, then turned to the right and, by a field path, gained a grass-covered open space which dominated a great view.

Below at his feet lay the long village of Sutton Dering; beyond stretched an immense undulating plain, divided up into large fields interspersed with small thickets; on the horizon rose the Malvern Hills. Evening was falling. The gentle, even pensive softness of summer in England at the hour of twilight almost mystically informed and enveloped the whole landscape. The rising smoke from the village looked delicately mysterious. Its suggestion of quiet lives, bounded by narrow horizons, was somehow pathetic. A dog barked in a farm. Some birds flew in line across a strip of lemon-coloured sky. The Malvern Hills turned from a deep blue to a soft and velvety black. From a Passionist monastery to the right of the village rose the faint voice of a bell. And the silence which followed was soft and sad. Yes, there was something sad in this dear England!

Eustace stood there on the soft, almost spongy, grass with his cap in his hand, and the slight breeze feeling round his hair. He had come to this height driven by an impulse which he could hardly have explained, which perhaps he scarcely understood, the impulse of a man who has had a shock to get away from four walls, to get away from people and to be alone for a little while. He had had the sensation in the house that he was "in" for something hateful.

Now he looked down over the village and instinctively his eyes sought for Chilham Corner. Of course he knew exactly where it lay, beyond the village, and away to the right. The light was failing now rather rapidly, but presently he thought he descried it, that faint blur over there beyond a small darkness of trees, the copse at the end of the pond. Lena was there with that letter which she hadn't allowed him to read.

Since he had received the gold box and its contents from Enid, and since he had thought things over, he was back again with the horrible suspicion which had tormented him in London and which had died on his arrival at Easton after the writing of his letter to Enid. But now it was fortified by recollections which crept through his memory like dry and cold snakes, and it was made much more hideous by a curious change in himself, of which, so it seemed to him, he had only just become aware.

Suddenly he realized that since his return from London Lena had come to mean much more to him than she had meant before. Either she had changed or, knowing her in a different way, he had become aware of qualities in her which had previously been hidden from him. At any rate he no longer thought of her as a country type. She was to him an individual, unlike all other women. He felt her strongly as a definite human influence. There was something in her that he cared for and there was something in her that he could be almost afraid of. There was something in Lena surely that was stronger than anything in Enid.

The message which he had just had from Enid, like a touch from a long unfelt hand, had startled him into knowledge. He had been slipping into forgetfulness of Enid during the last few weeks. Her silence had distressed him at first. Afterwards it had piqued and angered him. But, lately, had he not been ceasing to bother about it? Had he not been looking forward instead of backward?

And now this bombshell!

If Lena had received that cursed letter, if all this time she had kept it, meaning at the moment chosen by her to reveal the fact to him!

He remembered that since his return from London she had often seemed to him subtly different from the woman he had known before. He had noticed a difference on the very evening of his return; a new intensity in her eyes when they were for a moment fixed on him, a new swiftness and consciousness in her manner. And when they had gone out into the garden after dinner he had said to himself that there was something decidedly strange about Lena. Now, as the light rapidly faded away, and the gathering darkness withdrew from his eyes all the detail in the landscape at his feet, he remembered vividly how, on his return home that night after the dinner at Chilham Corner, he had sat up and smoked his pipe and meditated over the evening and had thought strongly about Lena as he had certainly never thought before.

"By Jove, I believe she had had the letter, and that was why she seemed different to me that night!" he said to himself.

And he shook his broad shoulders in a shiver.

"That was why I puzzled about her—perhaps!"

A sort of horror came over him with the thought. But then Lena hated him, and all this time she had been acting a part.

And surely she could not mean to marry him?

Perhaps she meant to punish him. But how?

That letter of hers—what was in that letter? Eustace now felt convinced that the envelope he had been on the point of opening that afternoon had contained something which would have brought him enlightenment if he had seen it. But how terrified Lena had looked when she saw him with it in his hand.

He was afraid—but she too was afraid!

Something dark slipped by him in the gathering night. He started violently, and looked after it. What was it? A dog no doubt. He had not been able to see. But he now felt that the loneliness was broken. There was life up here. Probably a shepherd was approaching, someone whom he could not yet see. He turned sharply, left the grassy space and was soon again in the country road.

As he walked back to Easton the darkness of night fell, and with it there came to him an increasing depression of spirit. He felt like one on the very edge of calamity! He had lost Enid, and during the last few weeks mysteriously he had become accustomed to that loss, had become indeed, as he now knew, almost, if not quite, reconciled to it. Was he now to lose Lena? For years he had lived alone, and had been happy enough in his bachelor freedom and independence. His work, his friends, his occasional light and not too engrossing love affairs, with plenty of sport had sufficed to fill up his life agreeably. But now a change had come about. Now he looked upon such a life as he had lived and it seemed to him dreary and lonely, almost horrible. He saw middle-age in the distance waiting for him and a shiver went through him. He wanted to hang on to something. If his engagement to Lena were broken now he felt as if it would break him. There would be nothing left for him then. Evidently he needed a woman's love even if he hadn't love to give in return for it. And he had been so calmly certain of Lena's affection for him. But if she had had the letter she must hate him, she must have been hating him ever since she had had it.

That was an ugly thought—that Lena hated him.

He saw in the darkness the shining of a light in Easton. A light in darkness looks like a welcome. But who was there to welcome him home in Easton? Only Mrs. Green and the maids.

"I can't stand this!" he said to himself. "Directly after supper I shall go down and have it out with Lena. Anything's better than this cursed uncertainty."

And, full of this determination, he hurried on to the house.

VIII

When Eustace had left Chilham Corner Lena went upstairs to her bedroom, taking the letter with her. She locked the bedroom door, took off her dress quickly, put on a dressing gown, and bathed her face with cold water. Then she put some eau de Cologne on her throbbing forehead, and lay down on a sofa near the wide-open windows which looked on to the garden. The shock she had had made her body feel as weak as if she were an invalid. There was no strength in her legs. Her hands shook when she held them out in front of her. And she had an odd, horrible feeling that water was running through her veins instead of warm, red blood.

She lay still and shut her eyes.

Faint sounds from the garden came up to her. She heard two voices speaking; no doubt a gardener and one of the maids. Yes, she heard Susan's pale, careful voice saying something, then the laugh of a man, then again Susan's voice, less pale, much less careful, almost pert this time. The twitter of birds, in lively conversation before going to bed, reached her, and she remembered her sharp realization of the separated worlds in the garden and pond, on the day when she had the letter. She heard her dog, Henry, bark. Henry was a fox terrier and much given to chasing things. Even a butterfly was not considered by him as unworthy of his attention. No doubt he was after something now. She opened her eyes and they rested on the letter. The sight of it renewed all her fear. How terrible it had been to see that letter in Eustace's hand. And yet— wouldn't it really have been better if she had come in too late, if she had not been in time to prevent him from reading it? Something decisive must happen. Things couldn't go on like this. This perpetual uncertainty, insincerity, apprehension, necessity for acting, tore her to bits body and soul.

Although her body felt weak and exhausted her mind was in fierce activity. It seemed to her ablaze, urgent with fiery demands which she knew not how to obey nor how to resist. She lay there and looked at the letter, or rather at the envelope which contained it, and her mind told her to do the strong thing, to thrust through her fear at whatever cost and come out into the open of sincerity. But her nature still shrank, still recoiled, still clung to the miserable present in which at least Eustace was with her in body however far divided from her in spirit. A voice within her said obstinately:

"I can't give him up. I can't go back to my lonely life. I can't let him know me as I am."

It never occurred to Lena as possible that complete sincerity might not break forever her relation to Eustace. She saw at this moment only two alternatives: to go on pretending and retain Eustace in her life, or to be sincere and see him go out of her life forever. She longed for sincerity; she loathed the atmosphere which she had created and in which she had been living during the past weeks; it was wholly unnatural to her; she almost stifled in it; and yet she did not know how to face the result of going out from it. And the fact that she had so nearly brought herself to the doing of the strong thing and, at the critical moment, had not dared to do it, seemed to have put a hideous impotence into her. Perhaps for the first time in her life she felt that she was a victim to herself, that herself had made of her a slave.

She had the distinct consciousness just then of being two in one, and the true woman in her, the woman she had hitherto known as herself, was at the mercy of the tyrant she had raised up when she had for the first time thrust that woman down into the mud where she could never dwell happily.

"I've made my own monster," she thought. "I'm one of the Frankensteins of the world."

And she shuddered.

Lena dined alone. She had forced herself to the effort of leaving her room and going down to dinner. But she had not put on an evening gown.

Susan, who was waiting at table, reported in the kitchen between the soup and the fish:

"I can't think what's come to Miss Lena to-night. She's as pale as skim milk, and sits there frowning."

"Frowning!" cried cook, as she transferred a nicely browned sole to a silver dish.

"Yes. She's got a frown fixed on her face. It might 'a' been nailed there."

"Well, I never!" said cook. "Can they have quarrelled?"

"She was very funny to-day when I went up to tell her he'd come back!" said Susan. "She seemed to come over ill all on a sudden when she heard he was waiting for her in the little room."

"Whatever can it be?" said the housemaid, with round eyes. "A nice thing if they've quarrelled just before the wedding day!"

A few minutes later Susan hurried in and exclaimed:

"Whatever do you think, cook? She's ordered the carriage!"

"The carriage! What for? What carriage?"

"The pony cart! And she's going out alone after dinner."

"Going! Wherever to at this time o' night?"

"She won't say, just said she wanted air and she'd go for a drive and take Henry with her for company."

"There's something up!" said cook solemnly. "I'll lay they've quarrelled and she's off to Easton to make it up."

When her dinner was finished and she had sat still for a time, Lena put on her hat and a light jacket and went downstairs. Simmons, her groom, had brought round the pony cart and lighted the lamps. He touched his cap when he saw her.

"Don't you want me with you, ma'am?" he asked.

"No, thank you. I shan't be very long. But it's hot to-night and I've a fancy to get some air. Here, Henry!" She caught up the eagerly panting dog and put him down on the floor of the cart, from which he immediately sprang upon the seat, barking with joy at the prospect of an unexpected adventure.

"He's not afraid of it!" thought Lena.

And for a moment she envied the delightful ignorance of animals.

Then she patted the sleek brown pony, took the reins, and got in.

"What's the time, Simmons?"

"After nine o'clock, ma'am, I think."

He pulled out a solid silver watch.

"No, it's twenty to ten, ma'am."

"I ought to be back in about an hour."

She touched the pony with the whip and drove off briskly.

"I wonder where she's going," he thought, looking after her. "She's bound on some errand, that's certain sure." And he strolled off to discuss the matter in the servants' hall.

Simmons was right. Lena was bound on an errand. During the time which had elapsed since she went up to her bedroom and her coming down for dinner her mood had changed. As the evening came on she had felt more sharply the horror of her present situation. In the gradually diminishing light she had seen, like a huge and gaunt shadow, the monster which she had created looming over her, looming over her life, threatening her now and in the future; and suddenly the slave woman had been driven to desperation.

"It cannot go on!" she had said to herself; "this is unbearable. Anything would be better than this. I would rather be alone for ever with my self-respect than live with Eustace all the days of my life as I am now."

The reaction had been abrupt, sharp. She had not expected it. A moment before she had been in bondage, and had not felt the capacity to break her chains. She did not know how the fierce change had come about. She even felt like a puppet maneuvered by destiny, as much a puppet in her victory as she had been in her defeat. But she was now driven along the path of sincerity—and she knew that this time she would not deviate from it. She was going to tell Eustace the truth that night and there was nothing which could stop her. Never again would she lie down to sleep hating and fearing herself, as she had hated and feared herself ever since Eustace had come back from London.

She drove briskly on in the soft summer night and, while she drove, Eustace, by a field path, was walking towards Chilham Corner, spurred on by an almost feverish impulse to sincerity akin to that which was governing her. He had had enough of it, as she had. But his impulse had been caused by a shock; hers was the result of a slowly gathering sensation of personal degradation. And he suspected that she knew what he was going to acknowledge, while she believed that he was still in ignorance of her secret. He did not see the yellow lamps of her carriage in the darkness; she did not hear the beat of his hurrying footfalls. They passed each other at a short distance, and neither suspected the errand of the other. The link between them was not strong enough yet to carry the strange between mind and mind, between heart and heart.

At Easton Lena pulled up. There was a light in the window of Eustace's study. She felt sure he was in there, probably smoking his pipe, reading, or writing letters. She had his letter to Enid with her in the envelope she had addressed that day, and now she felt for it and found it with steady fingers. She was calm, was in complete command of herself. As no servant came, and the wheels of the carriage had evidently not been heard by either Eustace or the servants, she got down, still holding the reins, and pulled the bell. An interval of complete silence followed. Henry stood on the floor of the carriage with his ears cocked and his small white body tense. Lena rang the bell again. This time it was heard. Steps sounded in the hall and then the door was rather cautiously opened, and Mrs. Green's respectable face appeared.

"You—miss!" she exclaimed, in evident astonishment.

"Yes. Good evening, Mrs. Green. I want to see Mr. Henley."

"He's gone out, ma'am."

"Gone out!"

"Yes, ma'am. He went out directly after his supper and he hasn't come back."

After a pause Lena said:

"Do you know where he's gone?"

"No, ma'am. But I expect it's down to the village. I had a thought that perhaps he had gone to see you."

"Oh, I don't think so. He was with me twice to-day."

"He will be sorry to miss you, ma'am," said Mrs. Green, still looking respectably surprised.

Lena hesitated. She had the letter in her right hand. Her left hand was holding the reins. Now she looked down at the letter.

"I might—no I won't wait. It's getting too late."

Slowly extending her hand she held out the letter. Mrs. Green heard her sigh in the dimness. Then she said:

"Please give that to Mr. Henley directly he comes back."

"Certainly ma'am."

"I want him to have it to-night."

"Yes, ma'am, he shall."

"Good night, Mrs. Green."

She gave a long look at the house, which was his, which might have been hers too if she had not given that letter. Then she got into the pony cart, turned the pony's head, and drove quickly away.

IX

About this time Eustace rang the bell at Chilham Corner, which was immediately answered by Susan.

"Can I see Miss Wareham?" he asked.

"Miss Wareham has gone out in the pony cart, sir."

"Gone out driving so late!" said Eustace, astonished and feeling a sudden sense of relief.

"Yes, sir. She said she wanted to get some air."

"What time do you expect her home?"

"I couldn't exactly say, sir. But I believe she did say something to Mr. Simmons about being out for an hour or thereabouts."

Eustace hesitated. Should he ask to go in? Should he wait till Lena came back?

"Have you any idea which way Miss Wareham went?" he said at last.

"Towards the village, sir, I believe."

"Oh! Well, I'm sorry I've missed her."

"Would you like to step in and wait, sir?"

"I—I'm afraid it's a bit too late. No, I'll be off. I may meet her."

"Yes, sir."

"Good night."

And he was off, walking quickly.

But when he was out in the road he hesitated, and stood still.

Where could Lena have gone? What could have taken her out so late? He thought of the letter. Perhaps she had driven up to Easton? If so he had missed her by taking the field path. But it was very unlikely she would go to Easton so late. She might, perhaps, have driven to the post office to post that letter to him, the letter which she hadn't been able to give him that afternoon. He walked on slowly till he came to the stile where the field path to Easton began. There he hesitated again. If he took that way home he would certainly not see Lena.

He put his hand on the stile preparatory to vaulting over it; then he took his hand away.

"What a damned coward I am!" he thought. "I've come all this way and now I—"

And he walked on along the road, always looking before him into the darkness, always dreading to see the yellow lamps of a carriage.

Soon he was in the village. All was quiet. There was no traffic. People went to bed early in Sutton Dering even in summer time. But presently, close to the village club, he saw some people and he stepped out into the broad to avoid them. Near the chief inn of the village there were more people, and he heard voices and laughter.

"Goo-night, Mr. 'Enley!" called a voice.

He called out a brisk good night and walked on quickly, always looking straight before him.

He was almost clear of the village, and was beginning to feel pretty sure that Lena had not driven in the direction of Easton, when away high up in the darkness he perceived two yellow spots. As he looked they moved slowly downwards. A carriage was descending the hill.

His heart gave a thump. It was Lena. He felt positive of that. She had been up to Easton and had missed him. Why hadn't he taken the field path back? But anyhow, she wouldn't see him in the dark. He would get off the road on to the strip of grass at the side or, better still, on to the path. It was impossible to say what he had intended to say out here, or in the pony cart, if he were to get in and offer to escort her home. And it was really too late now, altogether too late, to drive back to Chilham Corner and go in. The servants would be surprised. People would talk. That sort of thing didn't do, even when one was going to be married. Better, much better now, to wait till to-morrow. He would find out why Lena had been up to see him, would know then much better how to act. It was always a mistake to be in too much of a hurry over things.

He was on the path now close to Sutton Grange, where the Arlingfords lived. As he passed the long Tudor house he heard distinctly the sound of approaching wheels, and saw two large yellow eyes staring steadily at him.

The pony was trotting, but slowly, for the carriage was not clear of the hill. He walked on quickly to get the thing over. Another minute and the carriage would have passed him.

"Eustace! Eustace! Is that you?"

The carriage was pulled up. Eustace stood still. "That's you, isn't it?" He came forward into the road.

"Yes. Lena! Where have you been?"

"Up to Easton."

"To see me?"

"I've left a letter for you. But I meant to see you."

"Yes?"

He was silent for an instant; then be said:

"How did you know it was I? Can you see in the dark?"

"No, I saw a figure. I felt it was you. You've been taking a walk?"

"I—funnily enough I went to call on you—I took the field path. That's how we missed each other."

The pony moved uneasily, began to back. Lena stopped him.

"Then you wanted to see me again?"

"Well, after dinner I just felt like having a talk."

"Will you drive back with me?"

"It's getting a bit late, isn't it?"

"Not so very."

The pony moved again. He was getting restive—was probably thinking hard of his stable.

"Do get up, Eustace. I'll send you back with Simmons to save us the walk."

He still hesitated.

"But the village gossip!" he murmured.

"I don't care what they say. Besides I don't think they'd easily say anything very horrid about me."

"Right you are! I only thought I'd just mention it."

He caught hold of the bar and was up beside her. She touched the pony with the whip. He started forward at a fast trot.

As they traversed the village neither of them said a word, but when they were beyond the houses and had turned into the dark lane that led to Chilham Corner, Eustace said:

"You left me the letter I saw on your table to-day?"

"Yes, I meant to give it you if you were in."

"Though you wouldn't let me take it this afternoon?"

"Yes. Since then I've thought things over."

Henry set up a bark. They were turning in at her gate. Simmons came forward as she pulled up the pony before the door.

"I shall want you to drive Mr. Henley back to Easton in about half an hour, Simmons," she said, as she gave him the reins.

"Very well, ma'am," answered the man, rather grimly.

"I shan't be long, Simmons, I give you my word," said Eustace with a rather laboured attempt at heartiness.

"It's quite all right, sir."

Eustace followed Lena into the house. She went into the drawing room, which was lit. The French windows were open on to the garden. She stood still; then, without looking at him, she said:

"Let us go into the garden."

"All right!"

She stepped out on to the terrace. But she did not stay there. To his surprise she walked on over the dark lawn.

"Where the devil's she going?" he thought.

She led the way to the semi-circular seat in front of the sundial. There she stopped and sat down. He stood for a moment. Somehow he didn't feel inclined to sit beside her just then. He felt almost afraid of her and horribly doubtful about himself. He didn't know what she was going to say or do.

"Smoke if you like," she said.

"Thanks! I think I will. I've brought my pipe."

From the seat she saw his movements as he felt for it, found it, filled it, felt for the matches, lit one, let it out, lit another and put it to the pipe bowl. The tobacco glowed. For a brief instant the lower part of his face was faintly illuminated. As she stared at it she thought it looked grim and very masculine. She wanted that face in her life, wanted it terribly. For an instant she was again stricken with a sort of shuddering cowardice. Perhaps, even now, if she had not left the letter at Easton she would have compromised with herself. But the letter was there. The irreparable thing was done. By her own action she had practically forced herself to be sincere now.

Eustace didn't sit down and she didn't ask him to. If she saw his face more distinctly it might be more difficult to say what she had to say. For just one moment she looked at his long lean figure, wishing it a secret and terrible good-bye. Then she said:

"I believe you think me a—"

She had been going to say "a straight woman"; but she stopped, hesitated, and finally said:

"Eustace!"

"Yes?"

"I wish you would tell me why you came down to-night, after being here twice to-day. You must have had a very definite reason. What was it?"

He took his pipe out of his mouth, shifted on the gravel, and then said:

"Tell me something first. Are you—are you really fond of me?"

She was startled. She hadn't expected such a question. But she was resolved now to have done with lies, however much truth might cost her, and she said:

"Yes, I am."

"And you've never—there've never been moments when you disliked me, hated me, even—perhaps?"

"There may have been. We human beings are so strange, aren't we?"

"I've never hated, never disliked you, Lena."

"Perhaps not. But then you have never loved me."

"Why—what do you—"

But she interrupted him.

"And love and hatred are often very close together, I think. It's indifference and hatred which are always far apart."

"I think it's time I knew why you have sometimes hated me."

"Yes, it's time. What made you come down to-night?"

"When I got home before dinner I found something for me. It was sent by a woman I used to know well. It wasn't a wedding present. She returned something I once gave her—a box. In the box I found a note from her."

He stopped.

"Yes?" she said.

"The note showed me that—that a letter I wrote to her some time ago had never reached her. I must evidently by mistake have sent it to someone else."

"Yes, you did. You sent it to me."

He stood quite still and said nothing.

"That was the letter I prevented you from opening this afternoon."

He still said nothing. Now that the blow which he had dreaded long ago, and then ceased from dreading, had fallen he felt for the moment oddly calm, almost cold, but also strangely stupid and dull.

As he did not speak, after a moment of waiting, Lena said:

"You know now that you made a mistake about me. I am not the straight, honest woman whom you described in that letter. I think I was, when you wrote it, but I suppose we can change very suddenly. I oughtn't to have read the letter, but I did read it. I was fond of you. You had said you were fond of me. So I read it, and from that moment I haven't been straight with you. Now you know me as I am, a woman who is capable of deceit, and of doing a dishonourable thing."

"Lena! Lena!" he said.

And just then there was in his voice a sound she had never heard in it before. He bent down towards her in the darkness.

"You blame yourself like that! And you don't say a word against me!"

"There's nothing hurts a woman so much as condemning someone she—she has cared very much for. It was cruel of you, but—I can understand."

He said nothing. His face had flushed in the darkness, but she couldn't see that.

"And you came down to-night—?" she asked.

"I came down to tell you about the letter. I thought perhaps you had had it."

"If you had felt sure I hadn't had it you would never have told me?"

"I don't think I should—certainly not now. After we were married I might have told you … if—"

"If what?"

"I scarcely know. But perhaps later on, if we had been very happy together, I might. It—it wouldn't have mattered then perhaps."

"I think I know what you mean. When two people are very happy— really happy—together they can tell each other anything."

"Anything that's past and dead and done with. That's about it, I suppose."

"It must be easy to be truthful in happiness, I think," said Lena.

After a long pause she added:

"Now you know, Eustace, of course, you are quite free."

"Free!" he said in a startled voice.

"Yes. There will be a scandal of course. The village will talk and wonder. But we can bear that and keep our secret."

"You wish to break off our engagement!"

"I ought to have broken it off when I read the first words of that letter."

"But you didn't!"

"No."

"Why didn't you?"

"I hardly know now. Don't ask me. But for one thing—afterwards—I dreaded your finding out that I was not as straight as you thought I was. I knew you didn't love me, but I knew you respected me and believed in me. That was something. And I—didn't want to lose that."

He moved and sat down beside her.

"Lena," he said, "I've been a great cad, and a coward too, a moral coward. You say you were afraid of losing my respect. I did respect you. I do now—perhaps in a different way. I fancied you were a very ordinary sort of good woman. I know now you aren't. I had no sort of an idea of what you were. Lately, for some time, I've been realizing how much more there is in you than I had imagined. And I—I don't want to lose you. We've spoken out at last. I—I feel the better for it whatever happens. Can't you—is it absolutely impossible for you to forgive me?"

"But how can you care?"

"I do care." He took hold of her hand. "I do care. I want you in my life badly."

"But only a short time ago you loved another woman!"

"Yes—but in such another way. You—you—oh," he spoke almost with exasperation, "any man could understand how! But I can't explain to you."

"Perhaps I can partly guess," she said, soberly.

"Don't throw me over. I'll keep straight. I'll try to make you happy. I—I—it's damned odd, I can't understand it, but ever since you've been condemning yourself I've begun caring for you, you've meant ever so much more to me. You've seemed a real living breathing woman, instead of just a kind sort of creature. Perhaps you were more what people call good before, but I—I don't want you to be so infernally good." He put his arm round her. "You're awfully human to me now, Lena, awfully human—and I want you."

On the twenty-fifth of July Lena married Eustace Henley.

At present they are living at Chilham Corner. The village of Sutton Dering, which is fairly sharp as villages go, considers the marriage a great success.

The day before the wedding, when Eustace was tidying up at Easton, he burnt a letter.

A Boudoir Boy

I

"It is so impossible to be young," Claude Melville said very wearily, and with his little air of played-out indifference. He was smoking a cigarette, as always, and wore a dark red smoking-suit that, he thought, went excellently with his black eyes and swarthy complexion.

His father had been a blue-eyed Saxon giant, his mother a pretty Kentish woman, with an apple-blossom complexion and sunny hair; yet he managed to look exquisitely Turkish, and thought himself a clever boy for so doing. But then he always thought himself clever. He had cultivated this conception of himself until it had become a confirmed habit of mind. On his head was a fez with a tassel, and he was sitting upon the hearthrug with his long legs crossed meditatively. His room was dimly lit, and had an aspect of divans. Attar of roses scented the air. A fire was burning, although it was a spring evening and not cold. London roared faintly in the distance, like a lion at a far-away evening party.

"It is so impossible to be young," Claude repeated, without emphasis. "I was middle-aged at ten. Now I am twenty-two, and have done everything I ought not to have done, I feel that life has become altogether improbable. Even if I live until I am seventy—the correct age for entering into one's dotage, I believe—I cannot expect to have a second childhood. I have never had a first."

He sighed. It seemed so hard to be deprived of one's legal dotage.

His friend, Jimmy Haddon, looked at him and laughed. Jimmy was puffing at a pipe. His pipe was the only one Claude ever allowed to be smoked among his divans and his roses.

After thoroughly completing his laugh, Jimmy remarked:

"Would you like to take a lesson in the art of being young?"

"Immensely."

"I know somebody who could give you one."

"Really, Jimmy! What strange people you always know; curates, and women who have never written improper novels, and all sorts of beings who seem merely mythical to the rest of us!"

"This is not a curate."

"Then it must be a woman who has never written an improper novel."

"It is."

"And you mean to tell me seriously that there is such a person? To see her would be to take what *Punch* calls a pre-historic peep. She must be ingeniously old."

"She is sixty-four, and she is my aunt."

"How beautiful of her. I am an only child, so I can never be an uncle. It is one of my lasting regrets, although I daresay that profession is terribly overcrowded like the others. But why is she sixty-four? It seems a risky thing for a woman to be?"

"She takes the risk without thinking at all about it."

"She must be very daring."

"No; she's only completely natural."

"Natural. What is that?"

Jimmy laughed again. He was fond of Claude, but he and Claude met so often chiefly because they were extremes. Jimmy was a handsome athlete, who had been called to the bar, and persistently played cricket or football whenever the courts were sitting. He was cursed with a large private income, which he spent royally, and blessed with a good heart. Once he had appeared for the defence in a divorce case, which— lasting longer than he had anticipated, owing to the obvious guilt of all parties concerned in it, and the consequent difficulty of getting an innocent jury to agree about a verdict—had cost him a cricket match. Since then he had looked upon the law in the legendary way, as an ass, and spent most of his time in exercising his muscles. In the intervals of leisure which he allowed himself from sports and pastimes, he saw a good deal of Claude, who amused him, and whom he never bored. He called him a boudoir boy, but had a real liking for him, nevertheless, and sometimes longed to wake him up, and separate him from the absurd *chiffons* with which he occupied his time. Now he laughed at him openly, and Claude did not mind in the least. They were really friends, however preposterous such a friendship might seem.

"What is that? Well—my aunt. When you see her you will understand thoroughly."

"Does she live in Park Lane or in Clapham?"

"She lives in the country, in Northamptonshire, is very well off, and has a place of her own."

"And a husband?"

"No. She is a prosperous spinster, dines the local cricket team once a year, keeps the church going, knows all the poor people, and all the rich in the neighbourhood, and has only one fad."

"What is that?"

"She always wears her hair powdered. Come down and stay with her, and she will teach you to be young."

"Well—but I am afraid she will work me very hard."

"Not she. You would like a new experience."

Claude yawned, and blinked his long dark eyes in a carefully Eastern manner.

"I am afraid there is no such thing left for me," he said with an elaborate dreariness. "Still, if your aunt will invite me, I will come. Of course you will accompany me, I must have a chaperon."

"Of course."

"Ah!" Claude said, as a footman came softly into the room, "here is our absinthe. Now, Jimmy, please do forget your horrible football, and I will teach you to be decadent."

"As my aunt will teach you to be young—you old boy."

II

"Mr. Haddon has left, sir," said the footman, standing by Claude's bedside in the detached manner of the well-bred domestic. "Here is a note for you, sir; I was to give it you the first thing."

And he handed it on a salver.

Claude stretched out his thin white arm and took it, without manifesting any of the surprise that he felt. When the footman had gone, he poured out a cup of tea from the silver teapot that stood on a small table at his elbow, sipped it, and quietly opened the square envelope. The Northamptonshire sun was pouring in with a countrified ardour through the bedroom window. Outside the birds twittered in Miss Haddon's cherished garden. For Claude had come down at that contented spinster's invitation to spend a week with her, bringing Jimmy as chaperon, and this was the very first morning of his visit. Now he learnt that his chaperon had already "left," possibly to be a "half-back," or something equally ridiculous, at a local football match in a neighbouring village. Claude spread the note out and read it, while the birds chirped to the very manifest spring.

> "Dear Boy,—Good-bye, and good luck to you. I know you are never angry, so it is scarcely worthwhile to tell you not to be. I am off. Back in a week. You will learn your lesson better alone with Aunt Kitty. There is no absinthe in her cellar, but she knows good champagne from bad. You will be all right. Study hard. — Yours ever,
>
> Jim."

Claude drank two cups of tea instead of his usual one, and read the note four times. Then he lay back, wrapping his dressing gown—a fine specimen of Cairene embroidery—closely round him, shut his eyes, and seemed to go to sleep. All he said to himself was:

"Jimmy writes a very dull letter."

At half-past nine, Miss Haddon's house reverberated in a hollow manner with the barbarous music of a gong, the dressing gong. Claude heard it very unsympathetically, and felt rather inclined merely to take off his dressing gown, as an act of mute defiance, and go deliberately to sleep, instead of getting up and putting things on. But he remembered his manners wearily, and slid out of bed and into a carefully warmed bath that was prepared in the neighbouring dressing room. Having completed an intricate toilette, and tied a marvellously subtle tie, shot with rigorously subdued, but voluptuous colours, he sauntered downstairs in time to be thoroughly immersed in the full clamour of the second—or breakfast—gong, which he encountered in the hall.

"Why will people wake the dead merely because they are going to eat a boiled egg and a bit of toast?" he asked himself as he entered the breakfast room.

Miss Haddon was standing by the window, reading letters in the proper English manner. The sun lay on her grey hair, which she wore dressed high, and void of cap.

"You are very punctual," she said with a smile. "I was going to send up to know whether you would prefer to breakfast in your room. My nephew told me you might like to. I shall be glad to have your company. Jimmy has run away and left us together, I find."

"Yes, Jimmy has run away," Claude answered, beginning slowly to feel the full force of Jimmy's perfidy. He looked at Miss Haddon's cheerful, rosy face, and bright brown eyes, and wondered whether she had been in the plot.

"I hope you will not be bored," Miss Haddon went on, as they sat down together, the intonation of her melodious elderly voice seeming to dismiss the supposition, even while she suggested it. "But, indeed, I think it is almost impossible to be bored in the country."

Claude, who was always either in London or Paris, looked frankly astonished. In handing him his cup of tea, Miss Haddon noticed it.

"You don't agree with me?" she asked.

"I cannot disagree, at least," he said, "because, to tell the truth, I am always in towns."

"Probably you are happy there then," she rejoined, with a briskness that was agreeable, because it was not a hideous assumption, like the geniality that often prevails, fitfully, at Christmas time.

But Claude could not permit his hostess to remain comfortable in this utterly erroneous belief.

"Oh, please—" he said, with gentle rebuke, "I am not happy anywhere."

Miss Haddon glanced at him with a gay and whimsical, but decidedly acute, scrutiny.

"Perhaps you are too young to be happy," she said; "you have not suffered enough."

"I have never been young," he answered, eating his devilled kidney with a silent pathos of perseverance—"never."

"And I shall never be old, or, at any rate, feel old. It can't be done. I'm sixty-four, and look it, but I can't cease to revel in details, take an interest in people, and regard life as my half-opened oyster. It is a pity one can't go on living till one is two or three hundred or so. There is so much to see and know. Our existence in the world is like a day at the Stores. We have to go away before we have been into a quarter of the different departments."

"I don't find life at all like that. I have seen all the departments till I am sick of them. But perhaps you never come to London?"

"Every year for three months to see my friends. I stay at a hotel. It is a most delightful time."

Her tone was warm with pleasant memories. Claude felt himself more and more surprised.

"You enjoy the country, and London?" he said.

"I enjoy everything," said Miss Haddon. "And surely most people do."

"None of the people I know seem to enjoy anything very much. They try everything, of course. That is one's duty."

"Then the latest literature really reflects life, I imagine," Miss Haddon said. "If what you say is true, everything includes the sins as well as the virtues. I have often wondered whether the books that I have thought utterly and absurdly false could possibly be the outcome of facts."

"Such as what books?"

"Oh, I'll name no names. The authors may be your personal friends. But it is so then? In their search after happiness the people of to-day, the moderns, give the warm shoulder to vice as well as to virtue?"

"They ignore nothing."

"Not even duty?"

"Our duty is to ourselves, and can never be ignored."

Miss Haddon tapped a boiled egg very sharply on its head with a spoon. She wondered if the action were a performance of duty to herself or to the egg.

"That, I understand," she remarked briskly, "is the doctrine of what is called in London the young decadent; and in the country—forgive me— sometimes the young devil of the day."

"I am decadent, Miss Haddon," Claude said with a gentle pride that was not wholly ungraceful.

The elderly lady swept him with a bright look of fresh and healthy interest.

"How exciting," she exclaimed, after a moment's decisive pause, but with a completely natural air. "You are the first I have seen. For Jimmy isn't one, is he?"

"Jimmy! No. He plays football, and eats cold roast beef and cheese for lunch."

"Do tell me—how does one do it?"

She seemed intensely interested, and was merrily munching an apple grown in one of her own orchards.

Claude raised his dark eyebrows.

"I beg your pardon?"

"How does one become a decadent? I have heard so much about you all, about your cleverness, and your clothes, and the things you write, and draw, and smoke, and think, and—and eat—"

She seemed suddenly struck by a bright idea.

"Oh, Mr. Melville!" she exclaimed, leaning forward behind the great silver urn, and darting at him a glance of imploring earnestness, "will you do me a favour? We are left to ourselves for a whole week. Teach me, teach me to be a decadent."

"But I thought you were going to teach me to be yo—" Claude began, and stopped just in time. "I mean—er—"

He paused, and they gazed at each other. There was meditation in the boy's eyes. He was wondering seriously whether it would be possible for an elderly spinster lady, of countrified morals and rural procedure, to be decadent. She was rather stout, too, and appeared painfully healthy.

"Will you?" Miss Haddon breathed across the urn and the teapot.

"Well, we might try," Claude answered doubtfully.

He was remarking to himself:

"Poor, dear Jimmy! He certainly doesn't understand his aunt!"

She was murmuring in her mind: "I have always heard they have no sense of humour!"

III

"Mr. Melville, Mr. Melville," cried Miss Haddon's voice towards evening on the following day, "the absinthe has arrived!"

Claude came out languidly into the hall.

"Has it?" he said dreamily.

"Yes, and Paul Verlaine's poetry, and the blue books—I mean the yellow books, and" (rummaging in a just-opened parcel) "yes, here are two novels by Catulle Mendez, and a box of those rose-tipped cigarettes. Now, what ought I to do? Shall we have some absinthe instead of our tea, or what?"

Claude looked at her with a momentary suspicion, but her grey hair crowned an eager face decorated with an honest expression. The suspicion was lulled to rest.

"We had better have our tea," he answered slowly. "I like my absinthe about an hour or so before dinner."

"Very well. Tea, James, and muffins."

The butler retired with fat dignity, but wondering not a little at the unusual vagaries of his mistress. Miss Haddon and Claude, laden with books, repaired to the drawing room and sat down by the fire. Claude placed himself, cross-legged, upon a cushion on the floor. The box of rose-tipped cigarettes was in his hand. Miss Haddon regarded him expectantly from her sofa. Her expression seemed continually exclaiming, "What's to be done now?"

The boy felt that this was not right, and endeavoured gently to correct it.

"Please try to be a little—a—"

"Yes?"

"A little more restrained," he said. "What we feel about life is that it should never be crude. All extremes are crude."

"What—even extremes of wickedness?"

He hesitated.

"Well, certainly extremes of goodness, or happiness, or anything of that kind. When one comes to think of it seriously, happiness is really absurd, is it not? Just consider how preposterous what is called a happy face always looks, covered with those dreadful, wrinkled things named smiles, all the teeth showing, and so on. I know you agree with me.

Happiness drives all thought out of a face, and distorts the features in a most painful manner. When I go out walking on a Bank Holiday, a thing I seldom do, I always think a cheerful expression the most degrading of all expressions. A contented clerk disfigures a whole street—really."

Miss Haddon's appearance had gradually grown very sombre during this speech, and she did not brighten up on the approach of tea and muffins on a wicker table whimsical with little shelves.

"Perhaps you are right," she said. "I daresay happiness is unreasonable. Ought I to sit on the floor too?"

Claude deprecated such an act on the part of his hostess. Sitting on the floor was one of his pet originalities, and he hated rivalry. Besides, Miss Haddon was distinctly too stout for that sort of thing.

"I do it because I feel so Turkish," he explained. "Otherwise, it would be an assumption, and not naïve. People make a great mistake in fancying the decadent is unnatural. If anything, he is too natural. He follows his whim. The world only calls us natural when we do everything we dislike. If Rossetti had played football every Saturday, his poetry would have been much more read in England than it has been. Yes, please, I will have another muffin."

"But I think I feel Turkish too," Miss Haddon said calmly. "Yes, I am sure I do. I ought not to resist it; ought I? Otherwise I shall be flying in the face of your beautiful theories." And she squatted down on the floor at his elbow.

Claude had a wonderful purple moment of acute irritation, during which he felt strangely natural. Miss Haddon did not appear to notice it. She went on bombarding him with questions in a cheery manner until he began to be rather ill, but her face never lost its expression of grave sadness, a strange, inexplicable melancholy that was not in the least Bank Holiday. The contrast between her expression and her voice worried Claude, as an intelligent pantaloon might worry a clown. He felt that something was wrong. Either face or voice required alteration. And then questions are like death—extremely irksome. Besides, he found it difficult to answer many of them, difficult to define precisely the position of the decadent, his intentions and his aims. It was no use to tell Miss Haddon that he didn't possess either the one or the other. Always with the same definitely sad face, the same definitely cheerful voice, she declined to believe him. He fidgeted on his cushion, and his Turkish placidity threatened to be seriously disturbed.

The appearance of the absinthe created a diversion. Claude arranged a glass of it, much diluted with water, for the benefit of his hostess, and she began to sip it with an air of determined reverence.

"It tastes like the smell of a drag hunt," she said after a while.

Claude's gently-lifted eyebrows proclaimed misapprehension.

"When they drag a trail over a course and satisfy the hounds with a dead rabbit at the end of it," she explained.

"My dear lady," he protested plaintively. "Really, you do not grasp the inner meaning of what you are drinking. Presently the most perfect sensation will steal over you, a curious happy detachment from everything, as if you were floating in some exquisite element. You will not care what happens, or what—"

"But must I drink it all before I feel detached?" she asked. "It's really so very nasty, quite disgusting to the taste. Surely you think so."

"I drink it for its aftereffect."

"Is it like a good act that costs us pain at the moment, and gives us the pleasure of self-satisfaction ultimately?"

"I don't know," the boy exclaimed abruptly. To compare absinthe to a good act seemed to him quite intolerable.

He let his rose-tipped cigarette go out, and was glad when the dressing gong sounded in the hall.

Miss Haddon sprang up from the floor briskly.

"I rather admire you for drinking this stuff," she said. "I am sure you do it to mortify the flesh. A Lenten penance out of Lent is most invigorating to the mind."

As Claude went up to dress, he felt as if he never wished to touch absinthe again. The glitter of its personality was dulled for him now that it was looked upon as merely a nasty sort of medicine to be indulged in as a mortification of the flesh, like wearing a hair shirt, or rejecting meat on Fridays. He found Miss Haddon painfully prosaic. It seemed almost silly to be a decadent in her company. To feel Turkish alone was graceful and quaint, almost intellectual, but to have an old lady feeling Turkish, too, and squatting on the floor to emphasise the sensation, was tragic, seemed to bring imbecility very near. Claude dressed with unusual agitation, and made a distinct failure of his tie.

All through dinner Miss Haddon talked optimistically about her prospects as a successful decadent, much as if she were discussing her future on the Stock Exchange, or as the editor of a paper. She calculated that at her present rate of progress she ought to be almost on a level with her guest by the end of the week, and spoke hopefully of ceasing to take any interest in the ordinary facts of life, of learning a proper contempt for all healthy-minded humanity, and of appreciating at its proper value what seems to ordinary people, weak-kneed affection in literature, in art, and, above all, in movement and in appearance. Her bright eyes flashed upon Claude beneath her crown of powdered hair, as she talked, and the big room rang with her jovial voice.

The boy began to feel exceedingly confused. Yet he had never been less bored. Miss Haddon might be stout and sixty-four. Nevertheless, her net personality was far less wearisome than that of many a town-bred sylph. Unconsciously Claude ate with a hearty appetite, indulged immoderately in excellent roast beef, and even swallowed a beautifully-cooked Spanish onion without thinking of the committal of a crime. During dessert Miss Haddon gave him a racy description of a rural cricket match and of the supper and speeches which followed it, and he found himself laughing heartily and wishing he had been there. He pulled himself up short with a sudden sensation of horror, and his hostess rose to go into the drawing room.

"Shall we play Halma or Ek Bahr?" she asked; "or would they be out of order? I wish particularly to conform to all your tenets."

"Dear lady, please, we have no tenets," he protested. "Do remember that, or you will never become what you wish. But I do not care for any games."

"Then shall we sit down and each read a volume of *The Yellow Book?*"

She hastened towards a table to find copies of that work, but something in her brisk and anxious movement caused Claude to exclaim hurriedly:

"Please—please teach me Halma."

That night he went up to bed flushed with triumph.

Miss Haddon had allowed him to win a couple of games. Never before had he felt so absolutely certain of the unusual acuteness of his intellect.

IV

Three days later, Miss Haddon and Claude Melville were feeding chickens—under protest.

"I mean to give it up, of course," the former said. "It's a degrading pursuit; it's almost as bad as the 'things that Jimmy does,' the things that give him such a marvellous complexion and keep his figure so magnificent."

She threw a handful of grain to the frenzied denizens of the enlarged meat-safe before them, and added in a tone of pensive reflectiveness:

"Why is it, I wonder, that these actions which, as you have taught me, are unworthy of thinking people, tend to make the body so beautiful, the eyes so bright and clear, the cheeks rose-tinted, the limbs straight and supple?"

All the time that she was speaking her glance crept musingly over Claude's tall, but weak-looking and rather flaccid form, seeming to pause on his thin undeveloped arms, his lanky legs, and his slightly yellow face. That face began to flush. She sighed.

"There must be something radically wrong in the scheme of the universe," she continued. "But, of course, one ought to live for the mind and for subtle sensations, even though they do make one look an object."

Her eyes were on the chickens now, who were fighting like feathered furies, pouncing, clucking, running for safety, grain in beak, or, with a fiery anxiety, chasing the favoured brethren who had secured a morsel and were hoping to be permitted to swallow it. Claude glanced at her furtively out of the corner of his eye, and endeavoured, for the first time in his life, to stand erect and broaden his rather narrow chest.

Silently he resolved to give instructions to his tailor not to spare the padding in his future coats. He was glad, too, that knee breeches, for which he had occasionally sighed, had not come into fashion again. After all, modern dress had its little advantages. Miss Haddon was still scattering grain, rather in the attitude of Millet's "*Sower*," and still talking reflectively.

"We must try to convert Jimmy," she said. "I have a good deal of influence over him, Mr. Melville. We must try to make him more like you, more thoughtful, more inactive, more frankly sensual, more fond of sofas, in the future than he has been in the past. Do you know, I am ashamed to say it, but I don't believe I have ever seen Jimmy lying on a sofa. Poor Jimmy! Look at that hen! She is choking. Hens gulp their food so! And then, he's inclined to be persistently unselfish. That must be stopped too. I have learnt from you that to be decadent one must be acutely and untiringly selfish. The blessings of selfishness! What a volume might be written upon them! Mr. Melville, all chickens must be decadent, for all chickens are entirely selfish. It is strange to think that the average fowl is more advanced in ethics—is it ethics I mean?—than the average man or woman, is it not? And we ate a decadent at dinner last night. I feel almost like a cannibal."

She threw away the last grain, and was silent. But suddenly Claude spoke.

"Miss Haddon," he said, and his voice had never sounded so boyish to her before, "you have been laughing at me for nearly a week." He paused, then he went on, rather unevenly, in the up-and-down tones induced by stifled excitement, "and I have never found it out until this moment. I suppose you think me a great fool. I daresay I have been one. But please don't—I mean, please let us give up acting our farce."

"But have we reached the third act?" she said.

They were walking through the garden, among the crocuses and violets now.

"I am sure I don't know," he answered, trying to seem easy. "Perhaps it is a farce in one act."

"Perhaps it is not a farce at all, my dear boy," she said very gently and with a sudden old-world gravity that was not without its grace.

They reached the house. She put her basket down on the oak table in the wide hall, and faced him in the eager way that was natural to her, and that was so youthful.

"Mr. Melville—Claude," she said, as she held out her hand, clad in a very countrified brown glove, with a fan-like gauntlet, "of all Jimmy's friends I think I shall like you the best. People who have acted together ought to be good comrades."

He took the hand. That seemed necessary.

"But I haven't been acting," he said.

"Oh, yes, you have," she answered, "and I have only been on the stage for a week; while you—well, I suppose you have been on it for at least two or three years. I am taking my farewell of it this morning, and you—?"

The boy's face was deeply flushed, but he did not look, or feel, actually angry.

"I don't know about myself yet," he said.

"Think it all over," the old lady exclaimed. "And now let us have lunch. I am hungry."

Jimmy arrived that evening.

"How old are you, Claude?" he exclaimed, clapping his friend on the back.

"I am not sure," Claude replied. "But I almost begin to wish that I were sixty-four."

The Piano

I

Until I received her note, asking me to come to lunch to meet the great master, I had never realised that Mrs. Doremus was intensely musical. I will go further than that. I had never realised that she was musical at all. A charming woman! A delightful woman, with plenty to talk about, hospitable to a degree, sociable, friendly, full of good taste in the matter of house decoration, furniture, silver, a connoisseur in cooking—yes! Plenty of books lying about in her delicious African house and plenty of newspapers! Although she had lived almost perpetually in that African colony of the French ever since the death of her husband, she still took in *Punch* and read *The Times*, or seemed to, every day. Literary and political, but never boringly either—yes! And then—what a gardener! She really had a kind of genius for gardening, and although she kept sixteen Arab gardeners always looked into everything herself. The idea of lining both sides of the long drive which led to the Villa Karibi with double rows of arum lilies had been entirely hers. I had her own word for that. And it was she who, untold years ago, had had the inspiration to sow grass thickly in front of the white entrance of the old Arab house, and to dot fat palm trees about on that radiant lawn. The thrill it gave you on arrival, the sensation of Eastern opulence! And the Arab court with the papyrus and the fountains, and the enormous beds—fields almost they were—of carnations, and the pond with the island in it containing one gigantic coco palm, and the arbour covered up with bougainvillea, and the tea-house, framed by the vivid scarlet of salvias and double geraniums, and the hibiscus bushes, and the rose trees from Damascus, and the syringa, and that little bower smothered in—wasn't it really honeysuckle? —and the purple violet seas in spring! Oh, as a gardener she was without a rival. But I had never suspected her of being musical; and now the revelation was before my eyes; now she had let me into her secret.

"Music, as you know, has always been my greatest joy and consolation."

Odd how one can seem to know a woman for years and not really know her. The greatest joy and consolation of Mrs. Doremus had been hidden from me for all these years and I had never suspected it. Of course I didn't live in the Colony. I only came there occasionally from Europe. Still I must have paid at least fifteen visits there since she had settled down at the Villa Karibi, and I had been in and out of her house a great deal, and had had many long, and—as I had thought—intimate conversations with my hostess. And yet, looking back, I couldn't recall that music had ever been mentioned between us.

Her greatest consolation! Perhaps the subject had been too sacred to be touched on. Perhaps music had always meant so much to her that she simply dared not speak about it in ordinary conversation. But then how about that "as you know"? That seemed to imply a willingness on her part that I should understand and sympathise with this hidden source of intense artistic satisfaction. And really her little note was frankness itself.

Villa Karibi,
February 25, 19—.

Dear Friend,
Music, as you know, has always been my greatest joy and consolation. Imagine, therefore, if you can, my delight on hearing from dear Monsieur de Morisot that the great Master, Saint Sauveur, who is passing a few days at the Hotel des Gazelles, on his way to the Baths of Hammam Ziloutine, would be pleased to lunch with me next Thursday, the 28th, at 12.30, and has no objection to meeting a few of the choicer spirits of hereabouts. As I know your delight in good music I think it might please you to meet the great man, who is the glory of France and the doyen of the music world. If you can come please be punctual, as Monsieur de Morisot tells me the Master's digestion does not admit of his sitting down to table later than 12.30 to the minute. I am therefore begging everybody to be here at twenty minutes past twelve.

With cordial regards,
Yours always sincerely,
Henrietta Doremus (née Stackpole).

As she knew my delight in good music! As I knew that music had always been her greatest joy and consolation! My memory, I felt, must be treacherous. She and I must have discussed the greatest of the arts together, at some time, somewhere. But when, where? I gave it up. But I wrote an immediate acceptance. Saint Sauveur was a world-famous man, noted as a great pianist, a great organist, a great composer, a wit, a causeur, a raconteur, the Admirable Crichton among musicians. There was nothing he couldn't do, and practically nothing he hadn't done. His opera, *Hercules in the Augean Stables,* had been given all over the world. His pianoforte Concerto in D Minor had been played by every pianist of note for the last five-and-forty years. Many of his songs— "Clair de Lune," for instance, "Minuit," "Dans le Desért," "La fille du Soleil,"—were familiar to every prima donna and to every cultivated schoolgirl. His string music was as remarkable as his magnificent orchestral poems, such as "Eve at the Gates of Paradise," and "Pharaoh's Daughter on the Nile." And his imitations of Bach were so perfect that they had taken in the most accomplished professors. He could write like any composer past or present. And in addition he could write like himself, and that was best of all. He was now, of course, very old. Indeed he was said to be well over eighty. But his industry was still unabated.

He still composed. He still wrote poems. He still played the piano and improvised marvellously on the organ. He still travelled in Africa. And he was still the honoured friend of dear Monsieur de Morisot, seventeen times Préfet of the beautiful city that lies by the Mediterranean below the Villa Karibi.

No wonder Mrs. Doremus was pleased to have the chance of entertaining him. No wonder I wished that I hadn't come to Africa this time leaving my frock-coat reposing among moth halls in London. For I was sure—some instinct told it to me—that Monsieur Saint Sauveur would turn up on February the twenty-eighth in a frock-coat and not merely in a frock coat, but one that was braided. And what sort of figure should I cut in my neat dark jacket suit beside him? However, that couldn't be helped. A ready-made African frock coat, such as I could buy in the town, was out of the question. And possibly my instinct was wrong, possibly the Master was negligent in matters of dress. Oddly enough, I had never set eyes on him, though, of course, his name had been familiar to me from the cradle. But I imagined him as very precise, immaculate, more like a polished diplomat than a Bohemian musician. There was something in his music—I don't know! One gets ideas about great men and doesn't know why they come. My idea of the Master lunching at the house of Mrs. Doremus was this: a polished old man, perfectly dressed in severe and conventional style, with beautiful hands, the smile of a diplomat, the silver tongue of a practised orator, and the brilliant eyes of a charmeur.

And the frock coat would be braided.

II

It was pleasant to be numbered by Mrs. Doremus among "a few of the choicer spirits of hereabouts," and I confess to having felt quite unusually choice on the morning of February 28th, as I fastened my tie before the mirror in my charming room at the Hotel St. James, and placed a small, but exquisite, William of Orange rosebud in the left lapel of my dark jacket. From my hotel with me were going two other choice spirits, both of the female sex, Lady Ermyntrude Raineborough and Lady Carrò, with the accent on the last syllable. And we set out together to stroll to the villa exactly as the clock struck the hour of noon.

Lady Ermyntrude was one of those astounding old women who are only bred in America and England. At the age of seventy-eight she could see without glasses, walk without a stick, sit in a fireless room with windows open in all weathers, play bridge till midnight, be up in the morning to an early breakfast, do intricate embroidery, eat everything when she lunched or dined out, and sleep eight hours at a stretch without being surprised at it. She was a widow, like Mrs. Doremus, and wore mushroom hats specially made for her in Paris.

Lady Carrò was not a widow, but she didn't bother very much about her husband, who was Earl of Carrò and a director of companies in London. She was fifty-four, immensely vital and interested in everything, a great traveller, grey-haired, good tempered, eager to please, still more eager to have people please her, fond of company and celebrities, greedy for humour, kind of heart. She had a brisk way of throwing a joke at you, and then suddenly leaning forwards and sideways, with her head held obliquely, like Judy in "Punch and Judy." A most pleasant and genial woman.

As we walked along, through the hotel garden and down the hill towards the turn on the right which led to the drive of the Villa Karibi, I learned for the first time how intensely musical my two companions were. Lady Ermyntrude, it seemed, had a "passion" for Mozart, and had heard Mendelssohn's *Elijah* no less than twenty times. This was creditable. But Lady Carrò went much further than this. She had been among the first to go to Bayreuth, had been present at the initial performance of Strauss's *Rosenkavalier,* had, so she assured us, persuaded the beautiful Mary Garden to revive Verdi's *La Traviata* at the Opéra Comique in Paris, to show people what a great actress-singer could do with a stereotyped part, and had liked Scriabin at least a couple of years before anyone else had "found him out." She had also been an intimate friend of Massenet.

Both ladies (fortunately) had always adored the music of Saint Sauveur and both were all agog to know him. They had seen him on the platform. At least Lady Carrò had, and Lady Ermyntrude was sure that she had. But as she said he was a very tall, clean-shaven man "with a face like a weary bloodhound," while Lady Carrò assured us that he was not much over five feet two, and had always worn a beard "from young manhood up," I had my doubts about Lady Ermyntrude. Lady Carrò had heard him improvise on the organ at the Madeleine in Paris, and it was "the most absolutely wonderful thing she had ever heard in her life." All this, I thought, promised well for the success of the luncheon.

We turned in at the gate, and were walking between the double lines of arum lilies exactly as my watch pointed to the quarter-past twelve. Nothing could be better. We, at least, should not hold up the Master from sitting down to table precisely on the stroke of the half-hour. His digestive processes were safe in our hands.

But punctual though we were, we were not the first to arrive. Several enthusiasts had preceded us. The British Consul-General and his wife—both intensely musical, as I learnt that day for the first time—were already with Mrs. Doremus in the library which looked on the Papyrus Court, also the Admiral of the Port with his South American wife, and two Arab chieftains covered with decorations, the Agha of Beni Mora, and the Bach Agha of the Aurés, fine, dignified, bearded, speechless men in beautiful garments.

One felt at once that this was an "occasion." The Admiral was in uniform, the British Consul-General in a "morning coat." I began to be very conscious of my jacket, but hoped that the William of Orange rosebud would carry it off.

Mrs. Doremus, beautifully dressed in black with a bunch of marvellous violets in the front of her gown, her pretty yellow-white hair unconcealed by a hat, was as cordial and talkative and welcoming as ever.

"We are all musical here to-day," she said, in her cheerful, husky voice. "Monsieur Saint Sauveur will eat his lunch in the midst of an atmosphere of music."

An atmosphere of music! I glanced at the Admiral, a square man with the face of one who had doubled the Horn, and at the two Arabs with their eagle eyes, and I wondered. But just at that moment more people began to come in.

It was to be a luncheon of twenty-four.

We were already—for I counted—twenty-one in the library when my watch pointed to twenty-five minutes past twelve. The Governor and his wife had arrived, General Sarelle, who commanded the French troops in that part of North Africa, with his aide-de-camp, Mrs. G. F. Bethune, the American novelist, Comte de Montmorency, who had a lovely property at El-Aloui, Major Greyne, the British Administrator of vast regions south of Khartoum, who was spending a brief holiday among us, Mrs. Eleonora Bullock, the famous explorer, taking a rest after a journey in the South of Morocco, Monsieur Laroche, the semi-invalid, but wonderfully cultured, owner of the exquisite villa, Djenan-el-Mufti, which adjoined the property of Mrs. Doremus, and Count and Countess Faviacasa, charming Italians among us for a time on their way to Tunis. Mrs. Doremus's English butler entered the room, and murmured something into his mistress's ear. She raised and depressed her small, yellow-white eyebrows three times, turned to us all, said in a low voice, "*He* has arrived!" and went out quickly into the hall, while we stood facing the door full of expectation. There was a short and thrilling pause. Then she re-entered the room with a very short man at her side, followed by the towering figure, so beloved and familiar in the Colony, of dear Monsieur de Morisot, bony, long in the tooth, yellow, animated, and already in the full flood of discourse.

Monsieur Saint Sauveur looked exactly like an old Royalty. Although very short, his calm self-possession, his still dignity, were such that he seemed almost tall, and certainly in no way puny. He had the detached, masklike expression which Royalties often assume when sitting in a State landau and bending—it isn't really bowing—to a crowd. His grey hair was smooth and neatly arranged. He wore a moustache and a very small perfectly cut beard. His little hands were wonderfully refined and clever-looking. And—of course! I knew it!— he had on a braided frock coat, buttoned, and fitting his slight, trim figure in an almost sheath-like manner. In it was the rosette of the Légion d'Honneur.

After the Master had shaken hands slowly with the Governor and his wife, the General, and the Admiral and Madame Admiral, presentations began. Mrs. Doremus introduced all her guests, including myself, one by one to the Master, who shook hands slowly with each of us without uttering a word, and without looking at any of us. I noticed that his eyes were rather prominent and had a curious boiled look. The touch of his hand was dry and cold. His handsome face—he had regular features and a marvellously good complexion for so old a man—looked remote, not repellent. He seemed merely to be thinking about something with which we had nothing, could never have anything, to do.

As for us, we gazed at him, and most of us, when we shook hands, murmured something we hoped was appropriate. For instance, Lady Ermyntrude said, in her throaty Victorian voice: "The late Queen loved your music next after Mendelssohn's, cher Monsieur." Mrs. Bethune said, as she sketched a vague dip, not a curtsey, but a movement of the same family as a curtsey, "In the States we think a lot of you, Master." Countess Faviacasa murmured, *Maestro,* in a warm, overwhelmed voice. Lady Carrò, with her cheerful head held well forward and sideways, exclaimed, "Cher Maître, I have heard you at the Madeleine on the king of instruments. Two kings together!" Then followed the Punch-and-Judy movement so characteristic of her. As for me, I believe I said something about hoping that the baths of Hammam Ziloutine would prolong the life of one so precious to humanity. Rather too long and elaborate, as I realised when Mrs. Doremus somewhat hastily interposed with "Major Greyne, one of our most famous administrators, cher Maître."

When the last of us had been presented, the clock hastened to chime the half-hour, and Monsieur de Morisot exclaimed, of course in French:

"Just right! Just right! I said to the Master, order the motor for the quarter-past noon, allow three minutes, perhaps four, for the introductions, and on the stroke of the half-hour we shall all be ready to sit down to table."

And then there was an alarming pause. For we were not ready to sit down to table. Mrs. Doremus uttered her little cough, smiled, abruptly looked dreadfully grave, then smiled again. A guest was missing. Some outrageous person was not up to time. Who was it? Mrs. Doremus began hurriedly to speak about the African weather, and everyone began to look uncomfortable except the two Arab chieftains, Major Greyne, who had the sort of brick-red, weather-beaten face that can't look anything except weather-beaten, and the Master, who contrived to maintain the appearance of an old Royalty in a State landau.

"—and so the crops in the Bled ought to be exceptional this year, Kur-*rum!*"

Our hostess's voice tailed away, and then suddenly broke out in the sound that seemed half a cough, half a clearing of the throat. A silence followed, in which was audible the tick-tack of the black and gold lacquer clock on the marble chimney-piece.

"It has even rained as far south as El-Kantara. Hasn't it, Bach-Agha?"

A heavy mutter of smothered Arabic-French issued from the recesses of the Bach-Agha's mighty beard.

"And they say that—"

The Master turned his prominent eyes towards the clock, put one hand inside his frock coat, extracted a tiny round silver box, opened it, and swallowed a minute pill. Monsieur de Morisot bent down, abruptly halving his height, put his large, flexible lips—something India-rubber about them!—to the ear of Mrs. Doremus, and seemed to speak at great length, though where I stood his voice was inaudible.

"Yes, I know, my dear friend, I *know!* But it's—"

Whispering from Mrs. Doremus. More prolonged and emphatic lip movements by Monsieur de Morisot, his height still halved. A dusky red despair was invading our charming hostess, when the door opened and the twenty-fourth member of the lunch party entered the room.

Imagine my amazement when I beheld the most notoriously unmusical Englishman of his time, Lord Nottinghamshire, M.F.H., member of the Jockey Club, racehorse owner, presenter of the "Nottinghamshire Belt" to be fought for each year by British heavyweights, a big, red, laughing Philistine of a man, who, I was certain, had never even heard of the Master. How came *he* here? I learned afterwards that his steam yacht, *Brave Lass*, had come into the harbour the day before, and that Mrs. Doremus had at once dispatched a pressing lunch invitation to him. He was an English celebrity. She couldn't "leave him out" on such an occasion. So now we saw him come forward laughing, in a suit of loud checks and a bright yellow tie, and saying in his hearty voice:

"'Fraid I'm a bit late, eh? Couldn't get anything but a broken-down Ford to bring me here. Sparking plug all wrong. Had to tinker at things myself. Sorry!"

Mrs. Doremus presented herself.

"Delighted! No, not at all late. Let me—Lord Nottinghamshire— Monsieur Saint Sauveur."

As the Master gave his hand to the aristocratic sportsman, I noticed that for the first time he looked at a guest. Then, without any further introductions, we were—yes, really it came to that—we were hustled into the dining room.

III

The lunches of Mrs. Doremus were invariably banquets. Her food was the sort of food that insists on being taken seriously. Her wines could not be swallowed in a spirit of lightsome frivolity. And, besides, we were a mixed bag that day, what with the Arabs, the French, the English, the Italians, the South American wife of the Admiral, Mrs. Bethune from California, and Mrs. Bullock, who, as everybody knows, had a Scandinavian father and an Irish mother. Then a Governor, a Commanding General, the Admiral of a Port, a Consul-General, a couple of Oriental chieftains and the Glory of France, when mingled for the first time, could hardly be expected to be very light in hand. They were not. In the beginning only two voices were heard—so to say, really and unmistakably heard—among us; the voice of dear Monsieur de Morisot, who generally seems physically unable, despite any mental effort to the contrary, to stop talking, and the voice of Lord Nottinghamshire. These joined in a fairly strenuous duet, the respective themes being Wagner and Dempsey, with, as variations, Hadyn, Mozart, Tchaikovsky, Saint Sauveur, Carpentier, Beckett, Jimmie Wilde, and Kid Lewis. Mrs. Doremus occasionally interpolated a sort of muffled grace-note, or uttered her little "Kur-*rum!*" The rest of us were mainly silent.

I was seated between Lady Carrò who was on my left, and Mrs. Eleonora Bullock. Beyond Lady Carrò sat the Master on Mrs. Doremus's right hand.

I noticed that Monsieur Saint Sauveur, like many famous Frenchmen, took the midday meal in a spirit of high seriousness. With a napkin over his black satin tie, and bending forward over his plate, eyes front, he ate very slowly, masticating each morsel with patient care, and combining the various items simultaneously before him—as, for instance, venison, red currant jelly, puffed potatoes, French beans and green salad—in a masterly manner by means of knife and fork, with occasional aid, when in serious difficulties, from a carefully selected fragment of Toast Melba. Mrs. Doremus often looked rather anxiously towards him, or signed to the butler to take special care of him, but she evidently felt that the suitable moment to add a little conversation to the menu was not yet come. Not so my Lady Carrò however. By various symptoms on my left I gathered that she was increasingly desirous of getting into talk with the great man. She fidgeted, sighed, smiled, looked suddenly intelligent, animated, even roguish, assumed an expression of almost romantic gravity, put her head on one side, and several times opened her lips not in connection with food. But the complete abstraction of the Master evidently disconcerted her, and at last she turned round to me and murmured:

"Do you think I had better say something to him?"

I was secretly extremely doubtful on the point, but I took the resolute course, and said:

"Yes."

"Very well, I will!"

And she turned round to the left, braced up, leaned forward obliquely, smiled with raised eyebrows and widely-opened eyes, and exclaimed with her utmost briskness:

"At what age, cher Maître, did you discover that you possessed the marvellous genius for music with which you have delighted us all for so long?"

Monsieur Saint Sauveur retrieved a Brussels sprout, which seemed to be endeavouring to make its escape unperceived through a pool of brown gravy, dealt with it slowly and completely, slightly turned, and, without looking at Lady Carrò, replied in a clear, almost crystalline voice:

"At the age of two!"

He then turned calmly and redevoted himself to his meal, while Lady Carrò, apparently uncertain whether she had brought off a success, or fallen among the ruins of a failure, made a sharp movement sideways, still leaning forward after the manner of Judy. I, too, had been for an instant uncertain, but I speedily realised what her gallantry had achieved. The ice was broken. The Master had uttered a consecutive sentence in a voice which all had been able to hear. A small roar of musical conversation broke out. Lord Nottinghamshire's and Monsieur de Morisot's duet was succeeded by a chorus in which it seemed to me that everyone present took part, except the Master, who still ploughed his lonely furrow through Mrs. Doremus's marvellous lunch, and the two Arabs. But as—if my experience is to be trusted—Arabs never talk much, if at all, in mixed company, and are never vivacious in the house of a Roumi, there was nothing exceptional in their dignified silence. They had nothing to say, and very sensibly did not say it, in that reticence showing a wisdom akin to that of Monsieur Saint Sauveur.

I must confess, with regard to the last named, that his enormous self-possession began almost to hypnotise me. Although I had been going about in society for a great many years, I had never before met anyone who flatly refused—only by manner, look, general demeanour, it is true, but they in combination amounted to a flat refusal—to take any, even the smallest, part in the social entertainment. Of Monsieur Saint Sauveur at Mrs. Doremus's lunch party it could be said that he was an eating human being present in our midst. Nothing more could be truly said of him in his capacity as a social unit. Lady Carrò did not venture to address him again. Mrs. Doremus smiled over him, set the butler at him with second helpings and decanters of various wines, talked music to others so that he might hear and realise that he was in the midst of true devotees, but I never observed that she directly addressed him. And he continued calmly to select and to masticate, and to sip from the various glasses on his right, till the end of lunch. Only twice during that time did he raise his head from his plate, and seem for an instant to be aware that he was not alone. And on each of these occasions I noticed that he looked at Lord Nottinghamshire, who was sitting almost exactly opposite to him, eating and drinking with hearty good will, and talking genially to all and sundry.

After lunch we all went upstairs into the marvellous Arab drawing room, with its narrow arches, its columns, its small windows, guarded by iron grilles, its divans, brass-bound coffers, cedar wood and inlaid cabinets, mother-of-pearl coffee tables, wrought brass lamps, exquisite prayer carpets, Tunisian pottery and collection of Oriental china. For a moment I wandered away from the general company. My attention had been attracted by a new acquisition of my hostess, a Chinese pagoda fashioned in blue and white china, which had been placed on a carved bracket in a distant corner of the big room. As I was standing before it—aware of a roar of talk about music behind me—I heard a hearty voice exclaim:

"I say—are you English?"

I turned round and met the shrewd grey eyes of Lord Nottinghamshire.

"Yes," I said.

"Thought so! Well now, you can put me up to something. Who's the old boy in the frock coat, the chap who looks as if he ought to be behind eight cream-coloured horses, don't you know, driving to open Parliament?"

"That's Monsieur Saint Sauveur."

"Who's he?"

"The great French composer."

"What of?"

"The great musician, the Glory of France, the man who wrote *Hercules in the Augean Stables*.

"Stables! Does he know anything about a horse?"

"No, it's an opera."

"Never heard of him!"

"He really is famous all over the world."

"Queer kind of fame! I never so much as heard of him. But I'll do him the justice to say he can eat. I should like to get him to the Cheshire Cheese. Think he's ever been there?"

"I really couldn't say."

"Haven't I seen you at the National Sporting?"

"I go there sometimes."

"Good! Good! Thought I'd laid eyes on you there. And so that old boy wrote something about stables, did he?"

He seemed to hang on to that word as if it were very blessed.

"Yes, but only music."

"O Lord, I hate music! Beastly noise! One hears too much of it these days. It's a perfect curse. Wherever a fellow goes it's squalling, and fiddling, and hullabalooing. But anyhow the old boy's written about stables, eh? Well, that's all to the good. I thought somehow he'd got something in him. The way he stuck to his food, don't you know? Showed character! Showed grit! And now you tell me he's written something about stables—"

But at this moment I heard a fairly loud "Kur-*rum!*" behind us, and then Mrs. Doremus's husky voice saying: "Lord Nottinghamshire, may I give you some Arab coffee?"

IV

"Wagner," said Monsieur de Morisot, with elaborate lip movements, and the gestures of an accomplished orator, "has been, and still is, the curse of modern music."

A "circle" had now been formed in the Arab drawing room, in the midst of which, in an armchair made as Oriental by Eastern draperies as an armchair ever can be made, sat the Glory of France, with a coffee cup and a glass of yellow Chartreuse beside him, tranquilly digesting his lunch. So far as I knew he had not spoken again since his memorable remark to Lady Carrò, but by certain signs and symptoms, by a subtle brightening of the eye, a faint mantling of the generous blood in his cheeks, an occasional twitch of the lips beneath his well-trimmed moustache, I gathered that he intended presently, perhaps even quite soon, to say something to us. Meanwhile dear Monsieur de Morisot, unasked, gave us a discourse on the musical abominations of modern Germany, and compared with them the exquisitely clear, logical and melodious compositions of the French, headed by their doyen, who was quietly sipping Chartreuse before our very eyes.

Monsieur Saint Sauveur sat quite still, apparently listening like the rest of us, one small hand hidden in the breast of his coat, the other laid lightly on his left knee. Occasionally he seemed to me to send a glance across the room to a divan upon which Lord Nottinghamshire was lolling in an easy attitude, smoking an enormous cigar of a very special brand which he had brought with him. And it also seemed to me that Lord Nottinghamshire returned the Master's glance, and that some occult sympathy had sprung up between the two men, celebrities both of them, but belonging to two absolutely alien worlds. Yet how could such a thing be? Lord Nottinghamshire detested what Monsieur Saint Sauveur had spent his life for. I must be mistaken. Any sympathy between two such opposites must surely be quite impossible.

"The curse of Wagner is length. He never knows when to stop. He never knows when to—"

The Master applied himself to the Chartreuse, settled himself again in his chair, touched the rosette of the Legion of Honour with a pointed forefinger and faintly smiled.

"I'm *sure* he's going to begin!" Lady Carrò whispered to me. "I *feel* there's something coming. If only dear Monsieur de Morisot would—"

But dear Monsieur de Morisot wouldn't. He had got into his stride by now, and was listening with rapt attention to the admirable phrases which poured in a torrent from his lips.

"Compare the dreary and formless lengths of the *Ring* with the crystalline brevity, the conciseness, the marvelous form of our great Master's *Hercules in the Augean Stables.* Compare—"

There was a strong murmur of approval from the "circle," and Lord Nottinghamshire, I noticed, at the word "stables" leaned forward on his divan and seemed to be lending an attentive ear.

"Wagner, I repeat, was a monster, and has created only monstrosities. It is all very well to pretend that Wagner—"

A slight, but exceedingly definite sound from the armchair suddenly arrested Monsieur de Morisot's attention. He turned his large, dishevelled head, and saw Monsieur Saint Sauveur showing quite obvious signs of life.

"But who am I to speak about Wagner when we have here among us the great critic and merciless analyst of Wagner, the man who has opposed to the tremendous German muddle of dwarfs and giants, dragons, and shrieking women on horseback, broomsticks, or what not, a Hercules whom all can understand, an Eve fresh as the first morning of the world, a Pharaoh's daughter"—(again the sound !)—"Yes, cher Maître—yes?"

And Monsieur de Morisot hung over the armchair in a large attitude of sprawling attention, while we all leaned forward breathless.

"Wagner," said Monsieur Saint Sauveur, in a clear, small voice, "as even Nietzsche eventually found out, was a great—"

He paused for an instant, not, I am certain, because he was at a loss for the exactly right word, but because he was an accomplished speaker and knew the value a properly measured pause gives to the word which succeeds it. What that word was, or rather, was to be, however, we never knew, for dear Monsieur de Morisot fell heavily, like a lump of lead really, into the pause with a:

"What I have always said! What I have said from the very beginning! That was what Wagner was, and he could never be anything else."

And he proceeded to flow on with the genial turbulence so characteristic of him, while Monsieur Saint Sauveur, with slightly raised eyebrows, settled himself again in his chair and took another sip at his liqueur glass.

It was, perhaps, some ten minutes later that Mrs. Doremus, in desperation, broke in upon Monsieur de Morisot's lecture—for it had really become nothing less by that time—with a "Kur-*rum!*" so emphatic, so obviously intentional, that it had to be attended to.

"Kur-*rum!* Cher Maître—"

Monsieur Saint Sauveur bent slightly towards her, without, however, looking at her.

"I wish you to know that music, and especially *your* music, has always been my greatest joy and consolation."

The very phrase of her note to me!

"Your *Hercules in the—in the Stables*"—Lord Nottinghamshire took his cigar out of his mouth and suddenly looked keen—"has softened"— I believe she used the word "adouci"—"many a lonely hour for me. I just wished you to know that. And now—"

She got up. I knew what she was going to do. I knew she was going to suggest showing the Master over the gardens. When confronted by a social difficulty she always showed people over the gardens. But this time it was not to be. We were all on our feet, and the Bach-Agha of the Aurés, with the imperial courtesy characteristic of Arabs of the highest class, bending with dignity had assisted the Master to his, when a marvelous diversion occurred. Monsieur Saint Sauveur, standing erect, and looking more like an old Royalty in a landau than ever, for the first time since his arrival turned his eyes upon us, gazed steadily round from one to the other, as if taking careful stock of us all, and finally came absolutely and definitely to life.

"Where is the music room?" he said, with vitality.

I could see a thrill go through the assembly. Only Lord Nottinghamshire and the Arabs were exempt. Lord Nottinghamshire stood turning his cigar end about between his lips, and a bored expression showed in his clean-shaven, horsey face.

"The—music room, cher Maître?" said Mrs. Doremus, in a faltering voice.

"Mais oui! Mais oui! As you all love music so much I will play to you my pianoforte transcription of the great air of my Hercules, '*Lève-toi, grand soleil.*'"

A combined sound of ecstacy broke from us all—with the exception of the two Arab chieftains, of Lord Nottinghamshire and, strangely enough, of our hostess. Even the Admiral, being French and patriotic, joined in the demonstration. Even Major Greyne, warmed by wine, took his part.

"I—we—we all should love it! Such an opportunity! Such a—but, cher Maître, I grieve to say that there is no music room. You see, in these old Arab houses, no provision is made for—one has to put up with—"

Monsieur Saint Sauveur smiled. And his smile was quite kind, even cordial.

"*Je comprends! Je comprends!* Then take me to the piano. There is no need of a music room. Where is your piano, Madame?"

He was already in movement when an awful look in his hostess's face gave him pause. How can I describe that look? It was the scarlet horror of a "cornered" human being, of a human being found out in the face of the world. It seemed to make an impression even upon the supremely detached, supremely self-possessed Master. For he stood quite still, gazing, even staring, at his hostess.

"*Mais qu'est ce qu'il y a, chère Madame? Qu'est ce que vous avez?*"

"*C'est que—c'est que—*it—it— The fact is that these old Arab houses— in these old houses—these—Arab—these-these—"

"*Eh bien—chêre Madame?*"

"I am very sorry, cher Maître, very, *very* sorry! But—but I haven't got a piano."

Five minutes later Monsieur Saint Sauveur had taken his leave. There was a sort of general confusion among us, as there often is among people who have been involved in a common disaster, and I presently found myself in the hall just behind Lord Nottinghamshire, whose Ford was waiting at the entrance in company with the enormous limousine which had conveyed Monsieur Saint Sauveur and Monsieur de Morisot from the Hotel des Gazelles to the Villa Karibi. I was searching for my hat when I heard Lord Nottinghamshire's hearty voice saying:

"Let me give you a lift to the town, sir. My yacht's lying in the harbour. I should like to show you over her. She's a beauty. And I can promise you there's no piano aboard her. I don't pretend to be a musician. Tell the truth I hate music, can't stick it, never could from a boy. But I can give you as good a cigar and as good a drop of Scotch whisky as you've ever had in your life. Now what d'you say?"

What the Master did say I didn't catch. For the tumultuous voice of dear Monsieur de Morisot broke in with loud protestations. But it didn't prevail. For by the time I had discovered my hat and got out of the house, Monsieur Saint Sauveur, well wrapped up, was already seated by Lord Nottinghamshire's side in the back of the Ford, and as the little black vehicle started asthmatically down the drive, by the lawn edge and the fat assemblage of palm trees, I heard his lordship saying:

"This damned sparking plug's all wrong, but I'll get you to the yacht somehow, and once we're there, well away from all these musicians, we'll both have a jolly good—"

The rest of the sentence was lost to me between the double lines of the arum lilies.

The Worth While Man

"That's the difficulty in the country, unfortunately," said Mrs. Chetwynde Mason in her slightly hard intellectual voice. "Nature— well, one has the blessed power of choosing your Nature. If you like hills you look about till you find them. Valleys, rivers, plains, forests— the same. You search for them if you want them. You find them. There they are and down you can sit and enjoy them. You can even—if you've got the money," she added negligently, as if it were an afterthought, — "if you've got the money—build the ideal house and lay out the ideal garden...."

"As you have done here," said Lady Caroway, at this point.

"... As I have tried to do at any rate ... in the midst of the Nature which happens to appeal to your particular temperament. The choice is yours." (She stared for a moment at a remarkably fine specimen of a herbaceous border which stretched away in front of the two perfect garden armchairs in which she and her visitor were seated on a lawn of green velvet in the sunshine of summer.) "But when it comes to people, to what are called *neighbours*"—she made a slight gesture as if repelling an invisible something—"why then you are at the mercy of chance, fate, whatever you may choose to call it. There is nothing to prevent a rich pork butcher from settling down next door to a famous philosopher. There is nothing to prevent anyone from settling down next door to anyone. The most terrible propinquities can, and as I know from experience *do*, occur in the country, owing to the horrible power of choice which belongs to the most impossible people, to vulgarians, semi-idiots, cretins, the ignorant, the coarse, in fact to almost everybody. The most heavenly view, which in your natural selfishness you might wish to reserve for yourself and your choicest friends, may happen to attract dullards, even horrors. And what are you to do? *Neighbours!* Oh, my dear Eleanor, you who live almost perpetually in London can probably scarcely imagine the dreadful associations that word holds for some of us who happen to be sensitive, who happen to care only for the *worth while*, not merely in art, literature, and music, but in people."

"Well now, that gives me the courage to make a confession to you," said Lady Caroway, looking down at the green lawn with her bright blue, rather humorous eyes. "I've always rather wondered at your buying a property and building this lovely house so near to Brankhurst."

"To Brankhurst!" said Mrs. Chetwynde Mason, lifting her large intellectual head a little, and fixing her authoritative and slightly arrogant grey eyes on her pretty, curly, and petite friend. "What has Brankhurst got to do with it?"

"You are so sensitive about your neighbours, you are so easily affected by the wrong people, that I've always wondered that you cared to make your home—one of your homes—so near to a lunatic asylum. That's what I meant."

Mrs. Chetwynde Mason laughed, not merrily, but patronisingly.

"Lunatics are not neighbours, dear!"

"They live within a few miles of you."

"I know they do. But they might be in California for all one has to do with them."

"Don't you ever see them?"

"Occasionally I see poor Lady Glenbarley—the Earl of Glenbarley's wife—driving with her keepers, or Lord Brighton motoring with his. (Brankhurst is the most expensive and luxurious asylum in England). But lunatics are not at liberty to call on you, to invite you to their houses, to persist in expecting you to lavish hospitality on them. You can't make enemies of lunatics, as unfortunately you can of neighbours, if you give them the cold shoulder. Brankhurst doesn't affect me at all. Why should it? It's a lovely property and one has nothing whatever to do with its owners and inhabitants. I consider it an advantage. One might have some terrible plutocrat settled there, who might bore one to death with his well-meant, but pestilent, attentions. Lunatics! What are lunatics?"

"I think I should feel uneasy so near to them."

"Why?"

"Supposing one of them escaped?"

Mrs. Chetwynde Mason smiled, as only a very rich woman can smile.

"You evidently don't know much about Brankhurst. It's perhaps the most exclusive asylum in Europe."

"But—"

"They only receive the most exclusive lunatics there."

"Well, but how can a lunatic be exclusive?"

"Cannot a lunatic be well-born?"

"Oh yes, of course!"

"Cannot a lunatic be wealthy?"

"Yes, no doubt."

"Brankhurst is specially arranged and run for such lunatics. They have their own apartments, furnished according—"

"Not surely according to their own individual tastes!" interpolated Lady Caroway.

"No; according to the taste of their nearest relatives, or guardians. They have their own highly trained keepers."

"Are keepers trained—like setters?"

"You frivolous creature! They have their own carriages, horses, motorcars. Perfect cooking, I understand. The gardens are lovely and very large. Brankhurst is a beautiful retreat for the mentally afflicted rather than a lunatic asylum. Lord Brighton has lived there for over twenty years. He has a car and two charming-looking keepers. A place like Brankhurst is no disadvantage to me. No; it's the *neighbours* I suffer from."

"Are they so dreadful? I thought the county was full of interesting people.”

"It is full of *bores*," said Mrs. Chetwynde Mason emphatically.

"How unfortunate! But do they come and bore you?"

"They do. You see, I'm pretty well known."

"I should think so!"

"They've read about me in the papers. They've found out I had a *salon* in New York where all the famous men of the day used to come. Of course since my husband's death I've given it up but still—"

"But still—indeed!" murmured Lady Caroway, seriously. "Then my connection with Shakespeare has made me known over here."

"Are you a relative of Shakespeare?"

"No; but I founded a library in Kansas, and endowed a Shakespeare Chair in connection with it, and my press agent—I mean that there was a lot about it in the papers over here."

"To be sure!"

"The result of it is that all the bores for miles around, and they are many, call upon me."

"Hard lines!"

"Rectors and their wives call; stockbrokers and their wives call; publishers—the place swarms with publishers—come; socialists—there are lots about here in bungalows—come. A retired conjurer—"

"What!"

"A retired conjurer actually motored over and got in here on a Sunday, when I had Professor Smike and his wife from Oxford with me, and J. J. Hankup."

"The great writer?"

"Yes, of course! He just destroyed our Sunday afternoon. He simply assassinated it, and on the plea that he had been in the neighbourhood longer than I had, and so it was his duty to call upon *me*. His *duty!* Apparently in England the old inhabitant, however horrible, has the right to inflict his presence on the newcomer, however sensitive, even perhaps refined. *That* requires altering."

"Poor thing! I do genuinely feel for you."

"I don't want to be intemperate but one must call it disastrous. I hear that Professor Smike talks about it to this day—at Oxford."

"And J. J. Hankup?"

"Oh, he took it as a rare piece of raw human nature. But you know how delightfully eccentric he is. I shouldn't complain if the people about here were worth while. But they aren't. You'll forgive me for saying it, but really your English countryside contains very few fully educated people. There is very little genuine culture among them. Tennis and golf they understand. If it's a question of going out with the harriers or of drawing a badger they are up to the mark. But their minds, dear, are definitely dull. They have scarcely any conversation beyond what I call weather-conversation, which to me is intolerable. Intellectual movements are beyond their ken. *They* are not on the lookout for new comets. Although I have been here now for two summers I have not met a single really worth while man or woman who lives in my neighbourhood. All my artistic and intellectual sustenance comes to me from London."

"By boat, rail, and motor," murmured Lady Caroway.

"You must have your little joke, dear. But you see the situation! Oh—here's Barstow bringing some more bores to bother me!"

The large butler was visible in the offing proceeding at a leisurely pace towards them, his bald head glowing in the sunlight, followed by an elderly lady in black wearing a small cottage bonnet, and by a damsel in printed muslin.

"Actually a bonnet!" said Mrs. Chetwynde Mason. "You see, dear! Have I exaggerated?"

"I'm afraid not," said Lady Caroway, getting up to go. "I must rush off to town now. Barstow will tell my chauffeur."

"Mrs. Sampson and Miss Ellen Sampson! " announced Barstow, in a penetrating baritone voice.

"Barstow!"

"Madam?"

"Remember that from to-day nobody is to be let in without my knowing first who it is. You understand?" said Mrs. Chetwynde Mason, an hour and a half later, as Mrs. Sampson and Miss Ellen Sampson drove slowly away from Amber Grange in a dusty fly from the village of Amber two and a half miles away.

"Am I to say not at home, Madam?"

"Yes."

"Very well, Madam."

Barstow turned to depart and was near the drawing room door when Mrs. Chetwynde Mason said:

"Barstow!"

"Madam?"

"I think it will be better if in future you say to callers that you are not sure whether I am at home or not and that you will go and see. Take their names and then come to me—if I *am* in of course."

"Very well, Madam."

"That will do."

Barstow left the room and Mrs. Chetwynde Mason glanced round it with a sigh. It was a lovely room, full of beautiful things, large, with windows open to an exquisite garden. The scent of roses came to her. She heard the drowsy buzzing of a bumble bee just outside. A slight, soft breeze stirred the gold-coloured curtains. A shaft of sunlight fell on her favourite Correggio: *Christ With the Woman Taken in Adultery*. She looked down and her eyes fell on books by Edith Wharton, by Lothrop Stoddard, by Henry James, by Willa Cather, then wandered away to the open grand piano with a score by Stravinsky upon it. She thought of the view outside, a wide, blue, and lovely distance, an exquisitely varied foreground. And then she thought of Mrs. Sampson and Miss Ellen Sampson.

"What beautiful weather we've been having lately! My daughter won the silver spoon in the Amber tennis tournament. Didn't you, Ellen?"

"Yes, mother."

"Are you going to the garden party at Brankhurst? It takes place next week. We are going. Aren't we, Ellen?"

"Yes, mother."

"If this lovely weather holds the rector intends to have the annual Rummage Sale out of doors in the Rectory garden. Will you be there? Ellen's going to sell castoff garments. Aren't you, Ellen?"

"Yes, mother."

"If you have any castoff garments available it would be very kind of you to give them to Ellen for her stall. She can do with more than she has, and we country people ought to help one another, don't you think, and be neighbourly. I always believe in being neighbourly—"—etc., etc.

No more of it! Henceforth Barstow should guard the house from intruders. She hadn't spent nearly twenty thousand pounds in order that—

"What is it now, Barstow?"

For Barstow was again advancing from the door that opened into the inner hall of the mansion.

"A gentleman has called, Madam, and asked for you. At least he said to me"—and Barstow's baritone took on a more dignified tone—"Is your mistress at home?'"

"What name did he give?"

"He told me to say Lord Lionel Danesborough, Madam."

"Lord Lion—"

Mrs. Chetwynde Mason paused abruptly and mentally scampered through Debrett. Danesborough! Let's see. That was surely the family name of the Dukes of Hampshire. Yes! One never met the present Duke and Duchess in society. They were both notoriously shy, and lived in great retirement at their lovely place, Morton Abbey. The Duke had brothers—Danesboroughs. This must be one of them. She had never heard of a Danesborough living in her neighbourhood. Still—

"Lord Lionel! Oh, of course! Show him in, Barstow, and—"

"May I come in?" said a pleasant voice somewhere.

Mrs. Chetwynde Mason started and turned round. In the embrasure of one of the drawing room windows stood a very tall man of perhaps forty-five, with a long, large-featured face, and large brown eyes that held a rather melancholy expression. His brown hair was thinning on a curiously narrow but well-shaped head. He was extremely well-dressed in country clothes and held a soft grey hat and a gold-topped walking stick in one long-fingered hand. He was really an ugly man, but he was the sort of ugly man whose obvious high breeding and quiet assurance are full of attractive power. And he had, as Mrs. Chetwynde Mason noticed, a magnificent figure.

"I couldn't resist taking a peep at your marvellous garden, so I came round informally," added the very agreeable voice. And the splendid figure stepped into the room.

Mrs. Chetwynde Mason, rather surprised, but with her usual complete composure, held out her hand.

"Very kind of you to come, Lord Lionel. Bring tea, please, Barstow."

"Yes, Madam."

"Your lobelias are extraordinary," said the visitor, after pressing his hostess's hand. "Surely that must be a Correggio."

And he walked slowly towards the *Woman Taken in Adultery*.

"Yes, it is," said Mrs. Chetwynde Mason.

"Antonio Allegri," murmured the visitor. "A very fine specimen, too. The woman's attitude is masterly. You have been to Parma, of course?"

"Yes, of course—well, no, I haven't—yet," said Mrs. Chetwynde Mason in some slight confusion. "But I am going—probably this year."

"You ought to," said Lord Lionel, with a hint of reproach. "Until you have been to Parma and seen the cupolas there you cannot be said to know Correggio. By the way it is quite untrue that his people were rich. They were neither rich nor poor. But no doubt you are aware that his father was comfortably off. So you have a Burne-Jones, too. Do you know his *Love disguised as Reason*? But of course you do. My favourite picture—I'm speaking of *his* work—is his *Chant d'Amour*. There is a rare ecstasy of romance in that. Isn't there?"

"Indeed there is! Do sit down, Lord Lionel."

"Ah, you can get orchestral effects from this make," he said, walking over to the grand piano, beside which bloomed an enormous orange pink azalea in a tub of oriental china. "Are you fond of Wagner still?"

"Yes, very."

"So am I. But, you know, *les jeunes* are beginning to run him down. Bayreuth, so they tell me, is only frequented by the middle-aged now. There is no doubt that while the reputation of Wagner begins to wane the reputation of his adversary, Nietzsche, waxes. Do you remember that passage in Nietzsche's 'Nietzsche contra Wagner' beginning 'Richard Wagner, ostensibly the most triumphal creature alive, as a matter of fact, though, a cranky and desperate decadent, suddenly fell helpless and broken on his knees before the Christian Cross'—do you?"

"I'm not quite—let me see—"

"You don't," he remarked quietly, with just the least hint of intellectual regret. "No one can understand Wagner who has not studied Nietzsche's attack on him. The great Charlatan! The great Necromancer! Cagliostro in music! Have you been to Palermo?"

"Yes. I—"

"Giuseppe Balsamo—that was Cagliostro's real name—was born there, as of course you know. He died at San Leo. Cagliostro, Paganini, Wagner, there is an affinity between them. And Franz Liszt? What about him?"

He fixed his large, rather melancholy eyes on her dreamily, and yet enquiringly.

"You think that he—"

"Hadn't he a touch of the charlatan, too? Saintly and naughty! For you know Liszt was naughty. When he lived at Tivoli in his old age he had two female servants, and he used to embrace them. They said so themselves when they, in their turn, were old. 'He was very fond of embracing us.' Those were their very words."

"Were they really?"

"You didn't know it?"

Barstow and a saucy-looking young footman appeared with a sumptuous tea, and Mrs. Chetwynde Mason, conscious unusually of ignorance, begged her remarkable visitor to come to the tea-table.

"I am very fond of the music of Liszt," she said, striving after her usual authority as he sat down opposite to her. "His Hungarian rhapsodies—"

"Circus music!" said Lord Lionel quietly. "Thank you." (He accepted a cup of tea, and reached out gently for a bit of buttered toast). "The real Liszt, the ascetic libertine, the Abbé with illegitimate children—him you will find in such things as *Saint Stanislas* and *La Gondole Funèbre*. You are familiar with them of course? No!"

He sighed faintly, like a man disconcerted, as a school inspector might be by the ignorance of a child unable to remember who Adam was.

"Do have some strawberry jam, Lord Lionel," was the best retort Mrs. Chetwynde Mason could muster.

"Thank you." (He took some.) "Is that vase I see in the distance standing on an ebony pedestal Etruscan?"

"Yes—no! Which vase? Do you mean—"

He felt for, and put up to his eyes, a double eyeglass circled with rims of tortoiseshell.

"Oh, no, it wouldn't be Etruscan, would it? I thought you meant—"

"It *is* Etruscan," he remarked, putting down the eyeglass, and spreading some strawberry jam on his buttered toast. "Of the primitive period. Have you made a deep study of ceramics?"

"Oh yes! At least—well, *deep* is a strong word, isn't it?"

"No study is worth very much unless it is deep—and wide. At Morton, my brother Hampshire's place, there is an Etruscan Amphora imitating the Greek style. It shows Alcestis and Admetus. You remember who Admetus was?"

"Of course I do. He was loved by Aphrodite and was killed by a wild boar when hunting."

"You are confusing him with Adonis. Admetus was King of Pherae in Thessaly. Surely you remember his story? Euripides took it as the subject of his *The Alcestis*."

"Oh, to be sure!"

"And Browning—but, of course, you have studied Browning's *Balaustion's Adventure?*"

"Of course. Who hasn't?"

"A great many people, I'm afraid. Noble poetry isn't read much in these days."

"Oh, but think of the Sitwells!" said Mrs. Chetwyned Mason, with all the eagerness of one retaking a lost position.

"No," said Lord Lionel, almost with severity. "I shall think of Homer. I shall think of Horace, of Virgil, of Ovid, especially of Horace."

He closed his expressive eyes for a moment and murmured: "*Nec lusisse pudet, sed non incidere ludum.*"

He opened them and added:

"I hope you feel as he did about that?"

"I certainly do!" said Mrs. Chetwynde Mason, with anxious conviction.

"You understand the classics?"

"Well, yes—in a certain degree. That is, I don't read them fluently, but I can pick out—"

"It is not seemly to 'pick out' in the classics. But why be ashamed to confess ignorance of them? I say with Cicero, '*Nec me pudet ut istos, fateri nescire quod nesciam.*' When I do not know I am not ashamed to say so."

"But your knowledge, Lord Lionel, seems far-reaching, quite remarkable, if I may say so."

"Oh, I took a first in Classics at Oxford. But that's nothing."

"Some more tea?"

"Yes, if you are good enough to give me some. Are you fond of solving mathematical problems?"

"No," said Mrs. Chetwynde Mason, rather hastily. "I prefer the arts."

"Painting? Sculpture?"

"Oh, I love sculpture. What is your opinion of Epstein?"

"I know nothing about him. I have never heard of him. May I take some more of this delicious jam?"

"Do please! But surely you must have—"

"Never, I assure you. He hasn't come my way. I was brought up on Michelangelo, Donatello, Benvenuto Cellini, that rascal of genius. What do you think of Jacopo della Quercia?"

"Oh—well—of course he is very fine, very fine indeed."

"What do you think of his *Ilaria del Carretto* at Lucca?"

"Wonderful! Marvellous!"

He fixed his eyes on her in a look that seemed to be piercing. "You have visited Lucca?"

"Oh yes—at least—"

"You haven't visited Lucca. Go there, when you have the time, and study Quercia."

"I will most certainly. I have always intended—"

With a vague look he seemed, but very gently indeed, to rebuke her.

"Good intentions should be carried on into actions," he said, but not unkindly. "The philosophers tell us that fine thoughts should produce fine deeds. If you have always intended to go to Lucca in order to see the *Ilaria del Carretto* there you should yield yourself entirely to that intention—and *go.*"

He laid a rather startling emphasis upon the final word.

"Are you a great traveller?" asked Mrs. Chetwynde Mason hastily, to make a diversion.

"I never travel now."

"Indeed! And—and you live in England?"

He looked slightly surprised.

"Of course. I live in this neighbourhood. I have motored past your beautiful house several times and wished to enter it. But till to-day it has not been possible. So many engagements."

"Of course you must have! I thought I had seen you somewhere when you came in by the window with such pleasant informality."

"You have probably seen me motoring. I passed here only yesterday with a couple of men friends. You have probably seen us about together. We are inseparables."

He frowned slightly and looked out into the garden.

"Horticulture is evidently a hobby of yours," he said after a very slight pause.

"Yes, indeed! I am a great gardener."

"Do you believe in bottom heat?"

"Bottom heat?" said Mrs. Chetwynde Mason, in a rather blank tone of voice.

"Don't you know that gardeners call artificial heat applied to the roots of plants bottom heat?"

"Do they? Oh yes, to be sure! I remember now. Yes, I do believe in it— in certain cases."

"Which ones?"

"Well in—well—I—I think it depends a good deal on the nature of the soil."

"I don't. I think it depends on the nature of the plant. The *optimum* temperature best suited to a zonal pelargonium, for instance, is totally different from the *optimum* temperature which would give the best results with, say, an *asplenium bulbiferum*. Don't you agree with me when you really give your mind to it?"

"Yes, I do."

"What is your view on fan training?"

"Well really I—I possess a fine collection of fans, but they are in my house in New York."

"I was speaking of the training of fruit trees."

"Oh, I beg your—"

"The morello cherry, for instance. How do you treat your morello cherries? Do you subject them to the whole, the modified, or the half-fan training?"

"Well now, let me see!"

"Perhaps you have no morello cherries?"

"Oh yes, I'm sure I have, but—"

"I noticed as I came in that your fibrous rooted herbaceous plants are in fairly good condition. Your pentstemons are healthy looking. But do you think it wise to mix the purple aubrietia with phloxes, as I see you have done in the border which runs towards that small painted arbour?"

"Perhaps that *was* a mistake. I will speak to my head gardener about it. Do have a peach."

"Thank you. Peaches are very good for the health." (He took one.) "You remember Darwin's scientific interest in peaches?"

"Naturally!"

"You recollect his careful tabulating of the gradations between peaches and nectarines? It is very interesting. Do tell me your opinion on that old controversy as to whether the peach was introduced into Europe from Persia or whether its origin was in reality in China. That has always interested me greatly. Are you with Alphonse de Candolle or against him?"

"Alphonse de Candolle?"

"Yes!"

He leaned forward, waiting for her answer with evident interest.

"I am inclined to agree with him," said Mrs. Chetwynd Mason, but in a hesitating voice.

"You think the peach came originally from Persia?"

"Yes, I do."

He smiled with surely a slight touch of malice.

"But Candolle says it came to us from China, and was conveyed into Persia by the Chinese after the Sanskrit emigration."

"That's what I meant. That's exactly what *I* have always thought," exclaimed Mrs. Chetwynde Mason, who had become very pink about the gills. "Candolle was right."

"But then what about the name *Persica* which was given to the peach? And what about Aitchison's discovery in Afghanistan?"

"Aitchison's discovery—" Mrs. Chetwynde Mason's voice tailed off into a faint sound like the last twitter of a dying bird in the twilight.

"He found a form of wild peach there, as you must know."

"Of course he did! But still—still I hold to my original theory. Do have another peach, Lord Lionel."

"Just one more as you are so kind. That's a nice binding you have there. May I?" (He reached out towards a small table).

"Pray do!"

He picked up a book.

"This was bound in France. Possibly by Duru? Is it Duru?"

"Yes!" said Mrs. Chetwynde Mason, firmly.

He opened the volume and looked at the inside of the lower edge of the cover.

"No, you're wrong. This binding is by Bauzonnet. Here is his signature in gold lettering."

"Then we were *both* mistaken," said Mrs. Chetwynde Mason, with an attempt at a smile.

"But it isn't *my* book," said Lord Lionel, with a raising of his fluffy brown eyebrows. "Have you any Roger Payne bindings."

"I'm afraid not."

"Any transparent vellums such as Edwards of Halifax introduced in the eighteenth century?"

"No. I wish I had."

He turned the book over and looked at its title.

"I see it's Nietzsche's *Ecce Homo*."

"Yes. Poor Nietzsche!"

"Why poor?"

"Because he went mad. He was practically mad when he wrote that."

Lord Lionel's eyes became almost stern.

"Do you say a madman could have written this great yea-saying book?"

"Well, we know that—"

"We know that whippersnappers who couldn't write a line to save their souls, that men totally devoid of knowledge, and who knew not the meaning of culture, chose to *call* the great Nietzsche mad, as they call great men mad to this day. But that only proves their own madness. Genius always seems madness to the little strutting *bourgeois*."

He put the book down rather sharply and got up, stretching his splendid figure and looking round the big room.

"You have some very fine furniture," he said.

"Yes. I am rather a connoisseur of furniture."

"In that case I should like some day to take you over to Morton Abbey, my brother Hampshire's place. He has quantities of magnificent specimens."

"Oh, I should simply love to go with you!" exclaimed Mrs. Chetwynde Mason.

"The eighteenth century was of course the great period for furniture."

"Of course it was!"

"But Hampshire has specimens of almost every period. His Heppelwhites are the finest in England. But he has quantities of old Venetian furniture, as well as of course Chippendale, Sheraton, and so forth. French furniture is not lacking either. He has some marvellous Louis Quinze armchairs. Quite priceless. That's a very fine Italian Cassone you have over there."

He walked slowly towards the end of the big room.

"Of what period is it?" he added, feeling for his eyeglasses.

"*That!* Oh, well—that must be—yes—that must be of the seventeenth century, I think."

He put on his eyeglasses, leaned down.

"You are two centuries out. This is fifteenth century work. This gilded wood, this painted front, are pure fifteenth century work."

"Yes, that's it—fifteenth century. I meant fifteenth. You are perfectly right, Lord Lionel."

"Yes, you were two centuries out. What is this?"

He moved on, and paused before a tall piece of furniture like a cabinet— and yet somehow not exactly like a cabinet.

"That is a great treasure. It's an organ."

"An organ!" he exclaimed. "May I open it?"

"Pray do!"

"By whom is it?"

"Well now—let me see—"

"Good Heavens!" he said, opening it and pulling out a manual with black naturals and white sharps and flats. "This is a veritable Father Schmidt. You blow it with the foot."

"Yes. That's it—a Father Schmidt! And you blow it with your foot."

"You are lucky to have this. They are very rare. Even Hampshire hasn't got one."

He stood for a moment in a curious pose of attentiveness. Then turning abruptly he said:

"I must go. Thank you for a very pleasant tea. Directly—directly I can manage it I will call with my motor to take you over to Hampshire's place. He and the Duchess will be delighted to see you."

"Really, that will be enchanting!" said Mrs. Chetwynde Mason warmly.

He seemed to hesitate, staring at her.

"You—would you mind very much if I brought two friends with me?"

"Of course not."

"They may not—still they usually like to accompany me."

"Do bring them of course. Any friends of yours are sure to be delightful."

"They're really not bad fellows." (He spoke in a slightly deprecating voice.) "I think you will find them fairly all right."

"I know I shall."

"Then I'll let you know—when I can. Well, good-bye."

"Good-bye, Lord Lionel. I cannot tell you how much I have enjoyed making your acquaintance."

"Then I'll bring them with me. Good-bye. Don't trouble to ring."

He seemed to listen for an instant. Then he walked to the door into the hall.

"That's a Neuchatel clock!" he said, pointing towards a fine black and gold clock, which stood on a black and gold stand fixed against the wall. "Neuchatel—of about 1820 or so."

Then he opened the door and went out.

When Lord Lionel had accomplished his tranquil exit from her drawing room, Mrs. Chetwynde Mason stood for a moment looking round at all the beautiful things she had gathered together. How much more he knew about them than she did! What a marvellous mind! What culture! What knowledge! Was any mortal thing not known to him? He had really made her feel almost as if she were on a level with Mrs. Sampson and Miss Ellen Sampson, on the rummage sale level. She had not even been aware that the little old organ was a "Father Schmidt" until he had told her so. And he was going to motor her over to the Duke and Duchess of Hampshire with two of his intimate friends! He had chosen her out to—

A prolonged howl from somewhere in the inner or outer hall broke horribly upon her reverie. It was a human, not a dog's, howl, savage in its startled intensity, suggestive of fear, of pain, of outrage. Mrs. Chetwynde Mason turned pale and gasped. Something frightful must have happened to cause such a piercing outcry. And it hadn't been a woman's voice. Was it possible that Barstow had gone suddenly mad and tried to murder Lord Lionel, or that Thomas, that saucy-looking young footman, had attempted to strangle his superior? She trembled in the silence which followed the howl. She dared not go to the door to ascertain what had happened. Yet she was terrified at being alone in her haunting ignorance. Finally she sank down on a sofa and with a shuddering finger pressed an electric bell. In a moment the door opened and Barstow appeared looking painfully agitated.

"Yes, Madam?" he said, in a hoarse voice.

She signed to him to shut the door, which he did. Then she signed to him to come to her and he approached.

"Barstow!"

"Yes, Madam?"

"What has happened?"

"Happened, Madam?"

"Yes, in the hall just now? Who made that—who—who howled?"

"I'm very sorry, Madam. I hoped you hadn't heard."

"Heard! How could I help hearing? Who was it? Not—not his Lordship?"

"Madam, it was Thomas."

"Thomas! Why? What caused Thomas to howl?"

"I was downstairs in the servant's hall, Madam, for a moment when his Lordship happened to be leaving, and Thomas let his Lordship out."

"But why should Thomas howl in that dreadful manner when letting his Lordship out?"

"Not being there, Madam, I can't say for certain. But Thomas swears, takes his oath, Madam, that he did nothing to his Lordship."

"What do you mean? What should Thomas do to his Lordship?"

"I couldn't say, Madam. But Thomas *must* have done something."

"Why?"

"Because, Madam, so Thomas swears, just as his Lordship was leaving the house, with Thomas holding the hall door for him, he took a sort of run, and let out with his foot, and caught Thomas—well, Madam, I scarcely like to say it."

"Go on! Go on!"

"Caught Thomas a regular oner, Madam, in the hinder parts. Excuse me, Madam."

"Really, Barstow!"

"I'm sure I beg pardon, Madam, but you asked me."

"It's impossible, absolutely impossible!"

"So I said, Madam. And yet why should Thomas set up such a—such a—"

"It was a howl!"

"Such a howl, Madam, all for nothing?"

"Then you think—"

"By the look of Thomas, when I did get up the stairs, Madam, I think that someone must have caught him a rare one from the back. And there was no one to do it but his Lordship."

"Then Thomas must have insulted his Lordship."

"I couldn't say, Madam."

"*I* say he must have!"

"Certainly, Madam!"

"Give Thomas his notice and a month's wages. He must leave to-morrow. I cannot keep a footman who obliges a visitor of noble birth to assault him in self-protection, and then howls in that disgraceful manner. That will do, Barstow."

"Shall I remove the tea now, Madam?"

"Yes. I don't wish to see Thomas before he goes."

Barstow with dismal gravity collected the tea and went out.

When he had gone Mrs. Chetwynde Mason went to her writing table, sat down and wrote the following letter to her friend, Lady Caroway.

Amber Grange,
Amber.
Thursday evening.

My Dearest Eleanor,

I take back all I said to you to-day about the English countryside containing nobody of interest or culture. Since you left me this afternoon I have had a wonderful experience. It appears that a brother of the Duke of Hampshire, Lord Lionel Danesborough, lives in my immediate neighbourhood, though I didn't know it till now, and just after I had got rid of that dreadful old person in a bonnet and her daughter he came to call on me. He stayed for hours, and we had a really enthralling discussion about painting, music, Christianity, Etruscan vases, ceramics in general, the classics, poetry, sculpture, book binding, literature, horticulture, antiques, old furniture, and in fact almost every subject that can interest two omnivorous and far-reaching minds. We touched on Wagner, Nietzsche, Cagliostro, Liszt, Correggio, Horace, Virgil, Ovid, Cicero, Burne-Jones, Browning, and many others. We quoted the classics one against the other, each one as it were capping the other's quotations. I was able to give him some gardening hints, and to put him right once or twice about periods. (He was two centuries out in his attribution of my Italian Cassone, and made one or two other little mistakes which I was fortunately able to correct.) But do not suppose I am criticising him. We all make a slip occasionally, and I claim to be no more faultless in that respect than others. He is a wonderful man, perhaps even a man of genius. Naturally, being who he is, he is ultra-refined, and he has perfect manners. But in addition there is this marvellous culture, this far-reaching intellect, this critical acumen, and this quite amazing knowledge. Is it not wonderful to have such a neighbour, to have found at last living almost at my very door a worth while man? I cannot tell you, Eleanor, what a feeling of uplift I have this evening. My reaction to Lord Lionel is so vivid that I am almost dazzled, as if by a sudden blaze of light. There was only one thing to mar an otherwise perfect afternoon. You know Thomas, the saucy-faced footman whom you took quite a fancy to. When Lord Lionel left me Thomas let him out. And it seems that Thomas was so impudent to Lord Lionel that the latter was forced to correct him physically—in the hall. I heard Thomas howling—yes, dear, actually howling—sent for Barstow and enquired about it, and that was the explanation. Of course, Thomas leaves my service tomorrow.

> *Best love from*
> *Your ever affectionate*
>   *Tessie.*

P.S.—Lord Lionel is going to take me over in his car to see the Duke and Duchess of Hampshire at Morton Abbey in a day or two. He wants my opinion on some of the Duke's furniture. Two of his dearest friends will accompany us.

T.

This letter went to London that evening, and was received by Lady Caroway at breakfast time on the following morning. She read it over her tea and toast, and then turned to the morning paper. After glancing over the leading articles and the latest foreign news, she happened upon this paragraph:

Escape of a Lunatic

Yesterday afternoon at about two o'clock a dangerous lunatic, who was recently confined in the luxurious home for mental cases known as "Brankhurst," managed by some as yet unexplained means to evade the two keepers who were attached to his person and to get out of the large and beautiful grounds which surround the mansion. He was recaptured last night in the neighbouring forest after a prolonged search. The lunatic in question belongs to a famous English family, bears a courtesy title, and is a man of the widest culture. We understand that before being taken he paid a visit to a well-known lady who resides in a beautiful house near Brankhurst, and even took tea with her. His conduct while at tea seems to have aroused no suspicion, but we gather that when leaving the house he committed a savage, and entirely unprovoked, assault upon a footman who was letting him out. The name of the lady whom he visited is Mrs. Chetwynde Mason, well known for her literary and artistic proclivities....

Lady Caroway's bright blue eyes were smiling as she put the paper down and went to her writing table.

"I really must beg Tessie not to dismiss that nice-looking footman," she said to herself, as she took up a pen.

THE END

Robert Hichens Bibliography
(1864-1950)

Novels
The Coast Guard's Secret (1886)
The Green Carnation (published
  anonymously, 1894; republished as
  by Hitchens, 1948)
An Imaginative Man (1895)
Flames (1897)
The Londoners (1898)
The Daughters of Babylon (1899;
  with Wilson Barrett)
The Slave (1899)
The Prophet of Berkeley Square
  (1901)
Felix (1902)
The Garden of Allah (1904)
The Woman With the Fan (1904)
Call of the Blood (1905)
Barbary Sheep (1907)
A Spirit in Prison (1908)
Bella Donna (1909; reprinted as
  Temptation, 1946)
The Dweller on the Threshold (1911)
The Fruitful Vine (1911)
The Way of Ambition (1913)
In the Wilderness (1917)
Mrs. Marden (1919)
The Spirit of the Time (1921)
December Love (1922)
After The Verdict (1924)
The Unearthly (1925; UK as *The
  God Within Him*)
The Bacchante and the Nun (1926;
  US as *The Bacchante*)
The First Lady Brendon (1927)
Dr. Artz (1928)
On the Screen (1929)
The Bracelet (1930)
The Gates of Paradise (1930)
The First Lady Brendon (1931)
Mortimer Brice (1932)
The Paradine Case (1933)
The Power to Kill (1934)
Susie's Career (1935)
The Pyramid (1936)
The Sixth of October (1936)
Daniel Airlie (1937)

Secret Information (1938)
The Journey Up (1938)
That Which Is Hidden (1939)
The Million (1940)
Married or Unmarried (1941)
A New Way of Life (1941)
Veils (1943)
Young Mrs. Brand (1944)
Harps in the Wind (1945; U.S. as *The
  Woman in the House*)
Incognito (1945; Hutchinson)
Too Much Love of Living (1947)
Beneath the Magic (1950; U.S. as
  Strange Lady)
The Mask (1951)
Night Bound (1951)

Collections
After To-Morrow, and the New Love
  (1895)
The Folly of Eustace and Other
  Stories (1896)
Bye-Ways (1897)
Tongues of Conscience (1898, 1900)
The Black Spaniel and Other Stories
  (1905)
Snake-Bite and Other Stories (1919)
The Last Time (1924)
The Streets and Other Stories (1928)
The Gates of Paradise and Other
  Stories (1930)
My Desert Friend and Other Stories
  (1931)
The Gardenia, and Other Stories
  (1934)
The Afterglow and Other Stories
  (1935)
The Man in the Mirror and Other
  Stories (1950)
The Return of the Soul and Other
  Stories (2001; ed. S. T. Joshi)

Nonfiction
Old Cairo (1908; article)
Egypt and Its Monuments (1908)
The Holy Land (1910)
The Spell of Egypt (1910; orig.
  published as *Egypt and Its
  Monuments*, 1908)
The Near East (1913)
Yesterday (1947)

Plays
The Medicine Man (1898; with H. D.
  Traill)
Becky Sharp (1901; with C. G.
  Lennox; U.S. title: *Vanity Fair*)
The Real Woman (1909)
The Garden of Allah (1911; with
  Mary Anderson)
The Law of the Sands (1916)
Black Magic (1917)
Press the Button! (1918)
The Voice from the Minaret (1919)

Filmography [based on the novel
  unless otherwise noted]

Bella Donna (directed by Edwin S.
  Porter and Hugh Ford;1915)
The Garden of Allah (directed by
  Colin Campbell; 1916)
Barbary Sheep (directed by Maurice
  Tourneur; 1917)
Flames (directed by Maurice Elvey;
  UK, 1917)
The Slave (directed by Arrigo Bocchi;
  UK, 1918)

Hidden Lives (directed by Maurits
  Binger and B. E. Doxat-Pratt;
  Netherlands, 1920, based on a play
  by Robert Hichens and John
  Knittel)
The Call of the Blood (directed by
  Louis Mercanton; France, 1920)
The Woman with the Fan (directed
  by René Plaissetty; UK, 1921)
The Fruitful Vine (directed by
  Maurice Elvey; UK, 1921)
The Voice from the Minaret (directed
  by Frank Lloyd; 1923, based on the
  play)
Bella Donna (directed by George
  Fitzmaurice; 1923)
The Lady Who Lied (directed by
  Edwin Carewe; 1925, based on the
  story)
The Garden of Allah (directed by Rex
  Ingram; 1927)
After the Verdict (directed by Henrik
  Galeen; UK, 1929)
Bella Donna (directed by Robert
  Milton; UK, 1934)
The Garden of Allah (directed by
  Richard Boleslawski; 1936)
Temptation (directed by Irving
  Pichel; 1946, based on the novel
  Bella Donna)
The Paradine Case (directed by
  Alfred Hitchcock; 1947)
Call of the Blood (directed by John
  Clements and Ladislao Vajda; UK,
  1948)